The Accidental Psychic

Carol-Anne Mason

*To dear Sal
all my love
Carol.*

*Let's see more
of each other
in '22!*
xx
x
x

Copyright First Edition
Copyright © 2021 Carol-Anne Mason

The right of Carol-Anne Mason to be identified as the author of the Work has been asserted by her in accordance with the Copyright, Designs and Patents Act 1988

First published as an eBook in 2021

All rights reserved. No part of this book may be reproduced, scanned, stored in a retrieval system or distributed in any printed or electronic form, without the prior written permission of the publisher; nor be otherwise circulated in any form of binding or cover other than that in which it is published and without a similar condition being imposed on the subsequent purchaser.

ISBN 978-1-8384305-0-4
Cover illustrated by MIBLART

British Library Cataloguing in Publication Data.
A catalogue record of this book is available from the British Library.

Printed and bound in Great Britain
By Clays Ltd, Elcograf S.p.A

www.carolmasonauthor.com

For Andrew

"Don't be normal"

Prologue

Southampton
A cold morning in early spring 2017

Unbeknownst to Annie, a mundane commute to London on a train — will change her life forever. A fatigue crack in one of the front wheels of the train's control car had started to open up, and further up the frozen track, a set of points were waiting for the fail…

Chapter One

The Journey

'Oh God no ... not again!' Annie shouted, as she ran the last hundred yards. Her breath fogged, blasting into the freezing air.

The 6.59 train to London Waterloo pulled out of Southampton Central on time—but without her. She knew in that instant her job at Hollingsworth's of Mayfair was at risk, she'd already received her last warning from the owner of the gallery.

Melina, her boss, was a difficult woman at best. Although Annie had tried hard to forge a relationship with her, she seemed to turn her back on anyone who dared to get too close. And the timing error that day would most definitely have set a permanent wedge between the two of them.

Annie finally sat down on the 7.28 *and* in carriage number three, her lucky number. Maybe it was the good omen she needed to ease the tongue-lashing she was inevitably in for. She chose a rear-facing window seat, one of many superstitious travelling habits that had plagued her everyday life since she was a child. She placed her briefcase next to her as a deterrent to unwanted travel companions—

nearly always older men and rarely good-looking.

Annie suddenly realised that missing the 6.59 also meant she would miss the 'handsome guy'. She had exchanged smiles with the enigmatic man every morning for many months. And although they had never spoken, she was happy to leave it as it was, those briefest of encounters gave her enough fantasy ammunition to get her through her darkest days with Melina.

Annie remained optimistic about her love life, even though she was still unattached at thirty-two. Her forthright Lancastrian gran had told her more than once that she would be a barren woman—not having a man at this late stage in her life. But forgiving the old lady for her insensitivity was never a problem for Annie, Gran was the only ally she had within her strange narcissistic family. Her mother and father were different to her friends' parents, who showed their children love; Annie's were cold and impatient, and more than happy to offload their daughter onto anyone who would have her. But even invitations to stay over at friends had dried up, reciprocation had never been a word in her parents' vocabulary.

It was around that time that loneliness had prompted young Annie's conjuring of her imaginary friend, Ellie, who became her constant shadow and mischievous mentor. Her parents' acceptance of this fanciful playmate had, at the time, puzzled Annie. Years later though, she'd realised that Ellie was, in their eyes, the perfect distraction for their strange and irksome child.

The two seats opposite her had become unoccupied, so she stretched her legs under the table and propped her feet up on the seat cushions. *Not allowed, but I really don't give a damn today,* she thought.

It annoyed her yet again that first-class travel was out of her reach, her meagre wage was barely enough for a small mortgage on a semi-detached in Southampton. Her ambition to live in the big city, though, was still at the forefront of her mind, and the excitement of London living, without the mindless commute, kept her going.

The carriage had its usual plethora of characters that stimulated Annie's love of people-watching. Although she could see in her mind's eye images of the lives they led, she was convinced it was her extraordinary imagination working overtime as usual. But fantasizing about *their* lives was a good distraction from all that was going on in hers, especially today.

Annie's imaginings were suddenly interrupted by a foul smell. *It can't be sweat on a freezing morning like this,* she thought. The body odour was coming from a person sitting across the aisle from her.

She could see in her peripheral vision that it was a large man dressed in black. She couldn't help herself and turned her head slowly to the left, to catch a glimpse of this dark character. Simultaneously, he did the same and leered at her through protruding, veined eyes.

Annie knew all too well that he was a Catholic priest, as his clerical collar and silver cross made her stomach churn. His mouth opened as if to talk, but instead a vile grin appeared, exposing his stained yellow teeth. Droplets of sweat slowly trickled down his grey temples. Annie recoiled, bile rose up into her throat, and she whipped her head around towards the window.

Her ghost-like reflection was so different to the person she saw every morning in the mirror. Her long copper-red hair and aqua-green eyes were muted by the smoked glass, while the abstract countryside sped through her parallel image. But the imprinted vision of the priest's silver cross overpowered her thoughts, regressing her mind to her own miserable convent days.

Her father had moved her from a happy, mixed comprehensive to a religious all-girls school, simply because one of her best friends had got herself 'up the duff' at the age of just thirteen.

Annie's father used the fact that a pregnant friend would be a bad influence on his daughter to persuade her generous grandfather to pay for private education. More importantly, it was also a boarding school. He found a convent that would take fee-paying non-Catholics to boost their coffers. But her father mistakenly thought it was a virtuous establishment where his daughter would be safely tucked away from randy schoolboys. And, also, where he hoped she would gain the qualifications required for a decent job, or to get into uni.

It did all that—but it wasn't virtuous; in fact, far from it.

The nuns were spiteful and cruel, especially to Annie, who was a non-Catholic headstrong teenager. She would question the Sisters of Mercy regularly as to why they had chosen such an unnatural life. All married to one God, and seemingly living their lives *without* mercy or compassion.

She had spent most of her free periods at school reciting the Hail Mary prayer as punishment for her misconduct, whilst standing in Father Edwards's office. She remembered thinking at the time that using prayer as penance was odd. But then, everything about that school was strange—and so, too, was Father Edwards.

He would patrol the crucifix-strewn corridors with his hands clasped behind his back, seemingly feasting his eyes on the sisters and students. Annie had never before experienced God and religion until it had been forced upon her every day at that vile institution.

The train's Tannoy system crackled into life, with an overexuberant buffet-car attendant trying to peddle his wares. The announcement dragged Annie's mind back to the present, and rapidly planted the seed that she needed a zap of caffeine.

Leaving her jacket spread across the seat and a magazine on the table, she picked up her briefcase. Without looking at the priest again, she got up and weaved her way to the buffet car.

This coffee's gonna to have to do me until later, she thought. She was on a detox and the usual array of unhealthy but tasty calorie-loaded snacks were not on her agenda until at least Friday.

On her way back from getting a drink, she gasped in surprise, nearly choking on her coffee in the process. The 'handsome guy' was there, staring out of the window. He saw her reflection and immediately turned to face her. His usual sexy smile appeared—but then he *winked* at her, too.

Annie felt the heat rushing to her cheeks, and knew her pale complexion would be scarlet in seconds. She returned a nod in acknowledgement and rushed back to her seat, but was thrilled that he'd been so bold. It had made her miserable start to the day more bearable and had caused a strange *zing* to surge through her body, something she had never experienced before.

She sat, rested her head back and held her breath for a few seconds. She was curious as to why he was on the later train, too, and her imagination immediately started to wander into a romantic realm. His Mediterranean dark-bronze eyes, olive skin and close-cut facial hair were faultless; even his tousled dark hair with its natural highlights was groomed—but not too perfectly.

Then her senses were vulgarly smashed, the odour from the sweaty priest wafted over her again. She glared at the foul man. Thankfully, sleep had taken him, but she was still angered by his pungent intrusion into her exquisite daydream.

Annie scanned the carriage for characters to hone her people-watching skills on, and to take her mind off the unusual annoyance.

Most of the women were clearly heading for a shopping spree, their indecipherable babble an indication of their excitement for the day ahead. They were all dressed to annihilate, with coordinating handbags and boots, ready to descend on one of the best Meccas in the world for purchasing anything—from the most ridiculously expensive to the best bargains ever.

The men were mundane in comparison. Plainly dressed in suits and ties, and unlike the babbling ladies, quietly productive: either reading newspapers, texting on phones, or tapping on laptops. One of the gents, however, was talking way too loudly on his large mobile. He was enjoying the fact that everyone around him could hear he was purchasing a new Tesla car, for a 'vast amount of dosh,' as he tawdrily put it.

Although others in the carriage were raising their eyebrows and tutting at his crassness, a wave of compassion washed over her, and for some reason—she knew, deep down, that he was a lonely soul with no true friends.

She shivered unexpectedly, as a grim image of his mortality flashed through her mind. She was annoyed with herself for letting her imagination become creepy and intrusive, and she shook her head to drag her thoughts back to normality.

She sipped her bitter coffee, contemplating how the day would pan out, the carriage started to get a little busier. A group of noisy students had got on at Basingstoke, but she was relieved to see them crowding around four seats further up the carriage. Annie's attention was drawn to a pretty, slim girl whose unkempt brunette hair was knotting into early dreadlocks. Above all, her sad eye's revealed a despair that seemed incongruous amongst the cheerful teenagers.

Annie quickly looked out of the window, annoyed with herself for overthinking—yet again.

The speeding scene outside was spectacular, with the frost-laden countryside glistening whilst the weak winter sun slowly emerged.

Chapter Two

THE CRASH

The previous babble of voices had now risen to a headache-inducing hullabaloo, prompting Annie to put her earphones in to listen to her favourite track 'Human,' from the new Rag'n'Bone Man album. She closed her eyes to concentrate on the haunting words.

Suddenly, the train shuddered, then jerked violently. Annie sat bolt upright and yanked her earphones out. The carriage had fallen silent, everyone froze; all eyes widened just before fear kicked in. Then, an unprecedented sound as loud as an overhead thunderclap exploded through the carriage. The screeching of brakes set the students screaming and running for the exits, tumbling over each other like waves. Some commuters stood still, straddling the aisles, and holding onto anything that was bolted down.

Annie could only watch in terror and disbelief; none of it seemed real.

Then, the impact came. A jolt so violent it sent bodies crunching onto the floor of the carriage. Annie was forced backwards with a massive thud into her seat, knocking the wind out of her. If she had she been facing forwards, she would have been horribly smashed.

The screaming in the carriage had become unbearably loud, with commuters slamming into solid objects. The train rocked on its tracks and tilted violently over to her side; and just—kept—tilting.

Annie grabbed a pole on the aisle side of the seat and instinctively lifted her legs from the foot-well below the table, tucking them under her. There was a combined screeching and scraping, whilst brakes and metal sparked and twisted, before the train succumbed to gravity.

It was at that moment the priest was catapulted onto the pole Annie was holding, crushing her left arm as if it was matchwood. She screamed in agony as the bone in her forearm tore through her skin. Her hand opened automatically with the searing pain and she let go, crashing onto the window, which was now horizontal. Her head hit the glass.

Annie's eyes flickered open—as did her senses, albeit slowly.

There was an eerie silence at first; then came the odd groan and gasp that slowly grew louder, fear swept through the carriage like a tornado, drawing up screams from the shattered bodies.

Annie haltingly looked to her right, that familiar smell of sweat seemed so close by. The priest's glazed, unseeing eyes were fixed upon her. There was a large shard of glass protruding through his chest, with droplets of sticky blood slowly trickling from the anchored crucifix like the sweat had done earlier down his grey temples. His vast bulk lay against the shattered window, his legs crumpled and twisted around the smashed table.

There was a movement below him. Blood—like a river of black treacle—was draining away from his lifeless body, and meandering towards a gaping hole in the carriage.

Awareness of what had just happened started to break through her mind-fog, and she immediately knew she had to get out of this hellish nightmare fast. But her head was thumping so loudly; she could hear the pulsing of her own blood like tinnitus in her ears. She unwrapped the scarf that had been draped around her neck to keep out the cold and wound it tightly around her bleeding arm. How strange it was that her arm now felt so numb, yet she could see the white of her bone on the wrong side of her green jumper. Bile started to rise again.

Annie raised herself tentatively, but knew that although she had a nasty break to her arm and a bump on her head, she was relatively unscathed. At least she could move, unlike the priest, who was going nowhere.

'Help me.'

The voice came from behind her. Annie squeezed herself through the legs of the seating, which was now vertical. On the other side of the seat, a middle-aged woman was pinned between the window and the collapsed luggage rack. Part of a metal strut that had held the rack in place was embedded deep in the woman's right side, although there was very little blood escaping the wound.

Annie carefully moved over to her. When she gently took her hand, a flood of images ran quickly through her mind: a child, a mother, a house by a beach, and a smiling grey-haired man. For some reason, Annie knew that what she was seeing were 'end of life visions'.

'I'm dying, aren't I?'

'No, no you're okay ... really.' Despite her reassuring words, Annie could feel her slipping away.

'I'm not scared—I'm going to join them.' The woman slowly closed her eyes as if going to sleep, then her grip on Annie's hand eased.

It was the first time Annie had ever witnessed a person dying in front of her. One moment she was there, and the next she was gone—the transition had seemed so easy.

She stared at the woman's face for a while, trying to take in what had just happened. Then she gradually looked up as her senses returned to her.

There was so little room to manoeuvre with the train on its side, although there was a small gap between the headrests and the luggage rack, along the line of the windows. It was the only escape route towards the exit, Annie could see a sickening pile of bodies. Women and men, all crushed into a small area, a few trying to free themselves, some writhing in agony, and others, like the priest and the woman, deathly still.

Cries of help and deep moans invaded her senses; she put her hands over her ears, allowing for a moment of muffled silence in which to regain her composure.

Suddenly, an unfamiliar prickling sensation rose up the back of her neck and into her hair, it was as if a thousand pointed fingernails were digging into her scalp. She screwed her eyes shut waiting for the sensation to ease, but as she looked up—the 'dreadlock girl' was standing motionless amongst the bodies. Strangely, there was no fear on her face or in her eyes, just an extraordinary calmness that seemed out of place in the chaos. The girl gazed straight across at Annie and ironically smiled, then her body became ethereal.

Annie closed her eyes, and shook her head as if it would help clear her vision. When she opened them a split second later, the girl was gone. Confused, she was still staring at the space the girl had just occupied when a bright blue flash of light burst through the wrecked automatic door at the end of the carriage. Electrical sparks arced across the floor and into the motionless bodies, momentarily animating them.

One of the dead was the 'phone man,' crushed under a pile of metal that had forced its way through the outer wall of the carriage. Annie immediately knew that her earlier premonition of his mortality had been realised.

Her mind started to swim, and her ears buzzed as her senses cruised into slow motion. But the sound of sirens lifted her from the brink of a faint, abruptly focusing her mind. It was then her eyes fell upon the 'handsome guy'; he was looking straight at her.

'Are you okay?' he shouted above the wretched sounds.

Annie nodded her head, and tears started to well at this first kind gesture of concern. He had a nasty cut above his right eye and blood was staining his chinos below his left knee while he scaled the twisted seating.

Annie clambered over bodies towards him, now with tears streaming down her face—she had no control over her emotions as shock slowly seeped in.

Eyes hazed with tears, she stumbled over a woman who was lying in a disjointed heap. Her blonde hair was soaked red from the gouge in her neck, and her yellow Christian Dior coat was splattered from the same source. Her face, though, was serene and unblemished, and her perfect lips too; but they were—without breath.

Annie faltered and put her hand down to steady herself—straight into a pool of warm, viscid blood. And just as the sickening pungency hit her nostrils, two strong hands snatch her up and away from that moment of hell.

Swamped by an overwhelming attack on her senses, she fell into an all-encompassing—and welcoming—blackness …

Chapter Three

THE HOSPITAL

Annie see-sawed in and out of consciousness. She had no perception of time or space, but was aware of lights, sounds and intangible presences. So many people: shouting, screaming, and crying—there was so much crying.

A piercing light brought her back abruptly from an underworld of wretched sadness. Annie opened her eyes and was confronted by a grey-haired man in a white coat, leaning over her. He was holding a torch—clearly the source of the penetrating light that had been searching her eyes.

'Ah, young lady, you've decided to join us. How are you feeling?'

'Oh God.' Annie groaned, touching the bump on the back of her head.

'No, I'm not quite God ... you're still with us,' He seemed pleased with his quip.

But Annie frowned, unappreciative of his crass humour.

Realising his insensitivity, he cleared his throat and stammered, 'I ... I'm Doctor Lambert, you've been involved in a serious accident, do you remember anything?'

Even though Annie was still groggy, she knew all too well what had happened. The accident would be forever imprinted on her mind, although she had no memory of escaping the train.

'How ... did I get out of there?'

'You were rescued by a young man who accompanied you in the ambulance ... and apparently he helped a lot of others to safety, too.'

Annie looked around. 'Where did he go?'

'I think he went for stitches to a leg injury. Now, do you remember your name?' The doctor focused intensely on her eyes again.

'Annie ... Prior, I think.'

'Ah ... that's good. We found your ID, so we do know,' he said, scribbling on her notes.

'You've had a nasty bump to your head so we'll keep an eye on that, but it's the compound fracture to the radius in your forearm that I'm mainly concerned about. And it looks as if we're going to have to operate on it I'm afraid Annie. But, as open fractures go, it's not a serious one. Although, you may still have to have pins and a plate to stabilise it. None of that's going to happen though, until tomorrow now, we're simply inundated with ops scheduled for today already. Believe me, Annie, you were one of the lucky ones.'

Her throbbing headache was making it difficult to concentrate on the doctor's words, which seemed so trivial against the magnitude of what had happened that day. She desperately wanted him to leave, but he just kept talking.

'The good news is, Annie, you're in the right place, thanks to your hero friend. So ... I'll be seeing you bright and early in the morning. Oh ... and a nurse—*of sorts*—will be along soon.'

'Of sorts ... Doctor Lambert?'

'Oh ... you'll see. Anyway, he'll take you up to your ward after x-rays.'

Thankfully, the gauche doctor turned and left the curtained cubicle.

Weirdo, Annie said to herself, and closed her eyes. Immediately, crystal-clear visions of the crash flashed into her mind, and as the gory details vividly re-emerged, she shook her head again— to clear her thoughts. Although, what she was seeing in her mind's eye was clearer than it had ever been before. It seemed, her brain had been rebooted out of a fog, and the clarity of sight and sound seemed magnified way beyond the norm. Instead of those earlier daydream-like images, it was as though she was watching a movie.

She lay there wondering if the powerful painkillers had side effects that would cause this incredible lucidity. Then, the curtains parted slowly, and a familiar face peeked in.

'Hi ... didn't expect to see you sitting up,' the 'handsome guy' said as he limped in.

Even though Annie's new awareness had excited her momentarily, that same *zing* that she'd felt on the train suddenly coursed through her body again—sharpening her senses to an even higher state.

'Well, that was a hell of a way of finally meeting each other.'

Annie's cheeks coloured up. 'Yeah, it was crazy ... but how come you were on that train too?'

'I was going to ask you the same question. I literally missed our usual one by a minute.'

Annie sucked in a breath of surprise. 'That's so strange ... that happened to me as well.'

'Well, maybe it was meant to be.'

'What, a train crash?'

'Well, no ... I didn't mean it like that, Annie.'

'Oh, that's okay ... sorry... I guess I'm still rattled. Anyway ... how do you know my name?'

'The nurse told me after they found your ID ... and then she threw me out ... actually, to get my leg stitched.'

'Apparently, I need to thank you for rescuing me, but I must have passed out just before ...' Annie suddenly recalled what had happened prior to losing consciousness. 'It was you who caught hold of me ... just after I'd put my hand in that poor woman's blood.' She looked down at her hands and although they were now clean, she still wiped them together as if trying to erase the grim scarlet memory.

The handsome man, now with an emerging black eye, moved over to her side of the bed. 'Ooh, no, I see I'm gonna have to catch you again.' He smiled, which creased the corners of his striking brown eyes.

'No ... really, I'm okay now. What's your name?' Annie asked, wishing the flush of her cheeks would subside.

'I'm Thomas Tadros ... but call me Thos ... everyone else does.' He held out his hand.

Annie gently took hold of his perfectly masculine hand, barely believing that she was finally meeting this man.

'Thank you just doesn't seem enough for what you did,' she said, her complexion normalising slightly. She held onto his hand, and for a brief moment, saw a flash into his future. Curiously, she was there, too.

The curtains opened swiftly, making them both jump; a bleached-blond male nurse barged in, and, in an effeminate voice, said, 'Hi ... I'm nurse Mark, but call me Poppet or Pops, I'll answer to almost anything.' Then he turned to Thos and looked him up and down as if scanning what lay beneath. 'And you most definitely can ... call me, that is.' He giggled, then turned back to Annie. 'Come on, sweetie, I'm taking you up for x-rays and then on to ward twenty ... Lucky you, it's a mixed ward tonight 'cause we're so busy. But apparently, I've got to keep my eye on you with that *nasty* concussion of yours. Do you need any more pain relief for that arm, sweetie?' His words were almost indecipherable as they rapidly tripped of his tongue.

'No, thanks ... Poppet, I'm actually feeling a bit nauseous,' Annie said. She breathed out through whistle-shaped lips.

'Ah ... that'll be the morphine you had earlier,' Poppet said.

Thos seemed dumbstruck at the flamboyant nurse, and raised his eyebrows at Annie. 'I knew you'd have to have an op on that arm,' he said, trying to change the subject. 'I must admit it made it damn difficult carrying you off the train.'

She smiled back at the gorgeous man standing in front of her. 'I wish I could remember what happened after the crash; the doctor said you stayed with me in the ambulance even after helping others to safety. Why would you do that?'

Thos's Mediterranean skin flushed slightly. 'Ah ... well ... I needed to get my leg sorted out, so I hitched a lift; you didn't seem to mind as you were out cold.'

Thos ran his fingers through his messy hair and for a moment Annie was transfixed by his good looks. 'You'll probably be hailed a hero, especially after helping so many, and with your leg injured.'

'Na ... As for being a hero, I was one of the only limping wounded, so it was a no-brainer. But I've only had a few stitches; I count myself lucky.'

Annie grimaced. 'I know we got off lightly, from what I can remember.' Tears started to fill her eyes. 'I tried to help this poor woman who was impaled on a metal spike, but I couldn't do anything for her.'

'I'm sorry you had to go through that, Annie. There were so *many* badly injured ... Some of the things I saw were horrific.' Thos was about to go into detail.

'Please don't.' Annie said. She put her fingers gently against his mouth. He took her hand, and kissed it.

'Excuse *me*,' Poppet interrupted. 'I've got to tear you two apart and get this gorgeous lady up to x-rays … *if* you don't mind?' Poppet looked directly at Thos and winked.

Thos grinned awkwardly. 'I've actually got to go now too, Annie. But, would you mind very much if I came back tomorrow, just to see how you're getting on after your op?'

Annie made a silent wish. 'Really? Why on earth would you want to come back to see me?'

'Because, Miss Prior … you and I now have a connection that I would like to … well, follow up on, I suppose. Of course, that's only if you want me to.'

Annie's stomach somersaulted. 'Yes, I'd *really* like that.'

Nurse Poppet pushed Annie's wheelchair through the packed corridors. It was the first time she had left her bed since being admitted. But the sounds she had heard in her unconscious state were still in evidence: distressed and anxious people rushing through corridors towards Accident and Emergency, searching for their loved ones who had been on the train. Some of the relatives had clearly been given the worst possible news and were being comforted by nurses and family.

'Oh God, this is so awful,' Annie said, trying hard to hold back her tears. 'I can't tell you how horrific it was on the train, Poppet … There were so many dead and injured in my carriage alone.'

'Actually, Annie, I've heard you were really lucky to be in the third carriage. Apparently, there were only eight dead from there; all the rest came from the front two.'

Annie closed her eyes and thanked her superstition gods for keeping her safe, while Poppet veered the wheelchair through the packed corridors.

'I reckon you've landed yourself a *gorgeous* man today,' he added.

'I haven't *landed* him, Pops.'

'Oh, come off it, Miss Prior, anyone can see the two of you are meant to be together. It's sort of romantic, isn't it?'

'What do you mean, romantic?' Annie asked, but knew exactly what he was getting at.

'Well, he rescued you from a train crash, didn't he? That's romantic! It's the sort of stuff love stories are written about.'

Annie didn't dare to hope too much, but then she remembered her earlier vision and being part of Thos's life in the future.

'So, tell me, Annie, do you live in London?'

'No, I'm from Southampton but I work in an art gallery in Mayfair, so it's an everyday commute for me.'

'Ooh, lucky you … that would be my dream job. You see, I'm a budding artist myself, but nobody understands my work. It's all very weird, really … I suppose a bit like me.' He giggled.

For the first time since the crash, Annie laughed too. 'Seriously though, Poppet, I'd love to see your work one day; you never know, it might just be strange enough to hang in the gallery and …'

Annie was going to continue but stopped. Her heightened senses sent a familiar prickling sensation up her neck and through her hair. Then she recognised that same fetid stench of sweat. She shivered, not in apprehension, but because she was so cold.

'Poppet, STOP.'

'Ooh, bloody hell! What's wrong, Annie?' He pulled back on the wheelchair.

She could feel goosebumps rising all over her body. She looked through the throng of people walking down the corridor towards her, and focused on a vaporous figure standing in their midst. Using the right arm of the wheelchair to push herself into a standing position, Annie snatched in a breath; she recognised those same bulging, lifeless eyes.

The dead priest stood in the centre of the corridor, still with the blood-covered crucifix hanging from the glass shard in his chest. The living walked—oblivious— through his intangible body.

Annie fell back into the wheelchair, covering her face with her right hand; her ears started to buzz—then she heard his vile voice.

'They can't get me now,' he said, and then laughed grotesquely.

'ANNIE!' Poppet shouted above the noise in the corridor. 'What in the world is it?'

'He's not from this world ... It's the dead priest from the train, look—he's standing over there!'

Annie pointed to the middle of the crowd as if Poppet would be able to see the apparition; he automatically obliged, and scanned the corridor.

'Okay ... So, I think you're having a morphine episode, Annie. It can cause hallucinations if you're sensitive to it. Come on, honey, let's get you to the ward, you're freaking me out here,' Poppet said shakily.

Annie wondered for a brief moment if her visions had been drug-induced, but then realised that hallucinations couldn't stink.

Chapter Four

THE VISITORS

The surgeon realigned Annie's fracture without using plates and screws and fitted a splint so that the wound could be monitored for infection. Doctor Lambert was still concerned with her concussion. But after checking the amount of morphine that had been administered on admission, and a brain scan for possible bleeds, the doctor concluded that her hallucinations had possibly been brought on by post-traumatic stress.

Annie's stay in hospital over the next few days for observation was far from restful. She'd had too many visitors coming and going, and having to recount the story over and over again was getting her down. She also had to deal with uncouth journalists, who had been wheedling out gory information from unsuspecting patients every day.

But the thing that had really upset her was her parents jumping on the media bandwagon. Their concern for her welfare seemed distorted, they seemed more interested in the attention of the press; especially her mother, who had clearly over-preened herself for visiting. Annie was horrified to hear they had already been interviewed on a local radio station and been happily involved in a news conference before even visiting her. Her upset grew, she watched them enjoying the attention, clearly not giving a damn about *her* feelings or injuries. Her relationship with them had never been good, but for her mother to get involved purely for self-gratification was only widening the rift between them.

Annie got up and drew the curtains around her bed, and when she rested her head back tears trickled from the corners of her eyes. Weariness took over and she fell into a much-needed sleep.

Her tiredness was nowhere near erased; instead, nightmares crept into the depths of her slumber. Strange visions filled her mind: snow swirling around the bodies of the dead and lifting their souls upwards towards the brightest of lights.

Annie started to shiver in her sleep, and as she slowly rose to consciousness the cold that had engulfed her in her dreams remained. She opened her eyes, and through her freezing breath she saw a blurred vision of a young woman standing at the foot of her bed. Annie blinked heavily to clear the frosty film from her eyes, then realised that everything but the figure was crystal clear.

Memories of the crash came flooding back and a sudden recognition hit her hard: it was the 'dreadlock girl'. And for the briefest of moments the logical side of Annie's brain considered the apparition to be alive, but this was soon quashed. Her visitor was clearly unworldly, her outline wavered with the weak connection.

The girl looked pleadingly at first, then smiled. This eased the pounding in Annie's chest and caused a wave of peacefulness to wash over her, with any remaining unease dissolving.

'I don't understand what's happening. Why are you here ... why *me*?' Annie asked.

'Annie, I want you to tell my parents that I am finally happy and at peace. My sadness was not their fault, and the outcome of my life could never have been changed. The crash saved my soul ... and it helped you to see and hear, too. You now have the ability to save the souls of those like me, and help the living to understand that there is an *amazing* afterlife.' The girl lifted her hand in a leaving gesture; her outline wavered again and her ethereal body melted away.

Annie sat quietly on the bed, her mind trying to compute all she had just witnessed. *This doesn't happen in real life, and not to the likes of me,* she thought. But after her last hallucination, which had caused so much concern within the doctor's camp, she decided to keep this latest one quiet. After all, the medical profession was not best qualified to deal with ghosts, and they were more likely to have her committed. It was vital for her to handle this latest visitation by herself, even though she was questioning her own sanity.

She suddenly had a feeling of isolation and swept the curtains back, welcoming the busy ward into her senses. For a few moments, she forgot about her ghostly visitor. Soon, her momentary sense of calm was rudely interrupted by the worst vision of all—her boss, Melina, striding in through the doors.

'Oh ... Melina, how ... lovely of you to visit me,' Annie said, sounding uncommonly sharp.

Melina, being the master of sarcasm, took no notice. Instead, she looked oddly over-anxious, a demeanour that was not her norm.

'Are you okay?' Annie asked.

'Yes, s-sorry ... of course I am. In fact, I'm the one who should be asking you that. How *are* you, Annie?' Melina said in her usual monotone voice.

Annie was just about to start an empty conversation with her, when their eyes were drawn suddenly to the television screen in the ward. An image flashed up showing photos and the names of the thirty-seven fatalities from the crash. And there, in full colour, was the confirmation that the dreadlock girl, Millie Arnold, *had* died. Her name hit Annie hard; it personalised the soul she had just seen. Her eyes became teary, but she was not going to share her sadness with Melina, the woman with no heart.

Suddenly, a photo of the priest, Father Mellion Jackson, appeared on the screen. Annie flinched at seeing him, and glanced across at Melina, whose eyes were wide with shock and her skin a shade of waxen white.

'Did you *know* him?' Annie said.

'Oh God … I've got to go.' Melina turned and hurriedly left without saying another word.

'What the hell?' Annie verbalised to no one. She was now more confused than ever. What had already seemed a complicated situation was fast becoming an even deeper mystery.

She turned back to the television, not really wanting to see more, but thankfully an attractive woman reporter was interviewing Thos. She hailed him as a hero, although he was playing down his role in the rescuing of so many victims. He explained to the now flirty correspondent that he had been the least injured person on the carriage, and anyone in his situation would have done the same.

Annie had only known Thos for a short time, but felt proud to be associated with this amazing man. She loved his self-effacing humility, and even though he had helped so many, he was still reticent to acknowledge his part in the rescue. But he had saved her in far greater ways than just carrying her to safety. He was the calming and steadying influence she needed in her life right now. He had been her only connection to sanity since the crash, keeping her mind in the real world and showing her true concern. Something she had never been used to.

Four days in a place with so many reminders of her ordeal had finally got to her. She needed to leave and occupy her mind with trivia again, and not with Milly Arnold's ghostly messages or Melina's strange behaviour.

Annie was pursing her lips when Thos walked into the ward.

'Hi, gorgeous lady, how ya doing? Or is that a stupid question? By the look on your face, you've had enough.'

'Oh ... sorry, Thos. It's just that everything is so *weird* in this place ... I just want to leave, but the doctors aren't keen. Can you believe they're still worried about my supposed head injury, and they're now saying I've got PTSD or something along those lines? So, because of that they won't let me leave without someone being at home, and of course my parents are too busy to look after me as usual ... What a mess.' Annie took a deep breath to halt any further outpouring of emotion.

Thos stared at her for a few moments. 'Well, I've been thinking about all this. And I know this is gonna sound crazy, and probably is, but ... I could have the perfect solution.'

Annie crossed her fingers tightly under the bedcovers, not daring to hope too much. Thos bowed his head, his jaw muscles moving as he clenched his teeth together. Annie could barely contain herself—he looked so sexy.

'Okay ... so I have a very comfortable place in Peckham, where I live alone except for my Siamese cat, Mr Pong.'

Annie's heart had started to race. 'I never took you for a cat lover, but a guy who gives home space to any animal is okay in my book.'

Thos shuffled his feet. 'Actually, I inherited Pong from my grandparents. Although, he *is* pretty cool ... and I swear he's telepathic: he gets excited when I'm just *thinking* about getting his food.'

'That sounds like an animal's sixth sense to me.' Annie laughed.

Thos sighed heavily, as if he wanted to get something of his chest. 'Look, Annie, I know this'll sound strange, and we've only known each other for such a short time. But I'd be really happy to keep an eye on you back at my place.' He coughed nervously. 'I'm just genuinely concerned about you and your predicament and … obviously you'll have your own room … and your own space.' Thos stopped and glanced upwards towards the ceiling. 'Oh God, I'm sounding like such a weirdo. I promise I'm not a stalker or anything, it's just that I … really like you, Annie, and I wanna help.'

Annie couldn't believe what she was hearing. 'I like you too, Thos.' Annie clasped her hands together. 'Now, let me think about your proposition for a nanosecond … YES, *please!*' She knew she was being utterly uncool, but she had always worn her heart on her sleeve. She put her good arm around his neck and gave him a gentle but meaningful kiss on his cheek. 'Thank you so much,' she whispered.

Thos raised his eyebrows at her response. 'That's … great. Let's sign you out of this place and get you home, er, in a non-predatory way, of course.'

They both laughed, and any remaining ice was instantly melted.

Thos was quietly delighted; he had never met anyone like this girl before. She had got entirely under his skin after only a few days of knowing her. And every day after visiting the hospital, he could barely get her crazy aqua eyes out of his head. He knew it was a completely insane situation to get into—but it felt … right.

Chapter Five

New Beginnings

Annie was taken aback when they pulled up in front of Thos's home in Peckham. She had not given a second thought to whether his home was an apartment or a house, rented or owned. She really hadn't cared, but this was not what she had expected at all.

The house stood in a square of large, individually designed, detached properties, all standing in substantial private gardens and set back from the road. Thos's house was built from imposing red brick in the Arts and Crafts style, with its original leaded windows set into mullions of stone, and brow-shaped dormers in its vast roof. A large arch spanned the pillared porch, with a gnarled wisteria twisting over its entirety. The vine was still dormant, but Annie secretly hoped she would be there to witness its full lilac-blue beauty in the coming weeks. She immediately fell in love with this gorgeous home.

Can this get any better? She thought, and then saw the number 3—her lucky number—above the green, studded front door.

Mr Pong, the Siamese, welcomed Annie and his master into the house with a louder than expected *meow* for his diminutive size.

Thos laughed. 'He's very vocal. Chats all the time, bless him.'

Annie scooped up the inquisitive cat, kissed his purring head and told him they would be the best of friends. But the cat stopped purring momentarily and stared at Annie intently with his vivid-blue angled eyes, as if looking deep into her soul. When he was finished with his silent inspection he jumped down, flicked his tail, and continued his chatter.

Annie spent her first evening with Thos eating a Chinese takeout. They drank two bottles of Pinot Noir which didn't touch the sides, and chatted into the small hours of the morning. She was surprised he was so open about his private life and was honoured that he was comfortable in doing so. But then their relationship had been brewing silently for so many months on their daily trips to London, and all they needed now to cement their extraordinary connection was to find out each other's strengths and weaknesses.

Thos opened up about how he had made his money, buying large properties at auctions in need of complete renovation, and refurbishing them to a high spec. All this was enabled by a substantial inheritance from his adoptive grandparents, which had allowed him to buy without borrowing.

'So how come you had adoptive grandparents, Thos?' Annie asked, she snuggled into the fur throw he'd thoughtfully placed around her.

'It's a bit of a strange story really ... But, I guess you should know who I am and where I come from. So, long story short ... In the early eighties, Frank and Dorothy Townsend, who lived here, took in a young Greek student called Adelpha Tadros. Apparently, her parents were strict Orthodox so they organised a trustworthy couple to look after their daughter while she was at university here. But little did they know that in Adelpha's final year at uni she'd get pregnant by an English student. Of course, the lad disappeared as soon as he found out. And when I was a few months old, Adelpha, left me with them, and for legal reasons they brought me up as their adoptive grandson.'

'So why didn't she take you with her?'

'Yeah, well, apparently … it would have brought shame on her family to go back with a child and no husband, so she simply left, and didn't return. I never had so much as a letter; the only correspondence from her family was when I was nine, informing my grandparents that Adelpha had died after a short illness. But there was no mention of me in the letter, so … It looks as if she never told them I existed. I just wish I'd known more about her, although she was obviously not worth knowing. In fact, this is the first time I've told anyone about my mother, apart from my best mate, Max, and a trustworthy old girlfriend.'

'I can't believe Dorothy and Frank brought you up, that's an extraordinary thing for an old couple to do.'

'Yeah, I know. But apparently, they were never able to have kids of their own, and thought I was a gift from God. Anyway, babe … I promise that's the only sob story I'll ever tell you. Now, I want to hear all about you.'

Annie had moved from the sofa down to the rug in front of the log burner. Pong climbed onto her lap and curled himself tightly, his tail flicking in time with his kneading paws.

'My life isn't half as interesting as yours, but I do have a loving grandmother, who can be a little overprotective sometimes … but she really is amazing.'

'What about your parents?' Thos asked, he picked up both glasses of wine and sat on the rug next to her.

Annie took a dainty sip, although she would have preferred to gulp it down, before telling him about her mother and father. 'Oh, I don't really know where to start with them … and it's pretty boring stuff. But Mum and Dad were not at all loving; in fact, as far as I can remember, they were always too busy with friends and spending my grandfather's money.'

Thos tilted his head. 'Wow, I'm sorry about that. It's strange, 'cause I always envied other kids having real parents … I thought they all had what I was missing.'

'Well, mine didn't ever show me any love. But I was okay because I had my imaginary best friend, Ellie.'

'Really? Yeah, well … I can understand why you would. I probably would have had one too, but I had my best mate, Max, who is definitely real.'

'Well … Ellie was very real to me, too. And I know it sounds daft, but I swear I learnt a lot from her. Oh God, how embarrassing! I'm telling you my innermost secrets, and now you think you've brought a madwoman home.'

They both started laughing as Thos topped up their glasses.

'Go on Annie, tell me more. How did ya end up working in London?'

'Well, I had to get away from the parents somehow, and, I luckily got into Central St.Martins art school to study *History of Art,* then afterwards became a Blue Badge tourist guide—which was brilliant fun. I used to get *huge* tips from American tourists, who loved all the ancient stuff.' Annie stopped and pursed her lips. 'Then I made a huge mistake taking a job as an apprentice art dealer at Hollingsworth's—with Melina as my boss, and I've regretted it ever since. But, I'm loving this break!'

Thos leaned over and stroked the cat, as it nestled on Annie's lap. 'I never thought I'd be jealous of Mr. Pong.'

Annie raised her eyebrows and stared into Thos's eye's. 'Er, there's no need to be,' She twisted around and gently placed the cat back on the sofa. 'It's time you went to bed, puss.'

The disgruntled feline squinted his eyes at her; begrudgingly jumped down, and sloped off to his lambswool bed under the stairs.

Annie turned back, scrutinising a face that she had dreamt about for months, although she was only just getting to know the soul behind it. 'Be completely honest with me, Thos. Did you really want to get to know me before the crash, or was it just that our lives were literally thrown together?'

'Yeah, our lives may have been thrown together, but I'd been trying to work out a plan previous to the crash, but I didn't want to seem to be hitting on you. I hate that sort of thing. And honestly, I was devastated when I missed the first train that day. Then, of course, seeing you made up for it. And what did I do? I bloody *winked* … What sort of bloke does that? I really thought I'd messed up big time.'

Annie laughed. 'Well, I have to say I'm glad you did, 'cause you really made my day. But if that crash hadn't have happened … I wonder how long it would have taken for us to finally talk?'

'I dunno … but life's a strange old thing.' Thos leant over and gently put his arm around her shoulders. 'Do you mind?'

'No, not at all.' Annie's life had been turned upside down in less than a week. She had gone through every emotion that had ever been recorded. It was as if she had overdosed on some crazy new drug that had caused her to have a wave of feelings she had never known existed before.

The following day, Thos had a meeting with his project manager. He told Annie to get some rest and that he'd get the shopping on his way back. She was overwhelmed by his kindness.

If I'd chosen a man out of thin air, it would have been him, she thought.

She dozed on the sofa with a loudly purring Pong nestled in her lap, massaging her legs with alternating paws. Every now and again, a claw would dig a little deeper than Annie's pain threshold would allow, but a small tap on the offending paw would immediately calm his fervour.

She closed her eyes, and within minutes her mind drifted into a comfortable sleep with pleasant merging dreams, the first since the crash. Then a soft voice interrupted her dream, it called her name…

'Annie.' Then it came again with more conviction. 'ANNIE.'

As she was rudely dragged back to consciousness, there was a bitingly cold chill in the air. Then, a needle-sharp pain seared through her legs as Pong dug his claws in; then he screeched like a banshee and flew off her lap. Annie's senses rushed back faster than her mind could cope with. Her eyes then focused clearly and widened at the apparition before her. She knew immediately that this ethereal form was another soul from the afterlife.

'You don't you remember me, do you, Annie?' The visitant spoke with amazing normality.

Annie stared at her—and faint recognition seeped in. The spirit-woman was beautiful, with slim features and intense dark eyes. Her coal-black hair shimmered and floated.

'Who was your only friend when you were young?' the spectre questioned, almost as though it was a routine conversation.

Annie's mind flashed back to her early years, then all became clear. 'Ellie? You *can't* be real.'

'Well, I'm *hurt* by that, Annie.' Ellie smiled.

Annie was taken aback by the cheeky spectre. 'But my mother kept telling me you were just a fantasy … and that I was stupid to believe in you.'

'Yes, she did, didn't she?' Ellie said, scornfully pulling a face. 'She wasn't a very nice or loving mother. But, Annie, *she* was the stupid one, not you. Although I think you're slowly finding that out for yourself now, isn't that right?'

Annie, started to shake inwardly with the shock of seeing her imaginary friend again. 'Why did you leave me when I needed you most, Ellie?'

'You didn't need me at the time; it was *you* who chose not to see me. But I have you back now, and for good reason. You have to help me, and in return I will help you.'

Ellie smiled again as she evaporated like a mist on a breeze.

Flashbacks of Annie's childhood seeped in; it seemed that Ellie was in her every memory, both good and bad. She really had been her constant companion and best friend in her younger years.

But Annie's overriding thoughts were of the priest, the dreadlock girl, and now Ellie; they were all real—albeit ghosts. She could now see, hear and smell them, too, but she was confused about Ellie's request for help.

A key in the door turned noisily and brought Annie's mind back with a jolt. How on earth was she going to tell Thos about her unworldly visitor?

He unknowingly made it easier for her.

'Wow, you look like you've just seen a ghost … are you okay?'

Annie had to be truthful if the visions were to be a permanent part of her life; she had to share them with the man who had chosen to be with her, she owed him that much.

She spent the next hour explaining more about her childhood companion and all she had experienced since the crash, including Mr Pong's reaction to the visitation. She thought the cat's response would add gravitas to her story.

Thos quietly took it all in.

Annie sat forward on the edge of her seat. 'I promise you, Thos … It was all real to me.'

It was clear that he was confused, but he put his hands on hers and took a deep breath. 'Well, that's something you don't hear every day.' He shook his head smiling, although still with a furrowed brow. 'It's actually the strangest story I've *ever* heard, and believe me, I've heard a few.'

Annie tried to interrupt, but he stopped her.

'No, it's my turn to talk now, babe. You have to give me time to digest all this, but I'm not dismissing it as twaddle. After all, Pong *is* a sensitive cat.' Thos took her hands in his. 'But if you believe in all of this, there *is* someone I'd really like you to see.'

'You're *kidding* me ... not a psychiatrist?' Annie said, louder than she had meant to.

'Did I say that? I'd actually like you to meet a good friend of mine who works for the Spiritualist League in London.'

Annie's eyes widened in disbelief. 'Really?'

'Yes, really. Her name's Madeleine Upton. She used to be an old girlfriend of mine, but we both got over that years ago. Anyway, she's not one of those clairvoyants or whatever you call them, although you might think so. She professes to know everything about the subject. She's the secretary of the League, so I think she'll be just the right person to help. She's a good girl and can chat for England, but I'm sure she'll be happy to introduce you to the right person to help you further. What about it, babe?'

Annie shook her head. 'I just don't deserve you, Mr Tadros. That would be amazing ... You surprise me more and more every day. But are you *sure* you're okay with all of this?'

Thos grinned. 'I should have known from the first time I set eyes on you, you were gonna be trouble, and not the normal girlfriend.'

'Girlfriend?' Annie said, she put her arm around his neck.

Thos rolled his eyes. 'Yeah, well, we've actually known each other for months. So, why not?'

Chapter 6

∞

GRAN

After Thos had made an appointment for Annie to meet Maddy, she had googled the Spiritualist League of Great Britain. She hadn't realised that such a place existed until now. It was full of people like herself, with similar abilities, and there was so much going on: private sittings of clairvoyance and healing sessions held daily. More excitingly for Annie though, there were classes where she could develop her mediumship, and watch demonstrations by resident and visiting mediums.

Before she could dive into all that, she had to go back home to Southampton to collect some clothes and general girlie stuff. She had previously asked her parents to bring her personal items to the hospital, but her mother had simply thrown a few random things into a bag without any consideration for her daughter's needs. She was also disappointed in them for sounding relieved that someone else was going to be looking after her while she recuperated. It was just like them to pass the buck.

Annie had booked a National Express coach from Victoria to

Southampton. She was early, and had time for her favourite morning pick-me-up. A double espresso was just what she needed, and she enjoyed sitting in the smart new coffee lounge crammed full of individuals waiting for their day to begin. She scanned the various characters, which reminded her of that fateful morning on the train: normal people going about their everyday lives but not yet knowing the outcome.

A tall, elegant lady with platinum-grey hair got up and slowly walked over towards Annie with the aid of a walking stick.

She handed her a folded newspaper. 'I've finished with this, my dear, would you like it for your trip? And I hope you don't mind me saying, but your hair is *absolutely* stunning. I used to be a redhead when I was your age.'

Annie's heart melted at the empathic old woman. 'Well, I hope my hair turns out to be as beautiful as yours one day, too.'

'Thank you, my dear, I'm sure it will … We redheads all end up platinum white sooner or later.'

'Oh, and thank you for the newspaper, that was very thoughtful of you. I could do with it to keep my mind occupied.' Annie took the paper graciously, and in doing so, momentarily brushed the old lady's arm with her hand; it was just enough to send a rush of vivid images through Annie's mind.

She saw a beautiful ballerina with red hair on a stage, holding a large bouquet of flowers and curtseying to the audience. Then, a second later, an image of the ballet dancer lying on a road in front of an old Rolls Royce, with a distinguished bearded man kneeling down— comforting her. And a final fleeting image of the dancer dressed in white, sitting in the Rolls with the same man. Annie smiled as she ran through the story in her mind, but she still silently questioned whether it was just her vivid imagination or her new ability.

She sat on the coach and opened the paper; it made her shudder, they were still running stories about the victims from the crash. She had stopped watching the television and reading about the accident since leaving the hospital; she had seen and read enough. But just before she closed the paper, a small article caught her eye about a memorial for the victims. It was scheduled for the following day, to be held at a priory near Basingstoke. She simply had to go.

Her parents *hadn't* offered to pick her up from Southampton coach station, yet again, they were too busy preparing for a dinner party. It was their turn to host the evening for their bridge group, with the same old cronies they had been entertaining for years. But Annie had told them it was a fleeting visit anyway and that she would see them again soon. After all, she didn't want to interrupt their *important* gathering.

She caught a taxi back to her house from the coach station. Strangely, once inside, her little home meant nothing to her. She found it bizarre, as all she had ever wanted to do was to buy her own place. She had managed this by using part of her sixty-thousand-pound inheritance from her grandfather as a deposit, banking the rest for a rainy day. And although her new relationship was reasonably secure, keeping a separate home for her independence was hugely important—just in case that rainy day ever happened.

She had called her Gran to see if she could visit whilst in Southampton, and although the old lady had been under the weather, she was her usual open-hearted and welcoming self. She had meant more to Annie than her parents ever had; she had seen her through every milestone in her life—whether it was boyfriend problems or other occasions of much needed advice.

Gran's eyes lit up when she answered the door. 'Eee, it's my girlie.'

Annie couldn't help smiling at her Lancastrian accent. 'Hi, Gran, how are you?'

'I should be the one who's asking. I'm so pleased you're okay, love. Go on, tell me what's been happening.'

Tears welled in Annie's eyes. 'I don't really want to talk about the crash, Gran, it's been a strange couple of weeks.'

'That's fine, I don't want to know about that anyway … Just the new man in your life. You've got one, haven't you?'

Annie looked quizzically at her; nobody knew about Thos. 'Yes, I have … And he's lovely, Gran. He's incredibly caring, and just what I need in my life right now.' Then Annie frowned.

'What's up, love? It's not like my Annie to be down … Come on, get it off your chest.' The old lady put her hand on Annie's shoulder.

'You always knew when something was off-kilter with me, Gran. And I need to talk to you, 'cause you know I can't talk to Mum and Dad—they've never understood me. And as usual they're just too wrapped up in their own world to care about what's going on in mine.'

'Selfish, that's what I say. Your dad's not a bad man though, Annie, he's just weak. It's more your mother, she's never been interested in anyone but herself. I'd like to say they deserve each other, but your dad just needs to grow a pair and keep her in her place.'

'GRAN! *"Grow a pair"*? Where on earth did you hear that from?'

'Well, I think it describes your dad perfectly.'

They both laughed.

'Come and sit next to me, my darling girl,' Gran said. She plonked her ample bottom on the old sofa.

Annie remembered the threadbare piece of furniture so well. She sniffed it and smiled. 'Oh gosh, I'm having a real déjà-vu moment, Gran. I remember this smell from when I must have been about three or four. Don't you think it's sad that I don't have any happy memories from back at Mum and Dad's? This has always been my home—here, with you.'

'I know, love, it is sad. But do you remember telling your mum that you didn't want to live with them any longer? You stamped your feet in a temper at her.' Gran shook her head.

'God, yes I do. I was a little madam then, but if I remember rightly that's when you took over looking after me, so my tantrum must have worked.'

'Oh yes, it did that, my girl. You were always a feisty little thing, and you tried to stick up for yourself, unlike your father, bless him. Although he's my son, he's more like your grandpa was: scared of his own shadow. But I loved him all the same, he were a good man.'

'Yeah, I miss Grandpa so much. But all I can remember of him was that he used to sit in that old leather armchair over there constantly smoking cigarettes. Weren't they called Craven A and came in a red and cream packet?'

'My goodness, lass, you're right! How strange that you remember something like that.'

'Yeah, and I also remember climbing up on this sofa and sitting on the backrest. You were never cross with me when I was having fun.' Annie stopped talking for a while and smiled, reminiscing the past.

'Are you going to tell me what's been troubling you, love?'

'Yes, I suppose so, but it's a bit of a strange story. Do you remember Ellie, Gran?'

'Ellie? Of course I do, she was your little spirit friend.'

'What?' Annie was almost knocked off the sofa by her gran's comment.

'Your parents were having none of it, they wouldn't listen to me. In fact, they both insisted Ellie was just in your imagination, but I knew better. She was your guide, Annie, and I dare say she still is. Why, lass, have you seen her recently?' the old lady asked, as pragmatically as if she was talking about a living friend.

Annie flung her arm around Gran's neck. 'I do love you, Gran, that's just the best news ever. And yes ... I have seen, *and* talked, to her. How do you know about her?'

The old lady got up and went to her mahogany chest. She opened the top drawer and brought out an Edwardian beaded bag. 'Now, love, this belonged to your great-grandmother—on my side of the family, of course. I've not really talked about her much, because the family thought it were all a load of rubbish. She were called Mary Ellen Lockwood. Special, she was, just like you. She was a spiritualist, and the best medium and healer this country had ever seen.'

Annie's mouth was open, as she listened to the most wonderful news.

Gran continued, 'This purse contains Mary Ellen's healing crystal. She would have wanted you to have it, as the gift of seeing, hearing and healing is passed down through the female side of the family. I'm just a sentient, which has to do with feeling and perception. But you, Annie, are so much more powerful. You always have been but didn't know it. Now, you will have a lot to cope with as your new powers awake, but you're young enough to deal with each ability as it comes. Healing will be one of the last and coping with that will take more time and knowledge than the others, especially when it comes to using your crystal to enhance the power. But you'll feel it, my darling, and when the time is right ... you'll be exceptional.'

'Why didn't you tell me all this before, Gran?'

'Because the gift left you when you were young. But I knew it would return, it did with me, when I was about your age. So I've been waiting.' The old lady placed her wrinkled palm on Annie's cheek. 'You must go and help people now, love. Use this gift well, but take care. Sometimes you will see and hear things you don't want to. There are *evil*-minded and sometimes vicious spirits and imps amongst the good ones, and you'll have to guard against them, they can be *very* clever. But you'll be okay, my darling girl. As your power grows, you'll come to recognise the bad ones. Most of the time you'll be helping people with their grief and passing messages on from their deceased loved ones. Everyone has a calling in life, Annie, and this was pre-destined to be yours.'

Annie stared at her gran for a moment, she had never heard her speak so eloquently on any subject before. She looked at the crystal and held it close. 'This is the most precious thing you could give to me, Gran … Thank you so much.'

Annie turned to leave, Gran held her hand. 'I can die a happy old woman, now the gift has been passed onto you, love.'

'Oh no you don't, Gran, you're gonna have to hang around a lot longer! I need your help with all this.'

Gran kissed her cheek and stroked her long red hair. 'You don't need my help, darling girl. You have an unusual power, like my mother did, and her great-grandmother before her. And with this power you will help so many, both the living and the dead, to find peace in this world and the next. And one day soon you'll find out *why* your gift is so much stronger than that of those who came before you.'

'What do you mean "one day soon", Gran? Can't you tell me now?'

'No, Annie … It's too much for you to take in all at once; but you'll understand when your abilities have become more powerful. Now, go on with you, you take care and always remember your old gran loves you.'

Annie's trip back to London on the coach was the polar opposite to her inbound journey—which had been full of apprehension. Although her parents had disappointed her yet again, this had made her decision to leave them be so much easier. Then there was dear old Gran, what a woman! She had always been there for her in the most honest, loving way; but that day she had been a complete revelation and had made Annie feel as if she could cope with anything—at any time.

Chapter 7

∞

The Memorial

'I'm sorry, babe, but I can't make the memorial today,' Thos said. He looked down in embarrassment.

'Oh, sweetheart, I really wanted us to go together.'

'Yeah, I know. But … Apart from having a meeting with the planners this morning, the truth is, there's probably gonna be some people there I helped after the crash, and I can't be doing with thank yous and all that nonsense. Anyway, I bet the bloody press will be there, too. It's just not for me, babe—not today.'

Annie reached up and kissed Thos on the lips. 'Don't worry, it's probably best you don't come. But *I* have to. I don't know why, but I'm being drawn there for some reason, and God only knows what's going to happen.'

∞

Although the priory on the outskirts of Basingstoke was monumentally impressive, it still initially made Annie's stomach churn. She was well aware that it was her convent education that had converted her into a staunch non-believer and been the catalyst of a phobia for anything theological. But her passion for architecture had helped her overcome her aversion to religious buildings, and this particular priory was one of the finest examples she had ever seen. She had a huge amount of respect for all who had laboured for so many years on this incredible memorial to *their* God.

The vastly high ceilings were spectacularly painted with stunning Da Vinci-style murals. Celestial cherubs and angels surrounded Christ and his apostles, seemingly watching over their minions, while the large stained-glass window above the chancel glowed, illuminating their serene faces.

The nave was almost full to capacity, but Annie managed to find a space at the end of a pew near the back. *Thos was right,* she thought. There were many camera crews and journalistic photographers distastefully propped against every pillar—ready as always to get the 'tear rolling down the face' scoop. And although the memorial had obviously been organised by the well-meaning, it seemed to be fast turning into a parody. Many of the congregation were ghoulishly ogling the proceedings—clearly only there to replenish their need for morbidity.

Since the crash, Annie's dream-like visions had become more and more clear. And whereas before she had thought them to be part of her vivid imagination, she now knew, that they were irrefutable insights into the lives of those she did not know. And with that came a new ability to see auras emanating from all she studied. Although she had no knowledge of their purpose, she sensed their meaning. There were many auras in the priory, especially near the front of the nave, where the grieving families were steeped in ominous dark red shrouds—exuding immeasurable sadness.

Annie was scanning the congregation when her eyes were

suddenly drawn to a person standing in the aisle on the other side of the nave. She was not surprised, the contrastingly smiling face was the 'dreadlock girl,' clearly standing by the side of her distraught parents.

It was now clear, why she was drawn there that day. And although the service had started, she became preoccupied with how she would broach the fact that their daughter's ghost wanted to talk to them.

The congregation stood to sing a hymn, but Annie's lips were sealed. She had never been able to understand, on occasions such as this, why the bereaved would want to join in—praising God and thanking him for his mercy—especially when there had been so many lives lost. But it seemed she was in the minority, as almost all the congregation participated.

During the hymn, the families who had been affected by the crash queued down the central aisle to light tall white candles in honour of the victims. The candles gave out a warm, flickering glow, and together with the colourful beams streaming through the stained-glass windows, the church felt almost welcoming.

The two men next to her were clearly something to do with the press, they seemed uninterested in the service, constantly scanning the packed pews for a hint of a story.

The man sitting directly next to Annie whispered to her, 'I see you've got an injury, were you in the crash?'

The colour in Annie's cheeks rose up hot—with anger. 'Really?' she said, her eyes drew scathingly thin.

The other man butted in. 'In other words, mate, none of your damned business. Isn't that right, miss?' He laughed.

Annie lifted one eyebrow at him to affirm his interpretation. She was still fuming when she glanced back at the altar, but this time the sunlight seemed to be glowing through a shimmering veil. She looked up to see an impatient Milly Arnold, who was standing in front of her with the light from the windows shining through her ethereal body.

Annie jumped. 'Will you please wait, I'll be over when this has finished,' she said in a loud whisper.

Milly did as she was told and literally disappeared back to her parents, but Annie could feel the two men staring at her. She smiled to herself; both of them simultaneously slid along the pew in the opposite direction.

'Nutter!' one of them said.

The service continued for forty minutes with a bishop leading the readings and songs. He was clearly happy with his baritone singing voice, as it blasted out of the speakers, almost drowning out the choir and congregation. The service finally ended and the singing bishop with his tall white hat slowly walked back down the central aisle, nodding at the congregation as he passed.

People started to move; it would be now or never to deliver the promised message. Annie walked over to the couple, who must have been in their mid-fifties; their loss had clearly taken its toll on their drawn faces. Annie thought how normal they looked; not the sort of people to have a daughter with dreadlocks, although they probably had had no choice in the matter.

Annie approached them, and the mother smiled shyly, clearly realising that because Annie's arm was bandaged, she must have been in the crash too.

Annie's stomach churned. 'Hello … Are you Mr and Mrs Arnold?'

'Yes, we are … How did you know?' Milly's mum said with her head tilted to one side.

'Would you mind if we had a chat for a moment?' Annie asked, her heart thumping hard.

The couple looked at each other. 'No, that's fine, isn't it, Reg?' the woman said, she turned to her husband. But he shrugged, expressionless.

It was clear to Annie that the couple had been completely broken by the tragedy; they were unable to feel or to be bothered with anyone. Little did they know, their daughter was standing next to them.

'I expect you've guessed I was in the crash too,' Annie said, slightly nauseous.

'Were you a friend of Milly's?' the mother asked.

'No, I didn't actually know her. This is going to sound really strange, and I don't mean to upset either of you, but I have a message from her.'

There was hope in Mrs Arnold's eyes. 'Oh ... did she give you a message before she died? We were told she went instantly.'

Here we go, Annie thought to herself, and took a deep breath. 'No, she didn't. She gave it to me ... *after* she died.

Mr Arnold grabbed hold of his wife's arm, as if holding her back from getting too hopeful. Milly became agitated. 'Go on, tell them, *tell* them.'

Annie clasped her hands tightly together. 'Okay, so ... Immediately after the crash, I saw your daughter standing in the carriage. At first, she looked confused, but believe me, not as confused as I was at the time. Milly smiled at me, then literally vanished. But then while I was in the hospital, I saw her again, standing at the bottom of my bed. She told me that I had the power to see and hear the dead, and that I should help the living to find closure ... And the dead to move on by giving messages to their loved ones. That's why I'm here today to see you both.'

Millie's mother looked shocked, then turned to her husband. 'Did you hear that, Reg? I told you I still felt her around us, didn't I?'

But the father shook his head, as if he'd had enough. 'It's a load of old *rubbish*, Cynthia.' He spun back to face Annie. 'I've heard about people like you, and I hope you're not one of those coffin chasers.

But if you are the *real deal,* young lady—which I very much doubt—our girl would tell you something that only we know, as evidence that she's still around.' His voice started to sound choked. 'And I hope for your sake it's the latter, because we really have been through enough this week, and my missus can't take much more. So, say what you have to say, and then leave.'

'I was expecting that reaction, Mr Arnold, and worse, to be honest,' Annie said, relieved that they hadn't walked out on her already. 'Look, I completely understand how upsetting this must be for both of you ... But, as I said, Milly appeared to me while I was in hospital and told me to tell you both that she was finally at peace and happy. She said that all she had wanted for so long was to be on the other side, because she'd been unhappy for years. I guess she was trying to say that she'd suffered badly with depression.'

The mother put her head back and looked up at the large crucifix hanging above the altar. 'Thank you, God, she really is at peace now.' The woman's tears flowed freely.

The father stood staring at Annie, clearly shocked.

But Annie forged on. 'Oh ... and she also told me to tell you both that none of her sadness was your fault, and that you couldn't have changed the outcome of her life. She said the crash saved her soul, which I didn't really understand.'

The father sighed deeply. 'I think that's because we're Catholics, and after she'd tried to take her own life last year our priest came to see her. He actually told her that it was a sin to commit suicide, and that her soul could not be saved if she succeeded. So the fact that she died in the train crash ... did actually save her soul.' The man put his hand on Annie's shoulder. 'Did she say anything else?'

Annie started to shake her head negatively, but Milly interrupted. She leant forward and whispered in Annie's ear—as if telling her a secret. 'Give them this message and it will help them find peace, too.

Thank you so much, Annie.'

Orbs of light flickered around Milly; she smiled as she recognised old friends. Then a bright radiance from the stained-glass windows engulfed her—and she was gone.

Although Annie's eyes were filled with tears, she knew that what she was about to relay to Milly's parents was the evidence they needed to move forward.

'Milly has just whispered, "Tell them I'm so sorry for all the heartache I caused them and thank them for being such amazing parents."' Annie then looked at Milly's mother. 'She also said that her soul was there when you identified her body ... And that you put a small glass fairy in her hand.'

Both parents gasped, and the mother raised a handkerchief to stifle a sob.

Annie continued, 'She told me that she used to believe in fairies, but she realises, now, that they are just little angels. And the last thing she said was ... "Tell my mum ... fairies *are* real."'

Chapter 8

∞

THE AUCTION

Thos had a property auction to attend; and it was one he couldn't miss out on. Even though Annie had an appointment at the hospital which he should have taken her to.

A large derelict church in Dulwich had been on his radar for some time and had finally come up for sale. One of the local planners, who just happened to be a friend of Thos's, had given the green light for a change of use to residential. The derelict church, along with other neglected properties in the area, had become a beacon for vandals, pressurising the local council to ease planning laws and build in the affluent community.

Thos was unusually excited about this possible purchase; the guide price had been set at a million pounds and if he spent around eight hundred thousand on renovations there would still be a substantial profit in it. In fact, he had contemplated selling his grandparents' antiquated home in Peckham and moving into the church himself. Dulwich Village and the locale had always been an area he had aspired to. But because his private life had moved on apace, so too had his longings to leave his old memories behind and build new ones.

The auction was being held at a large hotel near Dulwich that had become a regular meeting place for London property developers, mainly old 'barrow boys' done good. Thos immediately bumped into a few of his rivals, all of them keeping their fancied properties close to their chests. They crowded around him wanting to know about his recent experience with the crash. Some congratulated him on his new status of 'hero,' while others who knew him as a friend took the 'gypsy's kiss'.

He was pleased that none of them had heard about Annie; he was determined to keep her a secret for as long as possible, especially from these reprobates.

The auctioneer called for all attendees to take their places. Thos, armed with his catalogue and lucky bidder's number, 137, stood in his usual spot at the back of the old ballroom, where he could keep his eye on known competition.

After a swift start, the auctioneer came to lot number 8, the Dulwich church. He started at six hundred thousand, but no one raised their hand. So down it dropped to five hundred thousand, which flushed two bidders out—and it was off. Thos held back, not wanting to show his cards too soon, and watched the opposition pushing the price up in increments of twenty thousand; then it started to slow. His heart was beating fast, which was unusual for him; he was generally known to be the 'cool operator' during auctions. The bidding stopped at seven hundred and eighty thousand. Thos waited for a few seconds—and up went his number. The auctioneer checked for bids online and then pointed to Thos.

'Ah, we have a celebrity in our midst. Mr Tadros, our very own hero from the train crash. Good to see you up and about, sir, and back here supporting our auction house.'

Although the ridiculous announcement made Thos inwardly furious, it seemed to have thrown the only other bidder off track. The hammer fell at eight hundred thousand, for bidder number 137.

Thos was inwardly delighted with his winning bid, but stayed calm. Although he was desperate to leave as quickly as possible to get back to Annie with the news, there was paperwork to sign and money to change hands. He knew he was stuck and ended up recounting his story repeatedly to all the reprobates.

Thos already had preliminary architects' drawings of the church to show Annie, but had been waiting to own it before telling her. Inwardly, he was more excited about this ambitious purchase than he'd been about any other property. Especially now that he'd snapped it up for two hundred thousand under the guide price.

He had already planned the big reveal to Annie, but first he was going to introduce her to his oldest and best friend, Max. He owned the finest Greek restaurant in London, where they would be dining on authentic homemade Greek fare cooked by Max's mama that evening.

∞

Annie was waiting in Orthopaedics for her turn to have an x-ray, along with many people like herself with broken limbs. She was daydreaming about her new life and how amazingly it was panning out, when someone tapped her on her shoulder. She jumped and let out an involuntary squeal.

'Ooh, sorry, Annie.' The offender giggled.

She turned around to see her favourite gay man. 'Poppet, I'm *so* pleased you're here, sweetheart. Have you got time for a chat?'

'No, I haven't … but that's not going to stop me from getting my daily ration of gossip.' And he squeezed in next to her with a feminine flourish. 'Now, how's that Greek *God* of yours, sweetie?'

'He's lovely, Pops.'

'I *told* you he was your man, didn't I? And what a hunk, I'm *so* jealous.'

'Hands off ... he's mine now.'

Annie was contemplating whether to ask for a favour; she had so many unanswered questions swimming around in her head. 'Poppet, sweetheart, what happened to the people who died in the crash?'

'Eww ... that's a strange thing to ask.'

'It's just that I wanted to know more about Father Mellion Jackson ... You know, the priest who died in the carriage I was in?'

'I know who you mean, sweetie: the chap you *thought* you saw in the corridor. You frightened the *bejeebers* out of me that day. I have to be completely honest with you Annie, I thought you very odd—but then, as you know, I like odd.'

'Thanks, Poppet; but that's a bit "pot calling kettle" don't you think sweetheart?'

They both laughed louder than they should have, and a few disapproving glances were thrown their way.

Annie tried to put her serious face on for a moment. 'Look, I *really* need some information about him, and haven't got time to tell you why. But this is *so* important to me, sweetheart. Could you find out some stuff, like where he's from, which church he was attached to, and maybe the names of any relatives who were contacted after the crash? I'd be *so* grateful if you could.'

'Bloody hell, you don't want much, Annie, do you? I can't just go *snooping* around in classified documents. But ... maybe I might just have a *little* peek... given it's for you, darling. As long as I get an invite to the wedding!' Poppet pouted his filler-enhanced lips.

'Stop it, you! There's no wedding, but I promise if there was to be one, you'd be at the top of my list, okay?'

'Oh goody. Well, I might have a gander at the odd record just for you, then.' Poppet winked cheekily.

They exchanged mobile numbers and hugged each other goodbye.

Annie was happy to have finally found the gay friend she'd always wanted. Gay guys had all the attributes Annie hoped to find in friends: fun, outrageous behaviour, loyal, and, unless they were bisexual, a safe bet. She'd never had many girlfriends, most were too much like hard work. Jealousy and bitchiness seemed to be a prerequisite for the women she knew, and although gay men were masters at being bitchy, it always seemed more tongue-in-cheek than in their female counterparts.

A nurse interrupted Annie's thoughts by pointing to the x-ray room. 'You're next, Miss Prior.'

After the x-rays, the nurse who had removed Annie's stitches remarked on how incredibly well her wound had healed, considering it had only been just under three weeks.

Annie remembered having a terrible gash on her knee as a child, after falling off her bicycle because her mother had refused her stabilisers. The family medic, Doctor Charles, had made a huge deal about how quickly her knee had healed, and how there was very little scarring after only one week. It was enough of an incident for Annie to remember it well, all these years later.

She waited in Orthopaedics for the results and was expecting to be there for hours—the department was heaving. She guessed that most of the outpatients had been involved in the crash too, there were so many in wheelchairs with casts on their legs, some with neck braces, and even one with both arms in plaster. She was thankful that her superstition gods had been watching over her … or had it been someone—or something—else?

Annie checked the rota to see who the orthopaedic doctor was that day, and was delighted it was Doctor Lambert, even though he had been slightly odd on the day of the crash—he looked even more perplexed when she walked into his surgery.

'Hello again, Miss Prior, how are you?' he asked, intently staring at her over the top of his fashionable wire rimmed glasses.

'I'm ... fine Doctor, thank you.' Annie shifted uneasily. 'Is everything okay with the x-rays, Doctor Lambert?'

'Well, Annie ... to be honest, I'm at a loss on what to say. Your radius, which as you know was an open fracture, should *just* have started to heal at this stage. Instead, it has almost completely healed with hardly any intervention.'

'Well, that's good news, isn't it?' Annie said with a huge smile.

'Yes, but it's been barely three weeks and you haven't even had a cast on it. I have to say it's most unusual; in fact, I can't remember another case like it. A compound fracture like this one would normally take at least six to eight weeks to get to this stage, and often months for recovery after that. You've either got an angel watching over you, Annie, or something in your blood that's accelerated the healing process, and as a scientist I'd rather it be the latter. Actually, if you'll excuse me for a moment, I'm going to consult a colleague about it.'

The doctor left Annie giggling to herself. *An angel watching over me ... little does he know.* She briefly wondered if it was something to do with her emerging abilities and the crystal Gran had given her.

Doctor Lambert came back ten minutes later, clearly more confused than before. 'Annie, would you mind staying a little longer and having some blood tests done? We're at a loss as to why you've healed so quickly, and I'd like to get to the bottom of it.'

Annie had no wish to remain at the hospital any longer than was needed and had to think quickly for an excuse. 'I'm sorry, Doctor, and it's nothing to do with you but I'm really not comfortable here.

It's just that I'm starting to feel a little anxious, you know ... memories and all that.'

The doctor looked down at her previous notes and saw her possible diagnosis of PTSD. 'Ah yes, I completely understand, Annie. Maybe when you're feeling a little less anxious, you'd be good enough to pop back again. My colleagues and I really want to know your secret.'

Annie was relieved but thought she would take the opportunity to dig for answers to her own questions. 'Yes, of course, no problem, Doctor. But would you mind me asking about one of the fatalities from the crash before I go?'

Lambert's face looked puzzled.

'Er, no, not at all, but if that person died on the train, then he or she would have been taken to a designated mortuary near the crash site. We only have information on fatalities if they die en route to the hospital, or post-admittance. Was it someone you knew?'

'No, but he died next to me in the carriage. I just wanted to get in touch with his family so I could let them know that he wasn't alone when he died,' Annie said, trying to sound compassionate about the hideous priest.

'That's a *really* lovely thought, Annie. I can put you in touch with a family liaison officer who's been in charge of this matter since the crash; she'll be able to help you.'

Annie left the hospital none the wiser, but she had a feeling that her digging would unearth answers that, for one reason or another, would change her life.

Chapter 9

∞

MAX

Annie had expected to come home from the hospital with a cast on her arm. Instead, she had been discharged with a full recovery letter, pending further blood investigations. It had got her thinking about her great-grandmother's healing powers and whether or not her new psychic ability included self-healing that was automatically triggered when she got injured. So many questions, with no real answers ... yet.

Thos had messaged earlier to say he'd been waylaid at the auction. It was to be their first date out at a restaurant together; their relationship had been moving on at a steady pace. Up until now, Annie had been doing most of the cooking in Thos's well-equipped kitchen, with him graciously complimenting her dubious culinary skills. He, on the other hand, was an amazing cook—Greek food being his speciality, and almost every dish delicious. The only ingredient that turned Annie's stomach was the slimy vine leaves that he wrapped fillings with; they were simply a step too far for her palate.

Although Thos was only half Greek and had never set foot in his mother's homeland, he had embraced the lifestyle fully. He had many

Greek friends, none of whom Annie had met, but that night was important to both of them—she was finally going to meet Max. He was not only the owner of Thos's favourite Cypriot restaurant, Celaeno, but he had also been his closest friend since childhood.

Annie walked in, and knew immediately what Thos was thinking, as his eyes had widened at seeing her without even a bandage on. But she skilfully evaded any in-depth conversation on the subject; the last thing she wanted was to overload him with her weirdness—especially at this early stage in their relationship.

∞

Max was everything Annie had expected of Thos's best friend. He was a colossal man-mountain with a booming voice, and his beaming rugged face and kind brown eyes put Annie immediately at her ease.

'Mama, come here ... it's Thos and his lovely lady!' he shouted.

His mother wobbled in, still tying a pristine white apron around her voluminous figure. She was surprisingly short in stature given that Max was her son, but made up for her lack of height with her width—and loud Greek personality. She was chubbily pretty, her plump unlined olive skin making her seem much younger than her sixty-plus years, but her emerging silver roots, edged with overly dark tints, betrayed her age.

∞

'*Hello,* my *darling,* Thos,' she said in a strong Greek accent. Then, surprisingly, she punched his arm hard and proceeded to give him a mouthful.

'Why you not come to see me before now, you bad boy?' She stretched up, kissing both his cheeks twice, and hugging him with a bear-like grip. She then turned to Annie. '*Ahh* ... I see why. You have been very busy finding this *beautiful* girl.' She grabbed hold of Annie's hand.

A strange inner vibration course through Annie's body, and she immediately saw an image of a large kind faced man standing behind the tubby little woman. He was Max's double—but older, and his strong Greek accent came across immediately.

'You have to tell my beautiful Leto I didn't mean to lose the money. I was doing it for her and our boy. Tell them both I *love* them with *all* my heart.' His image started to waver ... and then he was gone.

The visitation had happened so fast, that time—seemed to have stood still around them.

Mama looked quizzically at Annie, but she gently smiled and turned to Thos.

'I like this one, and so do you, I think,' she said, laughing loudly. 'Don't just stand there, Max-i-moose, they need food and wine ... Bring them mezze and Hatzidakis, now!'

Thos and Annie sat at a romantic table with a candle and a small vase of fresh cornflowers. The restaurant was exactly how she had imagined it. The interior was crammed full of white pillars and statues of Greek gods and goddesses. The chequered white and sky-blue tablecloths with matching blue hand-painted chairs looked typically rustic, and a Greek urn set into the wall—spouting water into a fountain base—rounded off the Grecian experience.

Annie intuitively felt that the restaurant had been designed many years before by Max's very Greek parents and had been kept the same as a memorial to his father.

Thos reached across the table, held Annie's hand and whispered, 'I know they're a bit loud, but they really are lovely people, babe.'

'Don't apologise for them ... I can see exactly why Max is your best friend, and I *really* like Leto, too.'

'Leto ... how do you know her name? Everyone calls her Mama.'

Annie sucked in a breath through her teeth. 'Ah ... well, I didn't want to spoil our evening, but ... her husband told me.'

Thos raised his eyebrows and flatly said, 'He's dead, Annie.'

Annie nodded. 'I know, but he came through when she was holding my hands ... He was a gambler, wasn't he?'

'Wow, that's spooky ... yeah,' Thos said. 'But nobody knows that apart from his family and close friends. He really did come through, didn't he?'

Annie was relieved that Thos believed her. 'Yes, and he also insisted that I tell Leto he was sorry for losing the money; apparently he did it for the family. Oh, and he said to pass on that he loves you all *very* much.'

Thos's eyes moistened. 'You don't know what this'll mean to them both ... and me, of course.'

Annie sighed with relief. 'Oh good, I hope it brings some comfort and closure. Tell me what happened to him, sweetheart.'

Thos sighed. 'Hmm, well, Alex died unexpectedly from a huge heart attack three years ago. And when Mama and Max were going through his finances, they realised he'd gambled thousands from their savings—on bloody horses, would you believe. They didn't even have enough money left for the funeral.' Thos stopped for a moment and looked pensive. 'So *I* paid for it, which was absolutely fine; he was like a dad to me. But he was a good man, Annie, and I know he didn't mean to lose their nest-egg, so of *course* I was going to help them. Max and Mama were both devastated, and *so* angry with him ... I never thought they'd get over it. But time moved on, and they finally forgave him. At least they still own the restaurant and apartments above, although they've both worked bloody hard these last three years to build up their savings again. They deserve success and happiness.'

'You're amazing, sweetheart, and I'm so glad you paid for his funeral. I felt he was a lovely man, and ... he was as *huge as* Max, too.'

'Yeah, he was ... I miss him badly, babe,' Thos said, shaking his head. 'It's *bizarre* that you've just spoken to him.'

'Well, I didn't actually speak to him, he spoke to me.' Annie thought for a moment. 'Maybe you shouldn't give them his message tonight. They don't know anything about me yet, and I think it'll be a bit strange telling them I'm a psychic with a message from Alex—especially on our first meeting.'

Thos nodded his approval. 'Yeah, that's a good idea. They'll be in tears when I tell them and I don't fancy that this evening, especially not in the restaurant. It'll be getting busy soon.' Thos took her hand. 'Now, can we change the subject just for a minute. I've got a surprise for you after dinner, and I'm so excited for you to see it.'

'Ooh, what is it?' Annie said, trying to keep her cool.

'It's not going to be a surprise if I tell you! But it's something I've wanted to own for such a long time.'

Chapter 10

∞

THE CHURCH

They arrived in Dulwich courtesy of Uber. Annie shivered and tightened the belt on her camel coat against the damp evening air. She scanned the leafy avenue, still none the wiser to Thos's surprise. The murky beams from the streetlights revealed very little apart from a large eerie church with a tower, looming in the midst of a graveyard. The time-worn headstones, drunkenly strewn in the overgrown plot, made it seem like something out of a Hitchcock movie.

'Oh, come on, Thos, what is it?'

'You're looking at it, babe.' Thos pointed and laughed.

Annie took one step back. 'You're kidding me ... The church?'

'Yeah, what do ya think?' His eyes were wide with excitement.

'It's ... *huge*! How many apartments are you going to get into that?'

'Er ... no ... I thought it would make a great private home.'

Annie was still a little tipsy from the wine and was slow on the uptake. 'Ha ... it's going to need a huge family to take that on.' Thos's words finally registered. 'Oh, sweetheart, I'm so sorry, I didn't realise: you've bought it for yourself?' Her heart beat quickened with embarrassment.

'Actually, babe, I've bought it for *us*. I know it's all a bit quick, but I just thought it would make a great home in which to start a new chapter. I don't want to carry on living in my grandparents' home, there are just too many memories there. And this could be just what we need, especially after what we've both been through. But you don't like it, do you?'

'No, no … I … love it. Maybe not as a church, but yes … it could be a great home. It's slightly ironic, though, an atheist living in one of God's houses.'

Thos laughed. 'Didn't think of that, but it would be *bloody* funny.'

'Could you really sell Dorothy and Frank's house, sweetheart?'

'That's just it, babe—it will always be their home.' Thos put his arm around her shoulder. 'Come on, let's have a look around and see what you think.'

Annie could see he was feeling anxious, and tried her best to look enthusiastic, but she had never been any good at concealing her true feelings. It didn't help that bad vibes had started to creep in.

∞

The huge Gothic porch sheltered a pair of equally impressive studded arched doors. Annie smiled when she saw the oversized key, which resembled a bottle opener.

'Well, that'll look nice on my keyring,' she quipped.

Thos laughed, appreciating her humour, and lifted his torch to find the light switches. Only a few of the many iron lanterns flickered on, inadequately illuminating the vast interior. Annie snatched in a breath—the scale of the building took her by surprise.

'Isn't it incredible?' Thos said. 'We could do so much with it.' His voice echoed back a moment later.

'Yeah, I'm sure we could … I'm just a little overwhelmed, there's *so* much to take in.'

Annie walked over to the centre of the nave, where she imagined packed pews had once stood. The vaulted ceiling towered forty feet above her, with carved oak beams braided through the ornate plasterwork. The side aisles were separated off by monumental, pillared arches, which stood in semi-darkness. But the grimy stained-glass windows allowed a faint light to trickle through from the streetlights, providing a warm glow.

Annie looked down at the engraved flagstone floor. 'Those look like tombs … Oh my God, are there actually people buried under here?'

Thos took hold of her hand and laughed. 'Yeah. I forgot to tell you about the sitting tenants … Do you mind if we share it with them?'

'No, I suppose not … as long as they're not too noisy.'

'Ha ha, that's my girl.' The deep wrinkle between his brows started to relax.

They walked towards a small oak door below the tower, where the bells had fallen silent many years before. Strangely out of character for this old building was a luminous hazard-warning tape wrapped around the base of the spiral staircase, cautioning potential buyers about rotting treads and years of bat guano.

Annie slowly made her way around this redundant shrine to a so-called god. The fact that it was superfluous was affirmation that people were leaving him in droves.

Although an atheist, Annie still felt a pang of sadness; she had always understood that people needed direction and a purpose to congregate en masse. The world was dividing, becoming selfish and cruel, with very little compassion. She disliked so much about religion and what it stood for, but also knew it was one of the only ways to bring like-minded people together peacefully.

Thos's demeanour was endearing. He rushed around, showing her the features of his latest acquisition and gushing with ideas for its future development. But Annie had a strong sense of foreboding, although she suppressed her fears for his sake. Thos unfolded the plans that had already been drawn up for the renovation. He was eagerly pointing out the ideas he'd come up with himself when his mobile phone suddenly rang, echoing around the vast walls.

'I'm so sorry, babe, I'm gonna have to take this, it's my foreman.'

'No problem, I'll have a snoop around myself.'

'Yeah well, be careful ... it's all a bit rickety.'

Annie smiled at his concern and picked up the small torch that he had brought with him. She scanned around and noticed another door at the far end of the nave. She looked back, but Thos had moved to the entrance to get a better signal. She walked towards the elaborately carved pulpit, she became aware of a pulling sensation; it felt like someone had grasped her hand and was drawing her closer to the door. She opened it with difficulty; the stiffened hinges resisted her efforts, and a sudden rush of air was drawn downwards, as though the chamber below had breathed in. But Annie was compelled to descend into its darkness nonetheless; the torch guided her down towards the unknown. Her heart thumped audibly, but she kept her breathing muffled, not wanting to disturb whatever was lurking in the shadows.

She reached the flagstone floor twenty feet or so beneath ground level, she lifted the torch to reveal more. The tall, arched tunnel seemed to run the full length of the church above, with smaller arches within its walls. Stone shelves held tell-tale remnants of rotting wood left over from coffins that had long ago been removed.

Annie squinted further into the catacombs, and could just make out a large, closed, ornate metal gate at the far end. But her waning light was not strong enough to penetrate the solid darkness beyond. The previously bright yellow beam had become a dim grey, with her shoes kicking up years of dust from the uneven flagstone floor.

A sudden chill of freezing air blasted through her, and a recognisable prickling sensation crawled over her entire body. Annie's eyes filled with tears, an immense feeling of sadness overwhelmed her; she knew it was a precursor to an unworldly event. She turned quickly back towards the staircase, and the light from the torch dimmed again; it fell upon the spirit face of a young, hollow-eyed boy.

Annie jumped with shock—dropping the torch onto the stone floor. It spun around, its beam rotating and seemingly attracting more despairing young faces. But before Annie had the chance to escape, a small voice whispered, 'He's here ... Please, help us get away ... we want to go home.'

That was enough for Annie. She sped up the stone steps and back into the welcoming air of the nave. Thos glanced up from his call and, seeing the panic on her face, raced over.

'Christ, what happened?'

Annie pointed down the staircase. 'Children ... there are *spirit* children down there.'

'Oh God, no ... not in my church.'

Thos' previous excited expression had disappeared; he looked angry.

Annie stared at him for a split second, incredulous at his reply. 'I'm so sorry, Thos ... but it's just too much for me. Can we go home, please?'

Their journey back from the church felt awkward; Annie recounted the story, while Thos kept silent throughout.

'So let me get this right. You saw the ghosts of children in the catacombs, and they were asking for *your* help?'

'Yes, that's about it. I know this is all so strange for you, sweetheart, but it is to me, too. Seeing and hearing the dead is something I just can't turn off at the moment.'

Thos pulled the car into the driveway and sat staring ahead at the garage doors. He was quiet again, which intensified Annie's apprehension. But she wasn't ready for his reaction.

'Your gift, Annie ... is becoming a bloody nuisance!' He got out of the car, slamming the door behind him, and stormed off to the house.

Annie knew exactly why he was upset, but couldn't help being disappointed in him all the same.

She followed a few minutes later. 'I said I was sorry ... what else can I do?' Her stomach was somersaulting.

Thos rolled his eyes. 'I'm just really *pissed* off this has happened, babe. You don't know how much this church means to me, Annie, and I was hoping it would to you, too. But this latest visitation has put a damper on the whole thing.

Annie held back the tears. She was cross with herself for not showing more strength of character after seeing the spirit children, but mainly for letting Thos get away with his temper tantrum. She had vowed from a young age that she would never let anyone speak to her the way her mother did to her father.

Thos looked down as he shuffled his shoes. 'Okay, babe, I've got a question for you. If we get this sorted ... whatever *this* is ... could you ever see yourself being happy there?'

'I have to be honest, Thos. Living in a church would *not* be my first choice, but if it means us being together ... then yes, of course I could. But please don't speak to me like that again, because I *really* won't hang around if you do.' Annie's heart was thumping so hard she thought he might hear it.

Thos looked momentarily shocked by Annie's retort, then half-smiled and shook his head. 'I'm sorry, babe, it's just that living in Dulwich has been a dream for me for such a long time, and then when the church came up for sale, I felt it was all falling into place.

But this whole ghost thing scares the bloody hell out of me. It's not the ghosts so much as, maybe, losing my dream. But I couldn't deal with losing you too … That's why I got so upset and mouthy. I'm crap at stuff like this.'

Annie smiled, a sense of relief washed over her, but also the realisation that she should have been more sensitive to Thos's feelings, too.

She leant in—to kiss him on the lips—but he got there first.

Chapter 11

∞

MELINA

Annie paced the Mayfair pavement outside Hollingsworth's Gallery; her heart pounded. Handing in her notice that day was the best decision she had made in a long time, but carrying it through was terrifying her more than any ghost could.

She checked through the window to see her boss chatting to a customer; now was her chance to get this over and done with. Annie wasn't surprised at the cold welcome she received—there was no change in Melina's demeanour.

'I'm busy—I'll be there in a minute, Annie.'

Annie slowly walked around the gallery checking out the newly hung works of so-called 'art'. She had never been a huge fan of abstract and couldn't understand why such paintings were easier to sell than figurative art—which she preferred. But her opinions had never carried any weight with Melina.

The gallery had been selling paintings ranging in price from five hundred pounds for limited edition giclée prints to over two hundred thousand for fashionably weird works. But the strangest of all the art selling for sixty-thousand plus on a regular basis was produced by an obscure German artist named Anilem—who apparently no one had ever seen. His reclusive life and the dark complexity of his work had left collectors from all over the world fighting for the ten paintings he produced each year. Even more bizarrely, Melina had exclusive rights to his work but had never divulged the reason why to anyone—least of all to Annie.

Something moved out of the corner of Annie's eye on the far side of the gallery, and for a split second thought it was another customer. But then those familiar goosebumps prickled, and the sudden chill was palpable. She was looking at a woman who was not connected to the world of the living. Her face was sorrowful, with dark, grief-stricken eyes. Annie glanced over at Melina and the customer, who were blissfully unaware that there was a ghost in the gallery.

Annie was getting used to seeing these unworldly beings, but this one made her feel unusually uncomfortable. She had an overwhelming awareness that this particular soul had a profound reason for her presence, and that somehow it was going to greatly affect Annie's future.

The spirit held out her hand. 'Tell my daughter ... I am *so* sorry for ignoring her cries for help. I was a terrible mother.' The spectre let out a cry of anguish and doubled over as if in pain; then the apparition faded.

Oh God ... it's Melina's mother, Annie thought. The resemblance was uncanny, albeit Melina was a slightly healthier-looking version.

Annie realised this was going to be a difficult message to give, especially to the only woman she had ever been scared of. She had two choices—she could either tell her, or not, although the latter was not an option, her strength of character had rarely allowed her to back down from problems that needed addressing. It was a stubbornness she had possessed since childhood, to the annoyance of her parents.

And it was needed more than ever that day; she had made up her mind where her future was going. Although her first dilemma was how to broach the fact that the ghost of her boss's dead mother was here, in the gallery.

Melina closed the door behind her customer and turned to Annie. '*What* is it, Annie? You're acting ... odd.'

'Yes, well, I'm not surprised,' Annie said aloud, having meant to keep it to herself. 'Okay, Melina, I have something to tell you, and I'm not sure how you're going to take it.'

'Well, *come* on ... spit it out.'

Annie had to start somewhere. 'You look... *so* much like your mother.'

Melina glared at her. 'What the *hell* are you talking about, and what do *you* know about my mother?'

Here goes, Annie thought. 'Apparently, I used to have a psychic gift, which I lost when I was a child, but because of the train crash it seems to have come back again, with a vengeance! And now, basically, I can see and hear the spirits of those who've passed.'

Melina's face changed. She suddenly seemed unsure, but then she scowled again. 'Are you telling me you've seen my mother? You know *nothing* about her, or my past. Are you for real?'

Annie started to feel she had made a huge mistake coming to the gallery, but had no option, and had to continue. 'Yes, Mel ... And for the first time in my life, I *am* for real, and I don't care what you think of me anymore. I have just seen and heard your mother here in the gallery, and she's seriously distraught. She wants to get a message across to you.' Annie recounted it word for word. 'Now, if you want me to leave, I'd be more than happy to oblige.' She turned towards the door.

'No ... Please, don't go, Annie.'

Melina's reaction was not what Annie had expected. Her boss's chin started to crinkle; tears filled her eyes, and the impenetrable exterior seemed to be crumbling in front of her. At that moment, her mother's spirit sensed her daughter's distress and came back stronger than before.

'Tell Mellie that I love her so much, but I was never as strong as she was. When her father died, it broke me, and I became weak. I should have listened to my poor girl ... and got rid of her stepfather. Tell her I did try, but he ...'

Annie suddenly lost her clairaudient connection, she saw Melina's mother distractedly placing a hand over her heart. She then vanished as quickly as she had appeared, taking with her the intense cold Annie had been cloaked in.

Melina slowly walked to the door and locked it, and when she turned back, her strong persona seemed to have changed to that of a tortured soul.

Annie quickly moved over to her and, without thinking, took hold of her hands. 'Your mum called you, Mellie.'

Melina's dark eyes widened. Annie could now easily read the thoughts that were flooding her mind. Melina realised that Annie was genuinely connecting with her mother and crumpled into Annie's arms; tears that had long ago dried flowed freely. Annie continued softly recounting the few words that Melina's mother had managed to get across before disappearing.

Melina's heartache seemed all consuming, her sobs snagged her breath. 'I don't understand how you do it, Annie, but I do know that you've just spoken to my mother. Nobody else knew what my parents called me, and only Mum and myself knew about that bastard of a stepfather. She was never actually married to him, you know, it just looked better not to have a live-in lover. Not that anyone around us really cared.' Melina breathed in deeply. 'I really did love my mum, but she left me to be mauled by that bastard. What mother does that?' Melina's eye's dropped, as if embarrassed for a moment. 'When I was …' She stopped and seemed to change her choice of words. 'If I was a mother, I would protect my child with my life, not like my mother did.'

Annie was confused by Melina's statement, but then everything that had just happened had baffled her. If this was the precursor to all her future otherworldly visitations, then she was in for a hell of a ride.

Melina's incongruous sincerity was something Annie had never seen before. 'I'm so sorry for being such a bitch to you all this time, Annie. I'm really not the hateful person you think I am. It's just that I had a such a bad time when I was younger, and I suppose being nasty to everyone who came into my life … was a self-preservation thing. I know you hate me, but please give me another chance? I need you to be here for me now.'

Annie was completely taken aback; she never would have thought she would see the day when Melina showed a sensitive side. And found herself feeling sorry for this woman who she had despised for so long.

'I'm *so* sorry you've had such a bad time, Mel. Do you want to tell me the whole story?'

Melina sat on the edge of the desk. 'You just don't realise, Annie, what a *hateful* and perverted man my stepfather was. He was my dad's so-called friend, but he had major issues. I was only twelve when Dad died, and even though I had enough sadness going on in my life, this awful man moved in on my mother … and she was too weak to say no. It didn't take long before he moved in on me, too, and my mum simply turned a blind eye to whatever he did. She wanted a man around so much that she let him take over everything we had, including our home. My poor dad had put so much into making it a wonderful place for Mum and me, and this *disgusting*, immoral man took it all … including my innocence. I tried to tell Mum again and again, but she ignored me. For *Christ's sake*, Annie ... that man got me pregnant when I was just fourteen! But Mum was too scared to stand up to him, and instead of being there through the worst time in my life, she disappeared.'

Melina shook her head then wiped her tears away. Her sadness turned to anger, but she continued. 'Shocking, isn't it? But not as shocking as when I was told two weeks later that Mum had been found in the Thames ... They said it was suicide.' Melina then shouted: '*She* chose to leave *me* ... when I needed her most. How can a mother be that selfish?' Melina put her hands over her face and wept again.

Annie was stunned at her revelations. For the first time in nearly seven years, she understood why this woman hated men so much. And why she was relentlessly nasty to anyone who seemed to get too close.

Annie's heart ached for her; she leaned forwards and put her arm around Melina's heaving shoulders, still with many unanswered questions swimming in her head: What did Melina know about the priest? Where was her stepfather now? And what happened with her pregnancy? One thing Annie knew for certain was that handing in her resignation was not going to happen that day.

Melina straightened her back, trying to pull herself together. 'I literally don't have anybody in my life, Annie. I have no relatives, and you know I don't have any friends ... But that's my fault. You've got to understand that after my mother died, I pushed everyone out of my life, including that man.' Melina's voice cracked, but then she laughed. 'I threatened to tell the police that he'd raped me if he came back to my father's house again. But he'd been acting differently for a while anyway and seemed to be scared of his own shadow for some reason. So, after my threat, he left, and thankfully I never saw him again. You see, I grew up so quickly because of all that I'd been through, and I suppose I looked and acted older than my years ... No one questioned why I was on my own. I had nobody to look after me, apart from Dad's solicitor, who wasn't much older than me then; and he kept quiet about it all too, and just helped me with legal stuff. From then on I looked after myself. That's when I started to get rid of all my bad memories and selling my parents' home to a developer for a crazy amount of money was the first step. Do you know, I hadn't realised that a house on a half-acre plot near central London would be worth so much. But it's now an office block. And because art and painting was the only thing that had kept me sane throughout my nightmare years, I knew exactly what I wanted to do with the money. And all these years later, here I am in my own five-storey freehold gallery, and I did it all before my twenty-first birthday.'

'It's an incredible story, Mel, but I wish you'd have told me this years ago. I could have helped, and we might even have been friends by now.'

'Yes, well, obviously my loss ... but I need you now, Annie.'

Annie didn't have to think about her answer, her heart was breaking for Melina. 'Well, I'm here for you, Mel,' she said. And wrapped her arms tightly around the woman who only an hour before had been her nemesis.

Melina stopped crying; 'We need to make up for lost time, so can I start by showing you my apartment upstairs? You've never been up there, have you?'

Annie shook her head, still shocked at Melina's complete reversal of character, although she was still expecting her to hiss at her. But no—Mel had changed.

Melina took Annie's hand. 'Come on ... In fact, nobody has ever been up there before, apart from my solicitor, so you'll be the second.'

'I ... feel ... honoured, then,' Annie said, still reeling.

Annie had only ever been up to the first-floor stock room where the excess art was kept. She had never expected to be allowed up to Melina's private sanctum. It was going to be a real insight into this woman whom she had known for years but who was only now allowing her into her life.

Annie had been desperate to have a nosey around; she already had visions of what she thought it would be like. She hadn't realised that her uncorroborated insights had been actually spot on.

It was a dark apartment, but on a massive scale. The semi-pulled blinds let just enough light in to see the muted decor and soft furnishings. Browns, blacks and beiges were cleverly used to draw in the high ceilings. And the walls were perceptively covered with Anilem's moody oils. All this contributed to the gloomy atmosphere, yet Annie still felt strangely at home.

'Isn't there another floor in the roof, Mel? I've seen it from the street.'

'Yes, but that's just full of stuff I took out of my parents' home, so I never go up there.'

'Funnily enough, this is sort of what I expected. It's dark but … stunning, Mel. Why don't you lift the blinds? I bet it's a great view.'

'No, I don't like letting London into my home, it's too frenetic … and I like to be quiet. It's been my sanctuary for so many years, I couldn't actually live anywhere else now.'

'I'm so sorry you've been through all that. It's just not fair that someone has to suffer so much in one lifetime.'

'You've got such a good heart, Annie, and I've treated you *so* badly, but I really need you now as a friend and to help with the gallery if you can. You're the only trustworthy person I've ever met, and now even more so. I know one hundred per cent that I want *you* to run the gallery for me. I've got to get away and start having a life for myself, otherwise I won't survive. How about it? *Please* do this for me.'

'Christ, Mel … I never expected you to say that. And I've got to be completely honest with you ...' Annie looked at the floor momentarily, then straightened. 'I actually came today to hand in my notice.'

Melina seemed shocked. 'You can't, Annie, you just can't!'

'I know that *now*. And of course I'll help, but would you consider someone else for the manager's role?' Annie had had an epiphany that had literally sprung from nowhere, almost like someone had whispered it to her. But it seemed to be the perfect solution if she could make it work.

'I trust you, Annie; if you can think of someone who could step into the role, then I'm up for giving it a try ... Anything to have a break.'

'Right, well ... I have a really good friend who is honest, sweet and *slightly different* ... but I think he would be ideal.'

'Oh God, you know I don't trust men, Annie.'

'Well, this one might just be perfect then. He's not a conventional sort of bloke, in fact, he's gay. I think you'll really like him. He just takes a bit of getting used to because he's really quite camp ... but lovely with it. Both of us can groom him into the gallery's ways, and I'm sure the clients will love him too.'

Melina seemed pensive. 'He might be just what's needed here, an injection of a different character and style. And I promise to be nice to him, Annie. But how much experience has he had?'

Annie was winging it now; she had no idea if he would even be interested, but she was having her usual good feelings about it. 'Ah, well he's a great people person, Mel. And don't worry about experience, he's quite passionate about art, and that's all the qualification he really needs. We'll teach him the rest, and you wait and see—he'll be absolutely perfect! I just need to talk him into it.'

Annie had jumped feet first into offering something she was completely unsure about. But then, that's what she had always done throughout her life. It was the only scenario she could think of, without having to give a definitive answer about her own future at the gallery. But there was one more question that was burning to be asked, and it was now or never.

'Sweetheart, I hope you don't mind me asking, but when you came to see me at the hospital, you had a strange reaction to one of the photos of a victim from the train crash. He was a priest who was in the same carriage as I was. In fact, he died next to me ... Did you know him?'

Melina's face changed. 'Oh ... I ... thought he resembled someone I knew a long time ago, but I was mistaken. Annie, I really don't want to talk anymore, I'm just feeling emotionally exhausted. And all I want to know right now—is that you and I are okay.'

Annie was disappointed not to find out more about Mel's connection to the priest, but she was delighted that her relationship with her old boss had finally been sorted.

She looked compassionately at her. 'We're all good, Mel.'

Chapter 12

∞

THE LEAGUE

Annie had been experiencing an overwhelming awareness of an intangible source of energy. As though she was being guided through adversity and lifted over every obstacle in her way. She now had the conviction that a guide, or team of them, was helping her through every moment of her new life. She just wanted to know who they were and hoped all her questions would be answered by the Spiritualist League, although she had been in two minds whether to go or not. How could she possibly involve one of Thos's old girlfriends in her future? But he seemed completely comfortable with the situation, it would be churlish for her not to be as well.

Her only other worry was that she had never met a fully-fledged clairvoyant medium before. She had spent time researching and watching many famous mediums on YouTube, but none of them seemed to have the same experience as she did when seeing and hearing the dead. Most of them perceived symbols, rather than observing ethereal beings who had changed very little from their earthbound self. But Annie did now on a daily basis. She was still worried though, that she'd make a fool of herself in front of someone she considered to be the real deal.

Her trip to the league in Holland Park from Peckham was mostly on the underground, although even after years of working as a Blue Badge guide, she would rather walk miles than 'tube it' anywhere. She had never classed herself as a true claustrophobic, but that pinch of panic always gripped her when travelling through the bowels of London, and now even more so since the crash.

The platform was crushingly busy, with swarms of blank faces staring vacantly ahead, and while she waited, she remembered her Blue Badge days—when she would begrudgingly bring foreign sightseers down to catch one or two connections. She would regale them with her knowledge of the various lines and the fact that the underground was the oldest metro system in the world, dating back to 1863. The Americans loved stories from the mid-eighteen hundreds and were always astonished that the Brits were building such incredible underground structures during the same era their ancestors were cowboys and Indians.

Annie smiled at her memories and found herself people-watching again. It had become less of a pastime and more of a necessity, mainly to keep her mind occupied; she was now hearing souls whispering most hours of the day.

It was chilly down in the maze of tunnels, but so much better than in the summer months when the air was stifling and thick with clammy bodies and hot exhalations. Annie was sure most of her coughs and colds were caught down there, after breathing in the recirculated and virus-loaded air.

Suddenly, her mind reverted back to the coldness, the temperature had dropped from chilly to arctic. The usual prickling sensation was making her stomach churn; she knew it was the precursor to yet another supernatural appearance. This phenomenon, although now an almost daily event, was still unnerving.

There was a sudden vacuum and rush of air that changed the atmosphere again; a train appeared from the dark tunnel and the throng of commuters surged forward. Annie's name was being called from behind; she swung around with her copper mane billowing over her face. She fleetingly glimpsed her spirit friend, Ellie, but with an obscure figure standing behind her. Annie's hair settled and dropped away from her eyes, horror filled her senses when she realised the other figure was the priest. She was dumbstruck and her mind swirled like her hair; her confusion grew.

Ellie screamed at Annie in a demonic outburst. 'Only *you* can deal with this priest ... get rid of him for me ... *and* for them.' Another drag of air seemed to suck her away—and she was gone.

But *he* remained, grinning and shaking his head. 'You will *never* get rid of me.' He laughed grotesquely, then returned to the obscurity of the shadows.

∞

Annie had been so shaken by Ellie's crazed outburst that the rest of her journey slipped by without any more phobic thoughts. But she was also bewildered about the connection between Ellie and the priest, and contemplated returning home for reassurance from Thos. But no, she had to go; it wouldn't look good if she didn't show up for her first meeting with Madeleine.

∞

The large grey Victorian building with Gothic overtones looked exactly how Annie had imagined it. Her research into the League had shown that the property had been bequeathed in the early part of the nineteenth century to a spiritualist sect by Wilfred Wright. He was a wealthy widower who had believed his generous gift would guarantee his place in the afterlife and that once there he would be reunited with his beloved wife again.

The story had made Annie think about her future life with Thos, and how wonderful it would be to spend a lifetime together and then to continue it on in the afterlife.

She climbed up the large stone steps, and although the property looked sinister, the very essence of the building was benevolent and welcoming. The entrance hall was of huge proportions, with a life-sized statue of Sir Arthur Conan Doyle centred in front of a sweeping staircase. Annie had researched his extraordinary life story and was delighted to see his striking effigy in such a prominent position. She remembered reading about his spiritualism and psychical research way before her own ability had reappeared; but even then, she had felt a strange connection to him. She smiled at his chiselled face. Although he was not a handsome man, his groomed handlebar moustache and his superior stance gave him an air of dignity and knowing.

'I feel as though I know you,' Annie said quietly to the statue. But her mind was brought back abruptly, she became aware again of visitational vibes, this time much stronger than before.

'Hello. Are you Annie?'

Annie turned towards the voice half expecting a spook, but was relieved to see a very tangible young woman. 'Yes, yes I am.'

'I thought so ... I'm Maddy,' the young woman said; she thrust her hand out, expecting a shake. 'It's so nice to finally meet you.'

Annie showed her relief by ignoring the outstretched hand and warmly hugging the stranger instead. 'I'm so pleased to meet you, too.'

Madeleine looked startled by Annie's unexpected embrace, but it seemed to have the desired effect, and she relaxed immediately.

'Thos has told me so much about you,' Madeleine said with clear sincerity. 'I must say he sounded happier than he has been for such a long time, and now I can see why. Come on, let's grab a cuppa and have a chat, then I'll show you around.'

Annie wasn't sure whether Madeleine was just nervous or a fast speaker, but she had an openness and an endearing bubbly demeanour, although her appearance was not what Annie had been expecting. She had an attractive moon-shaped face, framed by a short Joan of Arc-style bob and a heavy fringe, and a womanly figure that was the polar opposite of Annie's skinny size eight. But her dark blue eyes revealed a kindness of spirit and an empathy that Annie had rarely seen in a woman before.

'Thanks so much for meeting up with me, Madeleine, I'm so grateful ... 'cause I didn't really know who to turn to. But then Thos, bless him, told me about you and the League.'

'Oh, you're very welcome, Annie. I'm fascinated to find out about your abilities, and I'm sure we can help you. By the way, I hate my name, it sounds so formal, so please call me Maddy or Mads.'

'Thos told me you were special, and he's obviously still very fond of you—in a non-romantic way, that is.' Annie pulled an embarrassed face.

Both girls laughed, and Annie linked arms with her.

'Actually, Annie, would you mind having that coffee later? There's a clairvoyant meeting going on in the Conan Doyle Hall right now, and I'm sure we can slip in the back without disturbing anyone. I'd really like you to see Sam Hargreaves in action; he's one of our most intuitive and talented psychic mediums. In fact, almost all our clairvoyants aspire to be at least half as good as he is, although recently he's been showing his age a bit, bless him.'

Chapter 13

∞

THE CONAN-DOYLE HALL

The hall was much larger than Annie had expected. It had thirty rows of centre and side pews, with dusty folded chairs stacked around the walls waiting for a popular event. The hall had clearly been architecturally modelled on a church, but was devoid of crucifixes or stained glass. The atmosphere, although a little sleepy, was peaceful and welcoming.

The seated congregation were mainly a silver-haired ensemble, although amongst them were a few hopeful younger faces—also patiently waiting to receive evidence from departed loved ones.

Sam Hargreaves, the medium on stage, was in full flow, aiming his message at a grey-haired woman sitting a couple of rows back. She had a handkerchief covering the lower part of her face, poised for the incoming flood of emotion. Annie was trying to concentrate on the message, which seemed to be a little generic in its content, but she was eager to listen and learn.

The old medium could have been in his early seventies, but it was hard to tell, he seemed worn down by life and his yellow pallor gave away an underlying illness. Annie was confused about Madeleine's comment that he was one of the best psychics the League had ever seen; nothing he had said so far had been at all impressive.

'Maddy, are all of Sam's messages normally like this?' she asked, trying not to sound disappointed.

'Hmm, yes, well ... I think he's a bit off his game today.' Madeleine shrugged in slight embarrassment.

Annie scanned around. 'Why are so many people standing when there are loads of seats available?'

Maddy looked to. 'What people?'

Annie realised these seatless souls were not here to receive messages—but to give them. She had been so consumed with what had happened that day that she had forgotten the overwhelming visitation vibes she'd had upon arriving. Her sudden awareness brought the vibes flooding back, causing a sensory overload and a rising nausea.

'Maddy ... there are *so* many spirits in here.'

Her new friend was visibly shocked. 'Roughly *how* many, Annie?'

'Ooh, I don't know ... maybe ... twenty or thirty.'

'And you can see them all clearly?' Maddy's eyes were wide.

'Yep, and they all seem to be just as bored as the congregation.' Annie smiled.

'Yes, well ... he's doing his best,' Madeleine said in Sam's defence, still flabbergasted at Annie's revelation. 'I've never heard of any psychic, *clearly* witnessing multiple souls before.'

The medium stopped talking abruptly and pointed towards Annie. 'I'm being drawn to the young woman with long red hair standing at the back. I have so many spirits waiting to give messages, but there is one *entity* that's pushing them back and he won't let me speak to anyone but you.' The old psychic suddenly staggered forward, grabbing hold of the back of a chair; he looked even paler than before.

Annie knew immediately who was causing this disturbance; The priest creepily stepped forward from the deepest shadows into the light. The same disgusting grin appeared that had haunted the depths of Annie's nightmares. But for the first time in her life, she was overwhelmed with anger. The priest had invaded a sanctuary to infect the good with his evil. And without a second thought she yelled across the hall, 'How DARE you come here … you're not welcome … GET OUT!'

The whole congregation jumped in their seats and turned towards the source of the discourteous interruption. Even the ghostly priest seemed shocked by his admonishment, but soon regained his gruesome composure and pointed to Sam Hargreaves.

'You will be over here with me soon.' He laughed, and pointed towards Annie. 'And you … you stupid, meddling fool, you're not strong enough to get rid of *me*!' He snorted a laugh again, as he melted back into the shadows.

The congregation were clearly unaware that there had been a disagreement between two souls, albeit one of them dead. But thankfully the old medium intervened by clearing his throat loudly into the microphone, and slowly addressed the audience.

'We seem to be having trouble with an over-zealous spirit, so if you don't mind, ladies and gentlemen, I'm going to have to bring this exciting meeting to a close today. But hopefully we'll see most of you here next week … God willing. And thank you for your continued support.' He turned from the microphone, and beckoned to Annie.

The congregation got up to leave, most of them glaring their disapproval towards her. They whispered amongst themselves, disgruntled that their service had been cut short.

Maddy stood with her mouth slightly open. 'Good *God*, Annie, what just happened there? That was *crazy*.'

'Yeah, I'm really sorry, Mads. I just got upset with an evil spirit who keeps turning up.'

'No, please don't say sorry; it was amazing, probably the most excitement we've ever had here. Let me introduce you to Sam, I'm sure he's desperate to meet you ... especially now.' She hurried off towards the stage.

Annie was just about to follow when a diminutive silver-haired lady with a painfully bent spine walked slowly over towards her, blocking her path. She turned her head to one side and looked up. Annie was shocked to see that she had sparkling pale blue eyes, even though she must have been in her late eighties. The elderly lady gently rested her gossamer-like hand on Annie's.

'You, my dear, have an extraordinary ability ... but I'm afraid it will draw bad spirits to you because you are so strong. You see, they thrive on electrical energy, which you clearly have plenty of. You must learn to use your inner strength to cope with their malevolence. There will be many, just like that pesky priest, who will try your patience. But don't worry, my dear, you're strong enough to kick his large bottom and others' out of this world and back into the depths of hell, where they all belong.'

For a moment Annie stood in silence. 'You saw him too?'

'Oh, yes, my dear, very clearly. Many years ago I used to be up there on that very stage with Sam. But you'll have noticed, I have a slight curvature, which made it very difficult to see the audience, although I always had a great view of my feet. So anyway, I gave up the ghost ... so to speak ... and now I see souls all the time. And believe me, they're a bloody nuisance. But you, my dear, have something much more than I've ever had, and my only advice is to embrace your abilities and enjoy every minute of your charmed life.' The old lady's blue eyes glinted. 'Enough from me now, I do go on.'

Annie was energised and inspired by the wise words from such an enlightened old soul. She suddenly became aware that the congregation had filtered out without her noticing. The old lady was shuffling slowly behind them, and lifted her hand in a goodbye gesture.

'Goodbye, and thank you,' Annie said, but the old dear kept walking.

'ANNIE,' Maddy shouted across the hall—beckoning her to join them on the stage.

Sam was sitting down, looking even older than he had before.

'Hello, Mr Hargreaves, I'm Annie Prior. And I'm so sorry for my outburst, but my emotions took over ... I can explain.'

'Oh, please don't apologise, Miss Prior, and no explanations necessary,' Sam said, then reached across touching Maddy's arm. 'And thank you, Madeleine, for bringing *such* an extraordinary young woman along today.'

'You're very welcome, Sam, although I hadn't realised just *how* extraordinary she is. She actually saw about thirty spirits around the hall.'

'I'm not surprised. I can feel their energy, and yours too, Annie,' Sam said, looking a little less in pain than before. 'Would you stay and talk with me for a while? Oh, and Madeleine, would you be a star and get Annie and me a cup of tea. I know it's not in your job description, but I'd be *awfully* grateful ... I'm parched.'

'Of course I will, Sam, I need one too after what just happened.' Maddy left to do Sam's bidding.

'So, Annie, when did you realise you had this gift?'

'To be honest, Mr Hargreaves, I'm pretty new to it all.'

'Please, call me Sam, we don't stand on ceremony here. Madeline told me you were in that awful train crash recently, is that right?'

'Yes, I was, unfortunately. But that's when my psychic ability returned. Apparently, I had the gift up to the age of five, then it left me, and now seems to have come back much stronger.'

'Hmm, it sometimes can do that. But you have no real idea about the strength of that power, do you?'

'No, not really. I've never known anything about spiritualism and psychic powers until literally minutes after the crash, and even then, it took me a while to differentiate between the living and the dead.'

Sam laughed. 'Yes, I know what you mean, I still have that problem sometimes, mainly because the living can be so much more boring than the dead.' They both laughed. 'But you see, Annie, I have never visualised them in quite the way you do; for me it's more like a daydream. I have flashes of faces, and symbols that I have to decipher. And when I hear them speaking, their words are not that clear. In fact, there was only one person ever in all my fifty years of working here who had a similar ability to yours. She was an amazing clairvoyant medium. Alice—God bless her—only stopped her mediumship in her eighties because she had spondylitis of the spine and could no longer see the congregation.'

'Oh, yes, I know ... I met her after the service,' Annie said, pointing to where she had seen her. 'She has amazing blue eyes and such wise words, and still very much has the gift. She saw the priest as clearly as I did.'

Sam smiled and shook his head. 'The reason she could see the priest as well as you, Annie, is because she's no longer with us. Alice died when I was in my early twenties; in fact, I took over from her.'

'You're kidding me, Sam! You mean I've just had a full-on conversation with a blue-eyed, humorous ghost and didn't even realise she was dead? That's so bizarre!'

'Yes, it's crazy. But it just goes to show how strong your gift is. Now, I'm going to be totally honest with you, dear girl ... I have a problem. You probably realised after witnessing my terrible service today, I'm losing my mediumship abilities. I used to be able to see and hear a lot more than I do now, and that ability is rapidly leaving me. So I desperately need someone ... like you ... to take over.'

'What? I ... I couldn't do this, Sam. I've never stood on a stage, let alone spoken to a few hundred people about their deceased loved ones. I wouldn't know where to *start*.'

'Don't worry about that, Annie, I'll teach you everything you need to know. And with your energy and ability you could be the best ever, even better than old Alice.'

Annie was shocked by Sam's request, but guessed this was one of the reasons her abilities had returned. 'Have I got time to think this through, Sam?'

'How about five minutes, while we're waiting for our tea to arrive?'

By the time Maddy had returned with tea and biscuits, the deal was done. Annie had also unloaded her psychic-related burdens onto Sam. She told him how she needed help with purging the church of its hauntings, and that she suspected the priest of evil doings in the past. But she finally felt a weight had been lifted since her first visitation, having found someone who completely understood what she was going through.

Annie smiled, watching Maddy munch through half a packet of digestives, while Sam discussed Annie's possible undeveloped healing powers, which may have been passed down from her great-grandmother. Sam remembered reading about Mary-Ellen, who had been mentioned in the spiritualists' *Book of Esteemed Psychics*. She had been one of the best mediums and healers of her century, even though she had been investigated as a charlatan—she'd been later exonerated; no evidence could be found. Annie was delighted that one of her ancestors was still known amongst latter day psychics, and that *she* was going to follow in her footsteps.

She sipped her tea, listening to Maddy chatting excitedly about the future of the League, now that they had a talented new medium on board.

'I wish I had the tiniest amount of psychic ability in me, Annie,' Maddy said, pouting like a child.

'You do have abilities, Maddy, I felt them when I first met you. I believe it's called being an empath, and I'm sure you're an exceptional one.'

'Yes, I agree.' Sam nodded in agreement.

Maddy looked perplexed. 'Then why haven't you mentioned it before, Sam?'

'Er ... well, you know me, Madeleine, things tend to go straight over my head these days ...'

Annie suddenly realised that she had knowledge on the subject that she had never known about before. 'Maddy, are you hypersensitive to people's emotions?' Annie continued. 'Do you feel intuitive sometimes ... and that you can pick up on negative energies, and untruths? And, also, that you seem to be the person who everyone dumps their worries onto because you listen and know what to say to ease their problems? I bet people would rather talk to you than a psychiatrist, am I right?'

'Oh my God, Annie, you're spot on! How do you know all that about me?'

Sam had been listening and smiling. 'She knows, Madeleine, because she's an empath too, although she doesn't know it yet. The knowledge Annie has ... is deep within her soul.'

'Well, then, we've both learned something new today, haven't we, Mads?' Annie said. She was happy for Maddy; she needed a boost.

But then she looked over towards Sam and suddenly, a wave of sadness consumed her. She had started to hear whispering from a number of entities crowding into her space, and immediately knew they were Sam's deceased ancestors, telling her of his mortality—and that his time was drawing near.

He touched Annie's arm lightly. 'I know what you're seeing and feeling, Annie. I haven't lost all my abilities yet: I can feel them, too. But they will have to wait until I've sorted out my new protégée with her future career. Which is going to be incredible, my dear... So don't worry about me, I have a new fire in my belly which will keep me going for now. You see, I'm going to be advising and tutoring the best psychic this country has ever seen.'

Chapter 14

∞

FANNY JACKSON

Mr Pong had started sloping off every time Annie returned home because he'd had his wits scared out of him by the appearance of a ghost while on her lap. It saddened Annie that Pong blamed her for the loss of his wits that day, and regaining his trust was going to be challenging.

She made herself a coffee and relaxed on the sofa, a ritual she allowed herself to indulge in for a few minutes each day. It gave her that precious 'me time' to recoup her sanity from everything that was going on; her new life had now turned into weeks full of crazy experiences.

Her thoughts were interrupted by the landline ringing, seemingly louder than usual. It made poor Pong throw himself out of his bed, his tail flicking wildly in a show of utter disdain at Annie, as if it was her fault again.

She went to pick up the phone, and as soon as she touched it, a vision of Poppet dropped into her mind.

'Hey, Pops.'

'Ooh, that's impressive. You got caller ID?'

'Yeah, something along those lines ... Nice to hear from you, sweetheart.' Annie smiled to herself. 'Did you get my message about the gallery?'

'Wow, yeah ... My dream job, but I may have a problem handing in my notice in; it's going to have to be at least a month. Mind you, I'm on my second warning for being over-camp with the patients, so I could *accidentally* get a third. I'll see what I can do, Annie.'

'Thanks, sweetie, I appreciate it hugely.'

'All I need is an invite around to your place for a drink, so we can both sit and stare at your Adonis.'

'Will you please find your own boyfriend, Pops ... I'm getting worried about your interest in my man.'

The two of them laughed.

'Okay, girlfriend, but I was actually calling for another reason. I did what you asked and had a snoop through a few documents that just happened to be in a drawer that was open. And *bizarrely* I found out that although the priest had died on the train, he was still brought to the hospital mortuary to have a huge piece of glass removed from his chest. So his body has only just been released to the funeral home. I also found out that the only relative recorded as coming forward after his death was his elderly mother. Now *aren't* I a clever boy?'

'You're an absolute star, Pops! Don't suppose you have his mother's address, do you?'

'As it happens, yes ... But can I swap it for that drink at yours?'

'Let me have it now and you can come over whenever you like, my darling.'

'Okay, well, wait for it ... Her name is *Fanny* Jackson.' He sniggered like a naughty boy.

Annie squeezed every last bit of information out of him and was delighted that she finally had some details on the priest. She was happy, too, that she had made such a good friend in Poppet, and had a firm feeling he would be a great ally one day.

There was no time like the present, and a visit to the priest's mother that day would be perfect. Thos was working late, and Fanny Jackson only lived a few miles away at Norwood Park. So as far as Annie was concerned, she had the green light to go.

∞

Mrs Jackson's home was a large, detached house, albeit rather shabby from years of neglect. The seized hinges on the front gate had wedged it firmly open on the garden path, where weeds choked its last remnants of herringbone brickwork, with a jungle of blackthorn crowding in on its flanks.

The large front door and windows that had been dined on by every worm and insect that had a taste for wood, were in desperate need of a talented joiner. Even so, it was still obvious that this neglected house had been a grand home in its prime.

Above the old bellpull was a dirty lime-green copper plaque, which many years before would have been polished to a shining rose colour. It was inscribed with the almost indiscernible names of the house and its principal occupant.

THE OLD RECTORY
FATHER MELLION JACKSON

Annie stepped back into the garden to see if the church that the rectory had once been attached to was still there. It was, standing proud on the left hand side, set back from the road and surrounded now by formal gardens and a picket fence. The small church looked as if it had been sold off and converted into a private home. This prompted Annie to wonder how Thos's acquisition would look like if it had a similar revamp, and she felt herself warming to the idea.

She took a deep breath and tugged gently on the bellpull, which jangled a large brass bell inside. After a few moments, a frail but stern voice echoed.

'Go away!'

The voice was a grumpy old lady's; Annie could feel her own stubbornness rearing up; she wasn't going to take no for an answer. With wilful conviction, she tugged harder on the bell. It seemed to have struck a nerve: through the haze of the stained glass in the door she could see a small, hunched figure slowly walking up the hallway.

The old lady opened the heavy oak door. 'Are you deaf? I said *go away*! I don't buy or want anything, and I don't like cold callers, so *bugger off.*'

Annie smiled inwardly at this caricature of a silver-haired old lady with a potty mouth.

'I'm not selling anything, I promise. My name's Annie Prior, and I was on the same train as your son. I just wanted to put your mind at rest that he wasn't alone when he died; I was there with him.' Annie didn't know what to expect from this wrinkled old woman aside from a certain amount of visible grief—but there was none.

'Well, you'd better come in then, and *close* the door behind you. It's cold enough in this bloody fridge of a house.' The old lady turned and walked down the musty corridor, with its threadbare Persian rugs scattered on top of a filthy oak floor.

Annie followed, thinking that at any moment the priest would appear to protect his dear old mother from this meddling fool. But no, although the house was cold, it was not the chill from the visitation of a spook.

'I think you've wasted your time, Miss Prior. I'm really not interested in what you've got to say.'

Annie was completely baffled by the old biddy's comment. 'I just thought it would give you some comfort to know that someone was there when your son passed.'

'This might sound harsh, Miss Prior, but my son and I didn't get on. He wasn't a very nice boy when he was young, and he turned into an even nastier man. He was always grumpy and telling me to mind my own business.' The old lady scowled. 'I blame his father for passing on his hateful genes to Mellion; they're both better off dead, if you ask me!'

Annie's eyebrows involuntarily lifted; she had never heard so much hatred come from anyone—apart from maybe Melina.

'I'm so sorry you feel like that. But, surely you were proud that he was a priest?'

'Proud? What was there to be *proud* of? He was excommunicated from the priesthood thirty years ago, not that anything was ever proved.' The old lady stopped talking and looked over towards the parlour door as if someone was listening. 'Now I've said too much. I think you ought to leave.'

Annie wasn't going anywhere until she had dug a little further. 'Excommunicated? But he was wearing a clerical collar on the train.'

'I said, you're going to have to leave now; and don't ask any more questions.'

The old woman sneered, but Annie kept on. 'I'd really like to pay my respects at his funeral, Mrs Jackson.'

'They won't allow him to be buried because he was defrocked, so he's being cremated next week. And there's no need for you to waste your time. Anyway ... it's family only.'

The old lady got up, turning her back on Annie. 'Let yourself out, Miss Prior,' she said with contempt in her voice.

Annie was stunned, but had enough information to be going on with. She got up and walked to the front door, but as soon as she opened it, someone pushed her from behind. She twisted around expecting to see the old lady—but she wasn't there: just a bright orb of light.

Annie knew immediately it was him, but was shocked because she had no idea there could be physical contact between the living and the dead. She turned to leave; a curtain stirred in an upstairs window and she caught a glimpse of a balding man with a rugged face—before he stepped back out of view.

Chapter 15

∞

The Funeral

Although shocked by her experience with Mrs Jackson, Annie had a renewed eagerness to get to the bottom of the mystery behind the family. She contacted the funeral home and used the fact that she had been with the priest when he had died to establish when and where the service was to take place. She had already persuaded herself to have a snoop even though she was clearly not welcome.

She found a website containing the names of excommunicated priests, and the first piece of evidence that Father Mellion had been under investigation by the Catholic Church. There had been allegations about his possible sexual abuse of young teenagers at a convent in London. But the trail seemed to end there, as if there had been a cover-up by the hierarchy of the church. No doubt meant to save it from further humiliation and damage already created by so many of its clergy.

∞

A week later, Annie arrived early at West Norwood Cemetery, not knowing what to expect. She had never been to a funeral before, but found the place amazingly peaceful and quiet, especially amongst the mass of memorials and mausolea. But there were no spirits lurking there; she understood that the dead physical body held no ties to the departed soul.

A hearse drove past her with a woven casket and no flowers; Annie instinctively knew who was making their last journey. She walked towards the chapel, while Mrs Jackson slowly got out of a car nearby. Annie recognised the driver, who had jumped out quickly to help the old lady: it was the balding man she had seen peering from the rectory window the week before. He was about six feet tall, well-built but not chubby, with sloping shoulders that seemed weighed down by a heavy secret. His puffy, wide-apart eyes, punctuated with a bulbous red nose, reminded her of the priest.

She shivered and swallowed hard; she remembered the first time she'd seen Mellion on the train. *This man must be his brother ... He's definitely shaped out of the same disgusting mould,* Annie thought, she continued to follow the cortege.

Mrs Jackson turned, and upon seeing her, whispered something to the man.

He whipped around and scowled, then walked towards Annie, shouting. 'Mrs Jackson told you *not* to come here today. It's family only, so you're not welcome!'

Annie was taken aback by his outburst, but was determined to stand her ground. 'We haven't been introduced. I'm Annie Prior, and I was on the train with Father Mellion,' she said, holding her hand out in defiance. 'And you are?' she added calmly, although anger was rising in the pit of her stomach.

The man looked even more enraged and shouted louder. 'Who I am is none of your damned business. Mum already told you to bugger off ... now *I'm* telling you, BUGGER OFF! We don't want you here and neither would my brother.' He spun around and returned to Mrs Jackson's side.

Although Annie was flustered by the altercation, she was pleased to have gained a little more in-sight into Mellion's family. At least she'd angered him enough, for him to confirm his relationship to the priest.

As she walked back to her car disappointed not to have been allowed into the service. She heard another man shout. "Mr Selby, I'd like a word with you." Annie turned to see what was going on. The funeral director was striding up to Mellion's brother with his top hat under his arm, and looking like thunder. Annie was desperate to hear what he had to say.

"Excuse me, sir. I don't normally interfere in family politics at funerals, but I feel you have disrespected that young lady over there, who was with your brother when he died. And now, regrettably, I feel I must get involved. I suggest you apologise to her immediately and allow her to attend the service! Have I made myself quite clear, or would you like me to repeat myself?"

The brother looked stunned by the funeral directors rage, and simply nodded back speechless. Annie was delighted that the man had stood up to him, but was curious as to what Mellion's brother would do next.

Still shaken, the brother walked towards Annie with his head down. 'Apparently Miss Prior, I've been disrespectful towards you. Er ... you must understand it's been very traumatic these last few weeks.'

Annie could see he was back-peddling as fast as he could, but his eyes gave away the fact that his words were meaningless.

'Of course I understand it's been traumatic for you,' Annie replied. 'But, I *was* with your brother during his last moments, and that's why I would personally like to pay my respects, too. By the way, I didn't get your name.'

He seemed agitated and ignored her question. 'Well, if you're coming, we'd better get on with it.'

Mrs Jackson and her son took their places in the front row of the large, non-denominational room with seating laid out in a tiered semicircle. Annie was embarrassed for them. As apart from the family and herself there were only three others in attendance—two men standing together near the back, and a nun at the end of a middle row on her own. Although Annie still held no penchant for anyone with religious convictions, her curiosity got the better of her and she was drawn to the woman in black.

'Would you mind if I sat here?' she asked politely.

The nun looked around the pews as if silently pointing out that there were plenty of other seats, but she still obliged. 'Yes, please do.'

'Thank you ... I don't like to be on my own at occasions like this, do you?' Annie whispered.

'Well, I've had to get used to it over the years, it's part of my job description,' the nun whispered back.

An unusual warmth and kindness radiated from her, which was surprising; none of the sisters at Annie's convent had had any semblance of compassion.

'Hope you don't mind me asking, but how did you know Father Mellion?' Annie asked.

The nun was clearly uncomfortable by the question, but still replied. 'He used to frequent a convent school which I helped out in ... But that was many years ago. We lost contact soon after he was moved on.'

'Moved on?' Annie asked.

'Yes, but I can't speak about it now.' The sister continued reading a religious pamphlet.

Annie took out one of her old gallery business cards and handed it to her. 'I'd really like to find out more about him, it's quite important.

Would it be possible for you to call me, or I could call you …? Whatever's easiest.'

The sister nodded and read Annie's card. She wrinkled her brow, seemingly confused. 'I thought you were a journalist. Why would an art dealer want to know about Father Mellion?'

Annie explained briefly in a whisper who she was, and was just about to continue when a large, frumpily dressed lady stood by the coffin and addressed the sparse assembly.

'Mellion Jackson's family have requested this music for their dear departed son and brother. Please take a moment to reflect on his life by listening to his favourite prelude, Debussy's "Sunken Cathedral".' The woman frowned, perhaps at the choice of title, then stood with her head bowed while the music played.

Annie's interest was heightened; it had been confirmed that the balding man was the priest's brother, and the nun could be a new major source of information. But whilst she listened to the sombre music, a shiver ran down her back. She knew in her heart that the priest had been involved in something wicked, but it was still beyond comprehension that the family were to give no eulogy.

She spent her reflection time surreptitiously weighing up the two men standing near the back; the half-moon seating allowed her to see them clearly without turning her head. Her observational skills had been honed almost to perfection over the years by people-watching, and it didn't take long before she had both men sussed.

One was clearly a journalist who had all the characteristics of the trade: scruffy, highly strung and mentally recording every little nuance—but he held no interest for Annie. The other man, however, did. He was statuesque, and although middle-aged, he was ruggedly handsome. He was smartly turned out, which she had always appreciated in a man, and he was clearly more intellectual than the journalist. He had an authoritative demeanour about him that made it clear to Annie that he was something to do with the police, albeit in plain clothes. This sparked her interest even more, and she wondered why a police officer would be at the funeral of a train crash victim.

After the peculiar service, Mrs Jackson and her son left quickly, though not before being intercepted by the journalist. He was unceremoniously handed off in a rugby-style tackle by Mellion's brother. The journalist then left with a ripped notepad and damaged ego.

The nun had seemingly floated off hastily too, after telling Annie she would be in touch. But Annie's attention had been diverted to the presumed police officer, who was reading a memorial dedication in the graveyard and puffing on a hand-rolled cigarette. She was compelled to find out if her instincts were correct.

Once outside, she strode over to him and held out her hand. 'Hi, I'm Annie Prior. Are you by any chance from the Met?'

The man dropped his cigarette and stamped on it. 'Now, how did you know that?' the officer said in a broad Cockney accent while shaking her hand strongly. 'I'm Detective Inspector Dan Watts.'

'Aha! So I was right.' Annie was pleased with her intuition. She held on to his hand a couple of seconds longer and felt his strength and kindness flow. She smiled at him, and he could do nothing else but return her smile.

'Hmm ... Detective inspector ... aren't you a little over-qualified for mere surveillance work?'

'Yes, well, I've had an interest in this family for some time now and wanted to pay my respects in person. Can we chat for a minute, Miss Prior?'

'Of course, I'd like that. Great minds ...'

They sat on an old oak memorial bench set amongst the graves and tombs. Annie read the dedication carved into the gnarled backrest.

WILLIAM AND MARIE DEPARTED TOGETHER 1971 TO BE REUNITED ON THE OTHER SIDE OF LIFE AGAIN TO LOVE AND CHERISH AS HUSBAND AND WIFE

'I'd like to believe in all that stuff, but I live in the real world,' the officer said, shaking his head. 'And what if you've had two or three wives? Are they all there waiting on the other side of the Pearly Gates? That'd be like going to Hell for me.'

Annie laughed. 'I don't think they'll be squabbling over you, Dan. There's no jealousy or vindictiveness over there, just pure love.'

'And how do you know all this, Annie Prior?'

'Because, Dan Watts, I'm what's called a psychic medium.'

'You're kidding me, right?'

'No, really, I am, albeit an apprentice.' She wondered if she should have told him.

'Woah, this is proving to be an interesting day. Tell me more.' Dan grinned, unconvinced but curious.

They sat for a while discussing the afterlife and her psychic powers.

'So why did you come to Jackson's funeral?' he asked.

Annie smiled. 'I don't think you'll believe me when I tell you.'

'Try me ... I'm more open-minded than you might think.'

Annie proceeded to tell him what had happened on the train and at the hospital, and about the many ghostly visits from the priest. But she kept the spirit children to herself; she wanted to make sure he was genuine before disclosing too much.

'Well, that's some kind of a story, not something I've heard before.'

Annie could feel a huge amount of scepticism coming from him, which she had expected. 'I know it all sounds bizarre, but it *is* a hundred per cent true.' She tried to sound convincing.

'Look, I'd really like to believe you, miss, but with respect ... I do hear an awful lot of bullshit from the nicest of people ... *and* of course the scum of the earth, too. So I've learnt to believe nothing until I have absolute evidence.'

Annie knew at that moment she had to give Dan proof to get him on her side. She laid her hand on his arm.

'What ya doing?' Dan looked nervous.

'Please, let me do this.'

She could immediately feel her visitation vibes running throughout her body, although it was the first time she had welcomed them. She took a deep breath as she saw and heard from someone who was the validation she needed, but she knew this was not going to be an easy reading.

'Okay, so, I'm going to give you the information I'm seeing and hearing, I need you to believe in me, Dan. Are you okay with that?'

Dan lifted his eyebrows, and nodded silently. Annie squeezed his arm to ease his concern.

'You lost your older brother when you were in your early teens, is that correct?'

'Christ ... yeah, I did.'

Dan was just about to say something else, but Annie stopped him. 'Please don't say anything unless I ask you a question.' He looked pale.

Annie put her hand on her chest and screwed her face in pain, she knew it was Dan's brother showing her how he'd died.

'He's telling me that he died from an impact to his chest. I can see now that it was a car accident, and it wasn't his fault. He's saying it was a friend who was driving, and that he shouldn't have been at the wheel ... Was your brother in a stolen car?'

'Yeah, he was.' Dan gulped in air, trying to hide his emotions.

Annie smiled. 'He's actually really excited to come through. He says it's the first time he's had the chance to let you know he's still around, watching you and your mum. He's sorry that he got into so much trouble when he was young, but *it's because of him you became a copper* ... That's exactly how he's saying it.' Annie paused for a moment to catch up with the enthusiastic spirit. 'Ah, bless him, he's telling me that he's really proud of you. Okay ... Okay, I'll tell him, but slow down,' she said aloud to the spirit.

All the while she was talking, Dan was quiet. Then Annie heard something that would be difficult to pass on.

'Tell my bro, I'm not so sure about his new girlfriend. I know he's still hurting after the last one left him, but ... tell him not to be a daft bugger and make another mistake.'

'Ooh, okay, so I'm guessing your brother was quite opinionated when he was alive,' Annie said.

'Bloody hell, yeah, all the time. He used to say it how it really was, no holding back. Why...? What's he said now?'

Annie pulled a face as if it was difficult for her to talk. 'He's saying don't make the same mistake again.'

'Ah ... so he doesn't like my girlfriend.'

'He didn't quite say that, but if he *was* still here, would he have approved of your new lady?'

'Na, probably not, but I'm still going to give it a go.' Dan shook his head. 'That's definitely my big brother talking. God, I've missed him giving me advice—even though it was wrong sometimes.' He moved closer to Annie and put his big arm around her shoulders and hugged her like a long-lost friend. 'Is he still here?'

Annie looked around. 'No, he's gone ... I think it's taken an awful lot of energy for him to come through, especially with him chatting so much. But now he knows he can, I reckon he'll do it again whenever I'm with you.'

'That's bloody incredible, Annie. But I tell you what, I could really do with your help solving crimes, how about it?'

'Ooh, not so sure about that, Dan. But first, how about telling me why you're here at the funeral?' Annie wasn't going to give up on her own bit of detective work.

'You're like a bloody terrier who won't let go, Miss Prior. Okay ... this is generally for cops' ears only, but I know I can trust you after all that amazing stuff. Well, Jackson had been on our radar for a while before his death, 'cause we'd had information that he'd been snooping around a school in north London again. It was the nun who was here today who gave us the nod; she apparently helped out there thirty or so years ago. And of course now it's all a bit of a touchy subject after the James Saville thing. So anyway, back then when we investigated it, I was only eighteen and a rookie, although a bit like you, I was a proper terrier getting my teeth stuck into the case. Then, would you believe it, my bloody chief closed the investigation before we had time to come up with any evidence. It wasn't long after that I found out he was a devout Catholic himself. Maybe I judged him wrongly, but I was pissed off thinking he'd swept the case under the carpet for the sake of bloody religion.'

Annie paused for a moment, then grinned. 'Yes, I understand you must have been upset. But presumably, your chief is no longer around these days?' She winked.

'Christ, Annie, I want you on my team.'

Chapter 16

∞

THE LETTERS

Thos walked through the back door to the kitchen, only to be bombarded by a great smell. 'Hmm ... what's cooking, babe?'

'Hi, sweetheart ... Shepherd's pie, hope you like it. I know I'm not much of a cook, but I can rustle up this dish blindfolded. Gran used to cook it for me all the time, bless her. Mind you, like me, it was the only thing she could make.' Annie giggled.

'Well, it sounds ace to me, babe, I'm famished.' Thos put his arms around her waist, pulled her close and kissed her on the lips. 'You ... smell of ... onions.'

'Yes, well, you're lucky ... I'm saving on expensive perfumes.' Annie stroked his face. 'Sweetheart, while we're waiting for lunch to cook, can we have a catch-up? It's so easy to lose sight of us when so much is going on in our lives. We should always find time to talk ... What do you think?'

'Yeah, sounds good to me. Actually, I was thinking along the same lines too, babe.'

They sat at the kitchen table with Annie recounting all that had gone on at the crematorium, and how she'd met a police inspector who might be useful in the future with their church problem. They had just started discussing their next plan of action when Mr Pong screeched—like someone had stood on his tail—both Annie and Thos jumped.

'What the bloody hell's wrong with you *now*, Pong?' Thos shouted.

Annie's skin tightened, and the hairs on her arms and neck prickled. She held Thos's hand tight. 'I don't know who it is yet, sweetie, but you're going to witness a visitation first-hand.'

'Christ, Annie, not sure if I'm ready for this. Do I have to?'

But it was too late to choose; stood in front of them was the faint apparition of an elderly lady who had appeared a few feet away.

'Tell my Thomas I love him and always will,' the old lady said, with a tremor in her voice.

Thos looked as scared as the cat. 'Who is it, Annie?'

'Thos, it's Dorothy. She looks exactly the same as in the photos.'

'Oh Christ, really? I'm not sure I can deal with this.'

But Annie continued. 'Sweetheart, she's obviously here for a reason, or maybe simply to say hello. She's saying she loves her Thomas and always will … Hang on, she's trying to show me something.'

The elderly ghost pointed towards the old dresser in the kitchen, she seemed distraught. 'Give him the letters … I know he will never forgive me for what I did, but I did it because I could not bear to lose him. He was all I ever wanted.' She slowly evaporated into the background and was soon gone.

All the while, Pong had been glaring at the spirit with his back arched and tail vertical, his usual sleepy blue eyes wide with terror. Annie went to the dresser, and that was enough for Pong: he flew into the air and, upon landing, screeched out through the cat-flap.

'Christ, that bloody cat! My nerves are shot,' Thos said.

Pong had disrupted Annie's psychic channel and her mind bumped back to normality. 'I told you before, sweetheart, animals have a sixth sense, and from the way he's acting he could see Dorothy too. But anyway, she's gone now. But just before she left, she tried to give us some evidence. She pointed to the dresser and told me to give you the letters that are in there, and that you'll never forgive her for what she's done. Have you got any idea what she means, sweetheart?'

'Beats me, babe. And I can tell you for certain there are no letters in that damn dresser. I emptied the whole thing when Gran died. And she wouldn't have done anything to upset me, at least not something that I'd never forgive her for ... I don't understand any of this.'

Annie opened a door at the base of the dresser; it was full of man stuff, just as Thos had said.

'Well, that's all she came through with, and seemed pretty adamant there were letters in there.'

Thos got up. 'Listen, to tell you the truth, babe, my nerves are rattled and I'm a bit blown away by the whole spirit thing. I'm trying really hard to get my head around it, but I'm just not into this stuff. In fact, I'm gonna go and have a pint with Max if you don't mind, I need a bit of normality?'

Annie was taken aback again at Thos's sudden change of temperament. '*No*, no, that's fine ... It'll probably do you good, anyway. I'm sorry the message wasn't better, but that's all she said.'

'Yeah, well, you're gonna have to give me time with the whole spook thing, I've never been good with stuff like that. I've always believed when we die, the lights go out. I tell you what, you do your spiritual thing ... but best not involve me too much. I'll see you later.' He left, banging the door closed behind him.

Annie was deflated, mainly about Thos's weak reaction. After all, it was him who had pushed her towards the Spiritualist League and Maddy; why would he have done that if he was a complete disbeliever? But then, had she misinterpreted what Dorothy had said?

Annie went over and over in her mind on what had happened while staring at the dresser. 'What *did* you mean, Dorothy? What bloody letters? Come on, you've got to help me here.'

Annie leant forward towards the old piece of furniture and slammed the open door shut. With that, a framed photo of Thos as a child that had been perched on the plate rack fell backwards and slipped out of view, crashing down the back. Poor Mr Pong, he had just crept back in momentarily, then spun around and flown back out through the flap again.

'Oh, BUGGER!' Annie shouted as the glass in the frame shattered.

She jumped up and tried to peer around the back, but it was dark and full of cobwebs. She squeezed her fingers behind the heavy sideboard, pulling it as hard as she could, but it wouldn't budge. She grabbed a torch from Thos's man stuff and shone it through the small gap, revealing that the broken frame had caught on something halfway down.

She put her shoulder against it. 'Come on, I need a bit help here,' she shouted. And suddenly, it was as though she had conjured a heavy-duty spirit, the dresser moved enough for her to squeeze her slim arm through the gap. She carefully took hold of the frame so as not to cut herself and gently pulled it free, along with what it had been caught on.

She knew immediately what the obstruction was. The frame and glass were completely broken, but the bundle of letters was perfectly intact, albeit covered in thirty years of kitchen grime and cobwebs.

Annie sat staring at the package, which had been tied neatly with a now faded blue ribbon. 'Dorothy, you're going to have to help me here. I'm scared this is going to hurt Thos.'

Annie realised at that moment that talking to a spirit meant they could hear her, Dorothy reappeared almost immediately.

'If you love him, Annie, you will make the right decision and do what's best for him.'

'Thanks a lot, Dorothy ... Not sure that's what I wanted to hear, but ...' She looked up, and found herself talking to thin air again.

She was desperate to read the contents of the letters before Thos, so she could protect him from whatever life-changing messages they might've contained, but at what cost to their relationship was it going to be? She sat holding them, contemplating the right thing to do, when her mobile rang.

'Hey, babe, I'm going to spend the night with Max if you don't mind. Drunk driving and all that ... and it's been ages since we caught up, so I think it'll do me good. And, anyway, it's not like you're going to be on your own.' His tone sounded curt and uncaring.

'I hope you meant Mr Pong by that, Thos.'

'Yeah, course I did ... See ya tomorrow.' The phone went dead.

Annie teared up. 'Thanks a lot, Thos ... At least you've made the decision easier for me,' she said aloud. Her tears dried quickly and her sadness was replaced with disappointment.

She blew the dust off the parcel and marvelled that the letters were in such good condition, although slightly sepia in colour. She untied the blue ribbon and spread the envelopes out in order of their dates. They started from 1981, when Thos would have been only six months old, and the last was from when he was five.

All were addressed to Master Thomas Tadros, C/O Mr and Mrs Frank Townsend. The first of the envelopes felt thicker than the others, she opened it, and a faded photograph slipped out. It was of a beautiful young woman with jet-black hair and a lovely smile—a smile, that Annie knew all too well; Thos had obviously inherited it from his mother.

Adelpha sat on a whitewashed wall with colourful fishing boats floating in a turquoise bay behind her. There was a dedication on the reverse.

> To my darling Thomas
> From your Mummy who loves you xx

Annie was confused, she remembered Thos telling her Adelpha had gone back to Greece without him and had never contacted them since. She had a sinking feeling in the pit of her stomach about Dorothy. She read on, everything his gran had told him were lies. The simple fact that Adelpha had written 'I love you' did not suggest a woman who couldn't care less about her child.

There were two letters in each envelope, one to Dorothy and Frank, the other to Thomas, with a few more photographs tucked inside birthday cards.

Annie read the first letter to his grandparents. It gushed questions about Thomas, pleading for photos of him. There was a small amount of information about her life back on the island of Kefalonia: how she was working in her father's restaurant to make enough money so that one day she would be able to provide a good life for her boy. At the end of her letter, she spoke of her sadness in being away from him and her British family.

Annie was upset for Thos; his grandparents had deceived him from the moment he'd been old enough to understand and had fed him so many lies that he had believed wholeheartedly.

But she could not understand why his mother had not tried to return to collect her boy before she died.

She read on:

My Darling Thomas,

One day soon when I see you, I will be able to explain why I could not stay. My heart is breaking every minute I am away from my little man. You are the most precious thing that ever came into my life and I am so sorry I left you. I thought it was for the best, I was so young and my family would not have approved. But I know that Dorothy and Frank are looking after you well for me, and I've told them that I will be back to bring you home soon.

Always remember that I love you, my darling Thomas, and I send you all my hugs and kisses.

Your Mummy xxx

'Christ, Dorothy, what have you done?' Annie said aloud, but Dorothy failed to reappear.

All the other letters addressed to her and Frank sounded progressively frantic. Adelpha continually asked why they had only written a couple of times and pleaded with them to send photos. She also mentioned she had got engaged to a Greek man who made her very happy. And in the second from last letter there was a photo of her on her wedding day with her new husband and extended family.

Dearest Dorothy and Frank,

I have enclosed a photo of my wedding day with my darling husband, Georgios Galanis. He has known all about Thomas since the first day I met him. I told him how Thomas had amazing surrogate grandparents looking after him for me, until the day I can bring him home. Georgios is a very modern-thinking man and has agreed to welcome little Thomas into our family as his own son. I know this will be a difficult time for you both to give him up, but as you know, it was always my intention to have him back one day when the time was right.

I also mentioned to you in a previous letter that my papa sadly passed away last year, and I have now finally told the rest of my family about Thomas. Although they were shocked at first, they are very happy for me, especially, that Georgios is going to stand by me and wants Thomas to live with us as a family.

I cannot express the gratitude in my heart to you both for these past five years, caring for my precious little man. I owe you so much. I will let you know very soon about the date that I will be travelling over, and I would like you both to accompany him and myself back to see where he will be living, and for you both to meet his Greek family. We will pay for your travel expenses, and of course you will be staying with us for an extended holiday, so that Thomas can get used to his new home.

All my love to you, and of course to little Thos.

Adie

xx

The last letter had been typed, and was addressed simply to Mr and Mrs Frank Townsend. Annie had a bad feeling about it, and she was right: it had been written by Adelpha's husband, Georgios.

Tears poured down over Annie's cheeks at the sad contents. She decided then and there that she had to keep it all from Thos, until she had worked out a way to tell him the staggering lies that he had been fed all his life. And her not handing the letters over to him would be adding to the deceit—but she had no choice.

Chapter 17

∞

MADDY

For the first time since the crash, Annie felt down; she had so much going on in her head and trying to make sense of it all seemed nigh on impossible. She understood Thos's issues with her; after all, having a girlfriend who talked to ghosts on a daily basis was not the norm. And the fact that it had affected his plans to renovate his beloved church had clearly changed the dynamics of their relationship. She had also added to her problems by keeping the existence of the letters from him, even though she had done it with his best interests at heart.

∞

Annie met up with Maddy for a coffee before her meeting with Sam at the League. She was intrigued to get to know another woman who had held Thos's heart for a while. At first, she had been baffled as to why he had ended his relationship with this incredibly kind-hearted girl, but then Maddy's exuberantly chatty and inquisitive personality would have annoyed the hell out of him. It was also clear that since their break-up she had had a void in her life that needed filling.

'Has Thos introduced you to Max yet?' Maddy asked.

'Yes, and what a lovely man he is! I can absolutely see why Thos has him as a best friend.'

'Hmm, those two are more like brothers than mates,'

'Woah, where's this going, Mads?' Then Annie's intuition kicked in. 'Oh, of course, you like Max more than just a little, don't you?'

Maddy's face flushed pink. 'Well, I wouldn't say no, put it that way, but I couldn't … It's all too close for comfort, and it wouldn't feel right.'

'Bugger that!' Annie said. 'He's on his own, and so are you, *and* he's the ideal age.' Annie threw her head back and laughed. 'It's absolutely perfect: buy one, get one free.'

'What do you mean?'

'Take Max on and get a Greek mother-in-law into the bargain.'

'Oh … my … God, how scary is that! It never even crossed my mind.' Maddy wrinkled her nose, as though she had smelt something rotten.

They both screeched with laughter, cementing their friendship further.

'Look on the bright side, Mads. You land yourself a Greek god *and* we get to see each other as couples.'

Maddy seemed worried. 'That would be great … But what on earth would Thos say?'

'Leave him to me, he'll be cool with it.' Annie winked.

While they were scheming, Annie's links to the spirit world had quietly opened without her noticing. She could hear many souls talking over each other, clearly vying for her attention. But a clear male voice broke through the jumbled chatter, and a handsome young man's translucent figure appeared behind Maddy. He immediately started chatting, to get his message across quickly.

'I would have married Madeleine but she only saw me as a friend, and I never got the chance to tell her that I truly loved her.'

Maddy had seen Annie in this same trance-like state before at the league. 'You okay, Annie? What are you seeing?'

'Actually, Mads ... There's a young man standing behind you.'

Maddy quickly turned around. 'Silly me; thought I'd be able to see someone ... but I am aware of his presence, though.'

'I'm not surprised you feel him, he's full of love for you. And he's just said it was always more than the love of a friend.'

Maddy looked quizzically at Annie. 'I know who it is, but we were really only ever friends.'

'He knew that's how you felt, Mads, but he felt differently, and would have married you.'

'What? Why didn't he tell me when he was alive?'

Annie could see Maddy was shocked. 'Probably because he knew he didn't have much time, so he's only getting it off his chest now.'

'I can't believe he's finally come through, Annie. I knew him when ...'

'No, please don't tell me anything, Mads, let me give you the evidence he's bringing forward.'

The young man continued: 'I loved her because she helped me cope with my illness when we were teenagers. When I couldn't breathe to communicate, she would speak for me, and never left my side. Tell her ... when she needs someone, I'll always be there for her, just like she was for me.' Before he faded, he shouted his name.

Annie recounted every word and was interested to see Maddy's reaction, she had been expecting tears. Instead, Maddy seemed happy.

'Oh, and by the way, Mads, just before he left, he shouted, "Stan the man I am."'

'Wow, Annie, thanks so much. I know Stan has tried so hard to come through before, using different mediums, including Sam, but none of them ever gave his name or any details as you have. But somehow, I've always known he's been close by, protecting me like I tried to protect him when he was alive. He suffered *so* much with cystic fibrosis and struggled every day to breathe through the muck in his lungs, so when he finally slipped away, I was happy for him. I hated seeing him battle with that terrible disease, especially towards the end. I wish I'd told him before he died, that he was the bravest person I'd ever known.'

Annie hugged her friend. 'Stan knows that, Mads; he's been around you making sure you're okay since his passing. It's hard losing someone so young, especially when they should have had a full life ahead of them. But as you know, they really do move on to a much better place, surrounded by the extraordinary love of family and friends from their past. They leave their suffering behind and become the person they always wanted to be, by doing the things they couldn't do before their passing. So "Stan the man" is definitely happy, and I'm sure, now he knows he can return to speak to you at anytime, he'll be popping in to see the love of his life on a regular basis … for sure.'

Maddy leant forward and kissed Annie on the cheek. 'Thanks so much, my friend. We all need people who make a difference in our lives, as Stan did for me. And I feel you've been sent to help not just me to understand but so many others too.'

They finished the dregs of their coffee while Maddy reminisced about the short but incredible years she'd had with Stan and how much she had learnt about being brave from him, although she was disappointed about not being able to apply that to herself. Finally receiving a message meant so much to her, they had never got round to discussing their true feelings with each other—but she now felt they were both at peace with it.

Chapter 18

∞

SAM HARGREAVES

Whilst they were chatting about messages from the afterlife, Annie seized the chance to tell Maddy about the one she had received from Max's father at the restaurant—although she left out the gambling bit; she wasn't sure how much Maddy had been privy to.

The two of them—now firm friends—arrived at the Spiritualist centre twenty minutes before the meeting with Sam. Maddy offered to show Annie around; her last tour had been cut short due to the rude interruption from the priest.

Annie stood looking up at the ceiling. 'I can't believe the architects mixed Rococo with Gothic; it's so mismatched, but still seems to work perfectly, especially here.'

'How do you know so much about architectural styles, Annie?'

'Oh, sorry, Mads, that must have sounded a bit pretentious. It wasn't meant to … it's just that I did a history of art degree in my early twenties, and my favourite part of the course covered historical architecture, so I just can't help myself when I see this sort of thing.'

'Wow, a degree … You're a woman of *many* talents, then.'

For the first time Annie could feel a faint hint of resentment from Maddy, but she dismissed it and put it down to overthinking again.

'So, Annie, you need to know a little bit about the centre if it's going to be your second home.'

'Not sure about second home ... but I'm all ears, Mads.'

'Okay, so each area and room of advancement has been named after mediums and important people in the spiritualist movement—like the Conan Doyle Hall, for instance.'

Annie's stomach churned over with embarrassment. 'That's where I disgraced myself last time.'

'You didn't disgrace yourself at all. It was the first bit of excitement ever witnessed at the league. Honestly, people haven't stopped talking about it, but not in a derogatory way. There's been a buzz about you amongst the psychics, and it's all good because we need a bit of new blood around here.'

There was a strong feeling of acceptance towards Annie in this meeting place for like-minded people, both, from the living and spirit. Every corner of its vastness was perfectly serene, even though her goosebumps were working overtime because of the patient souls awaiting their turn to communicate. There were no evil spirits within the walls, just a residual spark of energy the priest had left behind. But even that was being quashed by the sheer love from the other spirits.

Annie and Maddy made their way to the David Richmond Room, named after the first man to open a spiritualist church in the UK. Sam was sitting in a comfortable shabby leather armchair reading a newspaper, with an empty cup of coffee next to him. His tired eyes lit up when Annie walked in, but his worn-out body took a few seconds longer to animate. Annie's heart ached for him; she knew his time on this plane was drawing to a close. She selfishly hoped he would be around long enough to help her deal with the church children and assist her in exposing the priest for his depravities.

She hugged Sam tightly, and he knew exactly what she was thinking.

He held her at arm's length; his old grey eyes searched hers. 'My dear girl, how are you? Has that pesky priest been bothering you again?'

'I'm good, Sam, and all's quiet from him at the moment. But you do have an awful lot of phantom squatters around here.'

Sam smiled broadly. 'Yes, I know what you mean. I used to see them too—but not in the same way.'

Maddy looked confused. 'Well, I don't know what you're both talking about. It's just not fair … I've never seen a ghost, and probably never will.' She pouted like a disappointed child. 'I think I'll be the tea lady again, that's all I'm good for around here.' She winked at both of them, took out her mobile phone and snapped a couple of pics before they had a chance to complain.

Sam had been studying Annie's face. 'It seems, my girl, that you have all the main psychic abilities. I would say predominantly mediumship—as in seeing spirits—and then the "clairs," as we call them: clairvoyance, clairaudience, clairsentience and claircognisance. But you already know that, don't you?'

'Yeah, I think so, Sam. I've read so much on the subject since I last saw you, and I recognise all those abilities. But I think I'm mainly clairvoyant and clairaudient; I see and hear spirits everywhere. But that's not what worries me: I just can't seem to turn them off at the moment.'

'You will, but it takes time to get the hang of it.'

Sam spent a couple of hours explaining chakras—the energy centres of the spiritual body which channel life force.

'Psychics mainly use their third eye, which has many names, like the sixth chakra, the mind's eye, and I'm sure you've heard of the sixth sense—and I don't mean the movie. This eye is to see spirits and the signs they use to communicate with. Closing down these senses takes practice but *should* be done, because if channels are left constantly open it's detrimental for both body and soul. You literally need to come back down to earth after readings or visitations, for the sake of your physical and mental wellbeing. In other words, Annie, we have to do it for our own sanity.'

Annie and Sam spoke in depth about her experiences since the crash. He was convinced that she was born with her powers and had somehow closed them down herself when she'd been young, only for them to resurface unintentionally with the shock of the crash.

Annie told him about Ellie, how she had been her constant companion from a young age, and that she had come back as a grown woman ... albeit a ghost with attitude.

'I must admit Annie, I'm slightly worried that Ellie might be a tricky soul. Quite often, these impish spirits attach themselves to individuals who have psychic energy, even from birth, and tend to hang around that person for life. She doesn't seem to have your well-being entirely at heart. Just be cautious my dear girl—hopefully I'm wrong.'

'She's always been impish Sam; she used to even get me into trouble—but I'm almost a hundred percent sure she's ok.'

'Well, there you are then, I am wrong. Now, Annie, I really think that all you need is my guidance, not tutoring. In my extensive career as a psychic, I've never come across anyone with your combined capabilities. My only worry is you being strong enough to deal with such powers. I *do* promise you though, that as long as I'm here I'll help guide and protect your physical being *and* your spiritual one, too. And then, of course, when I'm no longer here—which may be sooner than later—and if they let me in through those infamous gates—I promise faithfully to be your "guide from the other side" ... And a poet it seems, too.'

They both laughed, but Annie was quietly overcome with love for this old man. He had shown her more compassion than either of her parents had done in all of her thirty-two years.

'Sam, you're so special, and thanks so much for all you're doing ... But why me?'

He paused. 'Because, my dearest girl, I have spent my life up until now trying to be a good man by helping others. But I've never made enough of an impact on people's lives to make a difference either to theirs or mine. Yes, I've done my best in a small way, but helping a prodigy like yourself to be bigger and better than I ever was would make my existence worthwhile. *You,* Annie, have come into my life just when I needed to redeem myself most.'

Annie put her hand on his. 'You've already changed my life for the better, Sam, and I'd be honoured if you would always be my guide. But I need to be honest with you first ... and it may change your attitude towards me.'

'I doubt that very much, my dear, but carry on.' Sam said, and cocked his head to one side.

'I've noticed you're quite religious, Sam, and I'm afraid to tell you that I'm not at all. In fact, I'm an atheist, or whatever you want to call a devout non-believer.'

Sam smiled again and shook his head. 'Annie, my dear sweet girl, religion is not exclusive to God. Everyone needs to have faith in something, whether it's a particular god or deity—of which there are hundreds to choose from—or maybe even something or someone else that consumes your life for the better. Now, forgive me if I'm wrong, but I would say that you *do* have a religion. Spiritualism seems to be dominating the goodness in your life right now, and I would say that's a religion of sorts. You see, Annie, I don't judge people on what they believe in, just the goodness that comes from whatever it might be.'

'You're right of course, Sam, and I've never looked at it that way.

I just thought you'd be disappointed in me for not being part of the God Squad.'

'God Squad? I like that, I'm going to use it.' Sam chuckled. 'And of course I'm not disappointed in you Annie. I like freethinking.'

'A-ha! That's what I'm going to call myself from now on: a freethinker.'

'Actually, Annie, when I was a young man, I didn't understand the messages and visions I was receiving. But my parents thought at the time that what I had was some kind of a religious calling. So, long story short, I joined a seminary and studied theology to become a deacon, but I was never a full priest. Things are meant to be in life, though, and it turned out that one of my parishioners was a clairvoyant. She could see the messages I was receiving were not from God, but spirits who wanted me to talk with their loved ones, and to pass on their important messages. So ... against my parents' wishes, I joined the spiritualist church to learn how to use my gift. Now listen, Annie, an awful lot of spiritualists believe in God; and yes, they feel that's where their ability and calling comes from. And I suppose I do too, to some degree. But believing in God is not a prerequisite to becoming a spiritualist or clairvoyant. Don't worry about religion, simply let your heart guide you, and you'll do just fine.' Sam put his hand on Annie's arm.

Annie got up and hugged the old man. 'You're amazing, but I wish you were younger so that we could have many years together as friends.'

'Yes, wouldn't that be just perfect; but alas, my girl, my time is short. So we'll just have to play the cards we've been dealt, won't we?'

Annie was comfortable enough with Sam to discuss her problems with the catacomb children and the priest. She asked if he would go with her to the church in a few days' time; it was a little more than she could handle on her own, and Sam would be the only one who could possibly help. Maddy was also up for it; she had never experienced so much excitement before meeting Annie—and evidently wanted more.

Madeleine looked at Sam. 'Haven't you forgotten to ask Annie something?'

'Oh, you're a pain in my derrière, Madeleine. Okay, Annie, I was wondering whether you would be up for an open-platform event here; but you seem to have so much going on in your life at the moment, so I thought I'd wait till the next time we were together to ask. But I suppose time is of the essence, my dear.'

'An open platform sounds scarier than any ghost, Sam. What's that all about then?'

'You know how I asked you to take over from me soon? Well, I thought you could have a trial run at one of our evenings. It's just like an open mic session for new singers; I know that because my son is a musician and used to do it all the time. So, you see, I'm "with it." I think that's what you say when you're supposed to be trendy.'

They all laughed, but Maddy tutted. 'Oh Sam, let me do this.' She took over the conversation. 'Look, Annie, bottom line is Sam needs to take a rest. He can't carry on much longer … it's just too much for him to cope with, and he hasn't been at all well. And to be quite honest with you, we haven't got anyone who is good enough to keep our congregation happy. If they don't get the messages, they'll leave in droves, and you're better than any medium we've ever had—sorry, Sam. But I know you can do it Annie … *please* say yes.'

'Thanks for that, Madeleine,' Sam said. 'I wasn't going to put it quite that strongly, but she's right, Annie. I haven't got the draw or ability I used to have, and we desperately need new blood. You're the only one who can put this place back on the map. Please say you'll do it. I'll be there with you, and we could possibly work together. Anyway, there'll probably only be a handful of our congregation, just a few oldies—nothing to be scared of.'

Annie shook her head; because she knew she'd been backed into a corner with no way out. 'Okay, okay, I'll do it. But promise you'll be there and stand with me, Sam. I *really* can't do it on my own … When is it, anyway?'

Sam and Maddy looked at each other. 'You tell her, Maddy.'

'In three days' time, Annie. Thursday at 7 p.m. to be precise … Okay with you?'

Annie just grinned. 'Right … Cheers for that, guys.'

Chapter 19

∞

OPEN PLATFORM

The last thing Annie wanted that week was to add to her plate of worry. But with the future outcome of the letters up in the air, the church dilemma, and the anxiety of the open-platform evening, she had an idea she was being tested.

How was she supposed to prepare for such an event? It wasn't like rehearsing a song for an open-mic show, or memorising words for a speech. All she could do was stand on the stage and hope a spirit from the other side turned out to be a chatterbox.

She took Sam's advice and spent time meditating to open her channels before jumping in the car for the half hour drive to the League. Thos drove; he usually did around London, but the start of their journey took place in awkward silence. Although Annie was reasonably chilled after her meditation, she still had pangs of letter-guilt.

They both started speaking at once.

'Sorry, sweetheart, you go first,' Annie said quickly, hoping for another reprieve.

'Yeah, okay ... Look, babe, my selfish behaviour the other evening was well out of order, and I know that leaving to spend the night with Max was wrong. All I can do is apologise, but unfortunately it seems I have the ability to be a thoughtless git now and again. It must be a trait I've inherited, I suppose ... Well, that's my excuse, anyway. So ... are you going to forgive me for the other night? And you're well within your rights to give me a rollicking if it happens again.'

'I *love* you for that, my darling, and of course I forgive you. But I'm not perfect either, and I need a chat about the other evening too ...'

But Annie had yet another reprieve.

'We've arrived, babe. Bloody hell, there's a queue outside.' Thos sounded as shocked as Annie looked.

'Oh my God, I hope that's not for me and Sam; it can't be.'

'I'll drop you off here, and go and find somewhere to park. Anyway, what was it you were going to say about the other evening?'

'Oh ... nothing ... it can wait. I'll see you inside, sweetheart.'

Annie got out of the car, and soon forgot her undeclared confession. The crowd seemed to recognise her, and she soon knew why. There was a large poster on the noticeboard with a huge photo of her and Sam on it.

EXCITING LEAGUE NEWS

OUR TALENTED NEW PSYCHIC MEDIUM ANNIE PRIOR PAIRS UP WITH OUR BELOVED SAM HARGREAVES FOR A SPECIAL EVENING OF CLAIRVOYANCE.

THE CONAN DOYLE HALL
Thursday 7:30 p.m.

Maddy came rushing down the steps and took hold of Annie's arm, pulling her past the crowds and into the packed entrance hall.

'What on earth is this all about, Mads? And that poster outside! You and Sam said it wouldn't be busy. It's like a bloody Rod Stewart concert.'

'Oh, you'll be *fine* Annie … I didn't actually think anyone would turn up on such short notice. It's just that the photo I took of you and Sam on Monday was *so* fabulous, I thought I'd use it to advertise this evening. Please tell me you're not cross with me, I couldn't bear that.'

'No, I'm not cross with you, Mads, how could I be? Just a little *vexed* maybe.' Annie smiled, albeit forced.

They walked into the hall, she scanned around looking for empty seats. But apart from a few single ones that people were already jostling for, it was full to capacity. Even the dusty chairs that had previously been folded against the walls, had been cleaned and crammed into every vacant space.

Annie's heart pounded and her hands started to perspire; she climbed the five steps to the stage. But when she saw Sam's beaming smile, her somersaulting stomach landed. She knew he was there for her and everything would be fine … she hoped.

Annie had never willingly prayed in her life, but since Sam had so eloquently informed her that religion was not exclusive to God, and that one could choose who, or what, to believe in, she decided to have a quiet word with her spiritual guides—whoever they were—and ask them to bring forward at least one or two chatty souls.

She sat on a chair at the side of the stage to settle her wobbling legs. Sam tapped the microphone to make sure it was live. It was … but Annie visibly jumped at the sound of whistling feedback from the speakers, and so did the audience.

'Oops, sorry, ladies and gentlemen, I was just checking you were all ready for an exciting evening of mediumship.' Sam moved away from the speakers, avoiding any more disquieting interruptions. 'Thank you so much for this incredible turnout, although *alas* I know it's not all for me.'

The congregation tittered.

'As you all know, Thursdays are normally set aside for our open-platform events, where we have a few new psychics trying out their abilities. But tonight, we welcome to the stage a very talented clairvoyant medium, Miss Annie Prior, and I'm here to give her guidance and support as a fellow medium. I would like all of you to open your hearts, not just to Annie but to our dear departed friends and families, to help draw them close. Annie is an incredibly talented psychic, but with any extraordinary talent, there has to be a period of schooling and practice. So I ask you all to be patient this evening. And if you don't mind, I'm going to start this demonstration with a message for someone in the centre of the hall … there.' Sam gestured to a large, ruddy-faced woman, who was clearly smug about being chosen first.

Annie scanned the hall while he was talking. It was full of probing faces, mainly scrutinising her. They all seemed to be quietly imploring her to choose them for a reading. But her sweeping study of the congregation was interrupted by the sight of a familiar hairstyle near the back. The woman lifted her head and Annie's stomach churned, but then settled, she remembered the incredible day they'd recently shared. Melina smiled at her—a new experience for Annie.

She could hear Sam talking but had stopped listening to his words; she'd had her own message come through.

'You can do this, Annie,' a detached voice said.

She scanned the hall but could see no one to attach it to; then her precursor vibes kicked in, many spirits of the departed stepped forward out of the shadows. Annie had never been happier to see them.

She could see Sam struggling with his message.

'I ... feel your husband ... or maybe a father figure is here. But my connection is *very* weak, er, it'll come through in a minute ... I'm sure.' Sam seemed uncomfortable, and the woman looked disappointed.

Annie immediately saw the man Sam was trying to describe, standing behind the woman. Annie stood, walked over to Sam and touched his arm.

'Would it be okay for me to continue with this message, Sam? I think I know who's here for her.'

Sam was clearly relieved. 'Oh, yes ... thank you, my dear.'

Everyone in the hall was relieved too. Annie took the reins, and without faltering continued with the message.

'I believe your husband is here for you; in fact, he's standing behind you with his hands on your shoulders. He seems to be steering you in the right direction.'

The lady touched her shoulder, as if to feel her husband's unseen hand.

Annie smiled whilst she listened to the spirit convey his message. 'Okay, so this is slightly awkward, your husband has just told me something which I believe is personal to you. Are you okay for me to continue?'

The woman simply nodded, she had never received a message of any consequence before.

'Well, according to your husband you're wanting to get married again, but you're feeling terribly guilty about it as it's only been two years since his passing.'

The woman's mouth dropped open. 'Oh my God, you're right. How on earth ...?'

'I think you mean *he's* right,' Annie said with a broad smile. The congregation laughed quietly. 'Actually, he's giving you his blessing, and really likes your future husband. Was he one of your husband's friends?'

The lady nodded again in affirmation and put her hands over her face—her emotions erupted. It seemed that everyone in the congregation sighed and teared up too, including most of the men.

Annie began to feel an overwhelming surge of spirits pushing their way in, they had been patiently waiting for years to get their messages across and now finally had someone who truly understood them.

They all rushed her at once, and she put her hands up to stop them. 'Please give me some space, I can only deal with one at a time.'

The congregation clearly thought Annie was addressing them. Her outburst must have looked crazy.

'Oh, I'm so sorry. I didn't mean *you* ... the congregation. It's just there are so many spirits all wanting to chat at once. So I hope you've brought sleeping bags, ladies and gentlemen, as I do believe it's going to be a long evening.'

The hall erupted with the sound of relieved laughter from everyone. Annie glanced over towards Sam who put both thumbs up and winked. She could hear his thoughts above the spirits and was moved almost to tears of how proud he was of her.

As Annie turned back to the congregation, her attention was drawn to a child darting in and out of the shadows. She focused on this particular vision and mentally pushed aside all the other spirits for the time being.

It was a young girl of about six, with golden curly blonde hair and a pink, cheeky face. Annie also noticed a small brown and white dog, which had appeared next to the child. They both seemed to be the best of friends.

Annie scanned the hall to attach the dancing child to a family, knowing in her heart there would be many there that night who had lost their children. She didn't want to raise unnecessary hopes by mentioning the girl before she had found the family. This was one of those times she needed a little help ...

And, with that thought, Ellie appeared, standing next to the child. She took hold of the girl's hand and led her through the seated congregation, stopping in front of a young couple. Ellie turned and looked at Annie. 'Just think of me and I will always be here to help, my friend.' Then, she was gone.

Annie was quiet for a moment, processing what had just happened, then the child stamped her foot impatiently. Annie pointed to the couple she was next to.

'You've lost someone very special, as we all have, but ... losing a child is incredibly hard to deal with. I have your daughter here and she's with a little brown and white dog.'

The man put his arm around his wife. 'It's our baby.' He grabbed her hand.

'She's a busy little bee, dancing up and down,' Annie said, smiling. But the couple seemed confused. 'Ah yes, she says ... "Tell Mummy and Daddy I can walk and dance now, and Bobo's with me, too."' The child continued to dance around the dog.

'Your daughter was disabled before she passed, is that right?' Annie asked.

The couple nodded, and in a broken voice the man told Annie and the congregation that Molly, their little girl, had been born with cerebral palsy, and could only walk with aid. But she loved to watch dancing shows on the TV and had dreamt of having her own ballet shoes.

Annie glanced down at Molly's feet; she was wearing unusually bright pink ballet shoes. 'Were the shoes she wanted fuchsia pink, by any chance?'

Molly's mother was shocked. 'Yes, but we told her they weren't made in that colour.' Tears rolled down her cheeks.

'Well, I guess they *are* on the other side—she's wearing them now, and having so much fun dancing up and down the aisle in front of you with Bobo.'

Although the woman was crying, she stood and took a deep breath. 'This is so amazing ... All our little Molly ever wanted to do was to dance, and now she is. And yes, Bobo was her constant companion; he would never leave her side. My husband and I both said that after Molly left us, Bobo wanted to go too. And he did ... just two months after we lost her. We had both dreamt of her dancing many times, so I guess dreams really do come true. But we would never have known, if it hadn't been for you, Annie. Thank you so much ... What you do is wonderful.'

Annie's throat tightened with emotion. 'Please don't worry about Molly, she's incredibly happy now, and doing what she had always wanted. You know, it's not sad for those who depart this world ... it's only sad for the one's they leave behind grieving. We all have to cope with the emptiness when they've gone, which is so hard. But it's up to us to find a way of moving forward after we lose a loved one. If we don't, those souls will be anchored to this world by our sadness. Show Molly that you're happy for her ... and then she can move on, too. Although I'm absolutely sure she'll be popping in to check on you every now and again.'

The couple hugged each other and beamed with happiness at the knowledge that their daughter's soul lived on. The child danced up the aisle away from her parents with her little dog running in front of her—both slowly disappearing upwards towards the moonlit window.

'Molly's gone now ... but she's at peace, as she can feel that your sadness has finally been lifted.'

The child's elated parents held each other's hands tightly. Her father turned to Annie and mouthed the words, 'Thank you so much.'

A few people in the congregation started clapping, then the others joined in. Annie smiled in the knowledge that their appreciation was not for her but was a collective reassurance that a wonderful afterlife awaited them. The clapping gradually stilled whilst the audience composed themselves for more revelations.

'Right ... I think we're all in a better place now, after that amazing and evidential visitation from Molly; she seems to have lifted everyone's spirits, so to speak. *And* seems to have summoned many more in—I see.'

Annie looked over towards Thos and Maddy and was shocked to see that Max and his mother had joined them. Max's mum was dabbing her eyes with a handkerchief that Maddy had handed her. It made Annie giggle to herself, she knew exactly what Maddy was up to.

Sam walked over to Annie, grabbed her hand, and squeezed it. 'You are an *amazing* young woman, Annie, but are you okay to continue? It's a much larger congregation than I have ever performed in front of, and it must be draining you.'

'No, I'm really good, thanks, Sam. Are we okay for time?'

'It's completely up to you, my dear girl, but I wouldn't carry on too long ... this *will* wipe you out for days.'

'Okay, understood. I'm going to have to carry on for a while, though ... I have so many desperate souls waiting.' Annie stood next to the microphone again waiting for another connection. The congregation simmered down and fell silent, all watching her intently.

A young man's entity appeared who Annie thought she recognised; she had to think for a moment,

as her memory of spirits and their messages seem to fade soon after contact. But then it came to her, and scanned the congregation for Dan Watts, the handsome soul was his brother. Dan had snuck into the back of the hall with a diminutive older woman. Annie presumed the old lady was his mother, they shared similar features, although her face had been ravaged by grief.

Annie pointed towards her. 'This is for you, my dear. I have a young man here who I *have* actually seen before, and he's so eager to say *hi* to his mum this time. Your handsome son is coming forward with a rose and so much love for you.'

'I haven't brought a rose,' the annoyed spirit shouted.

Annie spoke back to him quietly in her mind. *No, you haven't, but I feel it was your mum's favourite flower, and it will mean so much to her. You men never learn—even when you pass over!*

'Okay, so that was a great idea … Well done, Annie. But please tell Mum to stop thinking about me all the time. I can't move on with her grief holding me back. Tell her to concentrate on Dan. He's been so strong for her since I passed, and she needs to remember she's got a living son to be proud of … I love her but she has to let me go.'

'Well, we have another strong message about moving on,' Annie said. She recounted it to the congregation but was aiming it at Dan and his mum. And whilst his mother snivelled into her handkerchief, Dan gave Annie a thumbs-up, with a broad smile.

For the next two hours, Annie passed on many more messages, but suddenly became weary, and her throat had started to feel scratchy and sore. She still had many spirits urging her to continue, but could feel her ability being compromised by the draw on her energy.

'Ladies and gentlemen, much as I would like to continue with this demonstration, I'm feeling rather tired now and I don't want to make any mistakes, so I'm going to have to bring this evening to a close.'

A collective sigh of disappointment rippled.

'But I'd be very happy to do this again next week; that's if … you would like to see me again.'

There was a resounding 'Yes' from the congregation.

Annie was about to finalise the evening, when the spirit of an elderly man came close to her.

'You can't stop now; I need to ask my wife something.'

Annie sighed but kept smiling and walked back to the microphone. 'Ladies and gentlemen, apparently I have to give one more message; I have a rather persuasive gentleman here who's not taking *no* for an answer. Okay, so ... I feel as if I'm being drawn to the lady in the front with the blue blouse.'

The woman looked around her to make sure she was the only one wearing blue. 'Oh, you mean me?' she said in a posh English accent.

'Yes, you, my dear. I have your husband here.'

'Oh ... I *don't* want to speak to him,' the woman said indignantly.

Annie was shocked at the old dear's retort, as was the congregation.

Annie laughed. 'Well, apparently he doesn't really want to speak to you either, but he has a question for you.' Annie was completely perplexed. 'This is most unusual ... I *think* he's just asked why you had those words engraved on his headstone.'

The old lady's face flushed a little. 'Well, I suppose I didn't have much time to decide on an appropriate epitaph for him.'

Annie laughed; the old man seemed cross at his wife's answer and was adamant that he was going to get more from her. 'Your husband's just said, "You know what you had engraved—isn't true."'

The woman seemed strangely relieved, and shook her head, smiling. The audience had started to stand to get a better view.

'Please tell us what it was that you had carved on your husband's headstone. We all really want to know ... Don't we, ladies and gentlemen?' Annie said.

The audience all shouted, 'Yes!'

The woman, elegant in her blue ruffled blouse and long skirt slowly rose to her feet. She turned to speak to the audience. 'I now know that our dear departed don't change their spots just because they've passed over.' She shook her head. 'My husband and I did *not* have a very good marriage, but it was in the old days, when divorces were unusual. You see, back then it was down to us ladies to keep our selfish husbands happy, which was hard when the last drop of love had already been squeezed dry. But when my husband thankfully passed on, I didn't for a moment think I would ever hear from him again. So, I thought I'd have the last laugh, and had a lovely gravestone carved with "Till we meet again" on it. Obviously, I didn't mean it, but now it looks like my Charles … has had the last laugh. At least, he's come back to confirm what I already knew. He won't be waiting for me when it's my turn to shuffle off. And I can't tell you how relieved I am.'

The whole congregation erupted with laughter, as did the old lady.

Although Annie was exhausted, she was delighted that the evening had ended amusingly and with no tears. She was also overwhelmed by the amazing reaction and warmth from everyone—it had surpassed all her expectations.

Sam put his arm around her shoulders and hugged her as hard as his frail body would allow. 'I knew you'd be good, Annie, but *that* was extraordinary. You don't need my help now, just my friendship. And I promise I'll always be here, in some form or other, with my hands on *your* shoulders and steering *you* in the right direction.'

'Thanks, Sam. How crazy was all that? I can't believe it went so well.'

He smiled, his moist eyes glistening. 'I'm so proud of you, Annie; let's talk in a minute. I'm going to have to put this evening's proceedings to bed now.' He stood in front of the microphone. 'Ladies and gentlemen, I'm sure you would all like to thank Annie for such a wonderfully informative and joyous evening.'

Before he could continue, though, Molly's parents stood and started clapping. The rest of the congregation followed and for the first time in the League's history of demonstrations, there was a standing ovation for the medium. Annie scanned the hall, overwhelmed with gratitude but also slight embarrassment. Then her heart skipped a beat; Melina was standing and clapping too.

Annie took the microphone from Sam.

'I can't thank you enough for the welcome I've received this evening, and I am so appreciative of your show of gratitude towards me. But please, let it be for all our loved ones who have managed to come through tonight and made our lives richer with their messages, wisdom, and humour. And I would also like to take this opportunity to announce—if it's okay with Sam—that I'll be stepping into his amazing shoes over the next few weeks, so he can take a well-deserved rest and spend precious time with his family.'

Annie turned to Sam and started clapping, and the congregation joined in to show their appreciation towards the elderly man who had been giving readings and joy for so many years.

Chapter 20

∞

The Nun

Although the open platform session had been a baptism of fire, it had gone better than Annie could possibly have hoped for. But more than that, the nagging question she'd had since her spiritual awakening—had finally been answered. She was more than capable of passing on coherent messages from those on the other side, and at the same time holding an audience enthralled—even though her emotions had taken a pounding.

She had been overcome by the incredible response from her congregation and friends, but more so the reaction she'd had from Thos. He had celebrated her triumph with the boyish excitement she had only once seen before, which was encouraging, considering his aversion to all things unworldly. All the credence in her abilities had momentarily tipped her emotions over the edge after the show, but she had managed to escape for a private weep, which had been the release—albeit temporary—she had needed before her newly found strength resumed to normality.

Her exhaustion the following day was expected; she deserved a chilled time pattering around the house. The overload of spirits from the previous evening had taken its toll, so she put her phone on silent, which was a necessity for her own sanity's sake. But it wasn't long before her sixth sense informed her she'd had an important missed call. A couple of messages had pinged through from Maddy, but there was another that had stimulated her inner curiosity—so she called back immediately.

'Hello, Miss Prior, thank you so much for returning my call so quickly. I'm sure you won't remember me ...'

Before the woman could finish speaking, Annie had a vision of a nun in her mind. 'Of course I remember you, Sister, we met at the priest's funeral.'

The phone fell silent for a few seconds. 'Yes, of course ... Well, I'm Sister Margaret and you wanted some information about Father Mellion. When would it be convenient to meet up?'

Annie seized the opportunity and immediately forgot any thoughts of a day's rest. 'This afternoon would be perfect for me, Sister.'

'Good, I was hoping for today. What about 3:30 in front of the All Saints Church in Blackheath? Apparently, it's going to be a reasonably warm spring afternoon, so we can chat while we take a stroll over the heath.'

'That sounds just perfect, Sister.'

∞

The All Saints Church stood like a solitary beacon towering over the sprawling countryside of Blackheath. It was a picture-postcard vista of a sand-coloured steeple drenched in sunlight. Annie's interest in religious buildings had been growing; she found herself, yet again, in awe of the architecture. The monumental construction had been perceptively set against a barren landscape, seemingly to overwhelm and inspire those in need of a place to give them strength. She also thought it was perfectly placed to encourage religion within the poor local community, by presenting them with the grandeur of God's house. And the architect of such an awe-inspiring building must have accomplished all he had wanted from his masterpiece.

'Hello, Miss Prior.'

Annie swung around to see the nun grinning. 'Ah, Sister Margaret.' Annie stepped forward with her hand outstretched. 'Please call me Annie, I can't bear formality,' she said, looking over at the expanse of heathland. 'Thanks so much for getting in touch and suggesting this extraordinary place to meet up.'

'Yes, it's one of my favourite haunts, so to speak.' The nun laughed. 'You'll see what I mean later.'

Annie cocked her head to one side. *This is going to be interesting,* she thought. The woman of God stood for everything Annie had hated since her own convent days, but instead of feeling animosity towards her, she had a strange degree of respect.

The nun smiled knowingly. 'I believe we share something in common, and it's not just that we both knew Father Mellion. You see, I have a clairaudient and sentient ability too, albeit meagre. I hear and feel, but I don't see. It's nowhere near the power you have within you, Annie. You're someone very special, but I, on the other hand, only use my gift occasionally to help in my work. But to be quite honest, it frightens me. I don't really understand things I can't see.'

Annie shook her head. 'But that's exactly why I'm an atheist, Sister. If I can't see something, I don't believe it's there. And the fact that *He* never shows mercy or answers people's prayers, is all the affirmation I need to discount his existence. Show me your God and let me talk to him like I talk to the spirits of those passed, and honestly, I'll wear what you're wearing too.'

They both laughed.

'I'm sorry, Sister. Any chance to have a go at him ... and I'm up for it.'

'That's quite okay, Annie, I do understand where you're coming from. At least you're passionate about your beliefs; you'd be surprised how many people live their whole lives without having faith in anything. It's those I worry about.'

The two women walked and chatted, completely unaware of the attention they were attracting.

Sister Margaret was cherub-faced, wearing a below-the-knee grey habit and a Maria Von Trapp-style wimple and veil, all rounded off with the obligatory unadorned wooden cross suspended by a leather lace around her neck. In complete contrast, Annie was a twenty-first-century vision. Her striking aqua eyes matched her pastel-blue jumper and pale denims, with her long copper-red hair lifting in the light breeze.

'How is it, Sister Margaret, that you're not locked up in a convent somewhere? I didn't think nuns were allowed to roam free.'

'Ah yes, well ... Most of the population think that. But you see, I elected to be an Apostolic Sister. It means I can travel and meet extraordinary people like yourself, Annie, and it also allows me to spread the word of God, and assist wherever I'm needed. Generally, most nuns spend their lives living in closed convents: obeying the vows of poverty, celibacy, and obedience. But as an Apostolic Sister, I've taken *simple* vows, which means I can keep my parents' estate—although I'm not allowed to gain revenue from it. But I still abide by the same vows as my fellow sisters who are locked away.'

'Well, I must admit, Sister, I'm humbled by your commitment, but I still can't get my head around what you do. Of course I admire you for your beliefs, but I don't understand why God the Almighty would expect a human being to abide by such harsh vows.'

'That's okay, Annie. It's a good job we are all different.' The sister smiled empathetically, as if warming to her. 'Now, the reason I wanted a meeting with you today was to talk about Father Mellion. I've thought long and hard about whether or not I should speak to anyone about him. But now that he's gone ... I want to relieve my burden through you. And I know in my heart that you'll act on my information.' The nun walked over to a bench and sat, patting the seat next to her—silently inviting Annie to sit.

The sister looked straight ahead and took a deep breath. 'The first time I met Father Mellion was in a Catholic school in north London that doubled as a base for youngsters waiting for foster homes. It was run by sisters and an elderly priest at the time, which was about thirty years ago now, although it seems like only yesterday. I was a very young postulant helping out wherever I was needed. I was so innocent to the world and its evils, and I have to be completely honest with you, Annie, when I first met Mellion I thought he was charming ... and was quite taken with him. He was the first person who'd shown any interest in plain old me. Most people choose to ignore nuns and never think of us as human beings with regular feelings like anyone else. So when Father Mellion told me I was attractive and intelligent, my head was turned. But one day, when I was on my own with him, he took advantage of my innocence and tried to sexually assault me. If I hadn't fought him off ... I don't know what would have happened that day, and I was too scared to tell anyone at the time. Nobody would have listened to a seventeen-year-old postulant's word against a priest's, anyway.' Sister Margaret took another deep breath as she laboured with her words. 'He disappeared for a few months so I was fine for a while, and then when he returned, he thankfully ignored me. But it was only a few weeks after that I realised he'd started to abuse some of the older children; they were about ten to twelve years of age at the time. I never actually caught him doing anything inappropriate, but I knew what was happening. I could see them becoming afraid of him, and I could feel their fear too. They wouldn't tell me anything, but I'm sure he'd threatened them with Hell and damnation if they spoke about it, as he had done with me. But that's where he deserves to be now.' The sister cupped her hands over her eyes trying to block out her memories.

Annie was stunned at the story. 'I'm so sorry you went through such a terrible ordeal, Sister. But tell me, why did you go to his funeral then?'

'Hmm, it must have seemed strange, but I had to lay him to rest in my own mind, so to speak. I know it's a terrible thing to say but seeing his coffin was probably one of the best moments of my life. He was dead and gone, and finally unable to hurt anyone else. *He* was the reason I continued on to become a sister, because as far as I was concerned, the world outside our convent was a wicked place and I was not strong enough to live in it. But the best thing I did back then was to pluck up enough courage to tell all I knew to the old priest who ran the school. Bless him, he wrote to the bishop of the diocese, after which there was an internal investigation. But because there was no evidence—only my word against Mellion's—it was all swept under the hierarchical carpet. Although he must have been in a lot of trouble beforehand, because soon after that I heard he'd been excommunicated from the priesthood. And of course I was asked to keep quiet about it—for the sake of God and the Church.' The sister looked down embarrassed. 'The only other person I've ever spoken to about it was a young police officer at the time; he used to come to the home on a regular basis. But he had the same problem with his superiors and was asked to keep quiet, too.'

'That must have been Detective Inspector Dan Watts?' Annie said.

'Yes, it was. He's such a nice man, and I was so sorry not to have spoken to him at the funeral, but hopefully he can be of help to you now. In fact ... you two would make a great team.'

Annie smiled; she knew the nun was right.

Sister Margaret continued. 'I'm sure that after Mellion was excommunicated he moved elsewhere to continue on with his evil sins. And I'm convinced he escalated his abuse to something more sinister. You see, Annie, in those days it seemed not to be such a hideous crime as it is nowadays, although it must have been prolific amongst people like Mellion who had access to institutions. If only he had been fully investigated then, he could have been locked up and stopped from whatever atrocities he's got away with in the last thirty years.'

'I'm sorry to say that he still is evil,' Annie said, and proceeded to tell her about the crash and how Mellion had died in front of her—only to reappear in the hospital and elsewhere. 'Did you know he had a brother?'

'No, I didn't. But come to think of it, he used to visit the home with another man sometimes, who looked just as wicked as he was. Please don't tell me there's another Mellion Jackson out there somewhere ... Having his ghost around still—is bad enough.'

'I don't know anything about his brother yet, but now that you've told me what you know ... Mellion might well have had an accomplice. Don't worry—I'll dig deep, and I promise you, Sister, I'll do my very best to find out what both of them were up to.'

They got up from the bench, Annie stood perfectly still and looked down at the ground. A strange vibration was coming from below her feet.

'Are you okay, Annie?'

'Yeah, I think so. I'm not sure whether I'm feeling my visitational vibes or we're having a small earthquake.'

The nun laughed. 'It's not an earthquake. You remember I said earlier this was one of my favourite haunts? Well, I was being literal. I've never actually seen them, but I know there are many lost souls here. Back in the seventeen hundreds there was a plague called the Black Death and *many* thousands died in London alone. And because all the cemeteries were overflowing, they had to find places for burial pits to take bodies en masse, and I suppose here was ideal.' The nun concentrated on Annie's reactions.

Annie realised the crowds of people she'd thought had been out walking were actually the souls of departed plague victims. She had been so engrossed in her conversation with the nun that she hadn't noticed the wandering ghosts who were wearing peasant clothes from another era.

Annie looked at Sister Margaret. 'I'm so sorry you can't see them … it's really quite a sight.'

'I wish I could. I come here regularly, because it's the only place I have otherworldly experiences. But although I can feel them, I can't help them, which saddens me.'

Annie watched the spirits closely. 'You know something, Sister, I don't think anyone can help these spirits. I honestly feel they've already made peace with themselves. And what you're feeling and I'm seeing is their combined residual spiritual energy from years ago. I believe their souls have already gone home.'

Chapter 21

∞

THE GALLERY

Annie signed for a special delivery letter, which was an unusual occurrence, what with emails and messaging. And as soon as she held it, an image of Melina sprang to mind.

Dearest Annie,

I hope you don't mind the formality of a letter instead of calling, but I felt I would get too emotional speaking to you, and a handwritten letter hopefully proves how important this is to me.

Firstly, I can't tell you how impressed I was the other evening; I had absolutely no idea how incredible your psychic ability actually is. And when you gave me the message from my mother at the gallery, I didn't realise just how difficult it must have been for you, especially because of the way I've treated you in the past, which was completely inexcusable. But I now find myself ...

not surprisingly ... without true friends, and it doesn't help that I'm missing you so much at work too. Although I completely understand your life choice at this time, and it's obvious that you must continue on with it. But please give me another chance, Annie, I really need you in my life again.

So, saying all that, I'd love to meet up and treat you to lunch, and hopefully straighten everything out. You mentioned that you have a gay friend who might help at the gallery, and I wondered if you'd had a chance to get in touch with him for me, I'm getting desperate now. If you could talk him into taking the job, it would be a great excuse to celebrate by having lunch together. I have a favourite restaurant in Mayfair which I know you'll love because the architecture is absolutely superb. Hopefully we can do this soon.

With affection,

Melina X

Annie was shocked by Melina's about-turn; she appeared to have changed beyond all recognition. It was as if she was a completely different person. All Annie had to do now was organise Poppet to fill her shoes. She needed to do something to help Melina out.

∞

'Pops, it's Annie. How are you doing?'

'Oh, Annie, my darling, thank goodness you've called. Would you believe I've just been dragged across the coals in Matron's office yet again for being too bloody camp in front of patients? So before she gave me a third warning, I handed my notice in with immediate effect. And guess what? I've just walked out, so I really hope the gallery job's still open, 'cause I'm *free*.'

'That's extraordinary, Pops! It's exactly the reason I called. How soon can you start?'

'Ooh, today? But you'll have to wait for me to put some slap on, sweetie—that's make-up to you.'

'Oh, right. Well, I'll meet you at the gallery at 11, and I promise you'll love it, sweetheart. And of course you won't be the only gay in Mayfair, either. But do me a favour, Pops, and go easy on the *slap* ... until she's got used to you at least.'

∞

Annie wanted to walk her old route past the high-end businesses she used to window shop in, so got her usual Uber to drop her down the road from the gallery. She was delighted to see her favourite homeless lady sitting in the doorway of a vacant shop.

Sandra was one of life's mysteries. Intelligent, articulate and definitely not an addict. Annie had never understood why she was on the streets, but when she had asked previously, Sandra had avoided the subject.

'Hi, Sandy, how are you doing?'

'Bit slow t'day Annie, but better now I've seen you. I've missed you being around these parts.'

'Yeah, I'm sorry, sweetheart ... My life's changed a little.' Annie took her purse out of her shoulder bag and handed Sandra three twenty-pound notes. 'I guess I owe you for about six weeks, don't I?'

'God bless you, Annie, you're my guardian angel; there's no one else who cares about me the way you do, but you don't need to give me so much.'

Annie held Sandra's hand and put the money in it. 'Yes, I do. If only I was in the position to help you more, Sandy, I would. Maybe one day ... you never know.'

Annie heard a familiar effeminate voice shouting from a little distance away.

'Yoo-hoo, darling, it's me!' Poppet shouted, attracting the attention of nearly everyone within earshot.

Annie watched her gay friend mince towards her down the high street. She had only ever seen him dressed in his male nurse's uniform at the hospital and was shocked by his flamboyant style. His fedora hat was perched to one side, and his pink shirt with an upstanding collar set off a black satin neckerchief that he'd tied with a flourish. A feminine black blazer with pink flecks over tight jeans rounded off his Quentin Crisp impersonation perfectly. He was obviously very pleased with himself, as he kept glancing at his reflection in every shop window.

'Hi, Pops ... you look incredible. I'd like you to meet Sandra, she's a friend of mine and somebody who is one of life's special people.'

'I'm not special, Annie; you are, though. But it's nice to meet you, Pops. Is that your real name?'

'No, it's just plain Mark, but I prefer Pops if you don't mind, Sandra. And lovely to meet you too, darling.'

As Poppet and Annie walked the last hundred yards to the gallery, she filled him in on a few 'must know' details on how to impress Melina.

'Are you actually wearing mascara, Poppet?'

'I most *definitely* am, it makes my blue eyes stand out, don't you think?'

'You *are* funny ... I have to say though, you look perfect for the job. The customers are going to love you. But please do me a favour just for now: don't gush ... just be cool.'

'I'm always cool, sweetie.'

∞

Melina looked like a different person. Her broad smile gave away her delight at seeing Annie and her newest member of staff making a vivacious entrance.

'You must be Poppet.' Melina held out her hand. 'I *love* what you're wearing ... I can already tell that you're just the right person for the job.'

Melina's previously bitter voice had a much sweeter tone. She turned to Annie, put her arms around her shoulders and gave her a tight hug. 'Thank you so much, I can't *tell* you how much this means to me.'

'You're very welcome,' Annie said, still slightly bewildered at Melina's U-turn.

For the next half an hour, Melina and Annie showed Poppet around the gallery. He enthused over every painting, giving an intelligent commentary on the meanings of the abstractions, and blowing Annie's mind with his knowledge of nearly all the artists—including one of Melina's favourites, Tom Cox, a talented young man who specialised in urban London scenes.

Poppet stopped at a wall containing six large paintings. 'I've not seen work like this before; it's so dark and mysterious ... I really like it. Who's the artist, Annie?'

Annie couldn't believe Poppet liked the work. 'Yes, well, it's not *my* favourite; his name's Anilem, from Germany. I've never actually met him or even seen a photo, but he sells really well. And please don't try to read his abstractions, Pops, they'll depress you ... I've been trying to work them out for years.'

Melina interrupted. 'Come on, Annie, stop bashing Anilem's work ... and let's leave Poppet to it for an hour, he needs to be thrown in feet first.'

'So does that mean I've got the job?' Poppet asked, anxiously looking at Melina.

'Yes, of course ... I just hope your sales acumen is like your personality Pop's, keep passionately confident— and you'll be simply perfect. Now, give either of us a call if you have any problems.'

After showing him how to do the transactions, Melina and Annie left the new staff member with an inane grin on his face. They walked a few hundred yards up the road, turning right onto Arlington Street and up the front steps of the Ritz Hotel. Annie stood in the foyer, overwhelmed by the art deco styling. She had wanted to visit the famous hotel ever since her university days, but had never felt she would fit in, let alone be able to afford it.

A grey-haired doorman, wearing navy tails with gold epaulettes and a striking top hat, strode over confidently to them. 'It's so good to see you again Miss Hollingsworth, how are you today?' he said in a strong cockney accent.

'Very good ... Thank you Charlie, and how are you keeping?'

'Oh, not so bad, Miss. I suppose I should be thinking of retirement soon though ... it's coming up to forty-five years since I first started here.'

'Yes, I know, Charlie, but you can't retire yet. What *would* I do without you? By the way, I'd like you to meet a very good friend of mine, Miss Prior.' Melina turned to Annie. 'Charles was here when my dad used to bring me in for afternoon tea ... I must have only been about eight years old when I first came.'

'You're making me feel old, Miss.' Charlie touched the rim of his top hat. 'Nice to meet you, Miss Prior. Please come anytime and I'll be sure to look after you.'

'Thank you, Charlie, I'll definitely do that.'

'Now—I believe you're both booked for lunch in the Rivoli Bar? Let me take you through. I'd recommend the seafood selection on the specials today, Miss Hollingsworth. It's the freshest seafood you'll ever taste.'

'Thanks, Charlie, you've sold it well.' Melina said, surreptitiously handing him a folded twenty-pound note. 'Have a drink on me.'

Annie was astounded that Melina was on first name terms with the staff, and that she had been visiting the Ritz for years. 'What's going on, Mel? I had no idea you knew this place, let alone that you're a celebrity here.'

'Yes, it must look strange, but Dad and I used to come here once or twice a week. He knew everyone including the manager back then, so we always got preferential treatment.' Melina looked sad for a moment and then smiled again. 'Nothing lasts forever though. But I never stopped coming, mainly for the memories ... but also because it's a great place to butter up clients and dealers.'

'Well, aren't you full of surprises, Melina,' Annie said squeezing Mel's arm.

She was overwhelmed by the interior decor, the likes of which she had never seen before. The lengthy entrance hall with its palatial arches and huge chandeliers took her breath away. But no more so than the Rivoli Bar, where they were to have lunch. One of the waiters dressed in a tuxedo immediately sashayed over and acknowledged the fact that he, too, knew Melina well. They were ushered, with reverence, to a window seat, although the bustling street outside had been cleverly obscured by Lalique-style opaque glass. Annie was amazed by the sheer opulence of the room, and the fact that one of her favourite architectural influences had been used to create such a visual overload.

'I worked for you for six years, Mel, and all that time I thought you led a quiet, dreary life ... You're a bit of a dark horse, aren't you!'

'No, you were right first time, Annie, I have led a very quiet life. But this place has been my escape, where I could feel almost normal for a while.' Melina let out an audible sigh. 'I wasn't really interested in anyone: you, men, friends ... Nobody could penetrate my world until that day at the gallery. You've added a whole new dimension to my life, and I can't thank you enough. I really believe you saved me ... I was definitely on the brink.' Melina stopped talking and took a deep breath.

Annie tilted her head to one side. 'You wouldn't have done anything stupid, would you, Mel?'

'Probably ... Like I said, you saved me. And here I am enjoying myself with you, who would have thought? So come on, let's forget all about those miserable times and order lunch; I'm famished!'

The Rivoli Bar was busy with 'those who lunch' midweek. And while Annie and Melina savoured their seafood selection with a crisp Sancerre to wash it down, Annie had the chance to absorb a completely different experience from anywhere else she had been. Expensive attire and accessories seemed the norm— promoting an air of affluence. It seemed like a Louis Vuitton convention, with the unmistakable monogram print in abundance. But even with all the obvious prosperity, the usual plague of worry and sadness still showed on many faces. Annie's intuition and senses intensified and her psychic awareness heightened yet again. The back of her neck prickled signalling the arrival of a visitor. Melina glanced up from checking her phone.

'What is it, Annie?'

'Don't worry, it's really nothing.' She didn't want to upset Melina by announcing the appearance of a spirit and wasn't sure of how she would react after her episode at the gallery. She scanned the restaurant and realised that a man who had been standing by the bar since they had sat was in fact an unworldly visitor. He blended in well, as if he was a frequent customer. He looked straight at Annie and then moved his attention to Melina.

'Tell my daughter I'm with her mother, but we've been so worried about our Mellie. She's been to Hell and back, and you are the only one who can help her, Annie. Get that bastard who raped her, for us.'

'Is my mother here, Annie?' Melina said, as she'd seen her in the same trance at the gallery.

'No, Mel ... Let's pay and go, and we can chat on the way back.'

Mayfair's streets were jammed with people shopping, busking and begging. The homeless had always hit Annie's heart the hardest. She had never been able to pass one by without leaving even a small amount of change. But that day she had to deal with Melina first. Also, she couldn't understand why she was getting such a strong spiritual awareness even though she had only seen Mel's father.

'Come on, Annie, please tell me. Who did you see?'

'It was your dad, Mel.'

'Oh my God ... really? My dad ... What did he *say*?'

'He's worried about you and asked me to help. Most importantly, though, he's with your mum, and they're just fine.'

Melina stopped in her tracks and looked up towards the sky. The sun sparkled in the tears brimming in her eyes, but she smiled. 'They're really together? That's all I've dreamt of since losing them both. I can't wait to be with them again.'

'Woah, don't you dare start thinking like that, Mel. Your mum and dad would be exactly the same if you died today or if you were a hundred. And they'll be waiting for you when it's your time. You've got everything to live for now—the start of a happy new life, and you've got me, too.'

Annie put her arm around Melina's shoulder and kissed her cheek. 'Poppet and I are both here for you now. And, actually, I need your help too with this whole psychic thing. Thos isn't keen on the subject so I could do with someone to talk to about it.'

'Ooh, yes, I'd like that, Annie. Any time.'

Annie and Mel walked back to the gallery to check on the new manager.

'Well, you two can just buzz off and leave me to it,' Poppet said with a camp flourish. 'You'll never guess: I sold a Tom Cox painting within the first half an hour for three thousand pounds—not bad for my first sale! And I cheekily called Mr Cox to bring a replacement in. He's on his way ... and *I'm* beyond excited! I just love his work.'

'Congratulations, Pops,' Melina said, delighted he'd earned his permanent position at Hollingsworth's. 'By the way, you get your basic wage, which is better than most, and five per cent commission on everything you sell. So you've just earned yourself an extra hundred and fifty pounds.'

'Really?' Annie questioned. 'I never used to get commission,' she added, smiling.

'Yes, sorry about that, Annie, new rules now.' Melina winked at Poppet.

Annie went into the stock room to make a cup of coffee and Melina followed.

'You know I told you I fell pregnant at fourteen, Annie?'

'Yeah, I was going to ask you about that, but I didn't feel like I could.'

Melina took a long, deep breath. 'You need to know all about me now that we're finally friends. I was too scared to tell anyone about the pregnancy at the time, apart from Mum. Then she disappeared, taking my secret with her, and leaving me on my own in the house with the man who'd raped me. When Mum's body was found I had my chance to tell the police, but I guess Mum dying was the last straw ... I just shut down and kept it all to myself. But of course, my stepfather was so clever at smokescreens and such an accomplished liar that nobody would have believed me anyway.' Melina laughed, but it was devoid of humour. 'I just kept my head down until I couldn't disguise the size of my stomach any longer. He went crazy when he found out and made me to tell the school I'd had a liaison with a boy from my year. Of course, the headmaster and governors thought I was shielding the non-existent boy and asked me to leave to protect the school's integrity. But even with all that happening, I was determined to continue with my education after the baby had been born.'

'Bloody hell, Melina, what happened?' Annie asked quietly.

'It was so strange ... I had weird thoughts and dreams during my pregnancy. You see, I didn't actually want her to live in such a hateful world, and for *him* to be part of her life. She knew what her mummy wanted ...' Melina paused for a few seconds. 'My little girl died a few hours after she was born ... They said she'd had complications with her heart, but I knew that, somehow, she was never meant to be. Of course, I was devastated; everything I had ever loved had been wrenched from me. But then I was strangely relieved too; my daughter was never going to be exposed to the vile perversions I'd known. I had said a prayer and she had answered it by taking herself away from this world. I wish you'd seen her, Annie ... she was *so* beautiful, with dark hair like her mummy. But I never got to see her eyes because she stayed asleep. She's my little angel and always will be.'

Annie hugged Melina tight. 'That's *so* tragic, sweetheart, I'm amazed you've survived it all. But your little girl really is your guardian angel and always will be.'

'I know, Annie, I can feel her around me when I'm low. And I know it sounds strange, but I'm sure I can smell her, too. You know ... that newborn baby powder smell. But it's probably just my imagination.'

'It's not your imagination, Mel, you can definitely smell those who've passed. I know I've had that experience, too. What happened when you went home, after the hospital?'

Mel let out an ironic laugh. 'Well, because I'd lost everyone that I had ever loved, I felt he couldn't hurt me anymore. And somewhere I found a strength of character that I never knew was in me. So, I started screaming and shouting at him every time he came back, until I saw less and less of him. He stayed away for weeks at a time, and on the rare occasion he returned, he looked so different—almost as though he was scared of something. He seemed to be on edge, and always sweaty, and wringing his hands; it looked like he was losing his mind.' Melina sipped her now cold coffee.

'I went back to school, determined to do well, but if it hadn't have been for my art, which I loved, I think I would have lost my mind too. And after all that, I left school with top marks in all my exams and got myself into art college. And even though I'd inherited a load of money, I still took part-time jobs in galleries to learn the trade. But I rarely saw my stepfather after that, although the last time he came back I plucked up enough courage to threaten him with the police ... if he didn't leave the house for good. Well, he did, and I never saw him again.'

Annie sighed. 'Well done you, Mel.' Annie was full of admiration.

'I told you before, Annie, I sold the family house 'cause I'd grown to hate it so much. But look what I've ended up with: a great business and an amazing home, plenty of money to buy all the art I need to fill the gallery with, and a fabulous new manager. And it's only now, all these years later, that I have a true friend to enjoy it all with.'

Chapter 22

∞

REST IN PURGATORY

She awoke from a restless sleep, filled with bizarre scenarios about their inevitable church visit. At first, Annie put it down to her usual night nudges, but her dreams were becoming reality, and seemed worryingly accurate about her old friend Sam. She blamed the night nudges on rising stress levels, although Thos hadn't helped by overly flapping about the outcome, too—although for purely selfish reasons.

Annie went to the League to pick up Sam for a private chat before seeing Dan, Maddy and Thos at the church.

'I'm really worried about you, Sam. I think it's best you don't come today.'

'Rubbish, my dear girl, I've been looking forward to it. And, anyway, this is the one thing I'm good at, and you're not taking that away from me. My only concern is that my old body is going to let us all down before I can be of any use.'

'Sam, I have to be totally honest with you … My premonitions have shown me—'

Sam put his hand up to stop her speaking. 'You don't have to tell me, Annie, I know today is probably going to be my swan-song. But I would rather leave this world on a high than be bedridden for months before I croak. So I'd like this to be my decision, please. Now, I have to tell you a story and then you'll understand the magnitude of what might happen today. You drive and I'll talk.'

'Okay ... but you're scaring me now.'

'No need to be scared, Annie, I'm just telling you this so that you're forewarned and therefore forearmed. I've been having my own premonitions and they haven't been this strong for years. The only other time I experienced them like this was in my early days as a seminarian. Part of my course was to assist a priest who was the official exorcist for the diocese, which as a young man I thought was tremendously exciting. Of course, we'd been called out before to a handful of hauntings— you know, the usual poltergeists and unruly spirits causing havoc. But this time I was asked by my priest to attend a family in dire need of help ... as a solo exorcist. The family in question had bought the property for a heavily reduced price, completely unaware of the reason why it was so cheap. The house turned out to have the darkest of secrets, kept confidential by its multiple owners. It turned out that forty years beforehand, a husband had caught his wife in a compromising position with another man in the house. He'd used a hammer to kill them both and dumped their bodies under the stairs, leaving them to putrefy for weeks until they were discovered. It wasn't until I entered the house that I realised it was pure evil. Its very walls seemed soaked in malevolence, and the pungent odour couldn't be disguised ... It seemed to permeate even through the veil of death. The spirits were those of the murdered couple who had continually fought off all who had set foot in their place of torment. It was as if they were punishing the man who had ended their lives there. Well, long story short, I tried to free the spirits. But they were too strong for me—even the official exorcist who returned later to prove to me that it *could* be done was struck down with terror. That experience, Annie, made me psychologically ill for weeks after. But during my illness, I realised that I had to gain the knowledge needed, to ease disturbed souls and to protect the living from their malevolent behaviour. Which I am fully expecting to have to do today… So, my dear girl, you're going to have to be very strong, for me and the others; I do believe this is going to be a battle to the death.'

∞

Thos unlocked the large, studded oak door, mentally crossing his fingers that the day would have a better outcome than he was expecting. They were all in agreement to start immediately, even though Dan was running late.

Maddy linked arms with Thos for her own support, and there was a perceivable tightness in the air that everyone noticed but didn't mention. Annie's heart started beating faster in anticipation of what was to come. Maddy and Thos both seemed uneasy, and Sam was worryingly pale.

'Are you okay, Sam?' Annie asked. She suddenly had an overwhelming feeling that he was failing.

'Not too good, my dear, but let's get this over and done with.'

The familiar pulling sensation had started drawing Annie towards the entrance of the catacombs. 'Can you feel anything, Sam?'

'Yes, an extraordinary energy field, Annie, the likes of which I've never felt before.'

Thos turned the handle and forced the resistant door open, and an audible sigh escaped from the tunnels below.

Maddy stepped back as terror swept over her face, and her short breaths gave her unease away. 'I'm not sure I can do this,' she said, and went to stand behind Thos.

Annie didn't register her friend's concern, she was already descending the stone staircase in a trance-like state. Thos had brought a large torch with him and walked closely behind her, lighting the way. The bright light was comforting, it illuminated all but the most shadowy corners.

A sudden pain shot down Annie's left arm, and she instinctively knew it was Sam's agony she was feeling. She swung around. 'Sam?'

He was holding his arm. 'No, Annie, I'm fine.'

'But you're so poorly, I can feel it ... Let's stop now.'

Although Sam's eyes were weary of life, he had a determination that she could not halt.

'We have to finish what we came here to do,' he said quietly.

Annie's senses had heightened again; an unknown source of strength was saturating her in waves. She knew someone or something was watching over her. She quietly wished it was Ellie.

'Yes, it is me,' a familiar voice said.

Annie stopped and looked downwards. Ellie was at the foot of the stone steps, clearly worried.

'Well, it must be bad if a ghost is scared,' Annie quipped, trying to lighten the atmosphere.

'This will be your most testing time, my friend, and your life will be changed forever after. But *my* strength and that of others is with you.' Although Ellie faded, her spiritual energy remained as a guarding orb of light.

'So I'm guessing you're talking to one of your guides, Annie.' Maddy sounded uneasy.

'Yep, and she's here to help, so don't worry. But look after Thos for me, Mads,' Annie said, hoping that it would keep Maddy's mind occupied.

'Yeah, of course I will ... But who's going to look after me?'

They descended into the depths of the catacombs. The rank odour—mixed with the dust of many years—choked them like a smog. The group became aware of a distant thudding noise, speedily getting closer. Panic gripped Madeleine again, and her eyes widened with fear; she grabbed hold of Thos.

'HELLO!' A mortal voice shouted from the top of the stone stairs. 'It's only me, sorry I'm late.'

'Oh, for Christ's sake, Dan, you scared the beejeebers out of me!' Madeleine shouted and loosened her death grip on Thos—he let go of his, too.

But Annie was still focused on the task ahead. She knew that her increasingly strong psychic vibes were the harbinger of a dark paranormal activity.

Annie could feel the troubled souls of the children gathering. 'I'm here to help you ... Please come forward, little ones ... Let me see you,' she said softly.

The dust started to swirl around Annie, her copper hair lifting and wrapping around her shoulders as if to an embrace. The startled group stepped backwards when a faint light appeared through the churning gloom—forming itself into the face of a young boy. His eyes were sunken, and his cheeks were drawn, his body was slight in stature and appeared faded with the dust shrouding his diminutive figure. He turned and summoned to the unseen; another boy and a girl appeared. It was difficult to gauge their ages as they too, were slight, and looked as though they had been starved before passing.

The children's eyes suddenly widened with fear. 'He won't let us go home. Help us.'

Their pleas of help passed through the psychic veil, and for the first time Annie's companions heard and saw the sad apparitions, too. A gasp of breath came from Madeleine as she lifted a hand to stifle a scream. Dan staggered backwards, suddenly unsteady on his robust legs, and Thos stood motionless, his last faint air of scepticism was blown into oblivion.

Sam stepped forward, taking hold of Annie's arm, and was just about to ask if she was okay, when the children shrank away into the shadows.

'He's here,' the boy whispered and then disappeared.

The ice-cold catacombs suddenly dropped to a numbing temperature, and the breath of the living became opaque clouds. The dirt on the ground before them bubbled like a quagmire; a black protuberance rose through the dark swamp, slowly reshaping into the abhorrent form of the priest. His appearance seemed to have changed, as though ravaged by the very malevolence that had consumed him in life, and now in death.

His corrupt voice split through the stench-filled air. 'I told you both not to meddle with me, you fools! Leave us be.'

Annie's anger surfaced and she surged forward towards the spectre, but her old friend held her back, and with his last rush of courage he held out a large, wooden cross. Sam faltered, and Annie grabbed his arm. With that surge of extra strength from her—his bent body straightened. He closed his eyes and tilted his head back.

'Saint Michael the Archangel defend us against Satan
and his plague.
Be our protection against his malignancy and black
heart,
Banishing all those who prowl this realm with him
So they may suffer torture alongside their heinous
Master.'

'Shut up, you weak old man!' the priest bellowed.

But Sam continued with his prayer of protection, while the priest groaned in pain.

'May God denounce Satan's existence, and all his minions,
Casting them down into the depths of the everlasting fire
Where he may remain with his heinous disciples burning for all eternity.
Amen.'

Sam spattered holy water from a small bottle over the priest. 'I cast thee out … I cast thee out … I cast thee out …'

Sam forced the cross forward and into the doomed spectre; the fading priest let out a demonic howl—but reappeared momentarily for his last despicable act, and launched his fading arm through Sam's chest. The old man staggered and Dan surged forwards to catch him as he fell.

There was a quietude—a sense of tranquillity, as all evil had ceased to exist. Then Madeleine's cry of anguish cut through the silence and she fell to her knees beside her dying friend.

'Sam, please don't leave us! We need you.' Tears erupted over her cheeks.

Annie knelt down next to her distraught friend, and placed her hand on Sam's.

The old man opened his eyes and looked momentarily concerned. 'Has he gone Annie?'

'Yes, he has … and you won the fight, Sam.'

'No, my dear girl, *we* won the fight. And you will go on to win many more, and become the best medium that has ever lived.' He feebly tightened his grip on her hand. 'But I'll always be there when you need me.' His eyes slowly moved to Maddy. 'My sweet girl, I would like you and Annie to look after each other. And for you, young lady, to continue to grow as an empath. You are more amazing than you know.'

Weariness finally took over, and a serene smile momentarily lit his face; his eyes gazed past his friends and into the afterlife. 'They've all come for me. And it's about bloody ... time ... too.' Sam seemed happy with his parting words. He let out a sigh of relief as peace swept through his tired body and his soul stepped effortlessly into the next realm.

The spirits of the children reappeared from the shadows. They, too, were free. They beckoned Annie to follow, their eyes dancing with excitement.

Annie kissed Sam's forehead for the last time then turned and grabbed Dan's hand. 'I think you need to come with me.'

Dan followed Annie and the eager spirits down through the arched catacombs. The heaviness in the air had lifted, and the previous turmoil had been replaced by an extraordinary calm. The children stopped at the edge of a chamber, pointing to the ground, which marked their last resting place.

A radiating light cut through the darkness at the far end of the catacombs, where celestial figures waited at the threshold between the two worlds—and Annie knew that in that moment the children were finally safe.

'They've come for you ... Go and be at peace now.' She pointed towards the welcoming glow. Although the spirits could no longer be seen by Dan and the others, they were reflected in Annie's eyes as they finally went home.

'Annie,' Dan said quietly. 'I've got to call this one in ... What with Sam dying and all this going on ... Christ only knows what I'm going to tell the guys.'

'It'll all be fine, Dan, I promise you,' Annie said.

He put his strong arm around her small shoulders and squeezed. 'You're something else, Annie Prior,' he said, looking at her for the first time with affection and pride. Then he turned and bounded back through the catacombs and up the steps.

Thos stood back a little way from Annie. 'I can't believe what just happened here; it was like watching a bloody horror movie. And I've got to be honest with you, babe, I've never been so damn scared in my life. And poor old Sam—what the hell?'

'Sam and I both knew this would be his last day, but it's what he wanted, Thos. He's a lucky man, because he chose his own way to leave.'

But Annie's sentiments fell on deaf ears—Thos's mind was elsewhere.

'Do you realise this is going to turn into a nightmare show now?'

'Yes, it probably is ... but all this was meant to be.'

Annie walked over to Maddy, who was still sitting in the dirt next to Sam, although her tears had stopped flowing.

'I do believe he's happy now ... He is, isn't he, Annie?' she said, her voice cracking.

'He really is, Maddy. All he ever wanted was to make a difference, and that's just what he's done here today. He saved the souls of those poor children and got rid of the priest. He's a hero, Mads.'

'Yes, I suppose he is, bless him, although you're the *real* hero, Annie. You were the one who brought us down here and potentially solved three murders.'

'Yeah, well ... not sure about that. We've got an awful long way to go before we can prove who murdered them. But that's exactly what I'm going to do. The priest got his comeuppance today, so it's one down and his brother to go ... We're gonna get him, too, don't you worry.'

Chapter 23

∞

Aftermath

'I've briefed the Forensic team on where to find the bodies … Christ, Prior, I really hope they're there. The guys at the office are quite rightly sceptical. So we really need concrete evidence to add credence to it all right now.'

'You were there too, Dan.'

'Yeah, I know, and I can't get it out my head. It's like I'm awake in the weirdest of dreams. I don't know how the bloody hell you're coping with it so … calmly, Prior.'

'Welcome to my world, Dan … that's how I feel all the time. Come on, we'll get through this together, but let's get to the bottom of the Jackson family first. I know that creep of a brother has something to do with it all.'

'Yeah, okay, you and I will sort this one out. But right now, you, Maddy and Thos are gonna have to tell the investigation team exactly how it all happened, and as crazy as it may sound to them, they'll have to take it seriously … so keep the stories tight, guys.'

The quiet church turned into a chaotic crime scene. Statements were taken, raising more than just a few eyebrows. Both Maddy and Annie protested that Sam's body had been left where it was, but the team wanted nothing touched until photos had been taken and they'd cleared a pathway of possible evidence; only then could the body be moved.

Outside was just as hectic, with journalists gathering like vultures ready to pick the bones clean, and local nosy parkers refusing vehemently to move—even for television crews.

Annie left Thos talking to one of Dan's detectives, and wandered down to the far end of the nave. She looked up at the only surviving cross, which had been carved into the oak arch spanning the sanctuary above the pulpit. Her heart was heavy with Sam's loss, and the deaths of the children just intensified the anger that was boiling inside her.

So ... God ... if you are there, can you tell me why the bloody hell you've let this happen in your own house? You really don't do yourself any favours, do you? Three innocent children were murdered here, and my dear friend who'd never hurt anyone in his life died here, too. He served you all his life and rid the world of a devil today—which I stupidly thought would have been your job. Go on, I dare you to tell me why people believe in you, when you let so many of them suffer under your watch. You simply don't deserve their love! And surprise, surprise ... you'll never have mine. But silly me, I'm talking to myself again ... 'cause you simply don't exist.'

A weight had been lifted off Annie's shoulders, as if she had put not only one—but two demons to bed. Even so, tears of frustration still escaped her eyes.

A comforting arm wrapped around her waist, Thos pulled her close. 'It's not like you to have a chat with God,' he said.

'Actually, it was a private one, sweetheart, albeit a one-way conversation. I just had to explode my feelings onto something or someone, and he was the obvious target.'

'Glad it wasn't me then, babe,' Thos joked, clearly trying to lift the heavy atmosphere. And for the first time that day, they both smiled.

'I'm so sorry this has happened in your church, sweetheart ... I didn't mean it to.'

Thos smiled at her. 'I can see that all this had to be sorted before anything could be done with the church anyway. I definitely wouldn't have wanted to share it with any ghosts. So don't worry ... I'm all good with it—now.'

They walked back to the vestibule, where the action was. Annie noticed a very sad, Madeleine, standing on her own. She turned to Thos. 'Sweetheart, I have an idea for Mads ... Do you think we could call Max to come and fetch her?'

'That, babe, is an inspired idea ... You wouldn't be trying to match-make those two, would you?'

'Well, if they did get together it would be great for both of them, and us.'

Thos squinted his eyes at her. 'Hmm, did you know Max fancied her?'

'Well, I did have an inkling ... and I thought it was a good idea from the moment I met them both.'

'You're just a bloody witch, aren't you?'

They approached Madeleine laughing. Thos winked at Annie, and walked away to call Max.

'Wish I could laugh like you guys about something,' Madeleine said, slightly confused at her friends' apparent insensitivity.

'Oh, I was just having a rant at God, Maddy.'

'Ah well, that's okay then, I was thinking of doing the same.' Her lips broke into a weak smile.

Annie glanced over towards Thos; he'd just got off the phone to Max and gave her a thumbs-up.

She took hold of Maddy's hands. 'Max is going to come and get you, sweetheart.'

'You're kidding,' Madeleine said, her face lighting up.

'Nope. He's concerned about you, so he's on his way.'

'I expect you've had something to do with this, Annie ... but thank you anyway; I could really do with him being around at the moment.'

With Maddy soon to be ensconced in Max's safe hands, Annie and Thos were free to concentrate on what was going on with the church. Although they had been cleared to go, they refused to leave until the bodies of the children had been found.

Dan had been authorised to take charge of the investigation, after his involvement from the outset with the priest. He was the ideal man for the job and Annie was proud to be associated with him. She was also glad to have someone legitimate on her team, as she was feeling an imminent storm from the press approaching. And having a DI on board would hopefully add gravitas for the sceptics who were bound to rear their ugly heads.

A member of the Forensic team ran up the staircase into the nave. 'Detective Inspector, you need to come and see this.'

Thos stepped back and shook his head. 'I'm not going back down there, babe ... You go with Dan and I'll wait up here for any news.'

Dan and Annie descended back into the catacombs, and a chill of recollection bore through them both. But the previously dark chamber was now illuminated so that every corner was visible, even though the stench of dampness and rotting still hung in the air. Heavy flagstones had been lifted and stacked away from the search area.

'We've found one,' said one of the Forensic chaps, pointing down into a deep hole.

The undeniable smooth roundness of a small pale skull, half buried in soil, was clearly visible.

'Christ, Annie, I've seen loads of bodies and skeletons over the years, but seeing this one seems to mean so much more. Especially because I heard *and* saw the child these bones belonged to today, it's so bizarre. And although Mellion's gone—thank God—if any of his surviving family have anything to do with these murders, you and I are gonna get them, Prior.'

'That's a definite!' Annie replied with absolute certainty.

Chapter 24

∞

THE MEDIA

Their quiet home was a welcome retreat from the mêlée at the church. Thos and Annie had refused to give interviews to pushy journalists, but knew it was only a matter of time before they had to relent and talk. Thos turned on the television and was not surprised to see his old church on the six o'clock news. The camera panned to a busy scene behind a female news reporter, where a Forensic team in white paper overalls continued their sweep in the cordoned-off graveyard.

'I'm standing in a quiet avenue in the depths of Dulwich outside this derelict church where, according to eyewitnesses, there has been some *paranormal* activity. A body believed to be that of an elderly man has been removed from the scene, but we have *no* information on the circumstances surrounding his death as of yet. We have been told, however, that a detective inspector has been working closely with a psychic *medium*, no less, in connection with the remains of up to three other bodies that have been uncovered in the catacombs.'

Thos struck the TV controls on the coffee table and switched it off. 'Well, that's put a stop to the renovations, I suppose … especially now that it's all over the bloody media.'

Annie understood his feelings and frustrations. 'Yeah, and I know how disappointed you must be, but we're just going to have to ride this out together, sweetheart.'

'Yeah ... Problem is, babe, the media's not gonna leave us alone till they get what they want. And I think because a clairvoyant's involved, you're gonna be the bullseye they'll all be aiming at.'

'Hmm ... I was thinking the same. But the question is ... Are you going to stand by me through all this, Thos?'

He avoided her eyes. 'You're here, aren't you? And I'm the one who bought the church ... So, yeah, we've both been thrown into looking after each other's back now.'

Annie's brow furrowed questioningly. 'Okay ... So, I'm not *really* sure what you meant by all of that, but I guess we'll see what happens. Look, I'm tired; today's been another train crash for the both of us. I just want to go to sleep and forget it all for now.'

∞

A doorbell rang, interrupting Annie's nightmare; then it came again, pushing her sleeping torment aside.

'Thos ... wake up, someone's at the front door.'

'Christ's sake, it's only six thirty. Who the hell is it?'

The previous day had taken its toll; exhaustion had ravaged them both. Annie finally answered the door to Dan Watts and another man, who she semi-recognised. Both of them stood by the garden gate, smoking and chatting.

'Morning, Annie. Sorry we're so early but you're gonna be invaded by reporters from all over soon. We've had the nod that everyone wants to know who you are. Oh, and this reprobate, believe it or not, is one of a rare breed of trustworthy reporters who work alongside the

Metropolitan; Fred Lowes, meet Annie Prior.'

'Yes, I remember you, Fred—you were at the priest's funeral.'

'I was, Miss, nice to finally meet you properly. Dan here's told me *so* much about ya.'

Dan dug his elbow into the reporter's ribs.

'Bloody 'ell, Dan, that hurt.'

The two men walked into the kitchen, Fred held out a newspaper to Annie. 'Fresh off the press ... and you've made the front page. Overnight fame, I think it's called.'

An eager amateur had snapped a photo of Annie emerging from the church, and the camera seemed to have caught a strange glow around her.

Fred pointed to the photo. 'See, someone's done a bit of photoshopping on that already. Makes you look like you've got one of those aura things round ya. Clever, innit?'

Thos lifted his eyebrows, but said nothing. Annie remembered at the time feeling a strong electrical energy, as if a force field had been protecting her.

Dan and Fred were right about reporters swarming the house; within an hour the quiet cul-de-sac had become impassable with both reporters and cameramen. All were waiting for Annie Prior the clairvoyant medium to emerge.

Dan sat at the kitchen table opposite her. 'I know you don't want to, Prior, but you're gonna have to give an interview at some stage to stop any adverse speculation. It *will* happen whether you like it or not ... Why don't you give Fred an exclusive, and he'll promise here and now not to bend the truth like all those outside would do. Look, Fred's a freelance journalist, but he won't pass the story to the rags to be pulled apart.'

'Okay, only to Fred then. But I'm going to be honest, Dan, and tell him exactly how it happened: the priest, the children and how poor old Sam died.'

Dan stopped her there. 'I'm sorry, Annie, but you can't say anything about the priest or the kids until after the investigation, so just go easy. Why don't you say something about how you came into your powers, and maybe when your next psychic event is gonna to be held? You may as well get some free advertising out of this.'

'Do you honestly think I'm worried about advertising, Dan? I've got enough to think about.'

'Woah, I didn't mean it to sound like that ... I really do have your best interests at heart.'

Annie leant forward and touched his forearm. 'I know you do, and I'm sorry. But you were with me in those catacombs, so you can back up my story by adding a bit of gravitas to it. And, anyway, having a detective inspector as a friend should come with fringe benefits.' She winked at him.

'Absolutely, Prior, but I'm afraid I've also got to follow police protocol on this.'

Annie recounted her story to Fred, but found it difficult to leave the priest out. Just to set the record straight, she still told him that an evil entity had been exorcised at the church by Sam Hargreaves, who was not only a brilliant psychic from the League, but her friend and a qualified exorcist.

Fred's phone had been on silent while he interviewed her, but it still buzzed almost non-stop with calls and notifications. He ignored all the calls, but answered when he saw it was the News Across London television company.

He put the phone down after only a minute. 'Okay, Annie, how do you feel about doing a live TV show this afternoon?'

She glanced over at Thos for a reaction, but he just shrugged.

'I'll leave that one up to you, babe.'

Before Annie could answer, Fred interrupted.

'Yeah, but you would be getting in there first before the sceptics have their say. Anyway I'm gonna start by getting your story written down verbatim, and then it'll be out tomorrow in the quality papers, although we can't stop the rags running their lies. If you do the show this afternoon, it'll keep 'em all happy. But definitely discuss your psychic powers with the reporter; then everyone can buy the papers tomorrow and see your point of view.'

'What do you think Dan, should I do it?'

'Yeah, why not? But keep it tight. If the priest's brother has anything to do with the kids' deaths, we can't give too much away—especially in front of millions.'

Thos and Dan flanked Annie as they ushered her out of the house and into the baying throng, with Fred leading the way, handing off his old colleagues.

'Bloody typical, mate, 'spose you got the scoop on this again, Fred!' A green-eyed reporter shouted.

'Yeah, well, at least I write the truth, unlike the junk you spout, mate,' Fred sniped back.

Annie's psychic calmness did not extend to being jostled by a mob of discourteous reporters. She was unnerved, and glad to jump into the back of Thos's car. Dan got in behind her, his chin set firm. Fred went with them to prep Annie for the interview and to show her how to handle herself on camera.

Chapter 25

∞

THE INTERVIEW

The outside of the studio looked peaceful, with its unassuming fascia and tinted windows. Once they got through the revolving doors, the noisy activity of a busy industry was apparent.

The News Across London show was not just a regular news report, but an immensely popular programme drawing the lion's share of audiences away from rival stations. The main reason for its popularity was its creator, the most audacious reporter of any show.

Barbra Amos was the viewers' choice and the reporter they loved to hate. Behind the scenes, too, her colleagues found her hard-faced and prickly—earning her the nickname 'Barbed Wire'. She would seek out the most unusual and dirt-filled stories to pull apart, belittling any poor soul attached to them. She would often be heard saying after one of her verbal attacks on a guest, 'Another lamb slaughtered.'

A stylish young man with blond tied-back hair walked over to Annie and the guys. 'Hi, I'm Bjorn—Miss Amos's PA. I don't normally come over to talk to guests, but I really wanted to meet you, Miss Prior.' He held out his beautifully manicured hand.

'Nice to meet you too, Bjorn.' As soon as she shook his hand, his mental anguish was apparent, and her visitational vibes started to rise. The face of another young Nordic man appeared behind Bjorn. The spirit wrapped his arms around Bjorn's shoulders, but Bjorn didn't seem to feel anything.

The handsome spirit looked at Annie and smiled. 'I asked him to marry me, but he had not told his family about us, and then it was too late.' He turned towards the glass screen dividing the huge entrance hall from the news team, and pointed towards a stern-looking woman whose red lipstick was more prominent than her features. 'She hates the likes of us … so we had no chance to be together.'

Annie's gaze returned to Bjorn, finding his intense scrutiny had not wavered.

'What is it, Miss Prior?' he said, just as his boss appeared and grabbed hold of his arm aggressively.

'I thought I told you to take them into the conference room, Bjorn. Do as you are told! You've got that bloody head of yours somewhere else again.'

She then changed her demeanour and turned towards Annie. A cynical smile appeared. 'And you must be the psychic … *Welcome* to my little empire.' She turned on her heel and snapped at Bjorn. 'Conference room, *now!*'

Annie had a déjà-vu moment as she and the guys followed the PA. Barbra Amos could have been Melina's twin—not in looks, but in attitude. Annie had had plenty of exposure to her style of bullying in the past, and was fully capable of handling this intimidating woman.

She touched Bjorn's arm gently. 'Can I have a moment with you afterwards, please?'

Bjorn glanced over towards his boss, then back to Annie. He nodded, but squinted his eyes apprehensively at her.

'It's okay ... I promise it's nothing to worry about.' Annie exuded her usual empathic vibes.

Barbra Amos walked briskly into the conference room. 'I'm so looking forward to this, Miss Prior ... I don't think I've ever interviewed a *psychic* before. And I have to be totally honest with you ... I don't believe in the afterlife or anything to do with the paranormal, it's all a load of crap as far as I'm concerned, but I will try to be unbiased. Although you must understand it's my job to wheedle out untruths and scams, so if I'm a bit hard on you, don't take it to heart, lovie.'

'Oh, please don't worry about me, Miss Amos, I don't have anything to hide, and I don't lie either. So, it looks like this interview is going to be a little boring for you.' Annie faked a smile, but was sick with nerves.

Barbra scowled. 'No, Miss Prior ... I don't think boring is going to be the adjective of the day— I'm fully expecting my usual triumph. After all, there'd be no point in me doing this job if I didn't *win*.' She turned and shouted at her PA. 'Bjorn, get the make-up department to sort her face out, and back here for 12:50 sharp everyone. Oh, and make sure you get another chair for the inspector ... Miss Prior may need a little help.' Amos strode out.

Bjorn touched Annie's arm. 'I'm sorry she was so discourteous, but well done for having a go ... She usually frightens the hell out of most of her guests, but I'm guessing you'll cope.' He winked.

'Apart from my knees turning to jelly, Bjorn, I'm sure I'll be fine.' Annie turned to Thos, Dan and Fred. 'Do you guys mind if I have five minutes with Bjorn on my own, please?'

Thos raised his eyes upwards. She could almost hear him say, 'Bloody spooks again,' but ignored it.

The men followed Fred, who showed them to the viewing suite.

Annie turned back to Bjorn and took hold of his hands. 'As soon as I met you, I could see the pain you've been through, and I know why. I'm so sorry for your loss ... he was such a handsome young man, just like you.'

Bjorn sat with a thump.

Annie closed her eyes. 'I'm hearing Steve, was that his name?'

'Oh my God, it was *Stefan*. Is he really here?' Bjorn scanned around the room.

'Yes, and he told me he asked you to marry him. But you hadn't told your parents you were gay.'

Bjorn's eyes filled with tears. 'I loved him so much ... but I've never come out to anyone, let alone my parents. Mamma and Papa would have disowned me. You see, I love them, too, but I've been so scared of disappointing them.'

'I understand, Bjorn, but they're not the only reason you haven't come out. Stefan told me you were worried about losing your job as well, because Barbra won't tolerate gays around her.'

'Hmm, I wouldn't have lasted five minutes if she'd found out, and I really need this job.'

Just then, Stefan reappeared. 'Tell Bjorn: we had our time together, but he must find strength without me now. If she won't accept him here, he has to move towards those who will, and they'll love him for the wonderful man he is. He's going to have a long and happy life, and after that ... we will see each other again.'

Annie recounted Stefan's words; Bjorn's eyes spilled over with joy and relief. She squeezed his hands. 'Do what he says and live your life. And why don't we keep in touch after today? I feel we'd really get on.'

'I'd like that so much, Annie; you don't know how much you've helped me today. I'd never really thought about the afterlife before Stef died. But now that I know there is one, and I'm going to join him one day ... But, as he said, not yet.' Bjorn leant over and kissed Annie's cheek in gratitude. '*Oh my God!*' He jumped back. 'I've got to get you and Dan to make-up! She's gonna hang me, or worse. Do me a favour, Annie, please—if you see any spirits around Barbed Wire, please tell her! And then just maybe it'll knock that huge chip off.'

Dan and Annie took their seats to the side of Amos's huge desk, with four cameras poised and production assistants fussing around making sure they were ready. Barbra preened herself too, applying her red lipstick perfectly. She straightened her pens, notepad and laptop in an almost obsessive-compulsive way, then looked over at Annie and Dan in the famous black leather 'execution' armchairs.

'We're on in five minutes, so *be* ready, everyone! I'm going to keep the audience riveted today,' Amos said, smiling at her own glory and rubbing her hands together.

Annie couldn't believe that a woman could have such a hedonistic attitude, but then her viewing figures revealed that the audience loved her gladiatorial character. The temperature in the studio suddenly dropped fast, and a clear, classy voice broke through the pre-show commotion. A primped elderly lady, dressed in a suit with a set of pearls around her neck, appeared.

'I must apologise for my daughter's behaviour; she's always been a bully, and so self-opinionated. I tried so hard to change her ways but failed miserably. I've just popped in to let her know that the few times she came to see me at the end, I was *actually* still there, even though my senses may have seemed to have left me. But no illness can take away the love of a mother, whatever her child is like.'

A deep sadness for this spirit touched Annie, but at least the woman was now free from dementia, the illness that had obviously taken her.

Dan had noticed Annie in a semi-trance-like state. 'You okay? You were somewhere else for a moment.'

'Hmm, don't worry, Dan, I'm fine ... now!' She smiled almost smugly.

The production assistant spoke loudly. 'Okay, everyone, stand by, ready in 5 - 4 - 3 - 2 ...' Then she silently pointed to Barbra and the cameras started rolling.

'By now, most of you will have heard about the mysterious goings-on in a derelict church in Dulwich. *Apparently*, a psychic medium led a detective inspector into the catacombs, where an exorcism was performed. After which an elderly man died and the remains of three bodies have since been recovered. Well, it all sounds a little far-fetched to me, and that's why my guests are here with me today to explain themselves. We have Detective Inspector Daniel Watts, the investigating officer from the Met. And Miss Annie Prior, an alleged medium who can apparently talk to the dead. So, let's find out what on earth happened there yesterday.'

Barbra turned towards her guests and three cameras followed her every move, with another two angled separately onto Annie and Dan.

'Miss Prior, please can you enlighten us on the events leading up to this *unbelievable* story, I'm sure there are many sceptics who want to make their own judgement as to whether you are ... what you profess to be,' she said with unsubtle contempt.

'Yes, I will enlighten you and your audience, Miss Amos. To start with, I did not lead the detective inspector to the church yesterday. I asked him to assist myself and another clairvoyant with spirits that I had previously picked up on. I'd been working closely with the clairvoyant at the Spiritualist League and recently taken over his public demonstrations. We all knew he was very poorly with a heart condition, but there was no stopping him yesterday. He desperately wanted to help, and did so very successfully; but sadly, it proved to be too much for him. We're all devastated at his passing and I've lost a very good friend, but he died doing something he was passionate about.'

Barbra Amos shook her head. 'Well, I'm sure his family would disagree with you on that point, Miss Prior.' She turned to Dan.

'Now, Detective Inspector, can you shed any *down-to-earth* light on what happened?'

Dan sat forward, his jaw firm. 'I can confirm that all Miss Prior has said is true. I, too, was a sceptic the first time I met her, but I am now a complete convert after witnessing Miss Prior's extraordinary psychic abilities, which give evidence of the afterlife. You see, Miss Amos, I'm in the business of believing only when there is indisputable evidence—and that's exactly what she has provided me with. But this case has only just been opened, so I would ask you not to delve too deeply. When I've finalised the investigation, I'll release the details, but not before.'

Amos's lips drew thin—as did her eyes. 'Can you simply confirm, then, whether the three bodies uncovered were those of adults or children?'

There was an unfounded animosity in her voice and demeanour that Annie found strange.

Annie touched Dan's arm, holding him back. She sat bolt upright, and looked straight into Amos's eyes.

'As the DI has just told you, Miss Amos, we're not at liberty to disclose any more information as of yet. But I, on the other hand, do have personal information from the other side for *you*. Are you okay with me passing this on in front of your audience?'

The reporter looked slightly rocked. 'Well, I'm sure I have nothing to hide *either* ... Miss Prior. Are you actually saying that you're in touch with a *spirit* who *knows* me?' She had directed her words to the camera—and not Annie. 'Well, it seems I'm famous on the other side, too.' She laughed, and shook her head in disbelief, but a flicker of uncertainty suddenly spread across her face.

Annie's skin started to prickle, her senses became aware of the spirit's presence again. 'I believe I have your mother here.'

Barbra stared at Annie as if in disbelief. 'My mother?'

'Yes, and she's an incredibly smart lady, both in her dress sense and in her mind. She told me earlier that she'd had some form of dementia before passing, and that you found it all very difficult.'

Amos's eyes were full of contempt, although she was keeping a perfect poker face for the cameras. She seemed as though she was inwardly screaming and wanting to lash out, as the realisation of losing in front of her devoted audience was more important than a message from her deceased mother.

'Miss Prior, when people become famous, like myself, our lives are laid bare to everyone. It's not difficult to find out private details about any of us. My audience and I are not stupid, you'll have to do much better than that.'

Annie could feel her skin flush a little, but she kept her cool. 'Okay, Miss Amos ... Your mother has just told me that she's finally free from the torment of being locked in her own body. And although she couldn't say your name when you went to see her, she knew deep down who you were. She said you thought you had lost her a long time before she died, but you hadn't.'

Barbra's strained smile was enough for Annie to know that the story was accurate.

'Nope ... I'm afraid that won't do either, Miss Prior,' Amos snapped back.

Barbra's mother now appeared beside her daughter wearing the same red lipstick, as if it was a badge of familial recognition. 'My daughter, Barby, is a hard one to crack, but this story will jog her memory. I asked her to bring me my favourite lipstick when I was in the care home, but she never did. I knew at the time she thought I'd forget about it ... Although that doesn't matter now, because over here we love unconditionally—and I hope with all my heart she will do one day too.'

Although Annie had been humiliated by the reporter, she had no intention of making Amos feel the same. 'It appears that spirits have access to make-up on the other side too. Your mother is wearing the same colour and brand of lipstick it seems. And she told me an interesting story about asking her Barby to buy her one of these expensive lipsticks while she was in the home, but I'll save that story for when the cameras are off … *if* you don't mind, Miss Amos.'

Amos had clearly been knocked off balance for a moment, she then turned to the camera—and not to Annie. 'Well, I … don't recall any of what Miss Prior has just told me, and especially not being called Barby by my mother—she would never have called me that! So, I will leave *you*, the viewers, to make up your own minds as to whether you believe in ghosts, mediums, and things that go bump in the night … or maybe none of the above. Alas, we've run out of time, as I have my *favourite* Labour Party politician waiting in the wings to impart his usual words of wisdom—or at least to *try* to. I shall see you after the break.' She kept smiling until the cameras cut, then immediately pushed her chair back and turned to Annie. 'I don't want to hear the rest of that ridiculous story, Miss Prior, but thank you anyway for entertaining us.'

Dan put his hand on Annie's shoulder. 'Why didn't you finish the story, Annie?'

'Probably because I realised that her veneer was already cracked. There goes a lady who is incredibly unhappy in herself, and she doesn't need *me* to push her further—especially not in front of her beloved audience. Anyway, Dan, I'm quite happy with the way it ended.' Annie walked around to Amos's desk and used her notepad to write down the conclusion to her story.

Chapter 26

∞

THE INVESTIGATION

'Morning, Prior,' Dan said. He stood in the porch dragging on a hand-rolled. 'Got time for a coffee and a chat?'

'Yeah, of course ... Everything okay?' Annie asked, already knowing he was on a mission.

'Firstly, Prior, I'm sorry about Amos. She was such a bitch, but you handled her brilliantly.' He laughed. 'Don't think you'll be invited back again, though. And I can't believe she bare-face lied to her audience about what her mother had told you.'

'Yes, I know, but thinking about it, her mother probably knew how much she hated being called Barby and knew I would relay it. So, maybe she was getting her own back a little. But I have to be honest, I actually felt sorry for her ... she's such a sad character.' Annie pulled a pensive face.

'Oh, don't even go there. You can't help everyone, you know!'

'Now who's reading whose mind?' Annie laughed. 'I know you haven't come here to talk about her.'

'No, I haven't ... Christ, Prior, I'm actually feeling sorry for Thos now. Poor bloke, he probably can't even open his eyes in the morning without you being inside his head. But you're right, I'm here on another matter.'

'Go on, then.' Annie handed Dan a coffee and sat at the kitchen table while he remained standing.

'Okay, well, while we were on the telly yesterday, Forensics found a necklace underneath one of the skulls with 'Hanna' engraved on it. And, of course, it didn't take my guys long to find a girl called Hanna, and two boys, who'd all gone missing together in the eighties. The only problem is ... their recorded ages put her at sixteen and the lads at fifteen, and that doesn't match the size of the skeletons we found in the church. So that led me to thinking whether you could help with your psychic whatchamacallits.'

'How on earth can I help with that?' Annie asked.

'Yeah, well, one of the guys at the Met who's interested in what you do, said there was something called psychometry. Apparently, it's where a psychic holds an object and can see things about the person who owned it. I just thought on the off chance you might be able to do that too, it could help. So, hope you don't mind me being presumptuous, Prior, but I've brought the necklace with me.' Dan held out a plastic evidence bag.

'I'll have a go, but I can't promise anything. Can I take it out?'

'Sure. It's been tested, do whatever you want.'

She carefully opened the bag and touched the dainty gold necklace inside—then suddenly jumped back, as though an electric shock had shot into her fingers.

'Bloody hell,' Dan said, jumping too.

But Annie was already falling into a trance-like state, her mind filling with sounds and visions, and found herself looking through Hanna's eyes. She was seeing a schoolyard with noisy children playing and laughing. Two boys, who she felt Hanna knew well, were laughing and pulling on her plaits, with a nun chastising them. The image changed to the three of them walking down a road and a car pulling up beside them.

Annie could hear a man. 'What are you kids doing out? Come on ... jump in and I'll take you back.'

Annie heard one of the boys say, 'Oh God ... not him!'

But the kids still got in the car, and she could clearly see the backs of two men sitting in the front seats. They both reached round and pushed the locks down on the back doors.

'Big mistake,' the driver said. He placed his large arm on the back of the seat and turned to face the children. Annie suddenly lurched forward and was yanked from her trance.

Dan's eyes were wide. 'What is it? What d'ya see?'

She shook her head. 'That evil bastard Mellion was there! And it looks like he, and another guy I couldn't see, gave the kids a lift. But Hanna and the boys were definitely the same kids from the church, although not around fifteen and sixteen years of age—they looked much younger. I don't understand why the interviewee said they were that age.'

'Yeah, strange ... But if you could please try again? We need every last bit of info to make a case, although you do know that any evidence we obtain through a psychic is inadmissible in court; but we can get around that, so don't worry.'

'Okay, I'll give it another go.' Annie gingerly picked up the necklace again, but there was no initial shock—just a tingling sensation. 'At least I can still feel something.'

She closed her eyes and waited until the darkness lifted a little. Distorted, misty images moved across her internal vision until they slightly cleared, although they were still shadowy. Annie realised the gloom was not to do with her connection but the dark room the children were in.

'Oh God, they're in the catacombs. I can hear one of them sobbing.' Then darkness descended again and her link was severed. 'That's it ... the vibrations have stopped. I'm sorry, Dan, there's no more.'

'Christ, Prior ... What you've given me today is bloody incredible, girl. You've just *got* to work with me as a psychic detective—and I'm definitely not taking no for an answer on this one.'

'So, I've got no say in the matter, then?' Annie half-joked, but after what she had just witnessed, she wanted to help more than ever.

'No, absolutely no say. You're on the team.'

'Okay, then, let's find out why the two interviewees lied about the kids' ages.' She stood from the table.

'Right ... Excellent, Prior.' Dan grabbed his jacket.

He seemed just as excited about them working together as she was. She stared at him for a few moments while he put his jacket on, but stopped her thoughts immediately; they were taking a direction she didn't want to go in.

Dan's mobile rang. 'Yep, what is it? I'm busy,' he said brusquely, but continued to listen for a while. 'Right, find out who the interviewees were, and their last addresses ASAP. And that means I want it like yesterday, Constable.' Dan ended the conversation with a huge smile on his face. 'You'll never guess, Prior: Mellion Jackson was interviewed after the kids went missing.'

'I *knew* it! From the moment I saw him, I just knew it. And I'm a hundred per cent sure his brother had something to do with it all too.'

'Yeah, well listen to this. Apparently, he said that he'd spoken to the *teenagers* about joining the school choir at the church, but they were uninterested and had only talked about their lives together. He gave their names, which corresponded with the statements from the nun and the elderly priest. And when asked what he thought had happened to them, he said they'd probably run away together. And that kids would be kids, and he wasn't at all concerned about them, and they were old enough to look after each other. But he failed to mention the fact that he'd picked them up in his car a week before.'

Annie fumed. 'I thought I couldn't hate him any more than I already did. But how come your lot at the Met didn't see through his lying at the time?'

'Woah! I'd been moved to a station in Devon back then, Prior, and didn't even know this was going on, so it wasn't my lot. But my old boss *was* in charge then, and he was the Catholic one I told you about. But he's long since dead.'

'Okay … So all I'm interested in now is Mellion's brother; we need to get him, Dan.'

'Yeah, I agree. That's why you're on board with this case. By the way, I pre-empted the fact that we were gonna work together and applied to the court for a search warrant for old Mrs Jackson's house. You've been authorised on the warrant, too.'

'You mean I'm now legally part of your team?' Annie grinned. 'That's pretty cool! And, actually, I've already got one of my vibes that we'll find something at Fanny's house. I can't *tell* you how weird she was about the priest; they obviously had a terrible relationship. In fact, it sounded as if she hated him, but weirdly not his brother. He was definitely her favourite and I feel she's now protecting him somehow.'

'It's like having my very own bloodhound.' Dan laughed.

'You may laugh, detective inspector.' Annie touched her nose. 'But I've always had a good nose on me. By the way, changing the subject: what are you doing this Saturday at 3 p.m.? I've got my second demonstration at the League, and I need a friendly face in the audience.'

'You bet, Prior … Wouldn't miss it for the world.'

Chapter 27

∞

The Search

Dan, Annie and two constables stood outside the Old Rectory in Norwood Park.

'I haven't met Fanny yet; heard she's a bit of an old bugger. What's she really like, Prior?'

'I'll let you make up your own mind on that one, Dan; after all, she's only a little old lady, how bad can she be?' Annie smiled, knowing full well that even Dan, the sturdy, stiff-jawed police officer, would be shocked by her rudeness.

∞

Fanny Jackson seemed even more objectionable than before. 'What do *you* want again? You're like a bad penny, keep turning up—nosing into my affairs.' The old biddy looked Dan up and down. 'And if you think bringing the coppers here is going to frighten me, they *won't*.'

'It's nice to see you again too, Mrs Jackson, or should I call you Mrs Selby-Jackson?' Annie said.

The old lady whipped round. 'You think you know it all, but you don't, Miss Prior. I saw you on that programme the other day. Load of old rubbish, that is.'

Dan heaved forward as if to protect Annie. 'Mrs Selby-Jackson, my name's Detective Inspector Dan Watts and I have a search warrant for this address. And for the record, I'd like you to know that Miss Prior here has been authorised to accompany me, too.'

'So you police need the help of psychics now? That's *got* to be a joke.'

'If you would be good enough to step aside, please, Mrs Jackson …And I would urge you *not* to obstruct us in any way. Oh, and a cuppa would be appreciated.'

'Bugger off! Not wasting my teabags on you lot.' The old dear stormed off, albeit slowly.

Dan and Annie, with the required rubber gloves, started their search upstairs, leaving the constables to comb the ground floor. Annie was particularly interested in the front bedroom where she'd first seen Mellion's brother at the window.

The house had an overwhelmingly bad feeling, more so than when Annie had previously been there. A shiver, like an ice-cold drip of water ran down her spine, and she contemplated how anyone would live in such a negative environment. Even her hard-faced partner was clearly uncomfortable.

'You okay, Dan?' she asked, interested to hear his take on the house.

'Your psychic whatchamacallits are rubbing off on me, Prior— this bloody place is giving me the heebie-jeebies. There's definitely something not right here.'

'You're having a taste of my world again… That's exactly how I feel most of the time,' Annie said, smiling at a very twitchy Dan.

She walked into the front bedroom, where the walls were stained yellow-brown, and the air was heavy with the smell of stale cigarettes. A shabby metal bedstead covered with frayed vintage floral bedding stood against the far wall. A cross no longer hung on it, but its presence was still outlined by nicotine. The dark oak dressing table, bruised with white rings, was also an indication of the slovenly character who had spent many hours there.

Annie walked over to the foot of the metal bedstead and wrapped her fingers around the cold ironwork. Immediately, a vision flashed into her mind of a young boy, bound to the bed by rope. His mouth and eyes were taped and his skin was a greyish blue. She knew in her heart that this was a vision of a child who had already passed.

Dan whispered, 'What ya seeing?'

Her concentration suddenly broke. 'A young boy died here … he'd been tied to the bed for a long time before he died.'

Annie's psychic awareness heightened. A sickly feeling churned in the pit of her stomach, as though the priest was still around. But her fears fell away when she recognised the shape forming in front of her. Ellie's apparition was a welcome sight.

Ellie's face was stern. 'The evil priest may be gone, Annie, but his equal is still amongst the living. All the evidence you need is out there …' She pointed towards the back of the house, and as quickly as she had appeared, she was gone.

'What just happened?' Dan asked. 'I know when you're having one of your moments now.'

'Thankfully, it was just Ellie confirming that the priest's partner in crime has been here, and all the evidence we need is out the back.'

'Right,' said Dan. 'Once we've searched this place, I'm taking that old biddy in. She must have known what was going on here. I'll have her for aiding and abetting at least, whatever age she is.'

The garden was as unkempt as the interior of the rectory; a tangled jungle of weeds ten feet high, strewn with hundreds of disintegrating cigarettes ends and discarded beer bottles. There seemed to be no boundary to the garden, and the land at the rear was hidden by a thicket. A well-worn path beneath the canopy had been hacked through.

Dan led the team, stooping below the arched brambles and holding them aside for Annie. She knew intuitively that the secret winding pathway had been designed to hide its end.

A hundred and fifty metres into the thicket, they came across a large shed, in good condition considering its surroundings. The new timbers and recovered roof revealed its recent renovation. The interior was obscured from prying eyes by blackout curtains, and the door was furnished with two large padlocks, top and bottom.

'Christ … it's more like Fort Knox than a garden shed. What's that all about, then?' Dan sent one of the constables to get a bolt cropper from the car.

Annie walked around the shed as far as she could, but the tangled greenery got thicker, barring her way. She persevered—pushing the prickly barbs aside with a discarded plank of wood.

'Dan, come and look at this,' she shouted.

'What the hell?' Dan said as he peered around the back.

There was another door with heavy-duty bolts, and a separate cleared pathway that disappeared through the brambles.

'We need to get into this damn shack,' Dan shouted impatiently. 'Where are the bloody bolt croppers? Hurry up, man!'

With the bolts cropped, they yanked the door open. The team stood on the threshold staring in; the walls, ceiling and windows were covered in what seemed to be black corrugated sponge.

'What's that, then?' Dan said.

'That's soundproofing, sir. It's what musicians use in their studios,' said one of the constables.

In the far right-hand corner was a single bedstead, similar to the one in the house but with no covers concealing its yellow, stained mattress. Frayed rope was still attached to either side of the frame, exposing its undeniable use. There were empty takeaway cartons on the floor, with open baked bean cans that were full of cigarette butts, and depleted beer bottles strewn under the bed.

The rest of the shed was bare except for a single shelf with a dusty shoebox perched on it.

'I want you to open it, Prior—see what feelings you get from whatever's in it.'

Annie lifted the lid gently, revealing a muddled pile of photos. Her heart sank when she touched them. Each photo was of a child of similar age to the catacomb children, and all had taped mouths and were bound by ropes. Only one of the eight photos was a girl, whose distant stare showed that her soul had already succumbed.

Annie teared up. 'At least one of the bastards got what he deserved.'

'Don't worry, Prior, we'll get the other one.'

'What about the path at the back, Dan?'

'Right ... we need the full team here.' Dan organised the constables to guard old Mrs Jackson and call for Forensics. 'Come on, Prior, let's see where the path leads.'

He cropped the bolts on the rear door and shouldered it open, expecting it to resist his efforts, but it gave way more easily than he thought and he stumbled out. The brambles and ivy that had covered the back had recently been wrenched apart, and the pathway was newly trampled. Dan forged forwards, with Annie closely behind.

The path seemed never ending, but after a couple of hundred metres it opened up into an orchard that had been left to grow gnarled, with an old fence and gate clearly visible thirty metres beyond. Dan ran over, but Annie stood still in the centre of the orchard. She closed her eyes, and the same tremors she had felt in

Blackheath had started rumbling beneath her, but this time, with visitational vibes pulsing through her, too.

Although the connection was weak, an adult male voice spoke. 'The rest are here, Annie.'

She didn't recognise the voice, but knew he was there to help.

'DAN!' she shouted. 'This is where the other kids were buried.' She pointed to the ground.

He ran back to her. 'You okay, Prior?'

The concern on his face made Annie suddenly feel safe—and needed.

'This is a lot for blokes to deal with, let alone a sensitive lass like yourself.'

Tears started escaping Annie's eyes. She knew they were mainly for the children, but also for the kindness and concern Dan was showing her. He wrapped his muscular arms around her, and for a moment Annie forgot what they were really there for.

Chapter 28

∞

An Audience

Annie's phone had been ringing off the hook from TV shows fighting to boost their ratings. She had declined them all, especially after her experience with Miss Amos. Even her own mother and father had joined the queue of hovering vultures, after a popular breakfast show had offered them money to coerce their daughter into appearing. Her disappointment in them continued to grow as they sliced up the last few remnants of their relationship.

The phone rang again; Annie leaned over to check the number, but already knew it was Maddy.

'Hey, Mads, what's happening?'

'Hi, Annie ... Er, not sure how to tell you this, but this afternoon's show is a *complete* sell-out, and that's including the standing room.'

'Oh God, really?'

'It's obviously because of your appearance with that Amos woman. I've had so many calls about you, even people offering to pay to get in. In fact, it got me thinking about maybe charging and giving the proceeds to charity … What'd ya think?'

'Yeah, I like the sound of that, but the fact it's free means anyone, rich or poor, can come at the moment. I'll have a chat with Sam about it when he decides to show himself.'

'I miss him so much, Annie; it won't be the same without him today.'

'No, it won't, but you'll just have to step into his managerial shoes, Mads … he wanted you to.'

'Do you really think I can do it?'

'Absolutely! So I'll see you there just before three, then.'

∞

Thos drove Annie to the League, but instead of his usual banter there was an awkward silence. Although Annie could generally hear and feel what people had going on in their heads, it was difficult with Thos, his mind was such a jumble of emotions.

'I know tonight means a lot to you, babe, but would you mind very much if I didn't come in? I've just got so much going on at the moment.'

'Yes, I can feel you have, sweetheart; anything I can do to help?' Annie tried not to sound disappointed in him.

'No, babes, you crack on and I'll see you later. Good luck.'

Thos leaned over, but this time his kiss didn't linger. He drove off without even glancing back.

Christ … I'm getting whiplash with his mood swings, Annie thought to herself.

Her stomach churned, but not from nerves this time. Then someone grabbed her arm from behind rapidly moving her thoughts on. She was relieved to see Maddy although looking panicked. 'Oh, thank goodness you're here, Annie,' she squeaked in a higher pitch than normal. 'The hall's *so* crowded already.' Maddy glanced behind Annie. 'No Thos'?

'No, I'll explain later. Let's get this started. By the way, you're going to have to be my rock tonight instead of Sam.'

'What ... on stage?'

'Yep, but don't worry, I'll do the introduction. I just want you to stand where Sam used to, so I'm not on my own out there.'

'I'd be honoured to,' Maddy said and hugged her in support.

They walked through the double doors leading to the hallway, the loud chatter from the excited congregation gradually silenced. Someone at the back started to clap in appreciation of Annie's appearance, which set up a growing ripple of applause. The sea of smiling faces calmed her churning stomach, and her worries dissolved as she walked slowly up the steps to the large stage.

Her psychic energy levels were rising—a precursor to a good evening. She smiled inwardly with relief when her paranormal vibes came in strong and fast, signalling the spirits' arrival, and with Maddy standing in Sam's spot everything was suddenly good.

Maddy nodded, as if to say, 'You've got this, my friend.'

The congregation retook their seats, and Annie tapped the microphone. 'Well, ladies and gentlemen, what an incredible turn-out. Thank you from all of us here at the League for your support, it means so much to us. And although we've lost our dear Sam, please know that he will be here in spirit.' Annie raised her eyes up to the ceiling and shook her head. 'But he's taking his time; probably having a well-earned rest. So, if you're there, Sam, we'd *really* appreciate hearing from you.'

At that very moment, Annie heard a familiar voice, but without the weariness. She looked over towards an oblivious Madeleine; her old friend was standing next her. His once tired eyes sparkled with enthusiasm, and his previously yellowing skin was illuminated with an otherworldly light.

'I'm so proud of you, Annie, my dear. I told you I would always be here for you.' He glanced around at the congregation. 'You can do this better than I ever could, but rather you than me today.'

Annie smiled. 'Well, ladies and gents, Sam *is* in the room, and he's very happy that I'm doing the reading and not him; I think he has well and truly retired.'

The congregation all laughed in appreciation of her humour.

Annie smiled. 'He's pointing out that he's still my boss and pushing me to get started. And of course now that he's part of our *spiritual* congregation, he's bringing forward many eager souls. So it looks like I've got my work cut out again this afternoon.'

She scanned the hall for the pull of recognition to join a pushy spirit to its connection.

'I have a large gentleman with a very shiny bald head here, and he's chortling about having a heart attack in a really *strange* place.' Annie pointed to a young blonde woman, who was obviously sitting with her mother. 'I feel he's here for both of you.'

The mother was obviously not expecting a message as her eyes were wide with shock, but the girl kept her composure. 'We'll take it,' she said, enabling Annie to connect them. The girl spoke to her mother, then nodded back at Annie. 'I think it must be my Uncle Laurie—he died in a bank manager's office after receiving news about an overdraft.'

'Yes, it's definitely him,' Annie said. 'He's been waiting for a long time to come through. Such a lovely man, with the broadest smile, and I feel a true gentleman, too.'

The girl's mother dabbed her eyes, but they were clearly tears of happiness.

Annie lifted her hand as if holding something invisible. 'He's bringing through some evidence, but I'm not sure what it is. It's a piece of china; like a mug in the shape of a man's head wearing a hat.'

Both mother and the daughter gasped. The girl stood. 'That's incredible! My godfather loved his antiques, and the week before he died, he gave Mum a Toby jug which is exactly as you described. You see, my mum and dad were old friends of Uncle Laurie's, and only Mum and myself knew about this gift. Thank you so much.'

'You're very welcome, but don't thank me—your uncle's the one who made the effort to come through. Oh, and he wants you and his family to know how sorry he was to have left you all too soon. But he's incredibly happy now and is still the same person he always was.' Annie was heartened to see the mother and daughter tearfully hug.

She scanned the packed hall again to take in the vast numbers. There were at least four hundred sitting and another hundred standing, and, indistinguishable from the living, many souls who were gathering around their loved ones. Annie thought, *If the living could see how many ghosts are around them, there would be a stampede.*

She was pleased to see a few familiar faces amongst the congregation. Poppet was there with Melina, both acting like old friends. He stood to wave to Annie, but Melina grabbed his arm and pulled him down, scolding him—although with a grin on her face. Annie was delighted that their collaboration had been such a success. She suddenly became aware of someone standing at her side and turned to see Ellie.

'I'm so proud of you, Annie ... but you still have one more job to do for me. Find the priest's brother and stop him.' Before Annie could say anything, she was gone.

'Great, Ellie, thanks for that ... talk about good timing.' She turned back to see a concerned congregation. 'I must apologise for the untimely appearance of one of my guides; she can be a little erratic sometimes.'

The audience laughed but were eager for her to continue.

'Okay, so where am I going with this one? I have yet another gentleman here who seems a little agitated at me for not getting to him sooner ... Apparently, he doesn't like queueing. These souls come through with all sorts of messages they want to pass on, and this one is rather unusual, although it will be stunning evidence of survival. This gentleman would have been in his mid-to-late seventies when he passed, and was a *very* handsome older man, with a full head of platinum white hair. I'm getting the letter J ... would it be John? He's attaching himself to a gentleman sitting at the end of the fourth row back.' Annie pointed to him. 'In fact, you look just like this soul, you've got incredibly similar features and the same colour hair ... so I'm guessing you're his son.'

The man in the audience was clearly accompanying his wife and not expecting a message for himself. But his wife eagerly shouted, 'We'll take it.'

Annie continued. 'So, your father has told me you sold his car after he passed, which was fine with him, but it still had his personalised registration plate on it. It had apparently been on all his cars throughout his life, and basically he wants you to get the plate back.'

The man's wife stood. 'John was my father-in-law, and yes, my husband did sell his car, but he was so distraught after losing his dad that he wasn't thinking straight. You see, it hurt him to see the car sat on the driveway every day, so it had to go. But actually, his dad has just spoilt a birthday surprise. It just shows that spirits can't see everything, because I've already bought the plate back for my husband's birthday.'

Everyone in the audience sighed.

The woman's husband took her hand. 'Wow! Did you really do that for me?' And then he silently mouthed, 'Thank you' to her.

He turned back to Annie. 'That story is word for word correct, but I bet my father has come through just for the hell of it ... to spoil the surprise; that would definitely be his sense of humour, and so typical of my dad. Thanks so much, Miss Prior.'

'Again, don't thank me, it's your father who made the effort. You know, spirits really don't change personality when they pass over. That's because our characters and memories are part of our souls not our physical bodies, so humour always comes through as well as wisdom.'

Annie's head was full of voices pleading to be next. But was drawn to a woman about the same age as herself, sitting a couple of rows back from the front. Confused images flashed through Annie's mind; she could also see the same woman on the other side. She thought for a moment that it might be a forewarning of the woman's mortality, but the answer to that unvoiced question came straight back as a definitive *no*.

'Okay, I have to come to the lady there.' Annie pointed at her. 'I must admit I'm feeling quite confused—have you lost a member of the family who looks just like you?'

The young woman nodded, but didn't seem surprised about the message. 'Yes, that will be my twin sister.'

'Aha, that explains it. She's telling me that you already know she's still around.'

Annie closed her eyes to concentrate on the speedily delivered words. 'She's saying that you had an NDE—a near-death experience to those who don't know. Is that right?'

The twin in the audience affirmed again.

'But she also says it wasn't your time ... and she's still cross with you, for some reason. I think I understand what she's trying to say, but are you okay for me to continue, or do you want to see me after the show?' Annie was concerned for her.

'No, I'm fine with it ... I need everyone to understand what happened.' The twin took a deep breath to keep her strength going. 'My sister's name is Maisie, and I'm Mae.'

Annie was interested at her use of the present tense for her departed sister. 'Maisie's saying that you need to tell us what happened, and that you know it'll be good for you.'

Mae stood, turned towards the audience, and took a deep breath. 'Well, my sister and I were inseparable, as I guess all twins are ... but we *really* were. We finished each other's sentences and knew what the other was thinking at all times. But we also felt each other's pain. So I knew the moment she fell ill, almost before she did. Then, when she was finally diagnosed with stage four pancreatic cancer in January last year, we both knew she didn't have much time.' Mae was pale and seemed full of despair, but she bravely continued. 'I know everyone grieves when a loved one dies, but I literally felt as though I'd been cut in half when she left me. I'd been feeling her pain all through her illness, which was exhausting. That pain obviously left when she died, but it was replaced by the excruciating pain of loss. Then depression set in, which I couldn't cope with. So ... stupidly I tried to end it all ... by walking into the freezing cold sea and drowning myself.'

The congregation gasped.

'Are you okay to continue, Mae?' Annie asked.

'Yes, I need to finish this ... she wants me to.' Mae stopped for a moment. 'So ... I had an NDE, which I believe has changed my life. You see, after I drowned, I had this incredible lucid consciousness. I felt myself floating up above the water and viewing my body below the surface. Then I watched everything that happened. Two amazing people swam out, and dived to find me, then after struggling back with my body, they dragged me back up the beach. After that, I entered another dimension: and saw many beautiful souls who I remembered from this life, and bizarrely from other lives too. And in front of them all—was my sister ... She seemed so real, and when we hugged each other, I felt her. But then she said I had to go back, and that it wasn't my time. I wanted desperately to stay with her.' Mae shook her head.

'She was always so stubborn, more so than I ever was, so of course she wouldn't let me stay. But she said she would be waiting for me when it was my time, not for many years to come, though. She also told me to live my life as if I had two lives, and to aim to achieve twice as much as anyone else.' Mae faltered. 'I didn't want to come back, but I had no choice. Although, thankfully, the people who saved me knew what to do with a cold-water drowning ... They did CPR but didn't warm me up till I got to the hospital, which apparently saved my life. But before I was revived, I was clinically dead for forty minutes.'

Again, people in the congregation gasped in shock.

Mae continued. 'I was lucky. Although my heart had stopped for that long, there was no permanent damage because the water had slowed my organs down. But I'm not that lucky, because I'm still grieving even though I know she's with me. It's only my loss, because I can't see or hear *her*, but she can still see and hear me—which isn't fair. So, Annie ... please tell me how I can fulfil her wishes—so I don't disappoint her?'

The hall was in complete silence with the whole congregation sat forward on their chairs.

Annie looked at both twins for a moment and knew immediately what the earthbound sister had to do. 'Thank you so much for telling us your story, Mae, we can all see how difficult it was for you. And I think I know what you have to do. Why don't you write a book about the two of you, and your lives together? Pour it all in: her illness and passing, and your NDE experience after the suicide attempt. There are so many people who would gain strength from what you've been through. And then after your book comes out, you could tour and do talks about your experiences to young people in colleges and universities *all* over the world, like you've done here today. There's so much despair that leads to high suicide rates amongst young people, and your story will show that although they may feel their lives are meaningless, fighting for it and making life worth living is the only option.' Annie stopped talking and scanned around the audience. So, how many of you would like to read a book like that?'

Without hesitation, hands were raised until all were up.

'There you are! Yours and Maisie's story will help so many, and you've already got an audience.'

'I don't know how to thank you, Annie, that's an amazing idea. I'll do it for her.'

'No ... do it for the two of you, and everyone else who it's going to help.'

Annie smiled at the congregation, who all looked heartened and upbeat. Mae, too, seemed at peace now, as much as her sister.

'Okay, ladies and gentlemen, that was a long message that we all needed to be part of. Thank you to Mae and Maisie. Now ... there are a couple more souls impatient to talk. So, where am I going this time?'

The audience all sat up, hoping to be chosen.

'Okay, I'm being drawn to the lady wearing a yellow cardigan, two rows from the back.' Annie pointed to a thirty-something woman. 'Apparently you have a young daughter who tells you she talks to her grannie every night, is that correct?'

The woman nodded. 'Yes, she does, but I thought it was just because she missed her so much.'

'Well, Grannie, *your* mother, is standing next to you, and she's telling me that she does speak to Amy every night. Oh, and ... you've woken up a couple of times thinking your mum was stroking your hair. Well, she was, and does most nights, apparently.' Annie stood listening for a few moments. 'Well, that was short and sweet: she seems to have left already, albeit very happily. But there's enough evidence there for you and your daughter to know that she's still very much with you both.'

The woman mouthed, 'Thank you' and nodded at Annie in appreciation.

'Okay, ladies and gents, I have only one more message, as I've overrun by an hour.'

The congregation sighed collectively.

'Now, who's this I have coming through? He's a father figure, but I don't think he's a dad. Give me a minute, please, the connection isn't terribly good with this one ... I think I'm running out of batteries here.' Annie closed her eyes to concentrate. 'Ah, yes, I understand.'

She looked over towards the standing congregation, who had been exchanging places throughout the evening with the seated, and pointed to a young man in his early twenties.

'I have a message for that young man standing by the pillar over there. My connection is slightly better now. I think you already know who I have here, don't you?'

The young man nodded.

'Good ... I wasn't sure who it was at first, because although he was your uncle, he told me that he brought you up from a very young age and was more like a father, is that right?'

'Yeah, spot on!' the young man shouted across the hall.

'He said you used to go lake fishing with him, and he wants you to know that he still goes with you. He's seen *all* the fish you've caught since his passing, and he's showing me how big the fish are, gesturing with his hands wide apart.'

The young man shook his head. 'That's incredible ... my Uncle Tom always exaggerated the size of fish I caught by doing that! But can I ask *him* a question, Miss Prior?'

'Yes, of course you can. But call me Annie, please.'

'Okay, Annie. See, my uncle gave me something that I take on every fishing trip, and if you can tell me what it is, then I'm completely sold on all this stuff.'

'Okay, I'll try ... *Although,* I think you're already sold. You'll have to give me a minute.' Annie's stomach churned, she was not sure she would get a reply from the other side. 'Your uncle's connection seems to be fading in and out. Ah, but he's just shown me something really *odd*. It looks like a stick—no, it's more like the small horn off an animal, with an inscription on it.' Annie shivered slightly. 'I'm really confused now; he's saying something about a priest.'

'That's crazy.' The young man looked stunned. 'Nobody else knew about that. It's the base of a deer's antler, which is used to dispatch fish after catching them. I think it's called a priest hammer, 'cause priests give the last rites, or something like that. And my uncle gave it to me not long before he died.'

'Oh, thank goodness for that.' Annie said, relieved that it had nothing to do with her priest. 'Your uncle is an incredibly strong soul, he's still trying to give me more information and I think he's excited that he's finally got his message across to you. All I can make out is "almost being caught"—do you know what he's trying to say?'

The young man laughed out loud. 'Wow ... the inscription on the priest hammer says, "Nothing makes a fish bigger than almost being caught."'

The congregation gasped in astonishment and all eyes turned to the young man, who was shaking his head in disbelief. His uncle was standing with his arm around his nephew while he spoke to

Annie for the last time. He then disappeared, along with all the other souls, who seemed to know it was the end of her readings.

Annie walked across the stage, down the steps and over to the young man, who was taken aback when she put her arm around his shoulder. She whispered to him, 'Your uncle Tom has asked me to give you a hug from him, and to tell you that he knows about the two bottles of beer you take with you every time you go fishing. One is for you ... and the other's for him. He told me to tell you, "Cheers, mate."'

Chapter 29

∞

A Weight Lifted

'Wow ... this is a nice surprise, Annie,' Max said in his bass voice.

It was awkward involving Thos's friend in her problems, but Annie needed to, for her own sanity.

'Thanks so much for seeing me on such short notice, Max.'

'No probs, everything okay?'

'Well, not really ... that's why I need to talk to you.'

Annie had forgotten how colossal Max was. His head just cleared the restaurant door and he had to stoop right over to give her a kiss on her cheek.

'I expect it's about Maddy and me, isn't it?'

'You and Mads? No ... No, it's not, although I'm keeping my fingers crossed for the two of you. I've actually come about Thos and, I suppose, me too.'

'Ah, right ... Great timing! Mama's out shopping so we don't have to worry about her nosing in. Come on, let's have a glass of wine—not too early for you, is it?'

Annie glanced at her watch. 'No, of course not. I love a glass to wake me up in the morning.'

Max fetched a bottle and a couple of glasses. 'Try this, Annie. It's my favourite white from Santorini, called Assyrtiko—most of my customers love it, too.'

They sat at a little table next to a large marble statue of a Greek goddess; Annie raised her eyebrows at her voluptuous breasts. 'I'm surprised you can keep your mind on your work, Max.'

Max guffawed loudly. 'My father had her brought over from their family home in Greece when I was in my early teens. The lads from school used to pop in just to have an ogle at her—and the odd grope, of course.'

'Your dad was a character, then?'

'Yes, and I must thank you for the message from him, Annie. It meant the world to Mamma and me just knowing that he's sorry for what he did, and it's really helped us to finally move on. Now we can miss him the way we should instead of resenting him. Your gift *is* extraordinary, but I guess that's why you're here. Thos isn't dealing with it very well, is he?'

'Er, no, he's not ... But that's not the reason I've come over this morning. In fact, I didn't even realise he'd voiced his concerns to you ... What's he said?' Annie was taken aback that Thos had talked to Max about their relationship, but then, that's what she had come to do, too.

'Oh God, I've put my foot in it. Sorry, Annie. It's just that when he stayed over, we had a few drinks and he told me about you seeing Dorothy. And then everything else that's happened with the church and the media has been a bit overwhelming for him.'

'Yeah, I realised early on that he's uncomfortable with my abilities. Although I suppose it was okay when he was with Maddy ... she was never as weird as I am with it all.'

'Yes, but Maddy wasn't Thos's type, really.'

'What, and I am?'

'Yeah, pretty much. But … changing the subject on purpose … What *can* I help you with, Annie?'

'I did something that I regret now, although I was only doing it to protect Thos. God knows what you'll think of me when I tell you.'

'Go on, then, I'm all ears,' Max said, topping up their glasses.

'Well, after Thos had left to come here, I found the letters that Dorothy had said were in the dresser. They'd actually fallen down the back.'

'Ah … Thos mentioned something about some letters. But he hasn't said anything since, so I'm guessing you didn't tell him.'

Annie pulled out the parcel of letters and laid them on the table. 'No, I didn't. Please read them, Max.'

Although Max's hands were huge, he gently took out each letter, slowly read it, and then replaced each one with the reverence it deserved. But he held on to the last one, staring at the words for a while longer. He swallowed hard and his eyes filled with tears. 'Bloody hell. I never liked Dorothy when we were kids, because she suffocated him with this weird sort of love that just wasn't normal. But I'm having trouble believing she lied so much to him … This was just pure bloody wickedness.'

'Now do you understand why I didn't give him the letters?'

'Yeah, I totally agree with what you did.'

Annie let out a huge sigh of relief. 'Oh … thank goodness for that.'

'You didn't make the wrong decision, Annie. What with the turmoil he's been going through, I don't think he would have coped with this, too. You know … although he acts like a full-on bloke who could deal with anything life throws at him, he's really quite insecure. I remember when we were kids and Dorothy told him his mother had died. He was completely devastated even though he didn't know his mum. He'd always talked about seeing her again, so of course he was massively affected by the whole thing. And it wasn't easy for him being brought up by an old couple either: Dorothy fussed over him all the time, and Frank was completely out of his depth with a young lad around. In fact, poor old Frank had no input into anything, Dorothy just did what she wanted to do. The only godsend was that she couldn't stop Thos from going to school. And of course, once he'd met me, I led him astray, and that's when his childhood really started. So, you see, Annie, it's not his fault he's a complicated character, and he's well worth fighting for. And besides, I want to be his best man one day, so you've got to hang in there.'

Annie jumped up and flung her arms around the man-mountain. 'Thanks so much, I really needed to hear that from you. Do you think he would ever want to marry me, Max?'

'Er, yeah, he'd be daft not to, but that's not for me to say. Let's get this problem sorted and then hopefully you can both move on together. So ... I've got a Greek friend who happens to be a private investigator as well as a chef. How about I give him all the information we have, and he can go and do some digging in Greece for us?'

'That sounds amazing, Max! I wish I'd come to you first ... I've been fretting all this time about what to do.'

'Well, let's see what my mate finds out. Hopefully it'll be something we can use to turn this situation around.'

Chapter 30

∞

GRAN

Annie was poaching eggs when Thos walked into the kitchen. Mr Pong, now more relaxed in her company, was snuggled on a seat nearest the hot Aga, purring his contentment.

'What's for breakfast, babe?'

'Poached eggs, wilted spinach and crushed avocado on toast.'

'Ooh ... that sounds a bit healthy.' Thos wrinkled his nose.

'I thought we'd have a change,' Annie said, but one look at Thos and she picked up on his thoughts immediately. 'What is it, sweetheart? It's not that you don't like my choice of breakfast ... It's something else, isn't it?'

'Bloody hell, babes, I wish I could keep my thoughts to myself sometimes. But you're right yet again. Look, I'm not great at saying sorry, but I owe you a huge apology.' His sincerity was unconvincing, though.

'Go on, Thos ... What's this all about?'

'It's been on my mind since the message from Dorothy. And I'm ... really sorry for the way I've been acting recently, but it's just that my life's changed *so* much in the last few weeks, and I can't quite get my head around it all.'

Annie was a little more than vexed by his comment. 'I really do understand ... but it's not just *your* life that's changed, how do you think *I* feel? You know I was completely unaware that I had this ability when we met, and I suppose I would have gladly given it up for the sake of our relationship then. But as much as you don't like it, this is who I am now.'

'So, are you saying I've got to like it or lump it, babe?'

'That's entirely up to you, Thos. There's no going back to who I was beforehand. But apart from my weird abilities, I hope I haven't changed that much.'

Thos was clearly unnerved at Annie's sudden grit. 'Yeah, yeah ... of course, I know, and I wouldn't want you to change who you are anyway. But I've got to be honest with you ... I'm finding the whole ghost thing really difficult to deal with. I fell in love with you the moment I saw you on the train, and I know that seeing spooks isn't your fault, but I've come to realise I don't like having the creeps around or sharing you with them.'

'So where does that actually leave us, Thos?' Annie could feel her future with him slipping away.

'I dunno ... All I'm saying is I love you, but I *hate* them.'

'Well, that doesn't answer my question ... Do you want to end what we have?'

A look of panic swept over his face. 'No, babes, I—I want to be with you, but I don't want to be involved with your paranormal stuff.' He walked over and grabbed her hand. 'Can we make that work?'

Annie couldn't hide her disappointment in him. 'Yeah, okay ... I'll try to ignore them when you're around, although it's not gonna be easy coming home after an audience at the League and not being able to share it with you. You know, Thos ... I listen to all your stories about the lads at work and your new projects, but it makes me sad that you don't want to listen to my stories anymore. It's a bit one-sided, don't you think?' Annie let his hand go and turned back to the Aga. She gritted her teeth.

She could feel Thos's discomfort as he lingered for a few moments behind her.

'Er… I've got to go out to see how the lads are getting on, babe. You *will* be here when I get back, won't you?'

'Yeah … I'll see you later.'

The now rock-hard eggs and shrivelled spinach were still bubbling away on the hotplates; she lifted the pan and threw it into the filled sink, with water hissing and splashing everywhere.

Her relationship was slipping away from her, but then she remembered the vision she'd had in the hospital. They had been sitting together on a bench overlooking a lake, but it was far into the future. 'That was probably just wishful thinking.' She said aloud.

She sat with Pong on the sofa, feeling deflated. Suddenly, she could hear Gran's voice feebly calling her name, and a sharp pain stabbing inside her head. She grabbed the phone and called her grandmother's landline—Gran didn't answer, but unexpectedly her mother did.

'Mum, what's happened to Gran?'

'Oh, I told Dad not to call you,' her mum said, sounding cross.

'He didn't, Mum. I knew there was something wrong.'

'Oh, that's a load of old codswallop, I wish you wouldn't talk about that sort of rubbish.'

'Whatever, Mum. You didn't seem to mind when you were being interviewed about me, did you? Anyway, I haven't called for an argument—what's wrong with Gran?'

'Don't be cynical, Annie, it doesn't suit you.'

'No, I hate it, Mum, but I've listened to you perfecting it all my life. Now, what about Gran?'

'I stopped your father calling you about her because you're always so *busy* nowadays, and anyway, we can sort it out.'

'Sort *what* out?' Annie was beside herself with anger.

'Your grandmother had a stroke a week ago and—' Annie interrupted. 'A week ago? And you didn't call me? What the hell, Mum, how could you? I want to talk to her now.'

'Well, you can't ... she's in Southampton Hospital.'

'What are you doing at her house, then?' Annie asked, feeling her frustration growing.

'The doctors said she wouldn't be coming home, so I thought I'd come and clear out her things. She won't be needing any of it anymore.'

'I don't know how I'm even related to you, Mum.' Annie slammed the phone down.

The coach would have taken too long, so she took an Uber from home to Waterloo. She was sick to her stomach, not because she was catching a train for the first time since the crash, but because her mother had shocked the hell out of her by being so insensitive.

Annie hoped her journey back to Southampton would be quiet, as it was late morning. Without thinking, Annie automatically sat in carriage number three, *and* with her back towards her destination. She was so angry with her mother that it wasn't until the train lurched away from the station that a feeling of déjà-vu washed over her. Her hands started to sweat and her back stiffened with fear, as it crawled up her spine; she clenched her fists and closed her eyes in an effort to calm herself. Then a tingling sensation gently landed on her shoulder, and before opening her eyes she knew it was her friend's hand.

'ELLIE!' Annie said aloud.

A few people looked to see who had disturbed the peace.

'You need me, Annie?' Ellie said with her usual serene smile.

Annie put her earphones in as though talking to someone on her mobile. 'Yeah, I suppose I do. It's Gran ... I think she's really ill, and Mum's being hateful. And of course, I'm on a bloody train again.'

Ellie shook her head. 'You'll be *fine*, Annie, you've been through a lot worse. You know now— that what happens in life is predestined. Some of the outcomes you can alter for the better, especially with your mother, but I'm afraid ... not for your Gran. If it's her time, you can't take that away from her.'

As usual, Ellie left as quickly as she had appeared, but again she had left wise words behind her.

∞

On arriving at the hospital, Annie was shown to the hyperacute stroke unit. She walked up to her gran's bed and took a deep breath in when she realised the severity of the stroke. Gran's face had been badly affected, with her mouth and eye drooping down on her left side. She was almost unrecognisable, but as soon as the old lady saw her granddaughter, the right side of her face lifted with relief.

'My Ann ...' She tried.

'Oh, Gran, what's happened to you?' Annie asked, trying to keep it together.

'Your mother ... out ... my house. Not ... want her there.' The old lady was agitated and clearly upset, with tears rolling from the corners of her eyes.

'Okay, Gran, I'll go and sort her out. Please don't upset yourself, I hate seeing you like this.'

Her grandmother grabbed Annie's arm. 'You ... have my jewellery ... not her.'

Annie suddenly knew someone was standing behind her and turned. 'Dad, you're here!'

'Hello, Annie ... I heard what Gran said, and it's only right that you have her jewellery.' He sat on the bed, took his mother's hand, and turned to Annie. 'Gran and your mother never got on, but that was never Gran's fault. I'm afraid Marjorie can be *so* difficult sometimes.'

'You think?' Annie spouted angrily. 'What the hell is she doing clearing out Gran's house anyway? Why would you let her do that?'

'Christ, Annie, I didn't know she was,' he whispered. Annie squinted her eyes at her father.

'Annie, I promise you … Really, I didn't know. Come on, let's go over there now.'

Annie looked down at the frail old lady. 'I'll be back very soon, Gran. Dad and I just need to sort something out.' She bent down and kissed her tear-soaked cheek. 'I love you, Gran.'

'I … love … you too, Ann …'

On the way to her grandmother's house, her father was quiet. But Annie was seething, and felt she needed to ask questions that had been nagging at her for years. Besides, it was rare for her to be alone with her dad without her mother interrupting.

'Why is it, Dad, that we've never had a father-daughter relationship? The two of you have only ever been interested in yourselves. What went so wrong, Dad?'

Her father kept his watery eyes on the road. 'I'm so sorry, lass. It's my weakness that's stopped us having a relationship. Your mother's always been such a hard woman … she was so jealous of the closeness Mum and I had right from the start. And of course, when you came along and I showed you affection, she became jealous of you too, and has punished us both for it ever since.'

'I never knew that, Dad. Why have you put up with her for so long?'

'Because, Annie, she's always been a bully, and I'm embarrassed to say she's scared the hell out of me all our married life. I can't help being weak and I *really* hate myself for it; in fact, I wish I was more like you.'

Annie had never seen her father look so vulnerable. She had always thought it had been both her parents who had treated her badly—but now she was finally hearing the truth. She suddenly remembered only ever hearing her mother shouting at her father, and never once him shouting back. She remembered the many occasions her dad had tried to stand up to her mum, but she had beaten him down with words every time.

'But why, then, did you send me to that awful convent? Especially when I was *so* happy at my first school?'

'That wasn't my idea, Annie, and I wish I'd stood up to her about that, as well ... but your grandfather wasn't a very strong man either, and he chose to listen to her and not me. He only paid for you to go there because he thought it was for the best.'

'Why haven't you told me any of this before?'

'Because, darling, your relationship was bad enough with your mother without me making it worse.'

They arrived at Gran's house but sat in the car for a few minutes. Annie's father put his arm around her. 'Please forgive me, lass.'

She tried hard not to feel sorry for him; she was still hugely disappointed that he hadn't showed any strength of character before that moment. But at least he was finally trying.

'Of course I'll forgive you, Dad, but only on one condition.'

'Anything, Annie.'

'Okay ... so you have to be strong from now on, and don't take any more nonsense from her. Do you still love her, Dad?'

Her father seemed embarrassed, and said nothing.

'Well, silence usually tells the whole story. Come on, Dad ... let's go and see what she's up to.'

They walked into the entrance hall of Gran's stunning Edwardian house. It looked like someone was moving out, with boxes littering the hallway. And when they walked through to the kitchen there were cupboards and drawers open in every room. They crept upstairs to the master bedroom, trying not to alert Annie's mother. Her dad stood in the doorway looking dumbstruck; he watched while his wife rummaged through his mother's jewellery box on the bed.

'What are you doing, Marjorie?'

His wife jumped. 'Ken, what on earth? You stupid man, you scared the life out of me.'

'That's my mother's jewellery ... You know she wants Annie to have it.'

'Absolutely not! I'm the one who's had to put up with her all these years,' she said just as Annie walked into the room.

'Don't you think, Mum, that what you're doing is inappropriate? Gran might get better, and you're packing her house up.'

'Even if she does get better, she'll have to go into a home ... *I'm not looking after her.*'

'You disgust me, Mum,' Annie said.

Marjorie grinned cynically. 'So what are you going to do, Annie? Move in and look after her yourself?'

'Actually, yes, I would do it in a heartbeat rather than see her in the sort of run-down home you'd put her in.'

'Ken, tell your daughter to *shut up* and mind her own business.'

'You damn woman, how bloody dare you ... and I won't tell Annie to shut up. It's because of you ... I haven't had a relationship with her all these years. And she's right—you shouldn't be rifling through Mum's stuff—it's disgusting. You never had any time or patience for my mum, and now you think you're gonna get all of her stuff ... well, you're wrong—on so many levels. This is *my* mother's house and I want you to leave NOW!'

Marjorie looked as if she'd been slapped. Then her eyes narrowed.

'How dare you speak to me like that, Kenneth! Have you gone completely mad?' She whipped round to Annie. 'You've put him up to this, haven't you?'

'No, Mum, I just think Dad's suddenly recognised the selfish woman he's been married to all these years.'

Marjorie got up and walked to the window. 'This is going to be my house when she's gone.'

'No, it's not, Marj, it's Annie's—all of it, including her jewellery. I took Mum to a solicitor to finalise her will recently, and guess what? You don't get anything. And I don't want you near my mother anymore,' Ken said, straightening his back.

'Oh, to hell with you both, I don't need any of this garbage, anyway.' Marjorie threw a handful of jewellery on the bed and stormed out, slamming the door behind her.

Ken slumped, exhausted.

'Well done, Dad.' Annie put her hand on his shoulder. 'I know that wasn't easy for you, but she'll respect you all the more for doing it.'

'Well, Annie, I'm not sure whether I want any of her respect, and I really don't think I want to be married to her anymore.'

'I wouldn't blame you for feeling like that, Dad, but I'd go home and see if anything's changed before you decide. You must promise me, though, that if you decide to stay with Mum, you'll never let her bully you again. And if you leave her, you must come and live here … I'd rather you have the house.'

'Don't worry, lass, I've made up my mind; she won't be bullying me again.'

Chapter 31

∞

THE SURPRISE

Thos left for work after kissing Annie on the cheek.

Her mind was in turmoil: although she finally had the relationship with her father she had always wanted, she was worried about her own. Her life had become so complicated, especially now, with her gran in such a bad way. But making the decision to move back to look after her was the right one—she needed to be with her for as long as she had left.

Annie had sorted out the minutiae of how living back in Southampton would work. Doing a couple of demonstrations a week at the League would not be difficult, but she could see it would possibly be the final straw with Thos; their relationship was already strained to the breaking point.

She didn't want any more hassle though, and telling him about moving out—*and* the letters—would have to wait.

She settled herself on the sofa and was happy that Pong had finally succumbed to his fickleness, by nestling into her lap—although his purring did sound bizarrely insincere. Annie scrolled through the messages on her mobile and it started to buzz. She had sensibly put it on silent, what with Pong reaffirming their relationship. The caller ID came up as International, and although Annie would normally see who the caller was in her mind's eye, she had absolutely no intuition or vision with that particular one.

'Hello?'

The line fell silent for a brief moment.

'Ah, hello,' a woman said in a strong Mediterranean accent. 'Is this the home of Frank and Dorothy Townsend?'

'Er, yes, it *was*, but they passed away a few years ago. Can I help? My name's Annie, I'm –'

The woman started to speak over her, as there was a slight delay on the line.

'My name is Thea ... I found a couple of letters from the Townsends, written in the eighties, about my stepbrother, Thomas.'

'I'm sorry—did you say stepbrother?' Annie asked, thinking she had heard wrong.

'Yes, I am the daughter of Adelpha and Giorgios Galanis.'

Annie stood in shock. 'That can't be ... We never knew Thos had a sister! In fact, I have a Greek detective looking for any relatives of his right now.'

'Really? Why would you do that? Thomas died thirty years ago,' Thea said, sounding almost indignant.

'Oh ... Thea, of course you don't know. Er, this is going to come as a huge shock to you, but ... your brother Thomas is very much alive.'

She could hear Thea gasp, and the line went silent for a moment.

'Who am I speaking to?' Thea then said in an audibly shaken voice.

Annie could now visualise a beautiful dark-haired woman with stunning but tear-filled eyes. 'I'm Thos's girlfriend, Annie ... I can't imagine how you must be feeling right now.' Annie's heart was pounding with excitement and shock.

After Thea recovered her senses, they spoke for over an hour about the past thirty years, and especially about how Dorothy had got away with telling so many lies to both families.

'I want you both to come to Sarantos ... Please, Annie, it would mean so much to us. I run the family business, the Hotel Galanis, and I would love you to stay.'

'That sounds amazing, Thea, I'll get onto it straightaway. Oh, and would it be okay if his best friend, Max, and girlfriend come along, too? They've been such a huge support to Thos over the years, *and* Max is Greek as well.'

'Oh yes, it would be lovely to meet them both. Please book your flights and let me know as soon as you can, Annie.'

'I will, Thea, but I'm going to try to keep it a surprise for Thos. What do you think?'

'Oh yes, there will be many tears that day.'

Annie immediately called Max and Maddy, who were both eager to help with the plans *and* to be in on the surprise. But she hadn't realised just how eager Madeleine was—within a couple of hours, she had booked four return flights to Kefalonia with ferry transfers to Sarantos. And Max had covertly called Thos to invite him and Annie on a long-weekend break with him and Maddy.

∞

'Hi, sweetheart, did you have a good day?' Annie said when Thos walked in through the back door.

'Yeah, it was great. Guess what?'

'What?' Annie said, expecting him to say something about the weekend.

'Well, I had a call from your inspector friend, Dan, to say they'd finished collecting all the evidence they needed from the church, and it's now free for us to get on with the renovations. Isn't that amazing?'

'Yes, that's wonderful news, sweetheart, I'm so pleased for you! When are you going to start?' Annie wasn't really bothered either way about the church, but the fact that Thos sounded so much happier than he'd been for a while was perfect.

'There's only one problem, babe ... Max called to invite us away for a few days with him and Mads.'

'Why's that a problem?' Annie asked, worried he was going to say no.

'Well, it's not really come at the right time ... I want the lads to crack on with clearing the site. And I've had permission to move the gravestones over to the walls, so I need to be there to oversee it. But typical Maddy, she's apparently booked flights already, obviously somewhere abroad. What d'ya think we should do, babe?'

'Well, I think a break's a great idea before you start the project. And anyway, I'm exhausted after all that's happened with Gran and Sam, and we both need some time together. And then we can come back refreshed and you can crack on with the church. It's only four nights.'

'How do you know it's only four nights?' Thos said, confused. 'Oh no, don't tell me—one of your spooks told you.'

'Yeah, something like that.' Annie laughed, relieved that he hadn't sussed her faux pas. 'I'm just grateful Maddy's taken control, otherwise we'd *never* book anything, and it'll be so good to spend quality time with them both.'

'Looks like I've got no say in the matter, then. Do you have any of your vibes about where they're taking us?'

'If I did, I wouldn't tell you. You told me no ghosts ... and that means no vibes, too,' Annie said, chuffed at her retort.

'That suits me fine.'

Chapter 32

∞

THE LONG WEEKEND

It wasn't until they had arrived at the airport and the boarding passes were handed out that Thos realised they were off to a Greek island.

'Why are on earth are we going to Kefalonia, guys? It's a three-and-a-half-hour trip.'

'Because we all need a break, it's hot there, and Max speaks Greek. And I expect I could think of a few other reasons, too,' Maddy said, her hands firmly planted on her hips.

'Woah, okay ... got it ... Sounds great.' Thos realised he'd sounded churlish.

Madeleine was more excited and chattier than usual, but that was a plus for Annie, she was loving the experience of just being with her new friends and Thos. And most importantly, a weight would finally be lifted by the end of their trip; Thos would finally know about the letters, and their relationship would either be on or off.

The plane trip with Aegean Airlines was set to be fun, with the four of them sitting together in the centre of the plane. Annie sat in an aisle seat, partly because of superstition but also to have Maddy next to her—and Thos with Max. The arrangement was perfect as she didn't want to have to answer any awkward questions from Thos about the trip; she couldn't bear lying to him again.

A couple of gin and tonics and a tasty business-class Greek lunch later, Annie got up to stretch her legs and give her ears a rest. Maddy had been non-stop chatting about her and Max, and how well she was getting on with Leto, his mom.

Annie walked up the aisle towards the stewardesses' workstation, where they were busily clearing lunch trays away. Although the three women and one steward were chatting in Greek, they were still productively working as if it was automatic. The women looked classy in their sleeveless black dresses with white scarves, and the steward was smartly turned out too, in black trousers and a white shirt with epaulettes.

One of the stewardesses accidentally bumped Annie's shoulder, immediately sending her visions of a horrific car crash. Annie's mind had been quiet for a few days, but the vision was incredibly vivid and could not be ignored.

'Excuse me, but could I have a private word?' Annie said, wondering what the woman's reaction was going to be.

'Yes, of course. How may I help?'

Annie was relieved to hear that the stewardess had a mixed Greek and American accent, which confirmed why she had seen an American car in her vision.

'I know this might sound strange, and probably not something you would have come across on a flight before, but I'm a clairvoyant medium.' Annie checked the woman's name badge. 'Ah, Dimitra, what a lovely name,' she added, trying to lighten the moment.

The stewardess looked confused. 'Do you mean ... you hear dead people talking?'

'Yes, I do, *and* I see them too.' Just as Annie spoke, the spirit of a young woman stood next to Dimitra. Annie knew she had the right connection. 'In fact, I have a message for you right now—would you mind taking it?'

'No, no, that's fine.' Dimitra checked around to see if anyone had heard. Then she spoke to one of the other stewardesses, who nodded in agreement and glanced at Annie quizzically.

'There's a couple of unoccupied seats at the back, we won't be disturbed there,' Dimitra said.

They walked past Thos and Max who were deep in conversation and didn't notice, but Maddy did—she mouthed the words, 'Are you okay?'

Annie put her thumb up, and Maddy, understanding what was happening, surreptitiously winked back.

They sat, and Annie looked straight into Dimitra's stunning dark eyes. She also had the smoothest olive skin, which seemed a prerequisite for Mediterranean people.

'Would you mind if I hold your hands, Dimitra? It helps with the connection.'

The stewardess pulled a face—clearly bemused. 'I'm surprised any ghosts would be able to come through at thirty-thousand feet, let alone six hundred kilometres an hour.'

'Yes, well, I hadn't thought of it like that, but maybe I'm getting a better connection because we're closer to Heaven.' Annie laughed, pointing upwards, and Dimitra joined in too.

'Okay, Dimitra, I feel you're a sceptic, and that's absolutely okay, but I'm sure this message will help you.'

'Don't get me wrong, Annie, I'm very interested in what you have to say, but as far as I'm concerned when we die that's the end of it.'

'Okay, that's fine … but let's see how we get on anyway. I've just been told you studied at an American college, and that's where you met three close girlfriends in your freshman year. Is that right?'

Dimitra's eyes widened. 'Yes, I did, I ...'

'Please don't say anything, I'd rather your friend tell me all about it. So, she says the three of you were involved in a car crash, and that's when she lost her life. But she's taking full responsibility for it and was glad no one else was hurt. She's saying she should have listened to her Dimi.'

Dimitra's hand started shaking. 'This is madness—you *are* talking to her.'

Annie squeezed the young women's hand.

Dimitra closed her eyes and sighed. 'We were all so wild back then, but Lindi was off-the-charts crazy; she always had to go that one step further with everything ... as she did that night. We'd been partying with a group of sophomores—the year above us—and of course we all ended up having way too much to drink. But because Lindi had driven us there in her father's car, she insisted on driving back. I tried to talk her out of it, but she refused to listen 'cause according to her she was never wrong. I even called a cab, but she cancelled it.'

'Ah, that's what she meant when she said she should have listened to you.'

'Yes, but ... I still blame myself for not taking the keys off her; she was always *so* stubborn.'

'Hmm, I can feel that from her too, but she's full of understanding now, and wants you to stop feeling guilty. She says you would never have won the argument, but she's sorry for the last few years you've suffered. Apparently, you left college after the crash to work for the airlines instead of becoming a bank teller. But she's just told me it was the right decision.'

'Oh my God, that's exactly what happened. I didn't want to stay on the course we were on, without Lindi, so I left and I haven't been back to the States since ... I just wanted to be at home in Greece.'

'Actually, Dimitra, I've either lost contact with her, or your friend Lindi's literally flown off somewhere else. But I guess she's done what she wanted to do and is finally at peace with herself.'

'That is so like her—doing exactly what she wants, then losing interest and moving on to something else.'

Dimitra sat for a moment in silence. Annie had expected tears, but instead Dimitra had a contented smile on her face.

'I didn't realise before now that I'd been carrying my guilt as a sort of punishment. But it's finally lifted, and I can't tell you how grateful I am. What an extraordinary experience ... you not only changed my life for the better but changed my mind about what happens to us at the end.' Dimitra leaned over and gave Annie a hug and then kissed both her cheeks. 'I feel I should give you something for helping me so much.'

'Absolutely not, I'm only too pleased when a spirit comes through with a meaningful message—even if it *is* thousands of feet up in the air.'

They both laughed.

'You've definitely converted me into a believer.'

'Well, that's a good job done, then,' Annie said, while they exchanged mobile numbers.

She went back to her seat happy that it had gone so well, but Thos didn't seem so pleased.

'Where've you been all this time, babe?'

'Oh, just talking to one of the stewardesses, she's such a nice girl.' Annie knew what was coming next.

'Please tell me you didn't give her a reading ... *not* on the plane.' Thos said, shaking his head.

'I can't just say no to spirits when they're desperate to come through, Thos.' Annie's heart started beating faster; she was embarrassed to be ticked off in front of her friends.

'Annie can't help it, Thos, so don't get onto her about it,' Madeleine put in.

'Okay, but please don't do it while we're away, babe. I'd like to be able to relax without being crowded out by foreign spooks as well.'

Annie sat, and thanked Maddy for having a go at Thos for her.

Five minutes later, Dimitra walked up the isle towards them with a bottle of Dom Perignon and four glasses. 'Hi, everyone ... This is not enough, but it's a small thank you to Annie for something very special she's done for me today.' Dimitra gave a champagne flute to each of them, and even Thos took one.

Max lifted his glass. 'Yasou, Annie! Great start to a holiday. Let's get another bottle in.'

The plane had started its decent into Argostoli, Kefalonia's international airport by the time they had finished their second bottle. But it hadn't helped to stop Annie feeling nauseous about the reunion though; it was all going to be very real—soon.

A taxi was waiting to take them to the fishing village of Sami. Thea had cancelled Maddy's pre-booked ferry and arranged for a friend with a fishing boat to take them the thirty kilometres to Sarantos.

Max was in his element, chatting to everyone in Greek, as he rarely used it at home. His many friends from the Greek community in London had replaced their mother tongue with a mixture of the new multicultural London English—and Cockney. Annie laughed every time she listened to him translate all that was being said, and then Maddy's humorous attempts at repeating the tongue-twisting phrases.

Captain Adrianos was waiting for them on his Cretan fishing boat, which had been adapted tastefully to take clients. The boat was much larger than the other fishers in the port and would easily take ten to fifteen people comfortably. But that day it had been commandeered for four VIPs.

Annie thought the Captain was in on the secret, as he seemed very attentive towards herself and Maddy, but she soon realised it was his overly flirtatious nature. They both enjoyed playing along and teasing him.

Max and Thos immediately moved to the stern to check out the oversized inboard engine, where the proud Captain explained the modifications he'd made to get more speed out of the boat.

'Look at the guys, Maddy—they're just like a couple of kids in a male-only toyshop.' Annie put her arm around her friend's shoulder and whispered, 'I'm getting really nervous ... Hope it all goes well.'

'I've absolutely no idea what's going to happen, Annie, but I'm sure it'll be fine. And I'm glad we're here for you.'

The weather couldn't have been better. Although it had been hot and humid at the airport, a dry breeze skimmed the coastline. Annie and Maddy changed into their skimpy tops and shorts using the wheelhouse as a changing room. They took it in turns to stand watch, making sure the Captain was not peeking.

Annie sat at the bow looking back at the mountains that towered above the village. 'Captain Adrianos, I was expecting to see ancient buildings around the port, but it all seems reasonably new. Why's that?'

'Ah, well, my lovely ladies, there was an earthquake the year I was born, in 1953. It hit a lot of towns on the island very hard, that's why none of it is old. But we have plenty of ancient ruins too. Although, if old is your passion, I'm nearly there myself,' the Captain said and puffed his chest out.

'Surely not, Captain, you must only be in your early forties ... If only we were single,' Annie sighed, turning to Maddy. 'Isn't that right, Maddy?' The girls stifled their laughter.

'This island is a very romantic place, ladies... Have you seen the movie *Captain Corelli's Mandolin*, Miss Annie? It was filmed in the mountains and around the coast of Sami,' the Captain said with a sexy accent and a cheeky wink aimed at her. 'Okay … is everyone ready to go to Sarantos?'

'Sarantos? Why don't we stay here? It's perfect!' Thos yelled from the stern.

'I've booked Sarantos, Thos, so shut up and try and enjoy yourself,' Maddy shouted back at him, pleased that she'd ticked him off again.

Chapter 33

∞

SARANTOS

The boat was nearing the small island of Sarantos. Annie recognised the fishing village from one of the photos in the letters. Centuries-old, whitewashed buildings with red tiled roofs gleamed against the deep blue sky. Tall, slender cyprus trees towered like green spears above the rooftops, and a single, white-domed Orthodox church stood proud amongst the colourful canopies.

The northerly Maltemi winds had picked up, thrashing the girls' hair around one minute then straight-lining it back the next. Although it was a hot wind, it cooled them a little by drying the perspiration on their bodies.

The boat neared the dock and Annie's stomach somersaulted again, making her feel queasy.

The Captain got up slowly from his seat, as if tomorrow would do for everything. 'Okay, Maximus and Thomas, take the fore and aft lines and jump off when I say. It's a little windy today, so take care.'

The thirty-five-foot boat was moored perfectly with the help of the lads, and tied off professionally by Adrianos, who made it seem so easy.

Maddy grabbed hold of Annie's arm and whispered, albeit loudly, 'I'm beside myself with excitement! Is Thea meeting us here or at the hotel?'

'Shh! At the hotel, I hope,' Annie whispered back. 'Oh God, Mads, have I done the right thing?'

'Well, we're here now ... whatever will be will be.'

The Captain walked up to Annie and put a leathery hand on her shoulder. 'Have a good stay, beautiful lady, and I will be here Monday morning at 9 a.m. to collect you all.'

It was the first time Annie had been in really close contact with the Captain, and even with the wind blowing she could smell a strong whiff of aniseed on his breath. *Smells like ouzo*, she thought.

'Thanks so much, Adrianos, how much do I owe you?'

'You owe me nothing ... This is on the house and you are very welcome, Miss Annie.'

The old seadog walked away, singing loudly in Greek.

'Did I hear right? He didn't charge us, babe? What's that all about then?' Thos asked, confused.

Annie was at a loss about what to say, but Maddy fortuitously butted in.

'He obviously thinks she's gorgeous, Thos, and I hear Greek men make romantic gestures like that all the time.'

A slight air of jealousy flashed across Thos's face, which was Madeleine's desired reaction; she elbowed Annie.

'So, where to now, Mads?' Thos asked, scanning the area.

'Be patient ... all will be revealed very soon.'

Annie glanced across the cobbled street to the stunning whitewashed façade of Hotel Galanis. Blue and white striped canopies shaded a large front terrace where old Greek men sat sipping coffee. A beautiful woman in a pretty floral dress stood with her hands on her hips staring across at them; she was smiling but was tearful too.

Annie put her bag down and, saying nothing to the others, crossed the street and walked up to the woman. They stood for a moment in silence, then flung their arms around each other.

'Will someone please tell me what the hell is happening.' Thos shouted.

Annie turned around with tears in her eyes and beckoned to him and her friends.

'What's going on, babe, who's this?'

Annie was just about to answer when Thea walked up to him.

'Thomas ... I'm your half-sister, Thea.' Tears were welling in her eyes.

Thos glanced at Annie, and she nodded. 'She really is, sweetheart.'

'I've ... got a ... *sister?*' Thos looked into Thea's eyes and saw an uncanny resemblance to himself.

She held out her arms. 'My brother ... I've found you at last.'

She hugged Thos, but he stood back, holding this stranger at arm's length.

'I don't understand, my mother died years ago. Someone's got to explain what the hell's happening.'

Annie placed her hand on his cheek. 'I only found out myself a few days ago, sweetheart, that's why Maddy booked it all so quickly. Thea wanted us to come here to the family hotel.'

'That still doesn't answer my question, Annie.' Thos said as the colour drained from his face. 'Can I sit down a minute? I'm feeling quite dizzy.'

They sat inside the empty restaurant; Thea had cleared it ready for this moment. She rushed behind the bar and got a jug of cold water out of the fridge.

Thos gulped a glass down, never taking his eyes off her. 'This is crazy. Please explain what's going on.'

Thea sat in front of him and took his hands in hers. 'I know it's difficult for both of us to understand, Thomas. I called Dorothy's home to speak to her, after I found letters she'd written to our mother. You obviously don't know any of this, but she wrote to say that you had died when you were five years of age, from an illness.'

'What? ... Gran told me my mother had died.' He looked up at Annie. 'Babe, please tell me Dorothy didn't do that.'

'I'm so sorry, sweetheart, but it's all true. And that's not all she did. You know the night you stayed at Max's? I found the letters down the back of the dresser that your mother had written to Dorothy and you. And I'm ashamed to say I read them ... but they were so awful I couldn't tell you at the time.' Annie lowered her head. 'I told Max and Mads because I didn't know what to do with them. So Max, bless him, organised a private investigator to find your family, but somehow Thea found us first.'

'So, what did my mother's letters say?' Thos sat forward on the edge of his seat.

'Your mother said how much she loved you, and how she had wanted you back desperately, but Dorothy obviously had no intention of giving you up, and ... well, that's why she told her you'd died.'

'What the hell? Tell me—what does all this mean?'

Thea held his hand and looked over at the doorway at the end of the bar. 'Papa ... we're ready.'

A middle-aged Greek man walked out smiling leading behind him an attractive grey-haired woman. Her eyes darted around at the gathering, then they fixed on Thos; she put her hand to her mouth and let out a loud sob.

'Thomas ... my son, you have finally come home to me,' she said, struggling to stay upright. Annie ran over and took hold of her other arm.

Thos slowly stood, staring at a woman he knew only from his dreams. He walked over; her kind eyes stayed fixed upon his.

'You're ... my ... mother?'

The woman only nodded; no words would come. Thos's breath caught, as shock thumped him in the chest.

'My mum?' He flung his arms around her shoulders. '*Mum!*' he said again, his heart releasing thirty-six years of pain.

Adelpha cupped his face in her hands, kissing his cheeks and forehead. 'I dreamt I kissed my boy every night, and you are finally here, my son. I'm holding my darling Thomas at last.'

Mother and son cried together, and so did everyone else in the restaurant.

∞

The deep blue early morning sky reflected in the mirror-still waters. The colourful fishing boats that had lined the marina walls the previous evening, had already departed with their optimistic captains.

Annie sat under the striped awning with a small cup of traditional foamy coffee Thea had made, while Thos talked with his mother upstairs on the balcony. Both Thea and Annie were quiet; so much had already been said, and too much alcohol had been consumed the previous evening—not only by them but by the whole village who had been invited to join in the celebrations too.

Annie held Thea's hand. 'This has all gone so well thanks to you. I didn't know how Thos would react. You see, I hadn't told him about the letters I found.'

'Yes, but there's something else going on between you two, Annie, isn't there?'

Annie thought it would be difficult explaining her abilities to Thea, but she was wrong. She was incredibly open-minded about it all. Thea revealed to Annie that she had been quietly into spiritualism herself but could see how Thos might be conflicted by Annie's powers.

'Oh, Annie, I think it's a marvellous gift you have! But there will always be disbelievers, or, like Thomas, those who are scared by your strength. I've only just met my brother, but I can see a family trait there, and that weakness will be difficult to overcome. But your ability is important, and he will have to learn to live with it. But I can see how much he loves you Annie, so I'm sure he will make the effort.'

'I do hope you're right, Thea … All I want is for us to be happy, and maybe spend the rest of our lives together, especially now that I've met his amazing family.'

'Yes! I, too, want you to be my sister, Annie.' They hugged. 'By the way, my christened name was Dorothea, obviously after Dorothy, but when Mum received the letter telling her Thomas had died, she refused to have any more to do with her, so I became Thea.'

Max walked around the corner hand in hand with Maddy. 'Hello, hello … what's going on here, then?'

'Morning, you two, where've you been?' Annie said.

Maddy seemed sheepish. 'Well, we've been having a look at all the amazing restaurants along the promenade.'

'Reason being?' Annie quizzed her, she was getting one of her feelings.

'It's just that I would like to bring Mama back home to live in Greece, Annie, and this place is so stunning,' Max said, staring out at the boats.

Annie sighed. 'Well, I thought as much.'

'Aha … it sounds like I may have competition.' Thea laughed. 'Actually, I have a good friend who's retiring and selling his restaurant. Believe me, there's enough trade to go around here, and sometimes a little too much. So, I'd be delighted to have new friends down the road. What about it, Max?'

Max squeezed Maddy's hand. 'Okay ... We wouldn't mind having a look. Thanks, Thea.'

Thos walked out into the sunshine with his arm around his mother's shoulders. 'Morning, all ... How's everyone this beautiful day?' He said with a huge smile.

Annie got up and walked over to Adelpha, kissed her on both cheeks, then stood on her toes and kissed Thos gently on his cheek.

Thos kissed her back, and this time he held her tight. 'I love you for what you've done for me, babe ... It's all so incredible.'

Annie was taken aback; after all her worries, it was not what she had expected. 'Really? Even though I didn't tell you about the letters?'

'Look, babe ... I'll never forgive Dorothy for the evil she did. But you kept the letters a secret to protect me, and that means so much. At least you did it with the right sort of love in mind.'

'Thank goodness you're okay with it; but as far as Dorothy's concerned ... I suppose, although there's no excuse for what she did, I think the fear of losing you destroyed any morality she had. But you can move on and leave that part of your life behind now; you finally have the mother you always dreamed of, *and* an amazing sister, too.'

∞

The rest of the weekend was full of sightseeing and meeting local characters. Annie and Thos joined their best mates viewing the restaurant and helped them plot their future in Sarantos. Annie was feeling quietly optimistic about her future with Thos, too, as there had been such a transformation in his manner, literally overnight.

The last evening soon came around. Annie, Thea, Adelpha and Maddy set a huge table in the restaurant, for Thea's cousins and extended family who were arriving from Kefalonia to meet Thos. And Adelpha's husband Georgios had asked a top Greek chef to cook for everyone. Max and Thos had been out all afternoon viewing the restaurant again, and had arrived back laden with flowers that Adelpha had asked them to get for the table.

Thos presented his mother with a beautiful bouquet. 'This is one of many bouquets that you will have, Mama. I want to make up for all the lost years we should have had together.' Then he gave another to Thea. 'And this is for my beautiful sister, who I didn't get the chance to bully when we were young—but watch out, 'cause I'm going to make up for that!'

Everyone laughed, while Thos went to the crate of flowers and lifted out a small but beautiful bouquet of deep red roses. He turned to Annie. 'And these are for my extraordinary girlfriend.' He handed her the flowers. 'Don't ever change *anything* about yourself ... And you know what I mean, babe.' He leant down and kissed her.

The rest of the family arrived and the noise in the room grew as they all started singing and shouting with Greek enthusiasm. Maddy walked over to Annie and put her arm around her waist.

'How are you doing, my friend?' she asked, cocking her head to one side.

'I'm really good, Mads, and I can't tell you how relieved I am that everything's gone so well. I couldn't have done it without you.'

'I'm so glad you're in my life, Annie, but I wish you and Thos would move out here, too.'

'I'd love to, but not with everything that's going on back home. And anyway, you being here will be a great excuse for us to come out on a regular basis.'

The evening was loud and boisterous, with many villagers popping in. Traditional music played, and the men folk showed off their dancing prowess by performing Zorbas.

Thos stood and chinked a wineglass with a fork. 'Could I have everyone's attention, please? I have a few words to say.'

Everyone clapped and whistled, then quietened.

'These last few days have been extraordinary for me, and of course for my gorgeous mother, Adelpha, and my beautiful sister, Thea. If it hadn't had been for Thea, and my special girlfriend, Annie, and also my dearest friends Max and Maddy, I would never have known that my family existed. You will all find out in time why we have been apart for so many years, but I must tell you now, that none of it was the fault of my mother or me. But we're together now, and nothing will take away what we have finally found. I would like to raise a glass to my family and stepfather, Georgios, who has been so gracious about all of this.' Thos raised his glass. 'Yasou!' he shouted, then threw the glass to the floor with force.

Everyone looked over to Adelpha and Giorgios as they raised their glasses, drank them down and likewise threw them to the floor. The rest of the crowd followed suit, ending up with a sea of broken glass at their feet.

Thos chinked his wineglass loudly again, shouting over the uproar. 'Everyone, please ... I would like to introduce you to my great friend, Max, who has something to say, too.'

They all sat and a hush descended again. Maddy, who was sitting next to Annie, looked confused, while Max stood and introduced himself in Greek, then continued in English.

'Thos and I have been close friends since our early schooldays, and have always been there for each other, especially during bad times. When I lost my father, Thos was with me through my darkest hours and even paid for the funeral ...' Max turned to Thos. 'Thank you, mate. I love you like a brother. Now ... I'm so happy that you've been reunited with your mother and sister, who you had no idea existed till a couple of days ago; I know how much this means to you.'

Max raised a glass to Thos and everyone else joined in. The crowd started chatting amongst themselves, translating what had been said.

'I haven't finished yet ... thank you,' Max shouted.

Everyone quietened down again.

'My girlfriend, Maddy, and myself are so honoured to be part of this incredible reunion. But I have another announcement to make which I would like you all to be part of.'

He took something out of his pocket and walked slowly over to Maddy. She sat back in surprise as he knelt in front of her.

'Would you make me the happiest man and marry me, Madeleine Upton?' he asked, with a huge but nervous smile on his face. He held out a beautiful sapphire and diamond ring.

Maddy looked like she was about to faint, and tears started to trickle over her cheeks, she nodded. 'Yes, yes ... of course I will!'

Everyone stood and shouted 'Congratulations!' in English and 'Nazesete!' in Greek.

Thos put his arm around the couple, with Annie joining the group hug. A huge sense of happiness engulfed the close friends, and an immense sense of relief for Annie, with all the loose ends were now securely tied.

Chapter 34

∞

Back to Work

As they walked through the front door, Pong stood in the hallway meowing loudly as if to chastise them for leaving him to be fed by the neighbour, whom he disliked.

'Nice to see you too, Pong. Stop being such an old grump and come and give your dad a hug,' Thos knelt down and held out his arms, but Pong turned his back and indignantly wandered into the kitchen, flicking his tail.

Annie laughed. 'He's definitely had several lives ... way too much attitude for only one.' She picked up the post and a newspaper. 'Christ, Thos, look at the title on the front page: "IS THIS THE HOUSE FROM HELL?" There's a photo of the priest's rectory; and look, photos of six missing children, including Hanna and the boys.'

'Doesn't take long to get back to normality, does it?' Thos said with a slight hint of cynicism. 'You'd better call your friend Dan to see what's going on.'

'Oh, come on, sweetheart, you know this is going to be our "normal" for quite a while, at least until the case is closed ... but I thought you were gonna be okay with it all now.'

'Yeah, I've got no choice, have I? But now I'm home I can't help feeling a tad jealous of Max getting away from it all, lucky bugger. Anyway, babe ... I've got to get back to *my* normal and see how the lads are getting on. I'll see you later.'

Annie couldn't help but tut, she was more than a little deflated by Thos's turnaround in attitude. *Maybe a moody boyfriend is as good as it gets.* But she had more important things on her mind—especially her gran.

∞

'Dad, it's me.'

'Hi, darling, how's your weekend been?'

'Yeah, all good, thanks. I've only just got back and wanted to find out how Gran was ... I haven't had any feelings that she's any worse; is that right?'

'Yes, she seems to be holding her own, bless her, but I'm afraid she won't ever be well enough to go home again. She's definitely going to need 24/7 care from now on, and you can't do that, my darling. She needs a specialist team around her now.'

'But I don't want her going into a disgusting home, Dad.'

'I absolutely agree, and she's not going to. I've found a beautiful private care home, with a ground-floor room and patio door leading onto the garden. And she's so happy that they're allowing her to take her own furniture too. So I made a quick decision and booked it. She's moving in next week.'

As soon as Annie hung up the call, the phone immediately sprang into action again. She and Pong both jumped, but he sat firm—he'd become hardened to the constant shocks. Annie saw the call was from Dan and answered.

'Dan ... just the man!'

'Wow, Prior, am I just the man?'

Annie's mood immediately lifted. 'Well, I couldn't think of anyone else I'd rather be speaking to at this moment.'

'You've just made my day too. I'm actually calling to fill you in on what's been happening, but ... Are you okay, Annie? You sound a bit down to me.'

'Are you getting soft in your old age Dan—you normally call me Prior?'

'Less of the *old*, please, Prior. Look, why don't I pick you up in ten, and we can go for a catch-up coffee?'

Annie looked at herself in the mirror and pulled her emerging crow's feet tightly back with the tip of her fingers. *I've got bloody wrinkles coming already*, she said to the tired woman returning her gaze.

She pinched her cheeks for colour and applied a peach lipstick. 'Why the hell are you getting dolled up to see a forty-eight-year-old police officer, Annie Prior?' She said to herself, staring at herself for answers.

∞

She sat in the passenger seat of Dan's unmarked police car; she leant over and kissed his cheek. 'It's really good to see you, Dan. I needed to spend time with someone outside Thos's friendship group.'

'Okay ... so I'm guessing a coffee's not gonna hit the spot, then. Let's go to a pub where we don't know anyone and have a quiet chinwag, and maybe even a tipple or two.'

'Stop reading my mind, *Inspector*.'

The pub was a hole-in-the-wall affair: small, with discreet nooks and crannies that people could escape into.

'This is absolutely perfect! I needed time to chill after such an emotional weekend. And here was me thinking I'd have my life completely sorted out by the time we got back ...'

Dan put a muscular arm around her shoulders. 'I'm not gonna ask what happened, let's just have a drink and I'll bring you up to date with the case.'

She felt completely protected and wanted to stay in the little old pub forever.

Dan told her that he'd had Fanny Jackson in for questioning, and that she'd denied all knowledge of what had happened at the rectory. She had also told him that she'd had a bedroom downstairs for years because of her dodgy hips and knew nothing about the goings-on upstairs or out the back because "her hateful son," Mellion, had constantly told her to mind her own business. She had also categorically told them that her younger son, Eric, had spent no time at the rectory as he had been living away from home for the past thirty years with various girlfriends. And that he and his older brother had never got on, because Mellion had bullied him for being a simpleton.

'A simpleton? We need to have a look at his medical records, Dan.'

'The lads have already done that, Annie, and apparently Eric's not so much a simpleton but a schizophrenic; he's been on medication for it since his teens.'

'Really? Well, maybe that's part of his problem. Look, I know we don't have any evidence to say he was involved in Mellion's crimes, but I really do feel he was. And I did see him in the upstairs bedroom of the rectory, which makes old Fanny a liar ... *And* he smokes, which means all the cigarette butts at the house and in the shed were most likely his.'

'I didn't know he was a smoker.'

'Yes, he is; I could smell it on him at Mellion's funeral. And when I was in the psychometry trance, the man in the front of the car was smoking, and he smelt just the same.'

'Don't worry, we'll find out, Prior. So much has been sent to the labs for DNA testing, including the butts ... so watch this space. Although we definitely need more evidence on the priest, too, 'cause even though old Mrs Jackson's mad for grassing him up, we only have his statement from thirty-odd years ago. The fact that all of us saw his and the kids' ghosts in the catacombs—well, that would be laughed out of court, and I'm getting enough stick from the guys at head office. So we'll have to leave the visitations out of it.'

Annie laughed. 'Sounds like I need to give all the lads at the Met a reading ... that'll sort them out.'

'Yeah, maybe. It'd be funny, anyway. But I've got full confidence we're gonna solve the case with your help, so all we need to do now is interview the nun who gave a statement all those years ago.'

'What about the old priest who was running the home, Dan?'

'He's long gone ... but *she's* still going, living in a care home for elderly nuns.'

Chapter 35

∞

ANNIE INVESTIGATES

Annie met Dan at the Mary Magdalene Home for Elderly Clergy, Monks and Sisters.

'Does the Met have facilities like this for retired officers, Dan?'

'No, don't think so, at least I haven't heard of one. Christ, I couldn't think of anything worse. A load of grizzly old ex-coppers chewing over case anecdotes ... Bloody hell, I'd rather pop off.'

They walked in through the front entrance and a strong odour hit them. Annie crinkled her nose. 'Ooh, that's not nice,' she said, putting a tissue to her face.

'Christ, Prior, I'm gonna have difficulty with my gag reflex here. The place smells of rear-end body fluids,' Dan said, then suddenly gipped.

'That's hilarious, Dan, after all the ghastly things you've had to deal with over the years.'

'Yeah, but I've never been good with bodily emissions.'

Annie laughed at him as they walked down the corridor to room 19. They had been directed there by an assistant who'd warned them that Sister Muriel would be either confused or non-verbal.

'It's going to be a complete waste of our time, Prior. Sounds like she's already in cuckoo land.'

They walked into the stark bedroom with a plain wooden cross on the wall above a single bed, and a faded reproduction print of Mary Magdalene on the opposite wall. The place was bare of furniture except for a bedside table with a bible on it, a small Edwardian wardrobe, and an old armchair. The chair was turned towards the window, although, not for the view, as the sill was above the old nun's head height.

'Woah, this is a bit basic,' Dan whispered.

'Yeah, it reminds me of my convent days.'

'Well, *that* explains a lot,' Dan said with a hint of sarcasm.

'Oh, shut up!' Annie said, then walked over to the chair and knelt beside it. 'Hello, Sister Muriel. My name's Annie Prior and this is Daniel Watts.'

The elderly nun sat still, gazing up at the cloud-filled sky through the window. Her full-length black habit covered her shoes, and the white wimple and veil appeared too large for her small, wizened face. She slowly turned her head towards Annie, her pallid eyes seemed to see no one.

Dan tutted. 'You've knocked and she's not in, Prior.'

Annie couldn't help smiling at Dan's weird sense of humour that day, but continued on with her gentle interrogation. 'Sister Muriel, do you remember working at the Convent of the Cross in London, caring for foster children?'

The nun gave no response. Dan walked over to her bedside table and picked up the old lady's bible, then looked over at Annie and shook his head, as though she was wasting her time. But Annie scowled back; she was not going to give up that easily.

'Sister Muriel,' Annie said with more conviction. 'Three children went missing from your school back in the late eighties and you gave a statement to a police officer at the time. Do you remember that?'

Although the nun continued to gaze at the sky, Annie could feel a hint of discomfort emanating from her.

'You said in your statement that the three children—Hanna Dawes, Edward Clark and James Murray—had run away, and that they were around fifteen years of age. Sister ... I need an answer please.'

The nun's jaw tightened, and her eyes started to glisten with tears, but she continued obstinately to stare out of the window.

'It's useless, Prior, she's out to lunch.' Dan said. It was clear he wanted to be elsewhere. 'I can't stand the smell ... I've gotta get out of here, Annie—It'll be your fault if I'm sick.'

Annie turned. 'For goodness's sake, Dan, just be patient for one more minute,' she said abruptly, as though disciplining a naughty child. Then she turned back to the sister and placed her hand on the old lady's arm. 'Sister Muriel, this is *really* important because those children didn't run away and were not that age; in fact, they were *much* younger—around eleven and twelve—and that's a vast difference. Did you say that because Father Mellion Jackson forced you to?'

The old lady's eyebrows lifted, and the tears that had been held back tipped onto her cheeks. She continued to stare at the clouds, which were now parting, letting a streak of blue sky through.

She sighed. 'He's the devil,' she said, and grabbed hold of Annie's hand. 'He said he would take me to Hell if I spoke about him and the children.'

Dan moved over; he had already clicked on his voice recorder.

Annie continued. 'Did he abuse the children, Sister?'

The nun squeezed Annie's hand. 'Yes, and may God forgive me ... those poor little lambs. He said they had run away, but I didn't believe him and then he got very angry with me ... I was so afraid of him. He told me to say they were older so the police wouldn't pursue the case.'

Annie glanced quickly up at Dan; she could see he was itching to ask questions, too, but was leaving her to it. 'Sister Muriel, why did old Father Frederick—who ran the school—give the same statement as you? Was it because Father Mellion threatened him too?'

The nun nodded but stayed quiet.

'Is that a yes, Sister?'

'Yes, he did. Poor Father Frederick was scared of him as well, and I know that the stress of it all was the cause of Frederick's heart attack. I don't care now if I go to Hell; I deserve it for lying and not telling the police how evil Father Mellion was.' The nun broke down.

'You won't be going to Hell, Sister—that place is reserved for the likes of Mellion Jackson,' Annie said, then suddenly a vibration of spirit interrupted her.

Another nun appeared at Sister Muriel's side and placed her hand on Muriel's shoulder. 'Tell my old friend we are waiting for her in the most beautiful garden of roses, just like the ones she tended at the convent.'

Annie smiled when the spirit conveyed her name, then vanished. She squeezed the old lady's hand. 'Do you remember Sister Bethel?'

The old lady's eyes widened. 'Oh, she was my dearest friend ... How did you know her?'

'I didn't know her, Sister. I'm a clairvoyant, so I see and talk to those who've passed. And your friend has just come through to say— that she and the other sisters from your convent are waiting for you in a beautiful rose garden, just like the one you used to look after.'

The old nun clapped her frail hands together. 'You've answered my prayers, young lady ... All I want to do now is be with my old friends again.' The nun lifted Annie's hand and kissed the back of it. 'Thank you, my dear.'

∞

Dan and Annie walked out of the home, and he put his arm around her shoulders. 'You did well in there, Prior ... I knew you would, girl. And that visitation was perfectly timed. The old nun was as happy as Larry when we left. All we've gotta do now is find Eric Jackson and get some bloody DNA from him. We got plenty of the stuff from both scenes, but only one to match it to, and he's out of the picture now. If we get a match with Eric, then we've got a case.'

Annie arranged to meet Dan the following day, but as she drove away from the care home she started thinking about Eric and how she could get his DNA. Maybe if she went to the rectory, she could use her newly acquired interview skills on old Fanny Jackson. She knew Dan would be furious with her, but he would have to be pleased if she found something.

She was expecting a frosty welcome from Fanny but was strangely looking forward to the confrontation with the old biddy.

'You again!' Fanny said. 'You're not going to get anything else from me, you know—your friend already tried.'

'I'm not here to question you, Mrs Jackson. I realise we got off on the wrong foot, but now I know the difficult times you had with Mellion, and that your poor Eric had medical issues, too. It's made me feel bad for being such a nuisance to you, so I wondered if we could have a quiet chat, just to clear the air.'

The old lady's hard outward appearance softened somewhat, and she seemed to weigh up her family's nemesis with a slightly more relaxed view. Annie tried to come across as being respectfully contrite, although she was finding it difficult.

'Well, you'd better come in then. But mark my words, Miss Prior, any questions about Eric and you're out.'

The last thing Annie had expected was to be invited in; she was going to have to be incredibly clever to keep the old woman sweet. They walked into the musty lounge that appeared as if it was from the forties—and hadn't been cleaned since. The threadbare floral sofa looked like a trap, with sunken cushions ready to swallow any unsuspecting derriere. Annie decided to sit on a casual chair—also threadbare, but firm. She was more than happy that no tea had been offered; the whole house had a major cleanliness issue and the thought of drinking from a filthy cup turned her stomach.

The few minutes it had taken for the two of them to settle down was enough for Annie to forge a plan. 'I must apologise, Mrs Jackson, for my discourtesy when we first met ... And, of course, at your son's funeral too. I think it was because I was still suffering with shock from the train crash. I'm not normally as insensitive as that.'

'Well, maybe I was a little rude too, but I don't generally like to be bothered by strangers.'

'No, I completely understand; it was just that, because your son died next to me, I felt the need to reach out to you.'

The old lady stared intently at her for a few moments. 'I've been wanting to ask you something.'

'Yes? Ask away.'

'Why do you insist that you're a psychic, Miss Prior? I don't believe in that stuff.'

'Well, everybody has the right to believe in whatever they feel is correct, Mrs Jackson. But don't you agree that if there's unequivocal evidence for something, then generally that's a validation of truth?'

'Well, I'll give you that, Miss Prior, but you see ... I don't *want* to know if there's an afterlife, because there's no one over there who I want to see again. When I die, I'd like the blackness to descend, and I never want to see a light again.'

Annie consciously had to close her mouth. She had never heard so much negativity coming from anyone; even her own mother was positive on rare occasions.

'Well, Mrs Jackson, I promise I won't try to convince you otherwise,' she replied, but could see small cracks appearing in the old woman's rock-hard shell.

'I'm going to make a cup of tea ... Do you want one, Miss Prior?' Fanny asked, somewhat ungraciously.

'Er ... that would be *lovely*, thank you,' Annie said, still thinking of filthy cups.

While Fanny was in the kitchen, Annie scanned the room for anything of interest. There, on the mantelpiece and almost completely hidden behind a redundant carriage clock, was an old photo of Mellion's brother, taken in his younger years. Annie jumped up, moved the photo out and snapped a pic of it on her mobile. She slid it back behind the clock and sat just in time before old Mrs Jackson shuffled back in ... with a mug of tea in each hand.

'Thank you *so* much,' Annie said, taking the tea from her while trying to work out how she was going to *not* drink it.

Mrs Jackson had just sat down, when the sound of a closing door came from the kitchen; the old woman glanced over at Annie to see if she had heard it, too.

'Oh, are you expecting someone, Mrs Jackson?' Annie said, smiling, but feeling slightly anxious. 'I'll go if I'm holding you up.'

'It's no one; the wind sometimes catches the door,' Fanny said, looking nervous herself.

'Hello, Mother,' a deep voice said, then Eric appeared in the doorway of the lounge. 'Having a tea party with Miss Prior, are we?'

His mother stayed silent while Eric walked across to the fireplace; he stood admiring his image in the large mantel mirror, and then turned.

'Well, isn't this nice. I'll have a tea if that's okay, Mum?'

Annie's heart raced; she wished she hadn't been so stupid coming.

'Now, Miss Prior ... Have you been trying to wheedle information out of my dear old mum?' Eric asked, then took his jacket off and threw it onto the back of the chair next to Annie. His eyes were dark with rage.

'No, I actually came to apologise to her for being insensitive. I've had a difficult time myself since the crash and needed to speak to others who'd been affected by it, too.'

Eric leant over close to her face. 'Well, I ... don't believe you.' He continued to stare into her eyes.

His mother walked slowly back in with a mug of tea. She glanced over to the window, which was partially obscured by old net curtains. 'Eric ... there's a police car outside,' she said with panic in her voice.

He dashed over to the window, although kept a short distance back, so as not to be seen.

'Bastard cops,' he hissed through gritted teeth, and turned back to Annie. 'It's your lucky day today, Annie Prior, but it won't be the next time we meet.'

He then ran out of the lounge and down the hall towards the kitchen. Annie heard the back door open; old Mrs Jackson shuffled quickly after him.

'Eric!' the old woman shouted, but he had already gone.

Annie shot up out of her seat, grabbed Eric's jacket from the back of the chair and ran out of the front door. She neared the police car, but it drove off—obviously there for another reason. Annie jumped into her car, locked the doors immediately, then tried to put a shaking key into the ignition.

'For God's sake, woman, pull yourself together,' a female voice shouted from the back seat. Annie whipped around to see it was Ellie.

'Oh, thank God ... it's only you.'

'Well, that's nice. I'm only here to help.'

Chapter 36

∞

GOING SOLO

Annie stood waiting for Dan in the foyer of the local police station. She paced up and down, still very shaken.

'Christ, Prior, are you okay? What's happened?'

'Don't shout at me, Dan ... but I went to see Fanny Jackson.'

'What the hell d'you do that for? She's under investigation, and we'd normally get her *in* to have a chat.'

'Yes, but I went under the premise of apologising to her; and I'm a civilian, so your rules don't apply to me!'

'They bloody well do if you're on my ticket, Prior. Come on, let's go into the office—too many ears round here.'

Annie had folded Eric's coat in on itself, hoping to have saved the couple of hairs she'd seen on the lapel. She was excited to give it to Dan when they walked into the office, and held it out to him.

'What's this, then?'

'Eric's coat.'

'What? ... How'd ya know it's his?'

'Because he took it off in front of me. Be careful, there are a couple of his hairs on the collar ... You said you wanted his DNA.'

'Jesus, Annie, what the hell? He's a dangerous bloke, he could have had you.'

'I know... he threatened that I wouldn't be so lucky next time.'

Dan picked up the phone to Forensics while Annie wandered around the office looking at the photos of Father Mellion, the missing kids, and an artist's impression of Eric.

'Forensics are coming up. Well done, Prior ... but I'm still bloody cross at you for going there on your own, girl. God knows what he might have done.'

Annie took her phone out and gave it to Dan. 'There's a photo of Eric on there from when he was a bit younger. Hasn't changed that much though—still as ugly as sin. Oh, and by the way, old Mrs Jackson's in on it too; she warned him when she saw a police car. That's how I managed to escape—after he'd run out the back.'

Dan put his arms around her and squeezed tightly. 'I would have been *so* pissed at you if he'd gone and done something.'

'Well, I'm here, aren't I? So stop fretting like an old woman.' Despite her words, Annie was loving the attention from a man she'd grown incredibly fond of.

∞

Eric had run to the safe house Mellion had bought thirty years previously. Not even their mother had known about it, just in case the coppers had got to her. The brothers had spent countless hours there plotting their abductions. Mellion was the one with the brains so had done most of the planning. But since his death, Eric had finally been free of the brother who had bullied him relentlessly. He had despised Mellion for it, but had also revered him for his intelligence and strength of character. Eric knew he was the polar opposite, with

Mellion constantly calling him either 'stupid' or a 'mummy's boy'. But being the latter meant his mother had always been on his side, although she was scared of Mellion, too. He'd used to scream obscenities at her for being audacious enough to reprimand him for bullying his younger brother.

Eric had always been different. A withdrawn and depressive teenager, he'd continually had bouts of despair and suicidal thoughts, especially following the death of his father. But in his twenties, he'd become more content after receiving a diagnosis of schizophrenia; he'd been able to blame his legitimate illness for his lack of fortitude. Also his sibling had eased off with the bullying, which was another upside to his diagnosis. For Mellion though, manipulating a schizophrenic brother into assisting him with his perversions had been much more fun.

Access to children for Mellion had always gone unchallenged, since wearing a clerical collar had given him the credibility he'd needed to open the doors of foster homes. His penchant for prepubescent boys had not been to Eric's liking, and neither had been his fetish for leaving his victims bound and gagged until they'd died of starvation.

The children of their past were presently visiting Eric in his nightmares, and their pleading eyes were etched into his mind during his waking hours. The sense of unease was exacerbated by not being able to collect his antipsychotic medication, with the police watching his frequented haunts. But apart from a few minor issues, he was finally in control of his own life, and with Mellion out of the way, he had no one to answer to.

His one enduring sadness was that he had never achieved anything of worth in his sixty-four years. He'd almost had a family of his own, until the stress of it had caused one of his severest psychotic episodes and he'd had to end his relationship before any more damage was done.

It was Eric's time to shine. His scheme was brilliant; even Mellion would have approved. But he was not doing it for his brother, it was purely for the meddling psychic. He was sure the all-seeing Annie Prior would not see *this* one coming. She'd been the bane of his existence since his brother's death, after leading the cops to the catacombs and the rectory. And now, after finding her wheedling more information from his dear old mum, she was going to pay heavily—by being the finale to his greatest plan.

Eric was fired up, delighted that his ideas were so brilliant, and he had the perfect venue to hide his victim-to-be. After this, no one would ever call him stupid again, and he would have accomplished it all without his brother's help. And most importantly, his mother would be proud of him—her only son.

Finding the victim was easy. As a matter of ritual, Eric had been visiting a local combined primary and secondary school most days at 3:30 p.m. He loved watching the kids pour out in their hundreds, spreading in different directions towards their homes.

He'd noticed on many occasions an awkward-looking girl who seemed to have no chattering friends to walk home with. She would stop at the local corner shop to buy sweets, and then cut through a disused industrial estate, which was awaiting demolition due to asbestos.

The girl was a stunted eleven or twelve-year-old, with a mousey ponytail that she would let down as soon as she left the school grounds. Although she was not a pretty girl, she had something intriguing about her. That didn't really matter to Eric, he simply wanted her as a lure *and* for the thrill of his first solo abduction. Although he hadn't thought about the end game for the child, he was concentrating on how he was going to take the psychic and himself out—with maximum effect.

When he and his brother had staged their abductions, Mellion had always been the driver; he was way too large to dash out of the car to grab a victim. Eric, who was on the skinnier side in those days, had always been the physical abductor; he hadn't minded though—it had been more exciting than driving. But this time, he easily did both, and the deed was done.

He didn't want to risk any screaming so he knocked the girl out with a heavy smack around her face. It had the desired effect; she blacked out immediately and was easily bundled into the boot, gagged with gaffer tape and bound with a rope, in no time at all. Eric slowly drove past his chosen venue, scanning the quiet road for signs of police activity—there were none.

'I knew it, and they used to call *me* stupid! Well, not anymore,' he said out loud.

Then a noise came from the boot. He quickly pulled in to the overgrown driveway and jumped out. The leafy avenue was reasonably quiet, because it was known locally as the 'grey area,' where wealthy retired couples bought their last homes.

Eric opened the boot. The girl squinted in the light and stared at him in terror; the tape he'd hurriedly put over her mouth had peeled half off.

'Please don't hurt me again, mister,' she said her eyes now wide.

'Don't look at me,' Eric said through gritted teeth when he realised that one of the sets of eyes in his nightmares had belonged to her. He quickly pushed the tape back over her mouth, but all the while she kept looking deep into his soul.

He lifted her easily out of the boot and, after checking around, dashed to the side of the building. He pushed his way through the dense bushes, down a slope, to an old oak door below ground level. He was safe there from prying eyes because the unkempt gardens had been freely growing for years. Nobody knew about the back entrance apart from him and his brother, who had used it many times without interruption.

Eric dumped the girl with force on the ground and pointed close to her face. 'You make a sound and you're dead.'

She nodded, but continued to intently scrutinise his face.

'I told you not to stare at me,' he said fumbling in his pocket for the key to the padlock. He tried to open to lock, but it had been replaced. 'What the hell!' he shouted.

Leaving the girl on the ground, he ran back to the car for bolt croppers. He opened the door, which led to a stone stairwell, and forcefully grabbed the girl's arm.

'You're gonna have to walk now, I can't hold the torch and carry you as well,' he hissed through his teeth, untying the ropes around her ankles.

Everything seemed to be going to plan, but he was uneasy about the girl. She had not struggled or seemed scared, and her eyes were getting to him; they were the same ones from his dreams. Voices griped at the edges of his sanity, and for a moment, everything seemed oddly coloured around him until it grew back into focus. The sudden shift of reality brought back a sinking realization—he was on the verge of a psychotic episode."

Chapter 37

∞

ETERNALLY FRIENDS

'Hi, Mel.'

'Oh, Annie, I'm so pleased you called! I was just thinking about you.'

'Yeah, I know, that's why I'm calling.'

'Oh, stop showing off,' Melina said, laughing.

'Look, I need some artistic advice on the church renovation, and thought of you first. Would you be interested?'

Melina gasped in delight.

'Really, Annie? I'd love that. Do you want me to bring some paintings along?'

'Ooh, yes, please, that'd be great! I was thinking of a couple of Anilem's limited editions … I know I've never really appreciated his style, but dark abstract would really work in the church.'

'Thank goodness your taste in abstract art has finally come of age, my friend. Just tell me when and where.'

'Well, I know it's a bit short notice, but what about this afternoon around five? Thos will be there about six-ish to meet up with Dan, and I thought it would be great if we could go for a drink in a local pub after. Hopefully, it'll cheer him up—he really needs it.'

'Everything okay between you two, Annie?'

'Yeah, I think so. I've just got to accept he's moodier than me. But more importantly, how's Poppet doing?'

'Oh, he's *absolutely* crazy! But the customers love him and so do I. *And* he's such a great salesman, Annie, he could literally sell a painting to a blind man.' They both laughed. 'I can't thank you enough for finding him for me. Oh … I've got to go … There's a customer on the other line. See you at five, Annie.'

∞

After her trip to Sarantos, Annie had made up her mind that she was going to make a huge effort to get her relationship with Thos back on track. The church meant so much to him, and her getting involved with it seemed the obvious way to begin healing their differences. She hadn't told him she was going there with Melina that afternoon for some interior planning, but a surprise would be a good start.

Annie's cab trip to the church gave her time to reflect on the last few weeks. Her complex life was finally unravelling the way she had hoped it would, with the issues caused by Dorothy's letters being resolved in the best way possible. And once Eric had been captured, the case could move on and she'd be finally free of him and his brother's vileness.

The cab turned the corner onto Church Avenue, Annie's stomach churned. It was a feeling she'd had many times before as a forewarning, but this time she thought it was just bad memories.

Melina's smart Range Rover Sport was parked opposite the church; Annie automatically glanced at her watch. 'Oh God, I'm late again, she's going to rinse me.' But she could see Melina standing next to her car grinning.

Annie pulled an apologetic face and held her hands up. 'Okay, Mel, I've done it again. It's so rude of me and I'm really sorry ... but my mind's all over the place at the moment.'

'You'll be late for your own funeral, Annie. Come and give us a hand ... I've got something in the boot for you.'

There were four huge bubble-wrapped paintings in the back of Melina's car. Annie could tell even before unwrapping them that they were not prints.

'Oh, Mel, I can't afford originals!'

'I know, but one of them is a peace offering for the six years I was so horrid ... a gift from me to you. And if you like the others too, you can pay the same price as prints for them. I owe you that much.'

'Crikey, Melina! This is way too much.'

'Well, Anilem may have painted them, but I'm giving them ... so shush.'

∞

Melina stood with her mouth open, gazing up at the ornate ceiling. 'Christ, Annie, it's *huge*. I thought it was going to be a quaint little chapel ... Thos could get at least ten apartments in here.'

'Yeah, I know, but he really wants it to be a home just for the two of us, although I'm still not a hundred per cent about it. But at the end of the day, it's what he wants, so I'm gonna try and make it happen.'

'Good for you, Annie, I hope he knows how lucky he is. Now, this painting's for you ... Go on, open it.'

Annie ripped off the wrapping excitedly and stared at the massive work of art. Although it was painted in Anilem's usual creepy style, he had incorporated beams of light radiating outwards almost as though they were the wings of an angel. But it could have meant almost anything, with his signature style of abstraction being so deep.

'I really can't accept it, Mel ... It's got to be worth tens of thousands!'

'Oh, shut up, Annie, and just take it. It'll make me feel so much better about myself.'

They both laughed. Annie knew there was no point in arguing further. 'Thanks so much, sweetheart ... We'll discuss it all later over a drink; I'm sure Thos will love it.'

They hugged each other tight for a few moments, making up for lost time. Then Annie's stomach churn again, and she let go of Melina.

'You okay? You're incredibly pale, Annie.'

'Ooh, I'm not sure ... I'm having some of my weird feelings. I'll be fine, though; it's probably just memories creeping back. Come on, let me show you what's here ... It's quite an extraordinary place.'

They walked around the vast area. Annie explained about the tombs under the floor of the nave, and that the worn inscriptions carved into the flagstones revealed the wealth and standing the occupants had once enjoyed.

'The church must have stunk horribly with all those decomposing bodies down there,' Annie said, wrinkling up her nose.

'Actually, I heard somewhere that the reason for church flowers wasn't to make the place look pretty so much as to hide the stench of the rotting flesh.'

'Oh nice ... I'd rather not have known that, Mel.'

They both laughed again, then Annie had an image flash through her mind of a child's frightened eyes. She grabbed Melina's arm.

'Christ, what is it, Annie?'

'Not sure, but something's not right here.'

There was a muffled bang of a closing door, which seemed to come from below ground level.

Annie looked at Mel. 'That's coming from the catacombs below.' She had a strange awareness and unusual vibrations of otherworldly visitors, but also a premonition of an event that Ellie had warned her about. 'Mel, you have to leave now. Something's going to happen … and it's not good.'

'No, I'm staying with you, Annie. And don't even try to dissuade me from this one!'

'Okay … but I've got a really bad feeling.'

The door under the pulpit opened easily with all its recent use. And the stagnant air that had once filled her senses seemed fresher that day, as though a new source of ventilation had been introduced.

Annie knew Melina was close behind—her breath was heavy and hot on the back of her hair. She half turned towards her. 'Are you sure about this, Mel? You really don't have to come with me.'

'I'm fine … I've got your back now, and always will,' Melina said, placing a hand on Annie's shoulder.

Annie smiled—but with trepidation.

They reached the bottom of the stone staircase, and heard a stifled moan; both of them strained to see deeper into the catacombs, searching for any glimmer of light. They crept slowly forward without making a noise down the long, wide-arched corridor, and as they drew closer to the end chamber, there came another whimper.

Annie's mind kicked into action when she visualised a child. She quickly moved ahead, raising her phone's torch, with Melina close behind. There, in the corner, was a small, hunched figure, bound and gagged. The girl lifted her head slowly, seemingly afraid to see the bearer of the light. She had the very same eyes Annie had been envisioning.

'Oh God, it's a child,' Melina whispered.

The girl relaxed momentarily, but then her eyes darted past them and widened with fear. They both spun around, and a bright torch switched on, shining directly at them. The shadow behind the light was of a tall man with slouching shoulders.

He laughed with a smoker's rasp. 'Well, look who we have here—I've won the jackpot.'

Annie gasped when she saw who it was, and was just about to say his name, when Melina beat her to it.

'ERIC!'

Annie was stunned. 'You know him?'

Melina had reverted back to her embittered demeanour. 'Yes, unfortunately, I do. *This* is the man who raped me when I was fourteen, and the reason my mother took her own life.'

'Uh, no, he ... can't be,' Annie muttered, completely confused.

Eric turned the light on his face. 'Oh, I certainly am, and yes, I did rape her—and enjoyed *every* second. But I have news for you, little Mellie. Your mother never had the guts to kill herself, and you should have known she'd never have left her *perfect* daughter. But that stupid bitch threatened to tell the police about me, so I had to stop her. And do you know how easy it is to drown someone? I didn't ... until I held your mother under.'

Melina lurched forward, screaming. 'You bastard!'

She clenched her fist to hit him, but he smacked the side of her head, sending her crashing to the floor. Annie fell to her knees beside Melina, who was now groaning in pain.

A broken flagstone caught her eye, to the side of her hand. She grabbed it without Eric seeing, and slowly got to her feet, holding the stone down by her side.

Annie's strength was growing with her protective guides gathering around. 'You know you'll never get away with this, Eric.'

'Yes, but the thing is, *Annie Prior*, I don't *care*. You see, I planned that my life would end here today, and I was going to take you with me. But now it looks like I'm in luck ... and I can take Mellie and the child, too.'

A familiar voice suddenly broke through the tense atmosphere, as Ellie appeared.

'Kill him, Annie!' She screamed from the other side.

Annie lifted her arm and, with the force of many, struck the side of Eric's head with the sharp stone. He fell to the floor and doubled up in pain, cupping his hands over his spurting temple.

'You bitch!' he snarled, reaching out and grabbing her ankle.

Melina got to her feet. 'No, Eric, let her go.'

Ellie's apparition projected a bright light through the veil for all to see, and she moved in between Eric and Annie.

'What the hell is that!' Eric shouted releasing his grip on Annie's ankle.

Annie took hold of Melina's hand and ran for the stairwell while Eric was momentarily distracted. But he realised they were escaping, and got up and started after them, taking a flick knife from his belt.

'You won't get away from me this time, Mellie!' he shouted demonically.

Annie pushed Melina up the stone steps towards the open door, and just before they reached the top, Eric grabbed the back of her cardigan. He thrust the knife towards her, but Melina turned and pushed Annie out of the way. Eric forced the knife upwards—and in—as hard as he could.

Annie and Melina both fell, but Annie summoned her last ounce of strength and kicked out with force. Eric was lifted off his feet and flew backwards down the stone steps. There was a sickening double crack as his head hit the flagstone floor—snapping his neck backwards. A loud rasping breath rattled from his lungs, for the very last time.

Annie lay motionless, her eyes fixed on Eric's lifeless body at the bottom of the steps, just as she had done with his brother months before.

Her senses returned and she blinked slowly, recognising the smell of warm viscid blood again. She mentally checked herself for wounds, and after realising she was unscathed, she grabbed Melina's arm.

'Oh God, Mel! Are you okay?'

Melina groaned.

'No ... not you!' Annie said. She pulled herself up to the top step and dragged her friend out onto the floor of the nave and into her arms. Blood slowly pumped from the wound in Melina's side, Annie took off her cardigan and pressed down hard. Melina flinched with pain.

'Stay with me, Mel, *please.*'

Annie fumbled in her pockets for her phone when suddenly the main church door opened. Thos and Dan strode in, unaware of the horror they were about to find.

'Christ ... What the hell?' Thos shouted when he saw Annie on the floor, covered in blood, with Melina in her arms.

They ran over. 'What's happened?' Dan asked, immediately switching to police mode, and calling for back-up and an ambulance.

'It's Melina ... Eric stabbed her ... Please help her, Dan.'

He scanned the nave quickly. 'Where's Eric now?'

Annie pointed down the stairs. 'He's dead, and there's a child down in the chamber—she needs help, too.'

'Don't worry, they're on their way. But are *you* hurt, Prior?'

'No ... it's just Mel. Help her, please.' Tears flowed down Annie's cheeks.

Dan knelt beside Melina, gently lifting the blood-soaked cardigan to check the wound. 'Right ... I think she's going to be okay, and help's on its way.'

'Oh, thank God.' Annie looked down at her friend, who now seemed more at ease.

Dan moved closer to Annie and put his hand gently on her shoulder. 'What happened, Annie?'

'We were trying to get away from him, and before I knew it, he'd stabbed her! But it was meant for me, Dan.'

'What happened to him, Annie?' Thos asked, looking down the steps to the body.

'I ... guess I kicked him as hard as I could, and he fell backwards. I heard his neck break ... It was horrific.'

Annie glanced up at Thos, who was standing a little way away from them—with a stony face.

'Well, that's the end of the church,' he said flatly.

'What?' Annie was incredulous. 'I can't believe you just said that, Thos! You really are something else.'

Dan shook his head, astonished at Thos' reaction. Then turned back to Annie, gently moving the tear-soaked hair away from her face. 'You did so well, Prior; he deserved what he got. And don't worry, what you did was completely in self-defence.'

'Dan, you won't believe it ... but he was Melina's stepfather—the man who raped her when she was fourteen.'

'What?' Dan said.

Annie suddenly felt her skin tighten and prickle again. Ellie appeared swathed in light, and knelt by their sides. Melina's eyes flickered open and widened when she saw the spirit.

'My beautiful Ellileen, you're here for me.'

Annie looked at Ellie's face and then down at Melina's. 'How ... do you know Ellie, Mel? I don't understand what's happening here.'

Ellie smiled at Annie, that same empathic smile she had when they were children. 'Melina is ... my mother, Annie.'

'No, she can't be! I don't understand ... How come we're all connected?'

'I chose you, Annie, because you had such a strong gift ... I wanted you to rid the world of the brothers, with a *little* help from me.'

'What about the crash? You didn't ...?'

'No, I had nothing to do with that. It was destined to happen anyway, and using obstacles to change timings *is* acceptable. You had to be on that train for the rest of this plan to succeed.'

'And Thos?'

'Yes, him, too … The church was in his destiny anyway, and of course you two had to meet. But you alone, Annie, ended Eric's miserable life—which I will be eternally grateful for.'

Melina squeezed Annie's hand. 'I didn't know you were connected to my daughter, Annie … She's brought us together, and now you're my dearest friend.'

'Christ, Mel, it's taken six years to finally become friends with you, so you've got to hang around for me now,' Annie said holding her close.

Melina flinched in pain again.

'Dan, where's the bloody ambulance? She's not looking so good.'

Annie could tell from Dan's eyes—that he already knew the outcome. Annie could suddenly feel Melina's life energy fading, although her eyes seemed bright as she gazed past her—and into the next world.

'My mum and dad are here for me, Annie.' Melina's face beamed—the same beautiful smile as Ellie's.

Her parents appeared next to Ellie, waiting to be reunited with their daughter.

'If you have to leave me, Mel, please promise you'll come back when I need you.'

Melina nodded and whispered, 'Always … my friend.' Her head rested back into Annie's arms and her eyes slowly closed.

Ellie's aura changed with her outline diminishing in size. The little girl who had once played with Annie now stood before them. 'I'm finally taking my mum home with me, Annie … Thank you for being our friend.'

Ellie took hold of her mother's hand and gently lifted her soul out of her body—upwards towards the most magnificent of lights.

Chapter 38

∞

FAREWELL TO A FRIEND

Annie climbed the steep wooden steps to the pulpit, with the notes she'd made earlier tightly clutched in her hand. The meagre congregation were no different from her usual expectant crowd, except this time they were *not* there to receive otherworldly messages.

Most of them wore the requested flourish of colour, but those who did not get the code-of-dress memo were in the usual bleak funeral attire. Annie recognised most of the faces from local shops and businesses; the rest were clientele, artists, and other gallery owners, plus the usual crowd of freelance photographers waiting for their opportunity. Melina's and Eric Selby's deaths had been huge news over the past two weeks.

Annie was getting used to the photographers ill-mannered ways—and was ready for them, she didn't want this goodbye to Melina intruded upon in any way. She was also sad that apart from the media and business acquaintances, Melina'd had very few friends in life and now in death. Annie had tried hard to find Anilem's contact details amongst her vast heap of paperwork, she thought

Mel's most successful artist would have wanted to pay his last respects, too. But his details were absent—as *he* had been, the whole time Annie had worked at Hollingsworth's. The only person at the funeral who had been a long-standing friend of Mel's was Charlie, the old doorman from the Ritz. He had known Melina and her family since she was a child and was clearly genuinely upset. He was still wearing his navy top hat and tails with gold epaulettes, and had obviously come straight from work. But it was a fitting tribute to Melina, as she had only ever known him in uniform.

Melina had no relatives to organise the service and Annie had taken it upon herself to do so. Mel had had no religious convictions either, but had always loved this particular Mayfair church, with its magnificent frescos adorning every wall. Annie could now see how she had been drawn in on an artistic level, but she herself, was feeling remarkably at ease with her surroundings too. For some reason, churches had played heavily in her life since the crash.

Melina's coffin rested on a modest wooden stand below the pulpit. A large wreath covered its length, with tiny white buds of gypsophila blurring a sea of peach and white roses. Annie had chosen them as they were the flowers Melina adorned her gallery with every week. Her heart ached at the thought of having had such a short amount of time with her new best friend, but they had found a closeness that would not only stay with her, but with Melina, too.

Annie tapped the small microphone on the lectern, a habit she'd picked up from her other dear lost friend, Sam. She looked slowly over the faces of the congregation, gaining their attention.

'As most of you now know, I worked with Melina for almost seven years, and I can't lie ... they were difficult years. She was never the easiest boss to please, but I hadn't realised that there had been a valid reason for her behaviour. Her mental health had been affected badly by losing both of her parents when she was still quite young,

The Accidental Psychic

and the other horrific events she had to endure during that time were bound to change her, too. Sadly, I never got to know the true Mel until recently, after giving her a reading from a much-loved family member, which I'm glad to say helped turn her life around, and after that we became very close. But although we had such a short time together, we had found enough love for each other to last a lifetime ... and beyond. Nobody really knows about her early years when her parents were still alive, although she told me they were incredibly happy times. And when those times became difficult and she found herself on her own, she still wanted to make her parents proud. So, after studying fine art and selling the family house, she bought a gallery and home here in Mayfair, and believe it or not she achieved all of that by the age of just twenty-one. It was her sheer tenacity and determination that made Hollingsworth's the internationally renowned gallery that it is today.' Annie stopped for a moment and looked up at the arched ceiling.

'Melina loved this church, not because she was religious, but because of the stunning architecture and these *amazing* frescoes on the ceilings. No wonder she spent so much time here ... I think in a world full of madness she found some solace within these meaningful walls. Now, I'm sure you all know what happened just over two weeks ago now: Melina sadly lost her life at the hands of a madman, who the police had been looking for. But what you don't know ... is that if it hadn't had been for her bravery, this would have been my funeral instead of hers. The only consolation is that together, we managed to save the life of a young girl who had been abducted by this monster, and thankfully she's now safely back home with her family. And I can tell you with absolute certainty that Melina has also been reunited with her loved ones too, and they are all now finally at peace together. I would like to invite you all—but not the media, I'm afraid—to join us after the service at the Ritz Hotel for afternoon tea and a glass of Melina's favourite champagne. One of her true friends, Charlie, resplendent in his stunning uniform, will be there to greet you all. It will be a celebration of Melina's life in the only place that was full of wonderful memories for her.'

Thos and Poppet got up from the front row while Annie stepped down from the lectern. Dan, who was also in the front row, nodded, as if to say she had done well. They followed the coffin out of the church to the waiting hearse, which was there to take Melina's body back to the funeral home. The police had put a hold on her burial until the inquest had been heard.

Annie had a pain deep in her chest that she recognised from when Sam died. It was the sadness of how they had both lost their lives, but also for all the years of friendship they'd never had. Her only other consolation was that she knew their love would continue, from both sides.

Annie stood outside thanking strangers for attending, there was a sudden tap on her shoulder.

'Excuse me, Miss Prior.'

She turned to see who the posh male accent belonged to. It was a short, stout, middle-aged man, with his hand outstretched waiting for reciprocation. Annie didn't recognise him.

'My name is Roy Helliwell. I was Miss Hollingsworth's solicitor. I wondered if you would be kind enough to meet me at the gallery after the wake ... about 5 p.m., please. Miss Hollingsworth has bequeathed something in her will to you.'

'She's left *me* something? I wasn't expecting anything else, she already gave me a painting, bless her. I know this will probably sound unappreciative, but I'm absolutely exhausted, and ... if we could meet tomorrow instead, I'd be really grateful. It's just that by the time this has finished, I'm going to be on my knees.' Annie could see the solicitor was unimpressed.

'I can absolutely empathise with you, Miss Prior, but Miss Hollingsworth wanted this matter completed immediately after her funeral.'

'Are you telling me that she had this scenario organised?'

'Oh yes, Miss Prior, she was a stickler for order in her life, and I suppose she wanted that to continue ...'

'Okay, 5 p.m. it is, Mr Helliwell.'

∞

Charlie the Ritz doorman had rushed back, albeit only a few hundred yards, so that he was there to greet everyone who was attending the wake. It seemed that all thirty-two people at the funeral had turned up for afternoon tea and champagne, which pleased Annie, but it was also poignant that there had been so few to acknowledge Melina's life.

Annie was more than happy to pay for the funeral and wake for her friend, as she didn't feel it appropriate to take the money from Melina's estate for it. Although the Ritz's manager had kindly reduced the price significantly, in respect of the loyalty and custom the Hollingsworth family had shown over the years.

After welcoming the guests, Annie sat at a table with Thos and Poppet. He had cried throughout her eulogy, but Annie soon realised his tears were not only for Mel, but that he was also worried about losing his job.

'Pops, your mascara's smudged ... go and sort it out,' Annie said, laughing. It was her first light-hearted moment for a while.

Thos took hold of Annie's hand across the table. 'It's been on my mind, babe ... I guess I need to apologise to you again for that stupid comment I made at the church. It was unforgivable, especially after what you've been through these past weeks. You didn't deserve that.'

Annie pulled her hand away from him. 'You're right, Thos, it *was* unforgivable. And I have to be honest ... My worry is that you'll continue to say hurtful or inappropriate things at the wrong times, and then always expect me to accept your apology after. But really, today's not the right time to discuss what's happening with us; we need to sit down and decide where we're going with all of this.'

Poppet arrived back at the table. 'Oh my good *God*, Annie, have you been into the loos here? They're wonderful! I'm going to decorate my bedroom like it.'

'You really are so camp, Pops ... but I love you for it.' Annie leant across and kissed him on the cheek. 'By the way, you're coming back with me and Thos to the gallery to see what Mel's solicitor wants.'

'Absolutely, sweetie. You know me—I love a bit of intrigue.'

Thos stood. 'If you don't mind, Annie, I really don't fancy going to the gallery at five. You go with Poppet and I'll see you later.'

Annie watched as he walked out.

'What's going on between you two, Annie?'

'Oh, I don't know, sweetheart, but I'm getting whiplash with his mood swings again. I expect we'll sort it out ... or maybe not.'

Chapter 39

∞

THE BEQUEST

The walk back to the gallery from the Ritz was short but much needed. Annie had only had one glass of champagne, but it had gone straight to her head, afternoon drinking always did. She had forgotten just how busy Mayfair could be, but the walk with Poppet, who could talk for England, was doing her good by taking her mind off Thos.

'What do you think she's left you in her will?' Poppet asked, sounding more camp than ever.

'I don't know ... Maybe it's another of Anilem's paintings? But then, she's already given me a stunning one for the church.'

Poppet unlocked the door to the gallery, and Annie's stomach churned instantly. It brought back memories of the first five minutes of every working day, because Melina's moods were unfathomable. But she was more than disappointed not to see her friend's face this time; she would rather have had her back as her old miserable self than not at all. Her chest tightened with sadness again.

'What's going to happen to my job, Annie? I haven't mentioned it before now because I thought it was a bit insensitive, but ... I *am* really worried about it.'

'I don't know, Pops, none of us saw this coming. I'll know more after I've spoken to her solicitor. It wouldn't surprise me if she's put something in place to protect your job.' Annie grabbed hold of Poppet's hand. 'Don't worry, sweetie, I'm sure it'll be fine…'

Roy Helliwell arrived at five o'clock on the dot. Annie thought he was a complete caricature of a solicitor: punctual, OCD, and wearing thick-rimmed glasses.

'Hello, Miss Prior, and thank you for meeting me. Now, I wonder if we could go up to Miss Hollingsworth's apartment to go over the will?'

'Yes, of course. And can Poppet … I mean Mark … come too?'

'Er, no, I'm sorry,' the solicitor said, looking Poppet up and down as though he had never seen a gay man before. 'I don't make the rules— I just follow them. You see— only those who are named in the will are allowed to be in attendance, so if you could stay here in the gallery it would be much appreciated.'

'That's okay, I've got plenty of paperwork to be getting on with, and one knows when one's not wanted,' Poppet said, mimicking Helliwell's posh accent.

Annie led the way up to Melina's apartment on the second floor, via a newly refurbished staircase with a French-polished handrail. She opened the apartment door, and although it was a bit stuffy there was the aroma of an unmistakeable perfume that only Melina wore, almost like it had been freshly sprayed.

'Wow … Melina's perfume's still *so* strong,' Annie said, fanning her face with her hand.

The solicitor sniffed the air, looking perplexed. 'I can't smell anything, just a musty old atmosphere … We need to open the windows in here.' He walked towards them.

'No, please don't open them, Melina rarely did. She used to say they kept London out.'

Annie could still smell *Aromatics* by Clinique, her friend's preferred perfume. But instead of hating the smell as she used to, she breathed it in deeply.

She's here, she thought to herself, but neither saw nor heard Melina.

'Okay, Miss Prior, shall we sit at the dining table? I'll get the paperwork out.'

'I hope you don't mind me saying, Mr Helliwell, but this does seem a bit formal for just a painting.'

'Is that what you think you are getting, Miss Prior?'

'Oh … I'm sorry, I've probably presumed too much.'

'No, I think the opposite, rather. But shall we see?' The solicitor took out the will from his old tan leather briefcase, which had seen better days. 'So, Miss Prior, I had a meeting with Miss Hollingsworth just three weeks ago, and I must say she seemed happier than I'd seen her in many years. You see, the Hollingsworth's were my first ever appointment, when I was a green-behind-the-ears solicitor. Mr Hollingsworth, George, was extremely kind and very patient with me throughout, so consequently I looked after him until his tragic death. And then I continued looking after Mrs Hollingsworth's legal matters after George died. And I believe you know what happened to the family after his passing.'

Annie nodded. 'Yes, I do.'

'Yes, quite shocking. Well, Melina—Miss Hollingsworth—said, that she had told you everything about her past, and that you'd helped her to come to terms with all that had gone on.'

'Did you hear, Mr Helliwell, that Eric Selby not only killed Mel, but confessed before he died to murdering her mother, too?'

'Yes, I heard … It's quite unbelievably tragic, and it must have been a *terrifying* experience for you both. The only consolation I have is that before she died, Melina had found happiness and a true friend in you, Miss Prior, and that's why I'm here today. She instructed me as her legal representative to read her last will and testament.'

'Shouldn't you be reading it to all the beneficiaries at the same time, Mr Helliwell?'

The solicitor laughed. 'No, that only happens in the movies, with dramatic music and distant relatives who expect too much. But in *this* story, Miss Prior, you are the only beneficiary; Miss Hollingsworth has bequeathed her entire estate to *you*.'

Annie's mouth dropped open and her eyes were wide with shock. 'What? She ... she couldn't have. I knew her for almost seven years, but we've only recently become close friends. This is *crazy*! Are you *absolutely* sure?'

'Oh yes, I don't make mistakes. And besides which, it's all down here in writing, Miss Prior. I won't read all the legal speak, I'll just leave you a copy for your solicitor to deal with. But the gist of it is that she has left you Hollingsworth's Gallery and the entirety of her art collection. Which belonged solely to her because she purchased art directly from the artists, so they didn't have to wait for their payouts.'

'Wow, this is unbelievable! And I never knew that about Mel buying the art. You see, she ran the gallery and the sourcing of paintings ... I was here purely to sell them. Although, on rare occasions, she'd take on a new artist that I'd found.'

'Well, that moves us nicely to my next point Miss Prior. She also stipulated in her will that she would like you to continue helping the art community in this way.'

'I think that's a great idea, Mr Helliwell, but some of the art is extremely expensive, and ... the stock we carry is huge. So, I'm afraid I'm not in any position financially to be able do that.'

'Don't worry, Miss Prior, her estate is considerable, she was a very shrewd lady and made some lucrative investments over the years. This five-storey property alone is worth upward of twenty million, and I haven't had the chance to calculate the full amount yet, but she was definitely cash-rich too. And ... this is all yours now. But Miss Hollingsworth was hoping you would continue with the gallery and build on its success in helping the art community. Oh, and she also gave me this letter for you.'

The odd little solicitor handed over an envelope with 'Annie' written in Melina's unmistakable loopy handwriting on the front.

Helliwell got up. 'Goodbye, Miss Prior, and if I can be of any assistance to you in the future, please don't hesitate to get in touch.'

'Thank you, Mr Helliwell, I'm absolutely floored by all of this. But, I don't actually have my own solicitor, so I'd very much like to have you on my side. You know this business well, and if you could continue on with me ... I'd be very grateful.'

∞

Annie sat on her own, staring at the envelope, her eyes misted over with tears.

There was a knock at the door of the apartment.

'Annie, it's only me,' Poppet said.

'Come in, Pops.'

He walked in and immediately rushed to her side. 'Oh, sweetie, are you okay?' he asked, handing her a colourful handkerchief.

'I don't know if I am at the moment ... It's all a bit too much to take in.'

Poppet put an arm around her shoulders. 'Is that a letter from Mel?'

'Yes, and I suppose I ought to open it.' Annie held it tightly, visualising Melina writing it.

'Why don't I go down to the staffroom and make us a nice cuppa? It'll give you chance to read it on your own.'

'Good idea, Pops—and thank you.'

Poppet went downstairs looking worried. Annie took a deep breath and opened the envelope.

> My Dearest Annie
>
> You are reading this letter because I'm no longer with you. And you'll be sitting at my dining table, where Roy Helliwell, my solicitor, was with me while I finalised my will.
>
> I felt the need to explain to you why you are my sole beneficiary. There are a couple of reasons, one obviously being that I have no relatives—at least, none that I know of. But the main reason is that you were the only true friend I ever had.
>
> I've watched you over the years—before our friendship—and knew early on that you were special. Your exceptional kindness to people you didn't know, like the woman who begs for money two shops down from us. I stopped to give her a few coins once, and she asked after you by name. She told me that you gave her ten pounds out of your wages every week. That simple act of unspoken kindness alone helped me to understand that many people struggle in life and need those like you to make a difference. So, Annie, you're the reason that I started buying art from our artists instead of taking sixty per cent commission. I would pay them up front and gave them advances on future work too, so they could live a decent life without struggling.
>
> Unfortunately, you only really knew me then when I was that hateful person, which saddens me. But it was your kindness and your incredible psychic ability that turned my life around, and we finally became good friends.
>
> I know in my heart that you'll continue to help struggling

artists, and I'm sure you'll find many others to show your amazing kindness to. Of course, on the other hand, if you feel you can't cope with the enormity of my bequest, I've instructed my solicitor to help you disperse the estate to charities. But I believe in you, my friend.

I didn't leave anything to Poppet, Annie, I thought it would be best to leave that up to you. Please tell him from me, he was the first man—sort of—that I ever liked. Look after him, Annie, he really is a poppet!

Now, I know you've had a couple of shocks already. My passing, and being left the gallery and estate, it can't have been easy for you to take in. But there is one more surprise to come, I'm afraid. I wasn't completely honest with you about one of our famous artists … and myself. I'm sorry for deceiving you, but it was the only release I had in my dark world, before our friendship. I was going to tell you … but obviously events have taken over since.

If Poppet is with you, I want you both to go up to the top floor where the surprise awaits. I wish I was a fly on the wall right now—but then again, in a way, maybe I am.

What a day you're having, Annie!

Have a long and happy life, and I'll be popping in to say hi sometimes … I hope.

All my love,

Mel xxx

PS. Think *anadrome*

'Tea's ready … Have you finished reading it?' Poppet said, sashaying through the door with a tray.

'I have, Pops. Mel mentioned you in the letter, but I'm not going to tell you what she said ... yet.'

'Have I lost my job? Please tell me, I can't bear the suspense.'

'No, you haven't lost your job, Pops. In fact, you can be the manager for as long as you like.'

'Really...? How does that work? Who's the new owner, then?'

Annie grinned and didn't say anything, just raised her eyebrows.

'Oh ... my ... good ... God! She's left it to you, hasn't she?'

'Yep, and it's crazy, Pops. You're going to have to seriously help me with all of this; but we'll handle it, sweetheart. Although apparently there's another surprise in the attic waiting for us. She wanted you to come up with me. She said "think anadrome", whatever that means.'

Annie unlocked the door at the top of the staircase with Poppet peeping over her shoulder.

'Oh, hurry up, Annie ... I'm dying to know what's in there. Mel told me it was a store for her parents' stuff.'

As soon as the door was open, a strong smell of turpentine mixed with oil paints wafted out. They both stood at the entrance—speechless.

The vastness of the attic room struck them both. There were no internal walls interrupting the floor area, while the polished floorboards exaggerated the length of the room. There were four enormous floor-to-ceiling arched windows at the front, framing the London skyline of towering buildings in all their monumental glory, with the London Eye hazed by the early evening light in the far distance.

Around the perimeter of the room were completed canvases stacked against each other four to six deep, at least sixty in all. In front of them stood two large easels, on which were easily recognisable works. A large artist's palette sat on a splattered table next to the only unfinished painting, and there was a square plastic container with upwards of fifty hog brushes of all sizes, cleaned and waiting to be chosen. Annie and Poppet walked in slowly, both of them blown away by the attic's hidden treasures.

Poppet held onto Annie's arm like a scared child. 'There must be at least sixty of Anilem's paintings! Do you think Mel kept him in here, painting ... like in the movie *Misery*?'

'Oh, for goodness's sake, Pops ... She wouldn't have done that ... would she?' She walked over to one of the finished paintings on an easel, and stared at it for a few moments. 'Oh my God! Look at the signature, Pops—Mel said "think *Anadrome*". What's the anadrome of Anilem?'

Poppet quickly googled the word on his phone then checked the scrawled signature.

'Uhm.' He gulped in a breath. 'It's ... Melina.'

Chapter 40

∞

CHANGES

The enormity of losing Mel and finding out that she had been left the whole estate was almost too much for Annie to compute. At the same time, she was massively humbled by the bequest, and determined to measure up to Melina's expectations. But she needed to organise her life around the gallery a little more, and delegate most of the everyday running to Poppet. He'd shown his worth as a buyer, but also as an untapped resource for abstract art, even his own paintings had proved his extraordinary natural ability. So, involving him even more in the business, and giving him an incentive was her next step, and it was the time to lay bare her ideas.

The gallery was immaculately kept in every way, which was obviously down to Poppet's obsessive compulsiveness. That didn't surprise her, given that most of the gay men she had met throughout the years had been immaculate in both their personal and everyday life hygiene.

'Isn't this incredible, Annie?'

'Yes, and all thanks to Melina, bless her.'

'Well, I wouldn't say that exactly, darling. If you hadn't had been so good to her, she would have never entrusted her business to you. So, like it or not, it's got an awful lot to do with your generosity of spirit. And look what you did *pour moi*, for instance: you scooped little old me up and changed my life for the better.'

'Actually, I've been thinking about your life and future role in the business, Pops. And first things first: I know you have to travel an hour and a half every day, so I propose that you take a bedroom in Mel's apartment, and use the facilities as your own, rent free.'

'You're doing it again, Annie—changing my life for the better. Well, it would make such a difference, especially to my social life, which hasn't even got off the ground yet. And my odd little bedsit with its *lovely* view of a busy railway station costs me £600 a month plus the bills. Surely, I should pay towards the expenses here, too.'

'Absolutely not, Pops; although, if things keep going the way they are at the moment with me and Thos, I might just have to move in with you. We could be flatmates … What d'ya think?'

'Great! But what *is* happening with the hunk, sweetie? I'll have him if you don't want him.'

'You're incorrigible, Pops. But I'll keep you up to date with that, once I see how it pans out. Anyway, we've got so much to sort out here, I can't be doing with negative thoughts right now. Another idea that came to me was for you to use Mel's studio at the top. I'm sure she'll be delighted for you to work in there.'

'Annie Prior, I love you,' Poppet said, tearing up. 'But I still can't get my head around you using the present tense when talking about her—it's so strange.'

'She's still with us and always will be … But anyway, I'm glad we've got all that sorted. Now all we need is someone as a general help around the place.'

'Shall I put an advert in?'

'No, I think I know where to find someone. In fact, she's only a few shops down from here.'

'You can't poach staff from an empty shop, Annie! Have you lost your mind already?'

'Not yet ... But you'll soon see, Pops, leave it up to me. Oh, and the stock floor has loads of spare rooms and a shower room that we don't use, so I thought the new member of staff could live up there, too.'

'Sounds great. Why don't you give whoever it is a call and put it to them?'

'Better still, I'll go and ask her.'

Annie turned right out of the gallery and walked the fifty metres to the empty shop.

'Hi, Sandra.'

The homeless woman glanced up, and a huge smile spread across her face. 'Annie, my Mayfair angel, how lovely to see you. Oh, and I read all about what's been happening in your life ... I couldn't believe it. I'm so sorry to hear about your boss dying in such a tragic way.' Sandra got up and hugged her.

'Thanks, Sandy ...' But before Annie could say more, Sandra continued.

'Miss Hollingsworth was a little severe, but she still used to give me money sometimes; not like you, though. But today I've already made twenty-two quid, so you don't have to give me your usual tenner.'

'That's very honest of you, Sandy, but actually I have a proposition for you. I'd like to offer you a job at the gallery.'

'Tell me you're not joking ... are ya?'

'No, I mean it.'

The woman got up and flung her arms round Annie's neck. 'I said you were my angel.'

'No, I'm not, sweetheart. I promised you a while ago that if ever my circumstances changed, I'd help you much more than just giving you ten quid a week. And guess what? They've changed. So I'd like you to come and help the manager, Mark, with whatever needs doing, and that means cleaning as well, but also you'll be an apprentice, just like I was when I first joined.'

'Oh, Annie, all of my dreams have come true. Is this really happening?'

'Yes, absolutely. And you'll also need somewhere to live, so I'll kit out a bedroom on the second floor for you. But I think we'll start by going shopping for some new clothes and everything else you'll need to begin your new life at Hollingsworth's.'

Annie had ticked off her first act of kindness and was sure Melina would approve. But she was saddened that she hadn't felt or seen her spirit around, even though she *had* smelt her unforgettable perfume. It was still early days though, and Annie was hopeful that Mel would pop in to give her approval … or not.

Chapter 41

∞

GRAN GOES HOME

'Hi, darling, it's your dad.'

'I know, Dad ... It's Gran, isn't it?'

'Yes, I'm afraid so, darling. She's going downhill fast, bless her, and she's been asking for you.'

'I'll be there as soon as I can.'

Instead of catching the train, Annie ordered her friendly Uber again, knowing the cabbie wouldn't mind leaving the confines of London for a change, or putting his foot down if need be. They arrived at Southampton Hospital in just under an hour and a half, as the traffic was reasonable, and the cabbie drove like a maniac.

Annie walked up the hallway towards Gran's ward with that tight feeling in her chest. She thought that losing Melina and having to deal with Eric had been enough of an ordeal, but if anything was to happen to Gran, she would need every last ounce of strength to cope with it.

Good memories of growing up flashed into her mind, confirming the huge role the old lady had played in her life. She had virtually taken over Annie's parenting from a mother who couldn't be bothered. And even though she had a no-nonsense northerner approach to everything she said, she had also been Annie's only source of love. And with it came the fundamental principles of being a worthwhile human being.

Annie peered quietly through the curtains, which had been drawn around the bed, to see a nurse taking Gran's obs.

'It's okay, I've finished now ... Come on in. You must be Elsie's granddaughter, she's been asking for you,' the nurse said, then left, closing the curtains behind her.

'Gran, it's me—Annie.'

The old lady opened her eyes. Although they were pale and dull, they lit up momentarily.

'Our Annie, you're ... here,' she said slowly, and tugged on Annie's arm for her to sit on the bed.

'I'd forgotten your name was Elsie ... You've always been Gran to me. Even Mum, Dad and Grandad called you Mother.'

'Yes, *I'd* forgotten my name too, Annie. Actually, I had no idea who the nurse was talking to when she called me Elsie.'

'Oh, silly ... I'm glad you've still got your sense of humour. Your speech is so much better than last time. I suppose you've been practising on all those gorgeous doctors, haven't you?'

'Well, I may be on my way out, Annie, but I'm not made of wood.'

'You are extraordinary, Gran, and that's why I love you so much. Anyway, where's Dad? He said he'd meet me here.'

'He told me you were coming, love, so I sent him away. He understands that we need to talk.' The frail old lady held onto Annie's arm tightly. 'Now, listen, I have something very precious to give you. It's the key to your life ... and a legacy that has been handed down over four hundred years.' She took a deep breath to continue. 'It was last entrusted to Mary-Ellen, your great-gran, who died the year before you were born. But I'm too weary now to tell you more ... all will become clear. There's a box in my bedside cabinet, darling. I got your father to fetch it from one of those safety deposit thingys at the bank.'

Annie opened the cupboard and pulled out an old shoebox with a large elastic band tightly keeping the lid on.

The old lady sighed. 'I've been waiting all your life for the right moment to give you this, my girl, and I know you've already had the healing crystal, which was a personal possession of my mother's. But the contents of this box have been in possession of all the Keepers and Immortal Psychics in our family.'

'Gran ... I really don't understand what you're talking about.'

'You will, my darling, when you read the letter. It was written by the first Immortal Psychic who documented her life four hundred years ago. But there were many more before her who we'll never know about, unless *you* find it all out somehow. Now, I'm tired ... you're going to have to read it out to me.'

Annie opened the shoebox. A musty smell like no other took her breath away, and she quizzically looked over at her gran.

'Breathe it in, Annie. What you have in your hands is four hundred years of memories.' The old lady scrutinised her reactions closely.

Inside the shoebox was an intricately carved mini-chest, blackened by the years and held tightly closed by a well-handled brown leather strap and buckle; Annie was overawed by its antiquity. She brought the box close to her face and sniffed in the ancient scent again, and her mind was suddenly filled with visions of centuries past and flashes of lives that had long ago ended.

'Gran ... what am I seeing?'

The old lady smiled knowingly. 'They're the lives of your ancestors, and also yours.'

'Mine, Gran?'

'You'll see.'

Annie had fallen silent while she carefully unbuckled the strap and opened the lid. A scrolled letter that had been held by many hands before her—filled the box. She lifted it out reverently, revealing a small parcel hidden beneath, wrapped in ancient, fraying calico. It was much heavier than she had expected for such a small item.

'Unwrap it, Annie, and read the letter. It will explain everything.'

She slowly unfolded the calico wrapping, her heart beating faster, curiously, that she had done so before—many times.

A heavy, solid gold, elongated figure of eight emerged from the wrapping. It was the size of a large brooch, but with no pin. Annie put it between the palms of her hands until the cold, precious metal warmed. She recognised the feeling of its smooth symmetry and knew this was the key to her life, but there was still a veil shrouding her deepest memories and the complex images she was seeing.

'Gran, I know this ... I've held it before.'

'Yes, my darling. Now, read the letter.'

Annie unrolled it carefully, its edges were cracked and yielding from being stretched open. The spider-like words whispered of its author's distress at the time of writing, and an ink blotched page from an overfilled quill with sepia foxing spoke of its age.

'Go on,' Gran said, resting her head back on the pillow.

Annie somehow recognised the handwriting—and drew in a deep breath.

> *My name is Agnes Bardforthe.*
> *I wast borne in the town of Lancaster, in the year 1617. Thus, at the ripe old age of 67 and the year now being 1684, my life shall endeth t'day.*
> *I feeleth compelled to pen this account, fer a melancholy has befallen me. I am unable to expel myself from this deplorable predicament as my mortality draws close, so I must leaveth thee, my future descendants, with an explanation of thy past and future lives.*

I feeleth no sorrow today of my demise, my soul will be that of my great-granddaughter, who will be born a year hence, as it has been for generations past and will be for generations henceforth.

The readers of this account will be my future, every fourth generation female will be the reincarnation of their great-grandmother, and so on, and so forth.

Each new child of this fourth generation will inherit the culmination of powers from the female souls of her past lineage. Henceforth they will be known as Immortal Psychics. Whereupon each new female child of the fourth lineage shall be more powerful than before. Those born during the second and third generations shall holdeth lesser powers than those of the Immortals and be known as the Keepers. They shall watch ov'r the Immortals and be their earthbound guides.

A symbol of immortality is the Lemniscate, being that of infinite and eternal life. Therefore, I have commissioned this gold symbol which henceforth must be passed to each of the Immortal Psychics aft'r their power becomes apparent. This Lemniscate holds the memories of our past and future family. Warmeth in the palms of thy hands and thee shall rememb'r wh're thee cometh from.

I hast been accus'd this day of Witchery, having flame hair and the unfortunate features of being crone-like and sunken-cheeked. Also of possessing supernatural powers and the worship of Satan, all of which is naivety on the part of my accusers, mine own true powers are used only f'r the good.

My poor cat Tom, whom has hitherto been accused

an accomplice to my crimes and keeping of my company and the more, shall also walketh with me down the road of execution.
And so, too, my death will come at the end of a rope, but this is far m're favourable than my great-grandmother's demise from fire.
I must endeth this account of which I will pass to a Keeper en route to my end. Hitherto, I look forward to being part of your future lives.
May God have mercy upon my soul.
Agnes.

Annie sighed. 'Oh, Gran ... Although this all sounds so crazy, it explains everything I've been going through these past few months. So tell me, exactly *how* many Immortal Psychics am I the culmination of?'

'To be honest, I really don't know, Annie; they go way back before Agnes, but she was the first to document it. From Agnes till now there have been six Immortals including you, all with diverse abilities that will slowly become apparent throughout your life. I was born during the second generation, and I've been your Keeper and earthbound guide all your life, my darling. Here, take this—it's the names and dates of all the known Immortals and Keepers since Agnes's grandmother handed over this scroll. Each Keeper has kept this ledger up to date, and of course I made the last entry.'

'So, Gran ... All the women born in between the Immortals are like you?'

'Yes, my darling girl. But the odd one escapes the tradition, although that's to be expected over so many hundreds of years.' Gran took another deep breath, as if she had a lot more to say. 'The Keepers' duties are to pass on the knowledge and wisdom we all possess. But by comparison, our abilities are very meagre to those of the Immortals. Those abilities die with us, although if we wish to be reincarnated, that is our choice. But for me ... I'm happy with the one life I've had, and I'll be quite content to stay in the afterlife to keep an eye on you from over there. Until, of course, it's your time ... which won't be for many decades yet. And this is where the healing crystal will come in handy, it will protect you from illness and secure you a long life. But when you eventually pass, you'll join all the souls who will be born into your great-granddaughter.'

Annie kissed the old lady's forehead. 'So that's why you've always been there, quietly teaching me what I've needed to learn. I just want you to know, my darling Gran, that I love you and always will, and I thank you with every ounce of my being for everything you've done for me.'

The old lady looked heart-warmingly satisfied with her lot, and smiled contentedly while Annie sat on the end of the bed reading the other scroll.

Immortal Psychics and Keepers

Name	Birth	Death	Power
Agnes Bardforthe	1617	1684	Immortal Psychic
Wren	1637		Keeper All Knowing and Seeing
Elspeth	1658		Keeper Telepathy
Jenny	1685	1757	Immortal Psychic
Lilly	1706		Keeper Healer
Molly	1730		Keeper Channelling Medium
Willow	1758	1832	Immortal Psychic
Zelda	1778		Keeper Spirit Writer
Clementine	1803		Keeper Clairvoyant
Gwendoline	1833	1911	Immortal Psychic
Bessie	1851		Keeper Claircognisant
Alice	1873		Keeper Clairaudient
Mary-Ellen Lockwood	1892	1984	Immortal Psychic
Clementine	1914	1944	Keeper Astral Projection
Elsie Prior	1938		Keeper Clairsentient
Annie Prior	1985		Immortal Psychic

Gran held Annie's hand, squeezing it as tightly as her frail body would allow. 'My dearest girl, I've finally relinquished my job as a Keeper, and my work here has thankfully come to an end. You know ... it's not much fun having a mind that's active and a body that doesn't follow instructions.'

They both laughed, but the old lady seemed weary.

'I can't bear the thought of losing you, Gran. You've been the only person who's ever shown me real love.' Annie kissed her cheek.

'Your father loves you very much, my dear, and he really *is* a good sort ... just a little lacking in backbone sometimes. Be patient with him.'

'I heard that,' came a voice from behind the curtain.

Annie's father walked in.

'You know I meant it, son,' Gran said. 'You *do* have a good heart, you just need to learn to use it without that monster around your neck.'

'Say it as you mean it, Mother ... But you are right. Anyway, you'll both be pleased to hear I've grown a backbone and left Marjorie. But even more importantly, Mum, I'm going to keep an eye on our Annie for you now.'

'Oh, thank goodness for that, son. So I can leave you both to it, then.'

Annie held her gran's hand for the last time, her eyes blurring with the stinging tears. But the old lady looked serenely happy.

'I want you two—to do me one last favour, please.'

'Anything, Gran.'

'What is it, Mum?'

'Please say cheerio now and then go ... this part of my life is a private matter. It's just between me and God now.'

Chapter 42

∞

So Much More

'I'm not sure if I'm up for giving a mass reading tonight, Mads.'

'I do understand how you must be feeling, Annie, and I'm so sorry about your gran. It's been yet another terrible blow for you. But there are literally hundreds of people coming to see you later, and I'm not sure how we can cancel at this late stage.'

Annie sighed. 'Obviously I'm *not* going to let them down, sweetheart. It's just ... you would have thought a clairvoyant would cope better with losing friends and family.'

'Okay, under normal circumstances, yes, but you've just lost three important people in your life. And don't forget, I was there when Sam died and that was far from normal. Then Melina was murdered by a madman in front of you, and your amazing gran has left you during one of the toughest times of your life. So don't be hard on yourself, I think you're coping incredibly well.'

'You are lovely, Mads ... And I suppose, when you put it like that, I am surviving quite well. But I've been thinking that when the show's over tonight, I might just buzz off for a while to get my head straight.'

'Dare I ask ... Does that mean *with* Thos?'

'No, just me. I think we've come to a bit of a crossroads in our relationship. We're just so different, and I'm sure deep down he feels the same way.'

'Oh, Annie ... I'm not supposed to tell you this, but with the way you're feeling at the moment, I think you should know. Thos has flown Adelpha and Thea over for your show tonight.'

'Wow! Thanks for giving me the heads-up, sweetheart. But it's okay—it'll be so amazing to see them again, and it will definitely be good for Thos. So, don't worry about me, and I'll see you later at the League ... Okay?'

'Okay ... And I've got an amazing feeling that it's gonna be your best show ever.'

∞

Annie sat cuddling Pong, who seemed to have finally decided she wasn't the enemy after all.

She bent down and kissed him between the ears, increasing his already loud purr to a vibrating rumble.

Thos walked through the back door. 'Lucky cat ... he seems to be getting more affection than I am.'

'Yes, well, maybe he understands me better.'

'Ouch. I suppose I deserved that.'

Annie knew the time was right to set things straight. 'Thos ... Do you think we're forcing a relationship that isn't meant to be?'

He was clearly rocked by her candour. 'Well, you must be feeling that if you're asking the question, babe.'

'If you're being totally honest with yourself, sweetheart ... I think you do, too.'

Thos plonked down on the armchair opposite the sofa, completely crestfallen. 'I wasn't expecting to have this conversation now, babe, but

I suppose it's been coming. Look, I do know that I'm a moody and a selfish git sometimes, and I don't have anywhere near the strength of character you do. It's probably the reason all my previous relationships have bombed; but I'm pissed off that I didn't realise my shortcomings before I met you.'

'Sweetheart, you're an amazing man and what you did for me and for all those people on the train was exceptional, and I will always be grateful to you for it. But I think because of the accident, we were thrown together too quickly, and me moving in with you after just a few days was pretty mad. And then of course you've had to deal with my spooks, too, which I can see from your point of view has not been easy ... I don't think there's a man out there who wouldn't find it challenging.'

'You know, babe, that's not entirely true. Dan seems to understand you better than me ... And you have quite a lot in common, too.'

Annie stopped to think for a moment. 'Yes, I suppose we do ... But I promise you, Thos, nothing has been going on. Besides, I would never have done anything to hurt you.'

'Okay, so I'm sorry for jumping to conclusions, but you see I still love you, babe. Although ... if you're unhappy with the way things are, you must do what you feel is best. Maybe a break will give us both time to find out what we really want.'

'Well, now *you're* reading *my* mind, sweetheart... But you're right, I think that's the only way forward at the moment. Although I'm happy to stay and look after Thea and your mum while they're here.'

'Bloody hell, babe, who's reading whose mind? That's something I'm not gonna miss.'

∞

The Conan Doyle Hall was full to bursting. Blue bunting festooned every wall, and there was a large poster of Annie on an easel by the stage—courtesy of Madeleine's over-exuberance. Annie smiled, happy that her friend had fully taken on the running of the League and was making a success of it.

A sea of familiar faces beamed at her from the right-hand side of the hall, which had clearly been cordoned off by Madeleine for family and friends only. Annie's heart leaped as she saw Thea sitting in the front row with Adelpha and Thos. She blew them a kiss and Thos winked back, but this time his wink conveyed so much more than when they'd first met. She was just delighted to see him reunited with his family.

Max was next to Thos, with his mama, who was chatting loudly in Greek to Adelpha. And standing behind them, unseen, was Alex, Max's father, wearing the smile of a contented soul. In the row behind, Poppet was resplendent in his fedora, with Hollingsworth's latest recruit, Sandra, who had clearly been groomed to near perfection by her flamboyant boss. She looked stunning with a smart new hairstyle and make-up, obviously orchestrated by him. Sandra's face beamed with a newfound confidence that pleased Annie hugely.

She quietly congratulated herself for doing the right thing by her, when suddenly she became aware of a familiar perfume, and felt it was Melina's unseen spirit again, showing her approval too.

Annie strained to see who was behind Poppet and was shocked that it was Barbra Amos and Bjorn. Although Amos was clearly unimpressed so far, Bjorn was beside himself with excitement and gave a little wave. Annie could see there had already been a connection made between him and Poppet, who had quite clearly placed himself in the best position to get to know the handsome Scandinavian. Annie had a fleeting premonition of the two lads together—and it was all good.

Dan was sat with his mother, who gave a little wave too. Annie acknowledged it, but when her and Dan's eyes met there was something different between them—and she saw him in a new light.

Thankfully, her thoughts were interrupted by Sister Margaret, who was sitting on the aisle seat next to him; she incongruously put her thumbs up, gesturing that all was now cool in her world.

Annie climbed the time-worn steps to the vast stage that nevertheless felt so welcoming now, and eager spirits with meaningful messages crowded in. Her first meeting up there with Sam seemed from such a long time ago. Although her experiences over the intervening months had been life-changing, she understood at that moment that it had all been in her destiny. It was as though she had emerged from a long dream of no consequence, into a bright light of new knowledge and certainty about her life to come.

'My dear, sweet girl.'

'Oh Sam you're here.'

Hearing her old friend again, filled Annie's heart with love. He was standing straight and proud next to the microphone. Annie was unconcerned that the whole audience was quietly staring at her; after all, she had become renowned for speaking aloud to unseen souls. 'Sam, my dear friend, I knew I could rely on you.'

The old man had a look of huge pride on his illuminated face. 'You are more of a medium than I could ever have hoped, Annie, and I now know why. Your gran is ... quite a woman too.'

'Oh, have you spoken to her, Sam? Why can't I see her yet?'

'You should know, Annie, she's still in transition and not yet ready to come forward. But I was there when she passed—just as you requested—and I'm happy to report that she's delighted to finally be free of her mortal body, and will be with you very soon. Whenever you need help hence-forth, dear girl, you must turn to your many inner souls, as they are you ... and you them.' Sam turned and lifted his hand in a parting gesture.

Annie scanned around at the congregation. She shook her head and smiled.

'Well, ladies and gentlemen, that must have seemed very strange.

In fact, I was talking to our very own Sam Hargreaves, who popped in to say hello and to tell me that my recently passed grand-mother is doing okay.'

An en masse sigh of empathy rippled throughout the audience towards her.

'Sam was telling me that my gran was going through the transitional stage of the afterlife. In fact, we've all done that many times before, too, although none of us can remember. You see, all human beings are fragile vessels that contain our eternal souls. And although our bodies live and then die, the souls within us move on to a higher place, which is yet another stop on our extraordinary adventure called *eternal life*. Some of us, like myself, are lucky enough to have a small insight into this afterlife, and I can tell you with absolute certainty that we are all reunited with our loved ones from this lifetime and the many others we have lived. The only downside, which I am very aware of, especially now, is that we still grieve for those we've lost, although it will always be a natural process for the ones who are left behind, even for me. The thing is ... those who have gone don't grieve as we do, they can still see and hear us. So what we have to do on this earthly realm to stay connected to our loved ones is to honour them every day, and that means living our lives as though they're still with us. We must always keep them in our hearts ... because they keep us in theirs.'

Annie looked around the hugely appreciative congregation and finally felt at peace with herself.

Many souls had started to gather, and she knew it was going to be an amazing—message filled evening. 'Now, ladies and gentlemen, shall we get on with this show ... Because, believe me, there is *so* much more to come.'

Not The End ...

∞

Message from the Author

Dear Reader,

Thank you so much for choosing to read The Accidental Psychic.

I would like you to understand that although it's fictional, it is loosely based on my family's history.

My many life experiences were driven and supported by a strong belief in Spiritualism, which had been with me since my teens in the form of premonitions and intuitiveness. But after going through a traumatic time in my twenties, I actively sought solace from my local Spiritualist church in Bournemouth. All became clear in my forties after finding out from an old family member that my great-grandmother was a well-known clairvoyant and healer. Also around that time, my daughter was showing signs of psychic abilities as well.

Unbeknownst to me, that family member (my aunty), had been waiting to pass down a healing crystal to the only female in the Howard line, which before had been passed to my great-grandmother during the nineteenth century.

Over the last forty years, I immersed myself into finding out more, and continued to amass knowledge on the subject. So writing about it — albeit in fictional form — seemed a natural progression.

The protagonist, Annie Prior, is based on my daughter's looks and personality, and using her image with her amazing aqua eyes for the front cover simply had to be done.

All the characters' names apart from Poppet (Nurse Mark), have come from ancestors on the psychic side of our lineage.

Long before completing The Accidental Psychic, I realised there was so much more life left in Annie, my protagonist, and I am now in the process of spilling her adventures into the sequel, The Eternal Psychic.

All that being said, if you enjoyed the novel, please consider leaving a review at your favorite retailer to let others know your thoughts on the novel. Every review helps as an indie author and I greatly appreciate your support.

Best Regards

Carol-Anne

www.carolmasonauthor.com

info@carolmasonauthor.com

Acknowledgements

<u>Alexandra Padou</u> — Luna Imprints Author Services. www.lunaimprintsauthorservices.com Thank you for your amazing help, both on a professional and personal level. You have inspired me with your kind words!

<u>Martin Ouvry</u> (Editor Jericho Writers. Wingate Scholar and Hawthorn Fellow) Thank you.

Cornerstones <u>cornerstones.co.uk</u> Editorial Services.

<u>Arabella Sophia Derhalli</u> — Talented Editor/Author. For much needed advise and for being my knowledgeable friend throughout.

<u>Lucille Turner</u> — (Author of Gioconda. The Sultan, the Vampyr and the Soothsayer. Also The Dust of a Thousand Places. Thank you for all your professional advice, and for also being a good friend.

<u>Melissa Morgan</u> - Website designer - gweledol.com Melissa is also a writer and therefore understands everything an author needs in a website. Thank you so much for my beautiful site (carolmasonauthor.com) and your unwavering patience with a complete technophobe.

<u>Miblart</u> - My amazing cover designers. Thank you. miblart.com

Adam Croft Best selling English Author of crime fiction (Knight and Culverhouse, Kempston Hardwick Mysteries) For your invaluable FB site. The Indie Author Mindset. And for taking the time to advise me personally.

Matt Wilson — Social media Expert www.altomedia.co.uk Great job Matt — thank you.

Tom Cox (Talented London based Artist) www.tomcoxstudio.com Thank you for allowing me to use you as my real-life artist in the Gallery chapters.

Mark Hamilton (AKA Poppet). After knowing you for forty years sweetheart I had to use your wonderful persona in my debut novel. And although I may have changed your true profession in the book, Poppet (the character) — is all you.

Frances Vinycomb — for being an honest beta reader, and an amazing friend with a glass on hand when needed.

Debbie Cahill — Beta Reader and a wonderful life long friend.

Debs Blount — Helping with much needed 'law and enforcement' advise, and friendship.

Mum (AKA Gwen Howard) — for always being my greatest fan whatever I may be doing! And for being my most honest beta reader! Love you forever.

Tim Mason — My long suffering husband. I'm sorry for all the many hours I left you alone, and for all the times I told you to shush while

I was writing. I love the fact that you have still supported, and shown amazing enthusiasm for the storyline even though you are a sceptic in all things paranormal. Thank you my darling.

Frankie Mason my daughter (AKA Annie Prior the protagonist) Thank you for letting me use your persona and your image on the front cover. Once I knew who my main character was, she had to be modelled on you in every way. Not just your beauty inside and out, but your intuitiveness and empathy has moulded Annie's character, abilities and humour. Thank you also, for your full hearted support through every step of my writing … I love you for it sweetheart.

About the Author

It may seem that writing a debut novel at the age of 62 was leaving it a little late in life, but believe me ... it has been a long time brewing.

After having experienced numerous lives all rolled into one, I felt that my maturity, knowledge and passion (especially for Spiritualism) left me in a good place to finally put pen to paper. The Accidental Psychic has taken two amazing years to write. I say amazing because I've loved every minute, more so than any of my past professions... which were many.

During my youth I studied fine art (my primary passion), interspersed with writing copious amounts of poetry, some of which were published. Poetry led to writing songs and performing at events with my trusty guitar in tow. Another passion was dancing, and after a successful audition I moved to Europe to dance with a troupe for a year, which proved an amazing experience and worthy of another novel ... that may come later.

After finally coming home to settle in Bournemouth, I started two hair and beauty salons. I also taught the latter at Bournemouth College, and ran a nightclub in the evenings ... (obviously that's when I had plenty of energy)

I met my eccentric and highly amusing husband whilst running the club, and soon after had our two wonderful children. But when they flew the madness of the nest,

I kept busy by dabbling in antiques for a while, also using the shop to sell my paintings of still life and landscapes, and taking commissions for animal and people portraits. But throughout my many pursuits over the years, I continued writing poetry and short stories. It all finally culminated in the writing of The Accidental Psychic, and its sequel—The Eternal Psychic—due for release Spring 2022.